ANGRY UNCLE DAN

ANGRY
UNCLE DAN

by

JAMES YAFFE

CONSTABLE · LONDON

LONDON
PUBLISHED BY
Constable and Company Ltd
10-12 *Orange Street* W.C.2

SOUTH *and* EAST AFRICA
Longmans, Green and Company Limited
CAPE TOWN NAIROBI

AUSTRALIA
Walter Standish and Sons
SYDNEY

First published 1955

Printed in Great Britain at the St Ann's Press
Park Road, Altrincham

PART ONE

Twelve Hundred Lake Shore Drive

" Then Satan answered the Lord
and said, Doth Job fear God for
nought?

" Hast not thou made an hedge
about him, and about his house, and
about all that he hath on every side?
thou hast blessed the work of his
hands, and his substance is increased
in the land."

PART ONE

Twelve Hundred Lake Shore Drive

I

EVEN in my earliest memory of him, my Uncle Dan is waving his arms and yelling at the top of his voice.

That memory goes back over fifteen years, when I was a boy of ten. My parents sent me to Miami Beach, Florida, that winter, because I "got colds". As far as I can remember, I got just as many colds down in Miami Beach as I ever got up in New York. I was simply the type of boy who *got* colds, and that's all there was to it. But my parents couldn't see it that way. My mother was devoted to old Dr. Schlesinger, and at that period old Dr. Schlesinger's prescription for every sort of trouble was "go down South for the winter". He never stuck to the same prescription very long, of course. If I had happened to get my colds two years sooner, for instance, I would have stayed up North and he would have given me liver pills. And two years later he would have had me using a nose drip.

Anyway, it was the winter of my tenth year, and I spent it in Miami Beach. Mother and Dad didn't spend it with me, except for one week after New Year's. Dad was too busy with his office, and Mother was too busy with her committees. I stayed at Dr. Porter's Boarding School, which was very expensive, because most of the pupils came from up North like me.

Uncle Dan and Aunt Sarah were living in Miami Beach

that year. I didn't find out why till later, and it didn't even occur to me to wonder. All I knew was, every other Sunday they took me out for lunch and to the beach. Aunt Sarah did, that is. Uncle Dan never showed up for more than a few minutes at a time. Maybe he'd pop into the hotel dining-room just long enough to gulp down a cup of coffee with us. Maybe he'd come striding on to the beach late in the afternoon, his bathing-suit showing what a pot belly and what short stubby legs he had. Then he's stretch out on the sand with a pair of dark glasses over his eyes, he'd take the sun for ten minutes, then suddenly he'd jump to his feet and go striding off the beach again as if he was in a terrible rush. Uncle Dan was generally in a terrible rush that winter. But that was another thing I didn't find out the reason for until much later.

The incident that really sticks in my memory though —every detail of it, as clear as if it happened last week— didn't take place till the end of March. It was my time for leaving Florida and going back home again. Originally Mother intended to send somebody down for me—the chauffeur, or my Aunt Goldie who wasn't married, or somebody. But at the last minute she was able to save the expense, because it happened that Uncle Dan and Aunt Sarah had to go up to New York too. And so it was arranged that they would pick me up at the school, and we would all ride on the train together.

I was completely innocent. What did I know of Uncle Dan's excitable nature? I had heard Mother and Dad joking about it from time to time. And once or twice I had heard Dad say, not so jokingly, "He's a wild man, that brother-in-law of yours! A wild man out of the jungle!" But I had never had any personal experience of this. How was I supposed to understand that there are people in the world for whom the simplest, most ordinary

8

situation can develop into a big crisis—playing bridge, driving a car through traffic, waiting for the menu in a restaurant, and most of all, hurrying to catch a train?

Nobody warned me. And so, when Uncle Dan and Aunt Sarah got to the school, I wasn't ready yet. I hadn't even finished packing my suitcase. I was quite a dawdler at the age of ten. (I wish somebody would tell me when I can expect to grow out of this habit.) With the empty suitcase lying on my bed, I had spent the whole morning with my friends, playing "Dr. Livingstone, I presume"—we used the palm trees on the front lawn to represent darkest Africa. Then it was lunchtime. I wasn't supposed to have lunch at the school—Aunt Sarah and Uncle Dan planned to take me into the diner on the train—but just the same, I wanted to sit and watch everybody eat. It was a great opportunity for me to be important. Since I wasn't being served myself, it was my privilege to " pick a number between one and ten million", and give away my roll and butter to whoever made the closest guess. And naturally I cheated a little, I sort of changed my number after the guessing was over, so that my best friend, Stanley Neidelman, would win.

Well, finally, in the middle of lunch, Mrs. Porter swooped down on me, with her finger wagging and that businesslike gleam in her eye. "What are you doing, dear?" she cried. "Your aunt and uncle will be here any minute, and you haven't even packed yet. Now, now, now, what will your aunt and uncle think of us?" Then she smiled her sweetest, most efficient smile and pointed at the door. Needless to say, I hurried to my room. If there was one thing we all dreaded in Dr. Porter's School, it was one of Mrs. Porter's sweet smiles.

For a little while after I got to my room, I threw things into my suitcase at a great rate. And then, gradually, my pace slowed up. I began to daydream. When I was ten, practically nothing in the world—no amount of outside pressure, street noises, music on the radio, yelling from the grown-ups—could break into my daydreaming. I sat down on the edge of the bed, and thought about what a fine winter it had been. I remembered all the fine times I had had—my performance as a Gentleman of Japan in the school production of *The Mikado*, the annual Christmas party where everybody ten years old or older was allowed to play games with the girls, the midnight frog-hunting expedition that I took with Stanley Neidelman, the lecture that we got from Mrs. Porter later on, in which she told us that she was "disappointed in us". It all seemed wonderful to me now. Even the lecture seemed wonderful. My eyes filled with tears. I was feeling almost as sad about leaving Miami Beach as I had felt four months ago about leaving New York.

The door burst open and broke into my daydreams. It was Mrs. Porter, beaming all over and announcing that my aunt and uncle had arrived. Even before I saw them, I knew that they were right behind her—because this was Mrs. Porter's special beam, her extra-affectionate motherly beam, which she turned on us only in the presence of parents and visitors. Sure enough, the next moment Uncle Dan appeared, moving fast, rubbing his hands together, looking energetic and brisk, with Aunt Sarah hovering a little ways behind him, as usual.

"All right, all right, how are you, nice to see you," he said, giving my shoulder a quick nudge in passing. "Now where's your luggage, have you got any luggage? Have to be hurrying along, you know."

Aunt Sarah bent down to kiss my cheek, but she never got there. Uncle Dan waved her away genially but commandingly. "All right, all right, no time for that foolishness. We've got a train to catch. The trains won't wait for hugging and kissing and fooling around."

"There's plenty of time, Dan," said Aunt Sarah.

But Uncle Dan had turned away from her: he was addressing himself to Mrs. Porter. His manner, though sharp and vigorous, was still polite. "Has he got a suitcase? Let's get his suitcase, and we'll be running along."

Mrs. Porter smiled at him and raised her finger in that expressive way she had, as if to say, "Patience, patience, you're in good hands now, just leave everything to *me*." Then she turned to the bed, and then she turned back to Uncle Dan. Her smile was sweeter than ever. "Now can you imagine that?" she said. "His suitcase is practically empty. What on earth has he been doing up here all this time? Such an absent-minded little fellow." She looked down at me fondly and indulgently, then up at Uncle Dan again, inviting him to share in the delightful joke.

But Uncle Dan didn't seem so delighted. His eyes narrowed. He smiled, just the smallest, tightest smile. He spoke in a very quiet voice. "You mean he isn't ready yet?"

Mrs. Porter laughed, that pleasant competent laugh of hers. "No, he isn't. Would you believe it? And he's had the whole morning to do it, too. Well, that's just what they're like at his age. No sense of responsibility."

"And sometimes," Uncle Dan said, his voice getting just a tone louder, "even when they're older than his age——"

"I'll pack the bag, dear," said Aunt Sarah, "as long as we're in a hurry." And as she spoke, she stepped between Uncle Dan and Mrs. Porter in the most deft, unobtrusive way. She was a tall, bony, long-legged woman, my Aunt Sarah, fully an inch taller than Uncle Dan, and usually her motions were a little bit queer and awkward. But this was one motion which she made as smoothly and expertly as a professional athlete. I didn't find out till later, of course, how much experience she had had in making it.

With Uncle Dan and Mrs. Porter neatly separated for the moment, Aunt Sarah moved on to the suitcase and quickly began to fold things into it. The tension was eased. Uncle Dan's smile grew a little less tight. Everything would have been all right, if it hadn't been for Mrs. Porter. As headmistress of the school, and therefore the person in the room of highest rank, she just couldn't let the subject drop without making it absolutely clear that no blame whatsoever could possibly be attached to her. So she turned her serene, superior smile on Uncle Dan and said, " Of course, I must tell you that basically this is a procedure I don't approve of. Here at Dr. Porter's School we don't do things for our boys and girls that they can just as well do for themselves. We like to encourage them to develop a spirit of self-reliance. We believe that the child's whole future attitude is somewhat more important than saving a few minutes here or there."

Uncle Dan snapped his head up at her. He was always given to quick, sharp movements, but this one was *so* quick and sharp that it made me blink. "A few minutes here or there? Is *that* how you feel about things? Is *that* the future attitude that you're stuffing into this child? You don't think it might be valuable, while you're at it, to teach your boys and girls how to get places on time? Or maybe you people don't know how yourself——"

Aunt Sarah craned her neck forward. "Dan, we'll be ready in a minute," she said, trying to calm him down, smile encouragingly at Mrs. Porter, and pile my clothes into the suitcase, all at the same time.

But Uncle Dan was nodding his head up and down very fast, and laughing in that quick sarcastic way of his. "You don't know how yourself. That's the answer. Absolutely. Or maybe you're under the impression that the trains are going to wait around in the station while you encourage my nephew to develop his self-reliance? "

"My dear Mr. Waxman," said Mrs. Porter, giving a little sigh—only somehow Mrs. Porter made you feel as small and mean with her little sigh as somebody else with a whole string of insults. "My dear Mr. Waxman, I appreciate your impatience, I truly do. After all, how can I expect you to understand our educational methods when you don't really have any experience in the field? However, I must ask you to remember that I have been running a school for over twenty years——"

"Running it into the ground." Uncle Dan's voice got another tone louder.

"All right, Dan, we're all ready now," said Aunt Sarah, picking up the suitcase with one hand, grabbing me under the arm with the other hand, and once again stepping between Uncle Dan and Mrs. Porter.

"Just a minute, Sarah," he said.

"We'll miss the train," she said.

Uncle Dan shoved his lower lip forward and glared ahead of him hard. I realize now that he was going through a terrible struggle with himself—on the one hand was the train, puffing and seething at the station, knowing perfectly well that Uncle Dan was expected, and therefore concentrating all its malice on breaking away and roaring off to New York without him: on the other hand was Mrs. Porter, her chin lifted slightly, her smile calm and triumphant, definitely not yet reduced to a pulp by Uncle Dan's crushing words. What to do, what to do? He battled it out inside himself a few seconds longer, then finally he gave a quick jerk of his head and muttered bitterly, "All right, let's get going, no use wasting any more time around here."

With Uncle Dan pushing and Aunt Sarah pulling, I was propelled out of the room, down the corridor, down the stairs to the front parlour. Outside, in front of the building, Uncle Dan had a taxi waiting, and he was already calling to the driver half-way down the stairs. "All right, all right, here we are, start up your motor!"

"Mr. Waxman," said Mrs. Porter—and since she had stationed herself between him and the doorway, Uncle Dan was forced to stop and listen to her, "your nephew is leaving us and travelling hundreds of miles away. We may not be seeing him again for a long long time. Don't you think he might like to say goodbye to all his little friends?"

Uncle Dan frowned at her, as if he couldn't quite make out what language she was talking. "Goodbye? What do you mean, goodbye? What little friends?"

Mrs. Porter had her hand on my shoulder, and she was moving me towards the dining-room. "You'll want to say goodbye to everybody, won't you, dear? They're just finishing dessert."

Mrs. Porter's words reminded me what a sad, sentimental mood I was in. What could be better for such a mood than one big, final goodbye scene while everybody was finishing dessert? So I ran through the dining-room archway and up to the table where all my friends were sitting. I was vaguely conscious of Uncle Dan and Aunt Sarah watching me from the parlour. Aunt Sarah's eyes were wide and worried. Uncle Dan's neck was beginning to turn a funny colour, sort of pink, like smoked salmon. I forgot all about him a moment later, as I moved around the table, shaking hands with everybody, telling them I'd be seeing them next year, returning their friendly wisecracks. Stanley Neidelman and I didn't make any wisecracks, though. We kind of avoided each other's eyes, and I promised to write him when I got to New York, and he mentioned that maybe I could visit him at Pittsburgh during the summer. It was the last time I saw him—I've always wondered what became of Stanley Neidelman.

I could hear Uncle Dan calling me from the archway. "All right, you've said goodbye, come on!"

I started back to him, but Mrs. Porter took me by the arm and turned me in another direction. "And the teachers, dear. You don't mean to say you're going to leave us without saying goodbye to your teachers?"

"Teachers?" said Uncle Dan. "Now who wants to say goodbye to teachers?"

But she brought me over to the teachers' table. I wasn't quite so enthusiastic about this particular duty. Still, it wasn't exactly unpleasant either. I walked around the table, politely shaking hands with each of them and giving stiff little bows, and it was really sort of surprising, how different they all seemed. There was Mr. Dunn, Phs.Ed., who always used to scare me to death at afternoon play period, the way he shouted at me, "Pull in your belly, stick out your chin, what kind of posture do you call *that*?" And there was dry old Mr. Whittaker, Arithmetic and History, who used such long words and never seemed to know that any of us kids were around, even while he was talking to us. And there was Madame Degrasse, Elementary French, who kept a couple of poodles—she was queerer than any of them, because she even talked to those *poodles* in Elementary French. But now, all of a sudden, they were all very ordinary, they shook hands and smiled and said goodbye just like ordinary human people. Mr. Whittaker even made a little joke—why, up to then I had never suspected that he *knew* a joke.

I felt a hand on my arm, pulling me back. "You can send them a letter, the rest of them you can send a letter." And before I had quite recovered myself, Uncle Dan had me out of the dining-room and on my way to the front door again.

By this time, though, I had begun to enjoy myself.

This rigmarole of marching from this one to that one, getting my hand shaken, being smiled at and talked to and generally treated quite differently than I used to be treated in the days when I was just another one of the pupils (yesterday, that is)—well, all of a sudden I didn't really feel like giving up this pleasant game so quickly. We were actually through the front door and standing on the front porch, when I turned abruptly and started back into the house. "The doctor," I called over my shoulder. "I forgot to say goodbye to the doctor."

"Now that's really very sweet of him," said Mrs. Porter, beaming away as our whole party followed me through the door. "He wants to say goodbye to the doctor."

"Doctor?" said Uncle Dan. "Who is he, this idiot doctor?"

Mrs. Porter turned to Uncle Dan quietly. "Dr. Porter is my husband, Mr. Waxman."

"Her husband." Uncle Dan was muttering to himself again. "Naturally she's got a husband." And outside the door of the doctor's study, he poked me in the ribs a few times hard. "So say goodbye, hurry up, what's keeping you?"

I knocked softly on the door, the way we always did before we went in to see Dr. Porter.

"Open it up, open it up," Uncle Dan said, and he pushed open the door before Dr. Porter even had a chance to say "Come in."

Dr. Porter looked up from his desk. He was a scrawny sad-eyed little man with a ragged brown moustache and a crumpled white suit and a yellow-paste complexion—everybody else might be getting rich Florida tans right and left, but Dr. Porter seemed to be completely immune to the sun. He spent most of his time in this cramped little study, doing God knows what—certainly Mrs.

Porter never allowed him, even by accident, to take any part in the running of the school. He looked up now, rather bewildered by the intrusion, and said, "Oh—ah——"

"I'm going Dr. Porter," I said, "and I just wanted to tell you——"

"Goodbye, Dr. Porter" Uncle Dan cried out over my shoulder. "Nice knowing you. Nice leaving you. Goodbye, goodbye, goodbye——"

And I felt myself being yanked right of the room, and practically dragged along the corridor to the front door.

Uncle Dan threw my suitcase into the cab, and then threw me in after it, and then asked Aunt Sarah, "Why the hell are you pottering around like that?" And then he slammed the cab door shut after himself.

Mrs. Porter stuck her head in at the window. "You see, Mr. Waxman, in reference to our little disagreement of a few minutes ago, as to our educational methods and so on, you see how the boy's attachment to the school——"

"Sure, sure, very interesting," said Uncle Dan. "Get going, what's holding you up? he shouted at the cab-driver. Mrs. Porter had to pull her head back sharply as the cab sprang into motion.

It was certainly the most frightening half-hour I've ever spent in a car. No matter how fast the driver went, it wasn't good enough for Uncle Dan. "Faster, faster!" he kept yelling at him. And he had his pocket-watch on his knee, and wouldn't take his eyes off it during the whole trip. "Faster! What's the matter, don't you know how to get a little speed out of this broken-down heap of junk? Faster! I'm paying my money, and you'll kindly follow my orders. You know, I'd just as soon step right out and get myself a *decent* cab."

Whenever we had to stop for a light, Uncle Dan went into a fury. He would poke his head out of the window, he would tap his foot, sometimes he would shout up to the light, "Change! Change, will you! My typical bad luck. The one day I have to catch a train, and the whole traffic light system of Miami Beach breaks down." Once, we turned a curve so fast that we had to swerve to miss a truck. As the truck disappeared behind us, Uncle Dan shook his fist at the back window. "Moron! Why do they give licences to such morons?" Another time, at a busy intersection, a policeman held up our line of cars for a few seconds after the light turned green. It was all Aunt Sarah could do to keep Uncle Dan from jumping out of the car then and there, and striding up to that policeman, and "giving him a good piece of my mind, public servant he calls himself, and all he does is prevent the public from catching trains".

And then, practically within sight of the railroad station, a terrible thing happened. Suddenly I gave a cry: "My polo coat. I forgot my polo coat."

"Your what?" Uncle Dan shoved his chin at me. "You forgot your what?"

"My polo coat," I said, a little shakily, wishing now that I hadn't brought up the subject. "It was in the closet—I hung it right up in front last night, so I'd be sure and not forget it—only everything happened so fast——"

"His polo coat," Uncle Dan said. "You hear that? He forgot his polo coat."

"Yes, dear," said Aunt Sarah. "Well, Mrs. Porter can send it to him up North."

"You forgot your polo coat?" Uncle Dan said, turning back to me.

"Yes, sir," I said, in a very small voice.

"Here's the station, Dan," said Aunt Sarah.

Uncle Dan was silent for a moment, sitting up very straight, glaring ahead of him, just sort of quivering a little. Finally he gave a nod of his head. "We'll go back for it."

"But Dan, it isn't really necessary. Mrs. Porter can——"

"Can a boy go up North without his polo coat? We're going back for it."

"But Dan, we'll miss the train——"

"Good. We'll miss the train. Driver, turn around and go back."

We turned around and went back. It was the same fast ride, the same careening around curves and racing down the avenues. Uncle Dan didn't say a word this time. He just kept on sitting up straight and glaring ahead of him. Finally we pulled up to the front of the school again and screeched to a stop. Mrs. Porter saw us and started slowly down the steps toward us.

"He forgot his polo coat," Aunt Sarah called to her, while she was still quite a distance away.

Mrs. Porter didn't let this upset her for a moment. She came right on towards us at the same leisurely pace, absolutely in no hurry. She stopped at the cab window and smiled in at Uncle Dan. "You're back," she said.

"We're back," said Uncle Dan, to the air. "We're back, she says."

"He forgot his polo coat," Aunt Sarah put in quickly. "Could you get it, please? We're really in a terrible hurry."

"Oh, the polo coat," said Mrs. Porter, laughing almost gaily. "Yes, we noticed that he left it behind. Dr. Porter has it."

"Dr. Porter has it," said Uncle Dan. "Big help. Dr. Porter has it."

"Yes. We noticed it just a few minutes ago, and I sent him down to the station to give it to you. He should be waiting for you there now."

"Waiting at the station," said Uncle Dan. Then without another look at Mrs. Porter, he leaned forward to the driver. "Back to the station," he said.

The cab turned around in the driveway, and for the second time that day I saw Dr. Porter's School fade into my past. The ride back was the fastest and wildest yet, and all the time not a word out of Uncle Dan. Aunt Sarah didn't say anything either. And me too—some instinct told me that I'd better keep my mouth shut.

Well, we got to the station, and Uncle Dan threw a bill at the cab-driver and didn't even bother to wait for change. We piled out of the cab, and ran up to the platform with Uncle Dan in the lead. We looked up and down the platform for Dr. Porter, and for a while we couldn't see him, and then we saw him. He was standing at the very opposite end, a lonely little figure with a polo coat slung over his arm. Uncle Dan went striding down to him, and Dr. Porter caught sight of us at the same time and came hurrying up to Uncle Dan. They met in the middle, and Dr. Porter extended the polo coat uncertainly, and Uncle Dan snatched it away from him.

"This is it?" Uncle Dan said.

Dr. Porter nodded. "And I'd like to say, Mr. Waxman——"

"This is the boy's polo coat?"

Dr. Porter nodded again. "And I'd like to say, Mr. Waxman——"

Uncle Dan turned to me. "You positively identify this as your polo coat?"

I was too confused to do more than gape at him, but Aunt Sarah answered for me. "It's his coat all right, Dan, now let's get on the train——"

"Just a minute, Sarah." Uncle Dan turned back to Dr. Porter. "You were saying something to me?"

Dr. Porter nodded and wet his lips and managed to speak up in a low voice. "I only wanted to say—that is, Mrs. Porter asked me to say—she hopes you haven't been inconvenienced by this slight mix-up. That's what she hopes——" His voice trailed off feebly.

Uncle Dan looked him up and down for a moment, and then he answered him. His voice was low too. "Mrs. Porter hopes I haven't been inconvenienced. Now that's nice of Mrs. Porter, isn't it? Now that's very considerate of Mrs. Porter. Well, suppose you give Mrs. Porter the following message." And then it happened, quick and sudden, with absolutely no warning at all. Uncle Dan's arms flew into the air, his chin started shaking up and down, the colour rushed on to his face—and it wasn't pink like a salmon this time, it was red, a deep brilliant red, like a lobster. And his voice—you wouldn't think it possible that such a loud voice, such a thundering roar of a voice, could come out of such a little man. "She's an imbecile, that woman! You hear me? You married an imbecile! Suppose you just tell her *that*."

Dr. Porter didn't seem to have an answer to that, and anyway Uncle Dan was roaring on. "And *you're* an imbecile! Do you know that? Did anybody ever give you that information before? Standing there goggling at me with your silly fish-face! And your whole school too, it's a school for imbeciles! And believe me, believe me——"

Aunt Sarah was plucking at his sleeve. "Dan—people are looking at you—Dan dear——"

"What do I care? I *want* them to look at me. I want them to hear what I got to say. Believe me, believe me," he gave a wide sweep of his arm, which included everybody in the station, and the rest of the world too, "Dr. Porter's Goddamned Boarding School is a goddamned stinking swindle and a pesthouse, and anybody who sends their little brats there ought to be locked up for cruelty to children!"

Uncle Dan finished off his outburst by slinging my polo

coat over his shoulder as if it were a knapsack, turning his back on the trembling Dr. Porter, and scrambling into the nearest car of the train—which was unfortunate, since our reservations were four or five cars down, and Uncle Dan kept stumbling over suitcases and people's feet all the way.

Aunt Sarah and I followed him back to our compartment. We kept a little distance behind him, of course, because he was cursing and muttering and glowering every minute. In the compartment, he flung himself into the seat, shoved his chin into his hand, and turned his head towards the window. Aunt Sarah and I timidly took our seats across from him. We all sat in silence. The train started off, the conductor came in to collect our tickets, the porter looked in to tell us that lunch was being served—and still nobody said a word. And so it went on for a whole hour. Surely that was the most uncomfortable hour that a ten-year-old boy could have spent. I didn't dare look at Uncle Dan, and yet I could hardly keep my eyes away from him. I didn't dare speak to Aunt Sarah, and yet I felt that I was dying of boredom and hunger. My knee itched, my nose twitched, the small of my back itched—and yet, so great was my terror of Uncle Dan's red face and his waving arms and his dreadful roar that only the most exquisite agony gave me the courage to scratch myself.

And then, around two-thirty in the afternoon, it all came to an end just as suddenly as it had begun. One minute Uncle Dan was glaring out of the window, the next minute he turned his back into the compartment and growled down at the floor, "I'm starved. Isn't anybody else starved? I suppose they've got enough sense to keep a diner on this train."

I looked up at him, amazed and confused. But the most amazing thing of all was the way Aunt Sarah took it. She answered him as quietly and conversationally as if nothing at all had ever been wrong. "Yes, dear, I *am* getting a little bit hungry."

"A little bit hungry." Uncle Dan threw his head back and gave a laugh—just as pleasant and genial a laugh as I had ever heard from him. "She eats like a bird." He turned to me and clapped his hand down on my shoulder. "These females, they eat like a flock of birds, every one of them. *We'll* show them a thing or two about eating, won't we?"

Then we all got up and marched back to the dining-car, and Uncle Dan kept his hand on my shoulder, and talked and laughed and winked at me. And during the meal he made jokes with the coloured waiter, and he told a long story about how he won a lot of money in a gambling-house. And during the dessert, he suddenly stuck up his chin, and put on a big false sugary smile, and blurted out in a high falsetto voice, "My dear Mr. Waxman, I must ask you to remember that I have been running a school for over twenty years." He slapped his knee and shook up and down with laughter, and I couldn't help giggling myself. And from that moment on, I forgot all about feeling sad at leaving Miami Beach.

As for the incident at the railroad station—Uncle Dan mentioned it only once more during the course of the trip. It was the next morning at breakfast. He sat for a while, looking thoughtful and letting his coffee get cold. Then he lifted his eyes and gave a little grin and said to Aunt Sarah, "That poor little doctor fellow—when we get to New York, will you remind me to send him a telegram?"

That's my earliest memory of my Uncle Dan. At the time, of course, I didn't know what it meant. With my dawdling and my daydreaming and my polo coat, I had no idea what was going on right under my nose. It wasn't till years later that I finally found out.

II

WHEN my Uncle Dan came to Chicago at the age of seventeen, he was, for all practical purposes, alone in the world. His mother and father, whom he used to live with back in Brooklyn, had both died suddenly, within the last year. His three sisters had been married and scattered around the country for a long time—and each one of them had shown the family trait of impracticality by marrying a man without money. His aunts and uncles were sympathetic, but they all had lots of children of their own. As for solid assets, Dan and his brother Herman, a year older than himself, were left with only four. Asset one—Papa's candy store—was sold to clear up Papa's debts. Asset two—the insurance money—was just enough to pay for the funerals. Fine, respectable, fancy funerals, "so you won't have nothing to reproach your conscience with," said Papa's brother, Uncle Meyer. Unfortunately Uncle Meyer wasn't offering to share in the expenses.

After this, there was only Asset three and Asset four— Mamma's first cousins, Simon and Wolfie. Cousin Simon owned a jewellery store in Manhattan, and Cousin Wolfie owned a Hats, Gloves, and Accessories business in Chicago, and both men were willing to give a chance to a promising young fellow who was also a blood relative. He would have to start off at the bottom, naturally, but always with the understanding that some day he might work himself up. The only problem was, which one should stay in New York with Cousin Simon, and which one should go to Cousin Wolfie in Chicago?

The aunts and uncles held a special conference to discuss this subject. It was a long, solemn, exhausting conference. There was a great deal of shouting and snorting back and forth. Several bowls of assorted fruit and a two-pound box of chocolate peppermints were gobbled up before it was over. All in all it lasted over three hours since everybody there had to put in his two cents—and lots of people were there. In fact, practically the only members of the family who didn't get invited to this conference were Dan and his brother Herman.

In the end, the following decision was made, and announced by Uncle Meyer in deep impressive tones. Of the two brothers, it was agreed that Herman was the reliable, dependable one. The jewellery business, therefore, with its high-class clientele and its glittering atmosphere, would be less likely to turn his head and give him delusions of grandeur. Dan, on the other hand, was considered to have a streak of wildness in him, a certain restless unrealistic little bug that made him a potential pushover for temptation. Much better he should go to Chicago and live a few years under the steadying influence of Hats, Gloves, and Accessories.

Less than a week later the two brothers said goodbye at the Pennsylvania Station. It was a difficult scene for both of them. They were very fond of each other, but at the same time they had never been able to carry on a conversation together—Herman was for ever expressing his disapproval of Dan's "complete lack of self-control" —which naturally made it harder than ever for Dan to control himself. And so, as they waited for the gates to swing open to Dan's train, they talked in awkward spurts about unimportant details.

Herman never got tired of playing the big brother, and on this occasion he was doing it up even more thoroughly than usual. He was full of advice and warnings about living alone in a big city—"from his many years experience as a world traveller", Dan thought. He was full also of worries about whether Dan was taking enough money with him, whether his ticket was safe in his wallet, did he have any magazines and books to read on the train, could he find his way by himself to the dining-car? In between all this, he kept asking Dan if he was *sure* that he remembered Cousin Wolfie's address. Finally, with only a few minutes to go, he cleared his throat, made his face especially long and serious, and launched into a speech about "upholding the family reputation with strangers".

It was because of his brother Herman that Dan, at the age of six, had found out what a terrible temper he had. For a couple of moments he was reminded of that incident now. He was reminded of how Herman, those many years ago, had put on just such a long, serious, superior look, and all of a sudden something had snapped inside of Dan, and he went charging into his older brother, fists flying, dreadful yells coming out of his mouth. He frowned and shook off this memory. One thing he didn't want at a moment like this was a fight.

The conductor was swinging the gates open. They made loud clanging noises that cut into Herman's speech. So he broke off with a little sigh, then solemnly held out his hand. "I'm counting on you, Danny."

Dan looked up at his brother's face. In an instant all the irritation, all the hidden anger, just melted away, and instead he was trembling with love and affection. He took Herman's hand, and shook it up and down enthusiastically, and blurted out, "We'll write to each other, won't we? We won't forget to write to each other?"

Herman was trembling too—Dan could see it—but only for a moment. Herman always made a big thing out of "not giving in to your emotions". He steadied himself with an effort, drew himself up a little, and spoke, very quiet and businesslike, from a height. "We're a couple of grown men now," he said. "Grown men have to accept the inevitable."

In spite of himself, Dan felt another one of those little pangs of exasperation. He turned quickly and hurried down the ramp to his train.

But the exasperation went away as soon as the train started to puff out of the station. Dan's feelings were mixed. One half of him was really sorry to go. Seventeen years of memories were staying behind him in New York. Seventeen years of playing with his gang, fighting with his brother, sneering at his teachers, exploring the backyards and vacant lots of Brooklyn, learning about life at the corner drugstore—seventeen years of developing his lungs to the point where he could hold his own at dinner-table conversations—seventeen years in those three tiny, dirty, noisy rooms behind the candy store, with the smell of soda pop in his nose every minute. And best of all, those wonderful tooth-and-nail family arguments that used to add spice to his life and keep him off the streets at night. There *was* no family now, they would never argue any more. And for a moment Dan thought he wouldn't ever be happy in this world again.

After all, he was only a boy. And the one thing a boy dreads is change. He likes to think that things will go on the same way for ever and ever.

But the other half of Dan didn't have a single regret. He couldn't have been more satisfied by what was happening to him. The train bouncing and shaking under him,

27

the steady clackety-clack of the wheels, the landscape whipping by the window. What a pleasure! What a relief! No more of those crazy, pointless family arguments to give him a headache. No more of that grey, sooty, dilapidated Brooklyn scenery. And no more soda pop. For the first time in his life he could stick out his chest and take a deep breath and definitely not get a nose full of soda pop. My God, that's what he called freedom! And there was more of it ahead of him—all sorts of wonderful developments, and spectacular ways of making money, and big-shots for dinner, and servants in uniform, and his name in the papers——

After all, he was only a boy. And the one thing a boy thrives on is change. He likes to think that money and fame and a beautiful girl, and most of all an exciting adventure, are waiting for him just around the next corner.

III

CHICAGO, at the turn of the century, must have been the liveliest, wildest, most exuberant city in the world. At least, to hear my Uncle Dan reminisce about it, you'd think it was. Of course, my Uncle Dan was livelier and wilder and more exuberant himself in those days.

" Speed," Uncle Dan used to say, talking to his nieces and nephews in one of his expansive moods. "That was the big thing about Chicago in those days—speed. Nowadays, of course, we take speed for granted. We're always moving around so fast, what with airplanes and television and instant coffee, we don't even notice it any more. Back in nineteen-o-three, though, speed was something special, something you stopped and looked at, and we used to point with pride at how much of it we had in Chicago."

And then, with a faint happy smile coming over his face, he would describe what happened to him within ten minutes after he stepped off that train, at the age of seventeen. First, a porter came along and tried to grab his big leather-strapped suitcase out of his hand, and Dan nearly got into a fight holding on to it. Then a man laughed at him—a man with a striped vest and a derby hat and a long heavy watch-chain, who was leaning up against the wall, idly looking over the scene. Then he was pushed by the crowd out to the street. It wasn't eight o'clock in the morning yet, but the city was as busy and full of noise as if it had been awake for hours. A newsboy shouted in his face. A woman poked him with an umbrella. A couple of nattily-dressed young fellows snickered at him from a doorway. A small, smoky, clattering automobile came whirling around the corner at a mad pace, splattering his shoes with mud. He found his way somehow into one of the new trolley cars which Chicago had just installed in imitation of New York. The bell clanged, and the trolley car jolted into action so sharply that Dan was thrown practically into the lap of a pretty girl. "Fresh!" she said, and slapped him square across the face.

That was the way my Uncle Dan told it, anyway.

He took that trolley to the only address he knew in Chicago, Cousin Wolfie's store on the South Side, which was located just across the street from Cousin Wolfie's home, and a short while later he got his first glimpse of Cousin Wolfie himself. He was a little stooped-over man, with a wisp of whiskers sticking out from his chin. He was in his fifties, but he looked to be in his seventies.

His face was old—a sharp little nose, thick pale lips, drawn down at the corners from perpetual muttering and grumbling, a pair of small, narrow, glittering eyes, bundled in wrinkles from years of squinting suspiciously at salesmen, customers, competitors, and relatives. His daily routine was old too. In fact it was the same routine followed by his father, his uncles, and his grandfather before him—prayers first thing in the morning, work all day, dinner at five-thirty, prayers after dinner, bed at nine o'clock. This routine was varied only on Fridays, when he shut up the store early and went off to synagogue. Then, for the next twenty-four hours, he celebrated the Sabbath—that is, he sat around the apartment, grunted orders at his family, and grumbled to himself in a low steady drone. Sunday was a relief to everybody, because that was the day Cousin Wolfie stayed in the back room of his store and played pinochle with his cronies. His wife and four daughters, who went around all week with their heads down and scared looks on their faces, had actually been known to lift up their chins and smile a little on Sundays.

But the oldest thing of all about Cousin Wolfie was his business methods. He was a good example of what is known sometimes, with a sentimental sigh, as " the old-fashioned type of businessman". That is, he stuck so obstinately, so pig-headedly, to the most antiquated, inefficient, inconvenient ways of doing things that he absolutely drove his customers and his employees crazy. The stock in his store, for instance, was arranged on the shelves in the most illogical way, so that everything was as hard as possible to get at. Derby hats, which were popular that year, were stuck way up on a top shelf, far out of reach. On the other hand, Prince Albert vests, which had gone out of style ten years ago, were right up there in front on the main counter. And why? Because that's where his father had kept Prince Albert vests, and what was good enough for his father was certainly good enough for him.

By the same reasoning, Cousin Wolfie never had a sale or a clearance, never got rid of old stock at reduced prices in order to make room for new stock. Practically the last thing his father said to him, on his deathbed, was "Wolfie, my boy, once you buy it, don't let go of it till you can sell it for a profit. This, my boy, is the secret of good business." The result was, there were pieces of merchandise on the shelves which had been there for twenty or thirty years. There was one box of four-in-hand ties which were already turning mouldy.

How Cousin Wolfie managed to stay in business under these conditions was a great mystery with everybody who knew him. And yet, he not only managed, he also grew richer and richer every year. Still, everybody predicted that he was riding for a fall. A man can't go on for ever, flying in the face of progress. The day would come when even Wolfie would be forced to catch up with the times, or go bust. And sure enough, the day did come.

It came during the First World War, about fifteen years after Dan's arrival in Chicago. It was Daylight Saving Time that brought about Cousin Wolfie's downfall. President Wilson passed a law, saying that you had to turn your clocks ahead one hour every spring. Under great protest Cousin Wolfie did this once; but when they asked him in September to turn his clock back again, he flatly refused. For forty years he had been opening the store at a certain time, and closing it up again at a certain time. And so had his father before him both here and back in the old country—and so had his father's father. So now, all of a sudden, because of some crazy law, was he supposed to change his whole life around? Was the world coming to such a state that a man had to get up in the morning and go to bed at night when

President Wilson told him to? Let them lock him up in jail if they wanted to, but he was a citizen of the United States of America and he was going to stick to his own schedule.

And so, for the next six months, Cousin Wolfie went down to his store every morning one hour ahead of everybody else. There was nobody on the streets but school kids and dogs, there wasn't a single customer in sight. But there he would sit just the same, on the high stool behind the cash register, with his little black skull-cap on his head, and his lips working silently. And at four-thirty in the afternoon, with the sun still shining on the streets and business at its height, Cousin Wolfie would close the store. It didn't matter how many customers were waiting, it didn't matter how loudly the cash register was ringing—Cousin Wolfie's watch said five-thirty, so it was time to close the store.

After two falls and winters like this, Cousin Wolfie went bankrupt. His customers got into the habit of going to his competitors down the street—and that habit stuck over the summer. And the more they stayed away, the more stubbornly Cousin Wolfie stuck to his point of view. "Compromise?" he used to say, in that peculiar way he had of grunting down at the floor, never raising his voice or his eyes. "Let *them* compromise." The following year his daughters sent him to the Jewish Home for the Aged, where he spent the last three years of his life muttering to himself about "these crazy modern ideas", and "the whole world is upside down these days".

But that was after Daylight Saving Time. Back in 1903, Cousin Wolfie was at his height. In fact, my Uncle Dan was scared to death at the first sight of him. He remembers still the way he came bouncing into Cousin Wolfie's store that first morning lugging his big clumsy

32

suitcase along with him, the way he went marching right up to Cousin Wolfie's stool, the way he stuck out his hand and announced with a big broad smile, "I'm your cousin Dan." And he remembers the way Cousin Wolfie just sort of squinted his little eyes at him, turned down the corners of his mouth, looked him over in silence for a long time, and finally gave a grunt. "Go put your things in the back room," he said. "And then you can sweep up the store."

After a few days, Dan knew that he wasn't going to get along with his new boss. First of all, he couldn't stand the dull, plodding, unimaginative way that Cousin Wolfie went about his business. No energy, no enthusiasm, no interest in expansion and new ideas. Every time Dan made a suggestion—even a tiny little suggestion, about putting an attractive display in the window, for instance—Cousin Wolfie just grunted and produced one of his sour inward smiles.

Second of all, Cousin Wolfie's slow, deliberate manner absolutely made Dan wild. You asked Cousin Wolfie a question, and what with frowning and shaking his head and mumbling to himself and creasing his forehead after every word, it took him about ten years to give you an answer. It was the same when Cousin Wolfie went to fetch something from one of the shelves. Slowly, painfully, he would lift himself off his stool—slowly, even more painfully, he would shuffle across the room in those big, moth-eaten carpet slippers that he wore all day. And then, there was the ordeal of Cousin Wolfie giving a customer change for a large bill. The way he counted out the coins—moving them one by one from his left hand to his right hand, his mouth working with each little penny—and then, chances are he'd lose count in the middle and have to start the whole thing all over again. My God, sometimes it was all Dan could do to keep from rushing forward, grabbing the whole pile of coins from Cousin Wolfie's hand, and throwing them into the customer's face.

But the most annoying thing of all was what Dan described as Cousin Wolfie's "high-handed dictatorial tone of voice". Specifically, this was a reference to Cousin Wolfie's way of turning to him, and grunting out very short and quiet, "Do this" or "Do that", and then turning away again without even waiting for an answer. "He's so positive I'll do what he wants," Dan said, "that he isn't even interested whether or not I say yes." The truth is, Dan wasn't used to taking orders from people. It was an experience he didn't like. He probably would have liked it just as little from a much sweeter, kinder, more sympathetic person than his Cousin Wolfie.

Not even the fuss that Cousin Wolfie's family made over him could reconcile him to this unpleasantness. He lived in the spare room at the back of their apartment—the board and rent was deducted each week from his salary—and Cousin Wolfie's wife, Cousin Martha, was constantly fussing over him, making his bed, washing his shirts, sneaking cold chicken and apple pie to him at night. What's more, Cousin Wolfie's daughters (the youngest was sixteen and the oldest was twenty-two) were continually trying to attract his attention—putting on new dresses for him, asking him artful little questions, quarrelling with their sisters for his benefit, showing off their piano-playing or their crocheting or their cooking. Naturally, this was all very pleasant—but it never quite succeeded in rubbing out the sting of Cousin Wolfie's "Do this" and "Do that".

After two weeks in Chicago, Dan decided that he was desperately unhappy. He wrote to his brother Herman and told him so. "Is this any life for a man my age?"

he wrote. "I am wasting away my youth. I am becoming old before my time."

Then the week-end came along. Desperately unhappy as he was, Dan spent Saturday going sightseeing with the youngest of Cousin Wolfie's girls. They walked all around town together—it was the Sabbath, so Cousin Wolfie wouldn't let them ride. She showed him the stockyards, and the business section, and the site of the old World's Fair. She showed him the Art Institute, which had been built ten years ago and already looked a hundred years old, and she showed him the auditorium, where the opera was going on now. Dan stared at this massive, sombre building for a long time. Opera, to him, was a word full of romance and mystery. It suggested women with diamond tiaras and men in evening clothes. What exactly went on in an opera house, anyway? His curiosity was aroused.

They finished up their excursion with a stroll along Michigan Avenue, past the ornate shop fronts, past the big fancy hotels, then across the bridge to Lake Shore Drive, with its spacious white mansions where the rich people lived. Dan was fascinated by it all. His mind was full of the contrast between this splendour and the squalid, grimy, brawling street where Cousin Wolfie, in spite of his money, continued to live. This time the emotion that Dan felt wasn't curiosity. It was a faint stirring of something much sharper and more provoking. Part of it was simple envy, and part of it was a kind of excitement, a kind of impatience, a little twitch inside of him that seemed to say, "Let's get going. What are we waiting for?"

On Monday morning, his brother Herman answered his letter. "I was very upset by your irresponsible attitude," Herman wrote, "though I must say it didn't come as a surprise. When are you going to learn that a man has to accept the good and the bad in this world? How do you expect to get ahead in business if you won't learn to take orders?"

This letter irritated Dan all morning. In every word of it, he could just see Herman's face, stretched out so long and serious and full of its own superior virtue. The more he thought about it, the more he was filled with a crazy desire to do exactly the *opposite* of what the letter wanted him to do. By the time he got back to the store from lunch, he was hoping, only hoping, for Cousin Wolfie to give him some kind of an order that he didn't want to carry out. He could just see himself drawing himself up to his full height—which was never very high, unfortunately—and telling Cousin Wolfie off. "I'm a poor relation," he would say to Cousin Wolfie, "so you think you can do what you want with me. But I'll show you that I've got a little spirit of my own. I'll show you that I'm not the type who lets people step all over him."

After this, Cousin Wolfie naturally wouldn't have anything more to do with him. He would tell him to get out of his store, out of his spare room, and out of his life. Dan would be alone in a strange city with no money and no friends, and what's more his family wouldn't have a bit of sympathy for him. He brought it on himself, they'd say, because he was a crazy, ungrateful no-good. He could almost hear Uncle Meyer's voice right now; "You made your own juice, Dan Waxman, so now you can stew in it." Which was perfectly fine with Dan. *He'd* show them in the end. He'd go out on his own and make a big name for himself, and one of these days Uncle Meyer would be coming to him to borrow money.

Sure enough, before the day was over, Dan had his chance to make the scene that he was spoiling for. Around the middle of the afternoon, a customer came in for a straw hat. Dan was in the corner, taking an inventory on suede gloves, when Cousin Wolfie grunted over at him, "Listen, climb up the ladder and bring down one of the number ten straws."

Dan stiffened a little. He didn't look up from the suede gloves, though, and he kept his voice very casual. "I'm busy right now."

There was a long silence. Then Cousin Wolfie's voice again, quiet and matter-of-fact, no more emotion than usual; "You can stop what you're doing."

This time Dan didn't answer him at all. He pressed his lips together very tight, and went right on counting suede gloves. Out of the corner of his eye, he watched to see what Cousin Wolfie would do.

After awhile, Cousin Wolfie started to his feet. Slow and painful, as always. He's afraid of a fight in front of the customer, Dan thought, with satisfaction. So it looks like he'll have to do some of his own work for once in his life.

Cousin Wolfie was shuffling across the floor. Slap-slap went those big, loose carpet slippers. Then he stopped in front of the ladder. He looked the ladder up and down for a moment thoughtfully, frowning a little, sizing it up the way he might size up a competitor. It's been a long time since he's made this particular trip, Dan thought. So it'll serve him right. He was getting too lazy in his old age. For a few dollars a week, he thought he could buy himself his own personal Chinese coolie.

Cousin Wolfie started up the ladder. One step at a time, the way he did everything else in the world. And the pauses between steps—well, you could read through the daily newspaper during one of those pauses. The ladder creaked and groaned under him all the way up. Going down was even slower and even creakier, because this time he was carrying a hatbox under his arm. So careful and cautious, thought Dan. He could be carrying the crown jewels of England, God forbid he should drop his load, and damage it a little, and maybe lose his profit on a piece of merchandise. A calamity like that, how could he ever survive it?

But Cousin Wolfie and the hat both got down the ladder safely. The customer tried it on, he liked it, he paid for it, he left the store. Cousin Wolfie went back to his stool behind the cash register.

And Dan, trembling a little with anticipation, waited now for the blow-up. His eyes and his hands and his shoulders all seemed to be concentrating hard on suede gloves—but his ears were keyed up sharply to take in the first stray rumbles from Cousin Wolfie.

The rumbles didn't come. Dan began to feel annoyed. What was the old man up to? Was he trying some new method of humiliating the poor relation? Was he playing cat-and-mouse with him? Well, this was one game Dan definitely wouldn't stand for. One thing he definitely didn't intend to be was mouse to Cousin Wolfie's cat. If the old man wouldn't start things up himself, all right, Dan was only too happy to oblige. There was a pair of suede gloves in his hand, which he now slapped down hard on the counter. Then he shoved out his lower lip and turned to face Cousin Wolfie, with his eyes shining, his cheeks reddening, and a spate of angry words all ready to burst out of him.

Well, he never brought out a single one of them. He was too surprised and bewildered by what he saw. Because the Cousin Wolfie who sat behind the counter wasn't the Cousin Wolfie he expected to see at all. Instead of looking at him with that shrewd little squint and that soft, thoughtful, mildly sarcastic smile, the old man was leaning way back in his chair, his eyes were shut tight, and he was gasping, just gasping and choking away as if he didn't have enough air, only without making a sound. But the worst of it was his face. It was white—Dan didn't know that a man's face could *get* so white. It was whiter than a sheet, whiter than chalk, whiter than any of the things that faces are usually supposed to be whiter than.

It brought a little cry out of Dan, that face, and he ran over to see what was the matter; "Are you all right? Can I do something?" With a terrible effort, Cousin Wolfie managed to bring a few strangled words out of his gasping. "A glass of water?" Dan said, and kept repeating it under his breath, "A glass of water—yes—sure—a glass of water," as he ran for a glass, ran over to the sink, ran back to Cousin Wolfie.

Most of the water dribbled down his chin. Just the same, it had its effect, because pretty soon Cousin Wolfie's gasps were coming a little less violently, and a touch of colour appeared in his face.

"What is it, what is it?" Dan asked, as soon as the old man had enough breath to answer him.

Always a man of few words, Cousin Wolfie wasn't turning into a public speaker overnight, just because of a small crisis. "It's the old business," he said, and that was all the explanation he gave. Then he motioned for Dan to help him into the back room, where he opened up his collar, stretched out on the couch, and told Dan to stop gaping at him and take care of the store.

An hour later Cousin Wolfie, looking more or less like his old self again, came out of the back room. He shuffled back to the cash register and took his seat on the high stool exactly as if nothing had happened.

Dan questioned the youngest daughter about it that night. He found out that Cousin Wolfie had been bothered for the last five years by a bad case of arthritis, very painful to him at all times, but especially when he

39

had to lift things or climb up and down stairs. "That's why Papa moves so slow all the time," said the youngest daughter. "He doesn't like to talk about it much, of course. Mamma says its very brave of him, and we shouldn't blame him when he acts bad-tempered sometimes. And I guess Mamma is right, though I can remember *before* he got his arthritis, and he used to act a little bad-tempered even then."

Dan had never been so ashamed of himself in his whole life. He just couldn't eat a thing at dinner. He couldn't even bring himself to look into people's faces. Cousin Martha noticed it, and worried about it all through the meal. "Are you coming down with a contagion?" she asked him. She felt his forehead, and even though he didn't feel "any more feverish than usual" she made him take a dose of paregoric, "only to be on the safe side".

After dinner, Cousin Martha and the girls went into the kitchen to do the dishes—all except the oldest girl, of course, who was too dignified for dish-washing. *She* went into the parlour to practise her piano. Dan and Cousin Wolfie were left at the dining-room table, finishing the last drops of their coffee. For a while neither of them said anything. Dan stared down at his plate, and Cousin Wolfie was perfectly content to sit back quietly with his hands folded over his stomach.

Well, finally Dan just couldn't keep quiet any longer. He raised his eyes, and looked at Cousin Wolfie, sort of sheepish and uneasy. "You don't have your pipe," he said. "Can I go into the parlour and get your pipe for you?"

Cousin Wolfie didn't answer for a while, then he gave a grunt and a nod. Dan knew him well enough by now to interpret this as a Yes. He jumped to his feet, and started out to the parlour fast. But he wasn't even through the door when he heard Cousin Wolfie's voice behind him.

"It's lying on the sofa," Cousin Wolfie said. "So you won't have to climb for it."

Dan couldn't keep himself from turning around and staring at Cousin Wolfie's face. But Cousin Wolfie's face didn't tell him a thing. The forehead was creased, the mouth was turned down, the little eyes were just as steady and unflickering as usual. There was no way of knowing whether or not he realized he had made a joke. So Dan gave a quick shake of his head and continued on to the parlour.

From then on, Dan never thought any more about picking that fight with Cousin Wolfie and striking out on his own. Well, maybe the blood did rise to his cheeks once or twice in the next few years—but he was always careful to leave the room before it could boil over. Come what may, he would stick it out a while longer in Hats, Gloves, and Accessories. He would save his money. He would take a few courses at a night school maybe—he didn't exactly know yet what subject he was interested in, though he was pretty sure that it didn't have much to do with selling derby hats to people. Whatever it turned out to be, he would read everything that was ever written about it, he would learn all there was to know about it, he would make himself some day into the most reliable, dependable, and responsible man in the field.

And it wasn't as if he was letting himself be intimidated by Herman's letter, either. As a matter of fact, that would be one of his chief pleasures in doing all this— because it was the last thing in the world that Herman and the rest of the family expected of him.

IV

By 1913, when he was twenty-seven, my Uncle Dan was rated as one of the most up-and-coming young fellows in his particular set. His particular set consisted of other up-and-coming young fellows about his own age and background. They were Jewish. They were in business —or occasionally in one of the more businesslike professions, like medicine or law. They were doing nicely, making more money than any of them would have dreamed of ten years before. They were confident that in another ten years they would be making a lot more still.

In their manner of life, they were all very modern, strenuously, unmercifully modern. They dressed themselves nattily, in the latest style. They sported ivory-tipped canes and straw hats. They wore morning clothes on Sundays. It was quite a treat to see them strolling jauntily along Michigan Avenue on a bright Sunday morning, with their wives (if they had wives) clinging proudly to their arms. Their way of talking was just as vigorously up-to-date. They learned all the latest, most popular slang expressions, and tossed them off casually with an air of long familiarity. If occasionally an oddly foreign turn of phrase, a tell-tale little intonation, maybe even some small but unmistakable word which nobody would ever find in any English dictionary, did creep into their speech, who could blame them for it? Because the truth about these up-and-coming young business-men was that back home most of them had a secret.

Sometimes the secret was a little white-haired gentleman, who sat around the living-room in his shirt-sleeves, smoked cheap smelly cigars, and liked to drink tea out of a glass. Sometimes the secret was a grey, pinched-up old lady with a perpetually worried look on her face, who was continually addressing the poor young fellow as "sonny boy". But more often than not, the secret wasn't quite so old or passive. The secret still thought of himself as being in the prime of life. He insisted on striding out into the world, maybe even showing up at Sonny Boy's office to slap the secretaries on the backside and announce louder, "All right, the old man is here, so let's hear about your problems!" Or if the secret was female, she could generally be depended on to charge into the biggest department store, the hairdresser, or the bank, and boast at the top of her voice about "my big business-man son, maybe you heard his name——?"

Well, an occasional moment of embarrassment certainly wasn't enough to destroy the general air of confidence, cockiness even, that clung to those energetic young fellows. They were the big men of the future, and they knew it. And being one of them, Dan knew it too.

He had left his Cousin Wolfie a long time ago. He had decided very quickly just where his interests and his talents lay. To spend his whole life in a store, selling things, would have bored him into an early grave. The kind of manœuvring and manipulating and spectacular lying that a salesman has to go through amused him up to a point, but what he couldn't stand was the other side of a salesman's job, the way you had to crawl and cringe for the sake of your customers, the constant bowing and scraping, and fawning and flattering, and generally making yourself small in front of other people. And if you managed to work yourself up and finally owned your own store—even if you turned out to be Marshall Field himself—underneath it all, were you ever anything but a glorified salesman?

Going into business for himself, however, had other disadvantages. What business could he go into, except to manufacture some product? In those days, advertising and publishing hadn't yet become big business, and there was no such thing as television—so what was there for a bright, ambitious, not particularly talented young man to go into? Underwear and pyjamas, coats and suits, ladies' handbags, and men's haberdashery, these were the growing items. But the thought of devoting the next fifty years to underwear and pyjamas made Dan feel sick. The trouble with manufacturing products was that all the products were so dull and ordinary to a man who was looking forward to big things.

There was one exception to this. There was one product that *did* raise his blood-pressure, set his heart beating a little faster, made him itch to plunge into action. That product was money. It was the only product that didn't have the dead hand of *usefulness* on it. You couldn't possibly use it for anything under the sun. You couldn't eat it, wear it, ride around in it, or furnish your house with it. All you could do was handle it, play tricks with it, buy it up cheap and sell it back expensive, coax it and caress it and baby it along, and let it reproduce itself. For Dan, there was a kind of fascination just thinking about this that he didn't get from anything else.

So as soon as he could, he enrolled in a night course in Banking and Public Accounting, and within two years he was licensed and certified and set up in a little office of his own. He did well right from the start. Business was good in those years, and a lot of his clients were faced with the necessity of keeping books for the first time in their lives. A page covered with figures was one great big baffling blank to them. They were badly in need of somebody to solve the puzzle for them—but they were also scared of whoever they might hire. Because they knew they were at his mercy. He could do anything with them. With those meaningless black and red scrawls in front of them, how could they protect themselves?

That was Dan's great qualification. He was not only good at his job, but his clients felt they could trust him. After all, he was one of them. Waxman was a nice, familiar, honest-sounding name. His Cousin Wolfie was one of the smartest merchants in town. His older brother was doing well in the jewellery business in New York. And Dan himself, with his thick, square nose, his active little eyes, his pleasant, homely, absolutely *normal* face— all you had to do was look at him, and you knew right away that you didn't have to worry about him. What's more, a man who could tell a story the way he did, with a good solid Yiddish punch-line—was it possible that such a man would steal your money? The reasoning was peculiar. After all, some of the same men who used it had themselves been known, from time to time——Well, it didn't really matter, because in Dan's case they were absolutely right.

Such was his luck during these years that even his excitable temper, which had always been such a problem to him, suddenly developed into an asset, a symbol of his good faith. Once for instance, he was approached by a man named Wardley who wanted him to do a little fancy juggling with a shady stock deal. The story was that Dan chased Wardley around the office three times, and finally caught him by the hair, and would have thrown him right out the window, except that Wardley's hair turned out to be a toupee. For a month afterwards it was the talk of Dan's set. People that he knew only slightly came up to him and shook his hand and slapped him on the back. In the course of that one month, he picked up seven new accounts.

His social life was a big success too. He discovered, as he made more and more money, that he had a taste for good clothes—and the style of that period, just a little bit flashy and extravagant, was so well suited to his temperament that he cut a better figure than many more handsome men. He was considered to be a highly eligible young bachelor. Which meant that he ate a lot of free dinners, did a lot of dancing, and was generally played for, cooked for, and crocheted for by a lot bigger game than Cousin Wolfie's daughters. His name was linked for a while with a Miss Neveloff, whose father had been a door-to-door pedlar twenty years ago, but to-day was a big-shot toy manufacturer and a patron of the Chicago Art Institute.

He discovered, in the course of these ten years, a number of new recreations that he had hardly even known about before. For instance, in common with most of the other fellows his age, he discovered golf. Well, to tell the truth, golf was actually a by-product of an even more important discovery that they all made—the country club. It didn't take them long to notice that the high-class crowd in Chicago—the rich Gentiles and the old snooty Jews, all of whom were thrown together by Dan and his friends, in one big bunch—kept up country clubs in the suburbs. All right, so wasn't it up to Dan and his friends to have a country club too? Didn't they owe it to the dignity of their new position?

Six or seven of the older, more distinguished, men got together to discuss the matter—and it was one of Dan's great satisfactions that he was invited to be one of them. They debated back and forth, they did some research with real estate men and architects, they sounded out their friends. As was to be expected, the preliminary discussion took about three times as long as it needed to take—but once the decision was made, the whole project

46

went into operation at double-speed. The money was raised, the land was bought, the building was put up. A name with the right mixture of distinction and cosiness was decided on—Pleasant Fairways. Then a grand opening was held. There were champagne and speeches, and a certain amount of rowdiness later on in the evening. Officers were elected—a Board of Governors, a House Committee, a Rules Committee, and most important of all, a Board of Admissions. Already there was talk about "keeping the standards high" and "only letting in the best element".

It was at this time, along with everything else, that Dan and his friends began to take lessons in golf.

Another new form of recreation that Dan discovered was the opera. He never forgot that Saturday afternoon when Cousin Wolfie's youngest daughter showed him the outside of the auditorium, and he never got over his curiosity about what went on inside. But to actually get inside, once he started in his own business, wasn't so very easy. He couldn't be sure how his clients would feel about an accountant who went to the opera. Who knows, it might completely undermine their confidence in him. Any man who would spend his own money on such foolishness, how much conscience would he feel about spending *other* people's money? Five years later, of course, this wouldn't be any problem for him. By that time, most of his set, Dan himself included, would be married, and the women would have discovered opera the same way that the men had discovered golf—and for the same reasons. Five years from now, a man who liked the opera could always get himself "dragged" there by his wife, with absolutely no loss of prestige. But that was five years from now.

And so, one night when he was by himself and didn't have anything else to do—he was between free dinners— Dan went down to the auditorium. He looked to the right and left before buying his ticket, just to make sure that nobody who knew him was there. He sneaked to his seat, and huddled up in it with his hand shading his eyes, until the lights went down.

Even with his hand over his eyes, he knew that he was starting in on something that was going to mean a great deal to him. There were more than enough tiaras and evening clothes to satisfy him. There was a sweep of boxes and balconies and electric lights as far up as you could look. There was a tremendous thick curtain, all covered with gold—the mental calculations that Dan automatically made under such circumstances showed him that this curtain must have cost a pretty penny.

But this wasn't it, this wasn't the reason for the funny little twinge of excitement that he could feel inside of him. It was what waited for him *behind* that curtain that tantalized him. It was the rustle of programmes, the buzz of voices, and then the sounds of the orchestra warming up, fiddles squealing sort of sad and whiney like Aunt Hortense who always imagined she was a sick woman, trumpets giving out breathy little bleats and blasts like an unsatisfied client, and that whatchamacallit that kept tootling away in the low registers, perfectly content with its own conversation and paying absolutely no attention to anybody else. Cousin Wolfie's youngest daughter to the life!

Then, all of a sudden, the lights began to get dim— and right away Dan's mood stopped being frivolous. With the hush that came over the audience, a feeling of tremendous solemnity filled the house. Then there was a rustle of applause, then it got louder and louder. Dan craned his neck to see what everyone was clapping for— but all he could see was this little man with a black beard threading his way among the violin-players, then stepping up in the middle of the orchestra, and making three stiff little bows to the right, to the left, and straight ahead. Then he turned his back to the audience and gave a quick little tap-tap with his wand. Right away the applause cut short, the hush was on the house again. The little man with the beard raised his arms over his head, he kept them there a moment—and Dan held his breath. Then the arms came sweeping down, and there was a crash of sound from the orchestra, and the red-coated troops of the Count di Luna exploded into my Uncle Dan's life.

He walked home from the opera. It was a long distance—Dan lived uptown in one of the more respectable hotels for young bachelors—and it was almost midnight, and it was chilly out. But he walked all the way, without noticing either the crowds downtown or the emptiness of the side streets leading to his hotel. He was thinking about marching armies and gypsy camps: about duels and serenades: about that mousy little man who seemed to gain a foot in height as his voice went soaring up to the top of the house: about that large, plump lady with the long black wig who died in such beautiful agonies that Dan could almost feel the breath being torn out of himself at the same time.

The next day at lunch, his friend Mort Meltzer, who was quite a joker, asked him what he was doing last night. "Tried to get in touch with you all night, Dan boy. Who's the chorus girl? Does she have a sister?" Dan blushed a little, and lowered his head, and murmured that he was sorry, she didn't have a sister.

But opera and golf weren't the only new forms of recreation that came into Dan's life now that he was making money. There was gambling—all-night poker games with the boys, or wild splurges of roulette at the downtown joints. Dan loved it, in spite of the fact that he was just about as bad a gambler as he could possibly be.

It was his old trouble, the thing that his brother Herman was always lecturing him about—no self-control. He threw himself into the game much too enthusiastically, he got involved in it as if it was a matter of life and death. If he picked up a bad hand, he gritted his teeth, growled, muttered under his breath. If he picked up a good hand, his whole face lighted up like a traffic light, and everybody else around the table could see that he was practically bursting to make his bet. Around the roulette table he wasn't any better. He concentrated on that little ball as if it was alive. He whispered to it pleadingly, he shouted orders at it, he heaped insults on it. Worst of all, he absolutely refused to admit it when his luck was bad. If he had a hunch to play number ten, then he would play number ten and play number ten, and go right on playing it, no matter how many times it lost. He was damned well going to *make* his hunch come true, even if he lost all his money at it.

Luckily he didn't go out gambling more than three or four times a year.

And then, in the spring of 1913, to celebrate his twenty-seventh birthday, Dan took up still another new form of recreation. He started to grow a moustache. It was his ambition to make it into a real thick, bushy, distinguished-looking masterpiece, and so he tended it lovingly for months. Every morning the very first thing he did was to stand in front of the bathroom mirror and twirl his moustache a little, then give it a clip here and a clip there, then stand back a ways and cock his head to the side and look it over critically. Naturally, he took a lot of kidding about this moustache from the boys at the club. "Why don't you admit that it's hopeless?" said his friend Mort Meltzer. "It won't do any good unless you grow one that's big enough to cover your whole face." Dan laughed at the kidding—sometimes just a little edgily, depending on the mood he was in—and he went right on with the moustache. *He* liked it, if nobody else did. And then, in the early fall, he suddenly got sick of it, and shaved it off.

It was a symptom. Because only a few weeks later, something happened to bring Dan's carefree, easy-going life to an end.

It began when he took a trip to New York for his Uncle Meyer's funeral. For the last few years Uncle Meyer hadn't been a well man. He had a weak heart and a bad liver, and the doctor advised him to take it easy. But everybody knew that Uncle Meyer wouldn't follow the doctor's orders. Right up to the end he couldn't resist running here and there to pick up and relay the latest gossip, telling his friends and relations what they should do "for their own good", giving lectures to people about how to improve their way of life—mainly by modelling it a little more after *his* way of life. You could almost say about Uncle Meyer that he killed himself with an overdose of self-righteousness. And he got his reward for it, too. The family gave him a fine funeral—just as fine a funeral as he was always recommending for everybody else, during his lifetime.

So Dan went to New York for the occasion. It was his first trip to New York since he left ten years before. He was amazed at how little he felt about it. No feelings of regret, no sentimental little tugs at his heartstrings, not a tear in his eye for the old familiar landmarks. Chicago was his home now. He knew it already. He didn't have to come back to New York to find it out.

It *was* nice to see his brother Herman, of course. In the last ten years Herman had been to Chicago four or five times—on business, and for the International Jewellers' Convention—and Dan was always glad to see him. How prosperous and dignified he looked. A little more prosperous and dignified every time. And now he was a married man, and a junior partner in Cousin Simon's jewellery business. For Dan it was a genuine pleasure just to sit back in silence and admire this brother of his—for the first day or so, anyway. After that, well, maybe his silence wasn't always quite so willing.

Anyhow, as soon as the funeral was out of the way, the family turned its attention to a problem which they had been discussing for many years, but which they had never had an opportunity to act on before—finding a nice girl for Dan. Twenty-eight was old enough for a man to stay a bachelor, it was about time he settled down and started having something in his life besides enjoyment. But they didn't have for ever to manage it. He would only be in New York for three days, and what sort of girl could he expect to pick up back there in Chicago? So they crowded as much into those three days as they possibly could— dinners, and lunches, and dances, and introductions until he was dizzy, until nice pretty Jewish girls from good families were practically coming out of his ears. But it wasn't a waste by any means. Because before the three days were over, my Uncle Dan had met my Aunt Sarah.

Actually the conditions were ideal. He was invited up to her apartment for dinner, and the whole evening was spent with Sarah—no family to interfere. That's because her mother was dead, her older brothers were all married and living away from home, her sister was still only a ten-year-old kid, and her father, old Liebstadt the diamond buyer, was the old fashioned German type who liked to eat a big dinner and go to sleep right after it. This gave Dan plenty of opportunity to discover what a sweet, pretty, and intelligent girl she was for only twenty-one. And what a wonderful conversationalist. All night long he talked about Chicago, and public accounting

methods, and the great times he had with his friends—
and except to nod her head and breathe out "Oh, how
interesting" she didn't interrupt him once. It was all so
pleasant and flattering, by the end of the evening he had
even forgotten that she was taller than he was.

Not that he proposed to her right then and there, of
course, or even during this particular trip. Such things,
the family knew, only happen in storybooks. He had to
be worked on a little. He had to be thrown together
with the girl. He had to make another trip or two to
New York—which, with Herman's co-operation, was
easy enough to finagle: Herman simply persuaded Cousin
Simon to turn his accounting work over to Dan. And
then, to clinch things, Sarah had to be sent out to Chicago
for awhile—also very easy: a little research dug up some
Chicago cousins of the Liebstadts: a little friendly bribery
got them to issue an invitation.

Exactly according to the family's plan, this trip to
Chicago did it. Sarah was with her cousins for over a
week, and Dan saw her every day. Instead of talking to
her constantly about himself, he began to notice a little
what *she* was like. So calm, so quiet, so steady and well-
balanced, with such tolerance and sympathy for other
people. So different from what he was himself—it was
good for him, to be close to somebody like that, somebody who wasn't a wild man from Borneo like *he* was——

One night he confessed to her, shyly, laughing a little,
how fond he was of the opera. And she didn't even smile
at him for it. She looked very serious, even a little
worried, because she hadn't ever been to an opera herself. But she would go to them from now on, she
promised him that, she would learn all about them so that
he wouldn't think she was nothing but a dope.

Another night he had a mood of discouragement.
They came over him occasionally, these moods, where

everything suddenly seemed flat and stupid, and he would never really get anywhere in the world, he would just be a nobody for the rest of his life. She smiled at him then, and told him he was much more than a nobody already.

And then, another night, he took her out late to a theatre, and they couldn't find a taxicab anywhere, and it began to rain, and he was getting madder and madder, hopping up and down, muttering about "the goddamned cabs in this goddamned city". And Sarah touched his arm lightly and spoke in a low voice, "It doesn't matter, Dan—I don't care about waiting——" And he whirled on her before he knew what he was doing and shouted at her, "You don't care about waiting. That's an idiotic thing to say. Are you dead or something, that you shouldn't care?" Then he saw her face, with the eyes wide and the lips trembling a little. All of a sudden it came over him, what he had just done. He turned red, he just turned completely red. Give him a gun, and he would have blown his brains out right on the spot. And just to make it as painful as possible, right then an empty cab stopped in front of them.

They got in, and they rode for awhile, and neither of them said anything. And then, from Sarah's corner of the seat Dan heard a noise. A soft little sobbing noise. It was more than he could bear. He turned to her, and grabbed her hands, and burst out all at once, "Sarah, I apologize—my God, I wouldn't hurt you for anything. It's something inside of me—it just seems to get into me—you of all people, don't you know it yet, you're the last one on earth I could ever want to hurt——"

Before they got out of that cab, they were engaged.

The wedding was held in New York in December. It was an ideal wedding from the point of view of Dan's aunts. The father had enough money to do things very nicely—and since the mother was dead, the females in the groom's family could meddle in the arrangements as much as they liked.

On the big day Dan was as nervous as men in his position are supposed to be. For an hour before the ceremony he snapped at Herman, who was his best man. And then, five minutes before the ceremony, he apologized all over himself, and told Herman he was "the best brother a damned fool ever had", and generally went off on such an orgy of mixed-up sentimentality that Herman had to cut him short firmly to get him into the synagogue.

Standing next to him in front of the rabbi, Sarah looked so beautiful, and so white, and so awfully young and helpless. With a pang Dan remembered the way he had shouted at her that rainy night in Chicago. He remembered that scared, uncertain look on her face. Never again, he told himself, as the rabbi droned on. Never again, as long as he lived, would he raise his voice to her. He made her that promise right now.

The promise was broken from time to time in the years that followed. But on the whole they had a happy married life together. They went to Florida for the honeymoon. Then he took Sarah back to Chicago, and threw a big party for all his friends, and introduced her to everybody. And they were all impressed with her, and she was impressed with them. And Mort Meltzer made jokes about how a man of Dan's "stature" was lucky to have "a wife that he can look up to". Two years later, Dan and Sarah had a little girl. Barbara they called her, not after anybody in the family, but simply because Dan thought that "Bobby" would be a nice pet name for a little girl. Two years after that there was a war, but Dan didn't have to go into it, on account of his age and his child and his high blood-pressure.

And then, when the war was over, the money really

started to pour in. Everybody was making it, right and left. Herman wrote that he was selling more diamond necklaces than ever before in the history of the firm— Herman was the head of the firm now, since Cousin Simon's death. And right here in Chicago, Dan's friend Mort Meltzer was a rich man overnight from mink coats. And Dan himself landed his biggest client of all, the great financial genius Martin Drexell, who was reorganizing the public utilities of the Mid-West. Out of all the competition, out of a hundred accountants with bigger reputations and Gentile names, the great Drexell picked Dan to handle his business exclusively. It was the most tremendous honour that Dan had ever received in his life— and the commission was nothing to sneeze at either.

On the strength of it, he moved into a new apartment— the penthouse apartment in one of those sunny new buildings along the lake. Twelve Hundred Lake Shore Drive was the address, and what's more, the apartment was a duplex. It was the final touch. It proved once and for all that he was on his way. So Dan and Sarah settled down in it, bought new furniture for it, built a playroom for Bobby in it, and pretty soon were so crazy about it that they could hardly imagine living anywhere else.

"The world is divided into two parts," Dan used to say, with a wave of his arm. "Twelve Hundred Lake Shore Drive—and everywhere else."

V

Observe my Uncle Dan in the year 1928. Follow him through an average day. Friday, March twenty-third, for instance, the day of old Abe Kugel's seventy-fifth birthday.

At eight o'clock in the morning, sharp, he comes down to the dining-room for breakfast. At the age of forty-two what an impressive figure he makes, dressed up for the office in his shiny, double-breasted blue serge suit. And yet, when you analyse it, isn't he still the same short little man with a thick nose? What's more, hasn't he developed a much more prominent pot belly than he had in the early days, not to mention that definite bald spot in the middle of his head? But just the same, what elegance, what distinction, what a fine handsome appearance! So fine that it rises above mere external accidents, like noses and bald spots. It comes from inside of him, my Uncle Dan's elegance. It comes from being a happy man.

His wife and daughter are waiting for him at the table. He kisses Sarah on the cheek a little hurriedly, then spends a lot more time enjoying a great big hug from Bobby. Bobby will be thirteen on her next birthday, but she's tall for her age. In this respect, she takes after her mother's side of the family.

"Excuse me, Daddy," she says. "I smeared you all over with strawberry jam."

"It was worth it," Dan says, as he wipes his mouth with the napkin. "How often do I get kissed by such a beautiful young vamp?"

Bobby laughs and blushes, turning her head to the side a little. Dan is crazy about the way she blushes. What a pleasure it is to have such a shy, sweet-tempered, good-hearted girl for a daughter. Sometimes he bawls her out for just these qualities. He tells her that she's too sweet and good-hearted for her own good, that people have to blow their own horn a little in this world, that she will grow up to be an A-Number-One sucker. But he tells her this only out of a sense of duty. Underneath, he likes her just the way she is. How much better than if he was cursed with a little show-off, like Mort Meltzer's Marilyn, with her bold manner, her sharp tongue, her loud laugh that you can hear ten miles away in a room full of people.

"Don't gulp your food, Bobby dear," Sarah said.

"I'm going to be late for school, Mommy," Bobby says.

"So be late for school," Dan says. "It won't kill them, if you drop in a little late once in awhile. Show them that you're independent. Show them that you don't just jump every time they snap their fingers."

Bobby's eyes begin to widen. "I guess I won't feel so independent when I get sent to Mr. Mortenson's office."

"I tell you what," Dan says "I'll give you a note for this Mr. Mortenson. 'Dear Mr. Mortenson, Please excuse my daughter Barbara Waxman for being late to school, as she and I were discussing important business matters. Sincerely yours——' "

"Oh, Daddy," Bobby breaks in with a wail, "Mr. Mortenson would *never* accept an excuse like that——" And then she stops suddenly, realizing that he was making fun of her. And the next moment she's giggling right along with him.

Dan get's a big kick out of kidding Bobby along like that. The way she looks so solemn and concerned for a while, and then, as soon as she finds out it's all a joke, her whole expression changes and she's just as delighted as she can be. This is a game that the two of them have been playing practically since she was a baby.

But now it's time for her to leave. She stuffs the last bit of toast into her mouth, leaves a trail of crumbs on her mother's cheek and her father's forehead, then dashes out the front door. She's on her way to school—the finest, most expensive private school in Chicago, naturally.

With Bobby gone, Dan turns his attention to the morning newspaper. Sarah reads the mail. Every once in a while, without bothering to look up, they exchange remarks about what they're reading.

"Politicians," Dan says. "Election time is getting close, so all of a sudden our fourflusher mayor is a big humanitarian. It says here he made a speech at a synagogue last night, how the Jews and the Irish should live together in peace and harmony."

"Here's an engraved announcement from Mort Meltzer," Sarah says. "The grand opening of his new fur emporium next week."

"The people that win the Irish Sweepstakes. It's a good thing they've got luck, because from the looks of them they were out of town when the brains were passed around."

"Oh dear, another one of those letters from my sister Goldie. She says Papa is giving her trouble again. He won't listen to the doctor. He keeps drinking beer when Goldie isn't looking."

"Did you ever hear of such a Market? Up, up, and up. How long can it last? Drexell only gives it another five years."

"I don't think I'm going to like the new spring hats. It seems like clothes are getting sillier and sillier every year."

A long pause. Only the sounds of chewing and sipping. And then, all of a sudden Dan raises his head from the newspaper: "Your father is a friendly, harmless old man. Why doesn't Goldie let him enjoy his beer in peace?"

Ten minutes later Dan finishes his coffee, and Sarah goes to the door with him. "Don't forget about tonight," he says. "Signor Mantini is coming for dinner. He's bringing that soprano and the new tenor."

"I'd better open an extra case," Sarah says.

After a pause, Dan smiles at her and says, "And what are *you* doing with yourself to-day?"

"Nothing special. I'm having lunch with some of the girls. And then I've got an appointment for a beauty treatment."

Dan laughs. "The way you spend my money. Now why should you want a beauty treatment at your age?"

Another pause, and then he kisses her on the cheek. "So I'll see you to-night." And then he goes out the door.

Dan has a car and chauffeur now, and both of them are waiting for him in front of the building. The chauffeur hops around and holds the door for him, and he gets into the car—but he doesn't think he'll ever feel right about it. The idea of being driven all over the place by a grown man, as if he was an invalid or a two-year-old baby or something. If it wasn't for the fact that everybody else is getting cars and chauffeurs nowadays—— One thing that Dan isn't going to stand for, no matter how much of a sacrifice it comes to, and this is that he should lag behind anybody else.

So he leans back in his seat and tries to forget his undignified position by lighting up a cigar. Smoking cigars is something else that Dan has taken up in these last few years, these fast, prosperous, high-living years. And if he does say so himself, he can manipulate a Corona De Luxe with the best of them. The way he snips off the end and sucks in on the flame, very intent and serious, like a man starting out on a highly important project. Then the way he waves it in the air when he's outlining an opinion, sort of casual an opinion, sort of casual and offhand, as if he's hardly aware that he has it between his fingers. And the way he can suddenly stop being casual and offhand, and grasp it firmly and make sharp little stabbing motions with it, to get across a point. Or the way he can clamp his teeth down on it hard when somebody comes into the office to sell him something, and lean back in his seat, and make that poor salesman feel like a worm. "In fact," Dan likes to tell himself, in one of his good humours, "I can do so many different things with them, it's a wonder I ever get time to smoke them."

But now, through the window of the car, he notices where he is. He notices the clutter and maze of the Loop, only a few blocks from his office. He leans forward and tells the chauffeur to let him out right here. "It's a nice day," he says, "I'll walk the rest of the way." Actually it's not such a nice day at all. There's a chill in the air, and it looks like rain. But every once in a while Dan gets the feeling that he'd rather not ride up to his building in that big fancy car with that big fancy chauffeur. Somehow he's a little embarrassed that the telephone girl or the office boy might see him.

And anyway, once he starts walking, the day doesn't seem so bad any more. Walking in Chicago has been one of his favourite pastimes ever since he took that first long sightseeing tour with Cousin Wolfie's youngest daughter, twenty-five years ago. He likes the feeling of plumping himself down in the midst of the city, with all its commotion and confusion, and striding through it, with his chin up and his cane working, as if he owned it all. He passes the fancy shop fronts, the big department stores, the skyscrapers, the traffic, and he remembers how it was when he first came to Chicago. Up-and-coming, yes, but nothing like what it is to-day. He feels somehow that he personally has been responsible for all this progress. This is *his* city, he feels. Then he looks at some of the people around him—that little man with the bowler hat, those three determined-looking women out on a shopping expedition, that puffy red-faced old lady selling pencils on the corner. He can imagine, with a chuckle, how *they* would react if he told them that this was *his* city.

"All right, so I'm vain and egotistical," he says to himself. "Who does it hurt?"

VI

DAN arrives at his office.

His office is no longer the dark little pigeon-hole that he started out in, with one dilapidated desk and a girl who came in three times a week to take dictation. Nowadays he works in style, just as he lives in style. He has a whole suite of rooms at the top of the newest, biggest office building in Chicago. Before you can get into his own private, personal room, you have to pass by two telephone girls and a secretary. Inside that room, which is wide and spacious, Dan sits at a large shiny mahogany desk covered with red leather blotters, two telephones, a dictating machine, fountain pens, important papers, and photographs of Sarah and Bobby in fancy frames. When he looks up from that desk he sees genuine oak panelling all around him. When he swivels around in his chair, right behind him is a magnificent view of the whole city, with smokestacks puffing and Lake Michigan gleaming far below. When he gets up from that desk to pace a little, his feet sink into the softest, most dignified, most expensive carpeting available.

His secretary, Mrs. Schultz, is in her forties, and has been with him for ten years. And she's just the sort of a secretary that a man of his importance needs. A tall, horse-faced Irishwoman (her maiden name was Brady) with a cynical outlook on life and a perpetually sceptical scowl. Besides being the perfect secretary to deal with cranks, salesmen, and people who want favours, Mrs. Schultz is also a wonderful tonic for Dan's self-confidence. He depends a lot on her tart, crisp, sarcastic comments about the daily routine, the people who come into the office, and life in general. Especially he enjoys her in one of her more personal moods, when she gets off on the subject of "that good-for-nothing bum" and the latest "trick" that he's been "up to". The good-for-nothing bum is Mr. Schultz, her husband, whom Mrs. Schultz has been supporting for twenty years.

Basically, the thing that tickles Dan about Mrs. Schultz's dislike of humanity is the way she manages to imply that he is the one exception to the general rule. "The whole world is crazy"—that's what Mrs. Schultz's manner seems to be saying—"all except you and me."

"And maybe," Dan sometimes adds to himself, "she isn't always so sure of me."

So now he comes marching into the office, enjoys the bright little squeals of the telephone girls and the earnest ambitious "Good morning" of the office boy, and disappears into his private room with Schultz behind him. Here they settle down to the work of the day—answering letters, going over figures, talking to clients on the phone. One letter is from the synagogue—they want a contribution to the Sunday School fund. "Fat chance!" says Dan, pushing the letter aside. "I gave them a hundred dollars last month. My God, can't those rabbis learn how to run their business?"

But now it's time to relax awhile. He listens to Schultz tell him how "the bum" just lost his latest job. "Janitor in a warehouse," she says. "All he had to do was sit in a little cubby-hole all day and read the newspaper, and every once in a while he might have to open the door for someone. So he's there a week, only one week, and yesterday the boss drops by and tells him his cubby-hole is filthy, he ought to sweep it out. So what does he do, that bum of mine? He gets up on his high horse, and he tells the boss he isn't accustomed to being spoken to in that manner, and he quits the job on the spot. And can I say a word to him about it? Can I admonish him for it? Oh no. All I have to do is start in on a tiny little bit of admonishing, and right away he's on his high horse with *me*. He's a German, you know, so right away he starts telling me how he went to the University of Heidelberg, and how his father was a personal friend of Bismarck. So maybe I get a little mad at this. That's only natural, isn't it? Maybe I answer him, 'Bismarck! No matter how you dress it up, that's still a piece of fish!' So he turns red in the face at this, and calls me a name in German, and talks about his pride. 'I have still my pride left,' he says. 'Everything else has from me been stolen, but I have still my pride.' And he won't talk to me again for the rest of the night. Those Germans, how would they get along without that crazy pride of theirs?"

"Why don't you walk out on him?" Dan says. "Get a divorce."

"I'd do it like a shot," says Schultz, "only it's against my religion. Besides, what's going to become of that bum if I walk out on him? Who'll he have to show off his pride on? No, I'm afraid I'm stuck with him for life." And Schultz lowers her head quickly and gets very interested in some papers in her lap.

After a moment, Dan speaks up. "Why did you marry him in the first place? What did you see in him, anyway?"

"What did I see in him?" Schultz raises her head and gives one of her sharp sour laughs. "I was eighteen years old, and he clicked his heels and kissed my hand. Believe

64

me, the last thing in the world I was using was my eyes." For just a second she lowers her voice, and her face grows thoughtful. "It might not be so bad, you know, if we could've had some kids." A second after, she raises her voice and laughs again. "Well, maybe that's a good thing too. With my luck, they all would've taken after him."

It's a hard world, Dan thinks, when Schultz goes away. And for the first time that day, he feels sort of depressed and uneasy. You're a lucky man, he tells himself. You've got money, and prestige, and a wonderful family. You should stop for a couple of minutes every day, and thank God for what a lucky man you are.

He searches through his papers for that letter from the synagogue. Then he makes out a cheque for a hundred dollars to the Sunday School fund.

At eleven-thirty, his work is interrupted. Schultz shows in young Mark Kugel from Kugel's Klothes for Kiddies, which has its offices next door. The boy is only in his early twenties, just out of the State University, but already he's practically running the business. That's because his father died in the War, and his grandfather, old Abe Kugel, the founder and president of Kugel's Klothes for Kiddies, is a man over seventy.

Not that the old man has his feet in the grave, or anything like that. He's a fine, tall, handsome old man, with all his teeth and a beautiful head of thick white hair, and he has enough strength left in him to run twenty businesses. But the fact is, as he often puts it to Dan when they ride down in the elevator together, "A young man I'm not, and the day will come when the boy will have to take things over, anyway. So let him learn how to do it now. He's a smart hard-working boy, and he deserves the opportunity. This is my philosophy of life," old Kugel adds, in a more serious tone of voice. "The old men have to step aside for the young men. Otherwise look at how crowded the world would be."

Dan feels a great admiration for this philosophy of life. With the wrong type of boy it's a philosophy that might turn into a tragedy—but Dan is sure that young Mark Kugel, with his thick glasses, his earnest, serious-minded air, his nice polite affectionate way of talking to his grandfather, is the right type of boy. Dan wouldn't be sorry if he had a son like that for himself, to take over *his* business some day. A son being impossible, a nice affectionate son-in-law wouldn't be so bad either.

So now young Mark Kugel comes into his office, nodding and smiling a little nervously. "Mr. Waxman," he says, "would you like to step across the hall? If you can spare the time, that is. We're about to begin the ceremonies.

"Ceremonies? What ceremonies?"

"For the birthday, Mr. Waxman," says the boy, very proud and pleased, and grinning shyly on account of it. "Didn't you know? To-day is Grandpa's seventy-fifth birthday."

"His seventy-fifth birthday? Your grandpa—he's seventy-five years old? My God, who could've believed it? He absolutely doesn't look a day over sixty!" And somehow this piece of news, though it really doesn't concern him personally at all, makes Dan feel just wonderful, his mood of depression goes away and his whole day brightens up again. "Can I spare the time?" he cried, jumping to his feet and starting around the desk. "Believe me, the time is spared."

He takes the boy by the arm, and they hurry out of the office together. And all the way across the hall, Dan keeps shaking his head and saying, "Seventy-five years—it's a miracle—it's a regular Fountain of Youth——"

As they start through the door of Kugel's Klothes for

Kiddies, the boy lowers his voice and says into Dan's ear, "Don't tell him what you're here for, Mr. Waxman. It's sort of a surprise. We're presenting him with a birthday present."

Dan nods and winks. "Not a word," he says.

And now they go into the outer office. It's full of people. Not just the usual staff—the girl at the switchboard, the office boys, the bright cheerful little old lady who has been old Kugel's secretary for years—but also a group of salesmen laughing at each other's jokes, the general manager and the assistant general manager shaking their heads over business conditions, the foreman from the factory standing uncomfortably in a corner, a couple of plump blushing ladies who represent the sewing machines. Dan is amazed at the sight of them all. What a crowd to turn out for the old man's birthday party!

At Mark's entrance, they all stop what they're doing and look up inquisitively. "So, so?" they say in loud whispers. "How about it? Let's get started."

"Right away," Mark answers, also in a loud whisper.

Then, while everybody hushes up, he steps over to the door that leads into old Kugel's private office, and he knocks on it softly.

"Come in, come in," says that familiar deep voice from inside the room.

"Would you come out, Grandpa?" says Mark. "I've got something important to show you."

"Problems, problems," says the deep voice, getting closer and closer. Finally the door is opened, and there stands old Abe Kugel himself, tall and impressive. When he sees the crowd gathered in the outer office, he shoves his long hawk-like nose forward a little and peers around, puzzled. "What's the convention, boy?"

"Just a second, Grandpa," says Mark. "We'll bring it

out right now." He gives a signal, and a couple of the office boys hurry out to the stockroom.

Meanwhile, old Kugel is squinting around from one face to another. "Mrs. Monahan, what's this all about? You didn't tell me I had so many appointments this morning. Jake, I don't follow, why aren't you at the factory? Has something gone wrong at the factory? Anything that goes wrong, I'm sure Mark here can handle it without my help."

"Nothing's gone wrong at the factory, Mr. Kugel," says the foreman, shifting on his feet and getting red in the face.

"The factory's just fine, Grandpa," says Mark, smiling at the old man, hardly able to control his delight.

Old Kugel smiles too. "Well, if the factory's just fine," he says, making his voice stronger, "I'd like you to tell me, please, why everybody is lying down on the job."

At this, there is suppressed laughter all around the room.

The next moment old Kugel catches sight of Dan. "More unusual events," he says. "Dan Waxman, will you explain kindly why you're neglecting your business and loafing around in here! If all your pencil sharpeners are broken, my secretary will be happy to help you out."

"My pencil sharpeners," says Dan, with exaggerated dignity, "are as good as any man's pencil sharpeners."

"So what is it then?" the old man cries, with a despairing gesture. "It couldn't be spring fever, it isn't even spring yet."

"Here it comes, Grandpa," says Mark. He turns and points to the door of the stockroom. Everybody else turns too, and the old man follows the general direction in polite bewilderment. A moment later, the door swings open and the two office boys appear, one of them looking terribly solemn and important, the other one fighting hard to control his smirking. Between them they carry a cake—a big round fat cake, all covered with white and green frosting, and a candle sticking up from the middle of it, flickering away in the entrance to the stockroom.

After a second of silence, the loud hoarse voice of one of the salesmen starts things off "Happy birthday to you! Happy birthday to you!" It isn't long before everybody else is joining in, and Dan himself one of the loudest, while the office boys march forward in time to the singing.

On the third line of the song, the voices become sort of jumble—"Happy birthday, dear Mr. Kugel—dear Grandpa—dear A-Abe"—depending on who's singing. But they all come together again for the fourth line, and bring the song to a triumphant finale:

"Happy birthday to-o-o-o-o-o you!"

Amid cheers and applause, the cake is set down on the secretary's desk in the centre of the room.

Various outcries from the audience; "Blow out the candle!" "Show us what a pair of lungs you got!" "Make a wish, make a wish!" Most of these outcries come from the salesmen, who are beginning to get warmed up to the occasion.

"Blow out the candle, Grandpa," says Mark, and he gently takes the old man's arm.

Old Kugel looks down at his grandson's hand. Then he looks around the room, blinking a little at all the smiles. On his face is that confused, embarrassed look that people usually wear at a time like this. "But it's such a surprise," he says. "How did you find out, all of you?"

The crowd laughs, very pleased with its cleverness.

"Come on, Grandpa, the candle," says Mark, and he helps the old man forward to the centre of the room.

"One candle," says old Kugel, with a little laugh. "Am I supposed to be one year old?"

"In spirit, Mr. Kugel," says his secretary, Mrs. Monahan.

"Why, you're not such an old man, Abe," yells out one of the salesmen—one who has been with the firm a long time. "I was talking with this girl from the Ziegfeld Follies the other day, and she says you're better than a young fellow in his twenties."

But now, as the old man gets ready to blow out the candle, the crowd hushes up again. The old man leans forward, looks around him awkwardly, then puffs up his cheeks and gives a blow. The candle goes sputtering out.

More applause. "So there's life in the old boy yet," says one of the salesmen.

"Now you have to make a wish, Mr. Kugel," says Mrs. Monahan, who has a deep sentimental side to her. "Quiet, everybody, Mr. Kugel has to make a wish."

Everybody is quiet. They wipe the smiles off their faces for this solemn moment.

Old Kugel closes his eyes briefly, and smiles a faint secret smile. A second later he opens his eyes again, and laughs. "All finished. The wish is made."

"What was it, Grandpa?" says Mark. "What did you wish for?"

"Now I'm not supposed to tell," says the old man. For a moment he looks down at his grandson, quiet and tender. "Otherwise it won't come true."

The tenderness hangs in the air. Dan can almost feel it there, and it gives him a little pang at his heart. And then, with a burst of exuberance from the salesmen, it goes floating away.

"The cake, cut the cake!" the salesmen are shouting. "Come on, we're starved, cut the cake!"

But Mark raises his arm and shushes them. "Wait a second. Ladies and gentlemen, before we cut the cake, there's an important matter to take care of."

The noises lower to a curious buzz. Mark reaches into his pocket and pulls out a small white package. He turns to his grandfather and clears his throat. "Grandpa," he begins nervously. Up to now he hasn't been the least bit nervous—but now, when he's conscious of actually making a formal speech, he suddenly becomes nervous. "Grandpa—all of us here—working with you every day in the office—we all got together, and—in token of how we feel about you—and all the nice things that we think about you—— Well, we got you a birthday present, Grandpa." And with that, he shoves the little package forward almost violently, as if he can't wait to get rid of it.

The old man takes it from him, looks down at it, then slowly begins to unwrap it. When the wrapping is all off, he's holding a small square box in his hand. He takes off the top, and reaches inside, and out of the box he pulls a cigarette lighter. And even from his place way in back, at the outskirts of the crowd, Dan can see the diamond inlays glittering on it.

For awhile, the old man just holds the lighter in his hand. Then Mark comes forward. "There's an inscription on it, Grandpa," he says. "Right there on the side. Why don't you read it out loud?"

Murmurs from the crowd; "Yes, sure, read it out loud."

The old man looks down at the inscription. In a low thoughtful sort of voice, more to himself than to his audience, he begins to read. "To Abraham L. Kugel. On his seventy-fifth birthday. With respect, and admiration, and friendship. From the members of his—the members——" The old man can't read any more. He presses his lips together and lowers his head. And for a long time nobody in the room says a word.

In the silence Dan looks around, he looks from face to face, from the wide, reddish, hearty faces of the salesmen to the timid, excited, embarrassed faces of the sewing-machine ladies. And on every face he sees the same thing. Respect and admiration and friendship, just like it says on the cigarette lighter. A funny little choking sensation rises to Dan's throat. He doesn't really know why it's there. He can't understand where it comes from.

And then the salesmen are shouting again; "Speech, speech! We want a speech!" "Let's hear from the birthday boy!" "Come on, Abe, you're not so shy when you've got a bawling-out to give us!"

Old Abe Kugel straightens up, throws back his shoulders, lifts his chin. Once again it's impossible to believe that this is a man of seventy-five. He seems younger, heartier, more full of high spirits and wild mischief than the salesmen even. "You want a speech?" he cries. "All right, I got two things to say. First of all, let me thank you sincerely for this wonderful present—I will think of you all, every one of you individually, whenever I light up my cigar. And second of all, why are we wasting the time with boring speeches? Let's get started on that cake."

At which there is general enthusiasm, and Mrs. Monahan magically produces a knife and forks and paper plates from the bottom drawer of her desk, and the rest of the morning is spent in eating, shouting, making jokes, slapping backs, and other pleasant types of noise and confusion.

VII

WHEN he gets to the club for lunch that afternoon, Dan is quiet and thoughtful.

His club is The Downtown Business-men's Social Club—known briefly among its members as The Downtown Club—and Dan is usually very alive and alert when he enters it, full of interest in everything that's going on around him. It hasn't been such a long time, after all since he and his friends have had this club. Only since the end of the War, to be exact. Until then they were willing to have lunch and play cards at the older, stodgier clubs, run by a generation they had nothing in common with at all. The founding of the club—the purchase of this three-storey building on State Street, and its transformation into a palace of plush carpeting and leather upholstery—was a big thing in all their lives. It was nothing less than the proof that they were finally independent and knew how to live like gentlemen on their own. And even now, almost ten years later, Dan still hasn't grown tired of looking around at this proof, admiring it, nodding his head at it with satisfaction.

Not to-day, though. He walks through the outer lobby with his head down, hardly noticing a thing. He doesn't even notice the new wallpaper—a red and brown bull-fighting pattern—though he himself is chiefly responsible for it. As Chairman of the House Committee he himself was the leader of the recent fight, against the die-hard reactionary element in the club, to tear down those grimy old Oriental tapestries.

He arrives at the dining-room, and follows the steward to his regular table by the window, where three of his friends are already sitting. On the way, he is greeted with waves and shouts from people that he passes. Everyone knows Dan Waxman, and everyone says "hello" to him. But instead of waving and shouting back, as is his custom, to-day he just smiles and nods a little vaguely.

And so he gets to his table.

"Greetings and salutations," says Mort Meltzer, getting up especially to poke Dan in the ribs. "Why such a long face? Did you lose a stray zero at the office this morning?"

Dan brightens up immediately. "Was I wearing a long face? All right, that's my privilege, isn't it? Do I always have to be a little ray of sunshine?"

He sits down across the table from Mort, between Nat Garfunkel, the real estate man, and Eli Glatz, buttons and laces. Nat gives him a quick nod and a sour grunt. Eli purses his lips up into that thin little smile of his and speaks in that high, prissy voice of his. "How are you, Dan? You *are* looking just a bit out of sorts. It isn't business, I hope. Drexell seems quite sound, according to the morning papers. Of course, you never can tell with these stock ventures."

What a contrast they make, the three of them—so Dan thinks, as he looks around the table at them. Mort Meltzer, the world's biggest life-of-the-party, always slapping you on the back, always telling a joke—and if nobody else would laugh at it, he wouldn't hesitate a moment to take care of that himself. And next to him Nat Garfunkel, the original Gloomy Gus, the fellow with the perpetual scowl, who doesn't have a good word for anybody or a cheerful viewpoint on anything, who believes there's only one thing worse than what's happening to-day, and that is what's *going* to happen to-morrow. Only, underneath it all, Dan has an idea that he isn't really such a terrible grouch. Having seen Nat with his wife and his twin sons that he's crazy about, Dan is pretty sure that he's a much more sentimental and human fellow than he wants you to think he is.

And then, to make the contrast complete, there's Eli Glatz. Dan always has to be very careful when he's with Eli Glatz, because Eli is one of the people who has the power of starting up his temper. Sometimes all Eli has to do is raise an eyebrow and put on that sympathetic expression of his—which somehow, underneath the sympathy, always seems to conceal a little gloat—and Dan's blood is boiling, his neck is red, he's on the verge of flying off on one of his rages. He usually manages to control himself, though. Life is going along so nicely for him nowadays that he hardly ever feels like getting into a fight. Only occasionally, for the fun of it, and to keep himself in practice.

"Honest to God," says Nat, with the arrival of the soup, "the food in this joint gets more uneatable every day. Will you look at this cup of dishwater?"

"Between you and me," says Mort, leaning forward and putting on a very confidential tone of voice, "my secret inside sources tell me that the Chairman of the House Committee has been up to a little hanky-panky with the Commissary Fund. Dipping his hand into the soup, you might say. I wouldn't want to condemn a man without proof—but there *is* something familiar about the taste of this soup——"

Dan laughs at this and says, "Well, it's your own fault, isn't it? If you were big enough suckers to make such an untrustworthy type the Chairman of your House Committee."

"Now really, I think this is terribly unfair," says Eli Glatz "If there's one thing I'm quite sure of about Dan here, that is that he's completely and absolutely honest, and the idea of stealing money from the club funds wouldn't even cross his mind."

Until Eli spoke up, the whole business has been a simple, easy-going joke. But now that Eli is finished, the joke seems to have turned a little sour, and there's a long uncomfortable pause.

Dan changes the subject. "Talking about money," he

says, "I've got a big favour to ask you fellows, and I might as well get it off my chest right now."

Very elaborately, Mort reaches into his pockets. "Any amount, Dan boy. Any amount you ask for. You can always depend on your old pal Meltzer. And all I'm asking for security is your wife's right arm."

"Now this is a pleasure," Dan says. "This is a real pleasure. I always knew that some day one of your jokes was going to backfire on you. What a pleasure, that I should be around to see it." Mort looks puzzled, so Dan laughs and rubs his hands together and goes on. "As long as you're so kind as to make the offer voluntarily, please bring your hand out of that pocket with a nice fat hundred-dollar bill in it—or better yet, *two* nice fat hundred-dollar bills. You see, I'm collecting money this week for the opera fund."

"The opera fund!" A loud hoot comes out of Mort, and a long low sigh of dismay from Nat.

"My God," Mort cries, "isn't it enough that Sarah drags you there every Monday night—now you have to collect money for them too. Every time Milly gets *me* into that place, I feel like *I'm* the one who ought to get paid for it."

Dan keeps up the bantering tone, but underneath he's a little more serious, because this happens to be a cause that's very close to his heart. "Just because *you* happen to be an uncultured barbarian who wouldn't know an aria from 'Hinky Dinky, Parley-Voo'," Dan says, "that's no reason to knock the opera. Plenty of people in this town are crazy about it."

"Plenty of people in this town are crazy," says Mort to the ceiling.

Dan gives an offhand shrug.

"Well, we manage to fill the house every night, so there must be a lot of lunatics around."

76

In his dry sour voice, Nat Garfunkel joins in on the conversation. "If you fill the house every night, how come you have to raise money every year?"

"How come?" Dan turns to him, working his hands a little. "Because you've got no idea the expenses that go into putting on an opera. All that fancy scenery, and that big orchestra, and those foreign singers. Even if they *do* fill the house every night, even if they could put people in the aisles and have them hanging from the chandelier, they *still* couldn't make back their expenses."

Nat shakes his head gloomily. "Doesn't sound like much of a business proposition to me. All you're saying is that it's licked ahead of time. Why should I put my money in an investment like *that*?"

"Who said you were putting your money in an *investment*? You're putting your money in a civic improvement. You're putting your money in a cultural force."

"Why should I want a cultural force?" Nat says. "Don't I have enough problems in my life?"

"Why should you want it? Why should you want it?" Completely forgetting about his lamb stew, Dan launches into his favourite speech, about the value of culture, and making this world a more beautiful place to live in, and showing a little pride in the development of your city, and turning Chicago into the artistic centre of the Mid-West, and who knows, maybe of the whole country some day.

Once, in the middle of this speech, Mort winks at Nat and Eli speaks in a low voice. "He's off on the Pride of the Mid-West again. The way he says that word 'Chicago', you'd think he was the mayor or the police chief or the president of the Chamber of Commerce."

"You'd think he felt guilty about it," says Nat. "You'd think he was a direct descendant of Mrs. O'Leary's cow."

But mostly, his friends listen quietly, politely, and even with a certain interest to what Dan has to say. And it makes an effect on them too. When he gets to the end of his speech, Mort and Nat are nodding and looking thoughtful and murmuring, "Well, the city *is* growing up, there's no getting away from that." "Culture isn't a bad thing in its way, I suppose—it keeps the women busy." "Well, a big city ought to have a big opera house, that I have to admit—even though you couldn't get me inside of it for money."

Only Eli Glatz still has some objections. He puts on his most earnest, judicious, and generally self-satisfied expression—the expression that never fails to get on Dan's nerves. "Of course I'm a firm believer in culture," he says. "Who has more right to be, after all?" This is Eli's usual subtle reference to the fact that he is one of the few men in their set who went to college—he graduated from the University of Pennsylvania Business School the year before he took over his father's firm. "And while I can't truthfully say that I'm a big music-lover myself," he goes on, "I do admit that there are many great musical geniuses in the world to-day, as well as out of the past. Beethoven, and Wagner, and the three B's, and *To a Water Lily*——"

"All right, all right, what's the point?" Dan says. He can't stand Eli's habit of making a Fourth of July speech out of every little remark.

"The point is, while I naturally approve of culture in principle, aren't you really exaggerating it out of all proportion? I mean, aren't there many *worthier* causes that we ought to take care of first? The Crippled Children, and the Home for the Blind, and the new Jewish Hospital, for instance. I mean, we should take care of those less fortunate than ourselves, shouldn't we, before we go spending money on luxuries and so forth?"

78

Dan raises his voice on this—he's annoyed at Eli's underhanded implication that, by collecting money for the opera, he somehow is snatching food out of the mouth of a crippled child. "We can take care of all those things too," Dan says. "Believe me, I give as much money as anybody to all those charities you mentioned." Then, with a hard look at Eli, "More money than *some*, if the truth got out."

"Oh, I'm quite sure of that," Eli says, raising an eyebrow and looking sympathetic. "Now you know I didn't mean you to take my remarks *personally*."

"Who's taking your remarks personally?"

"Go to your corners, go to your corners," Mort puts in. "All right now, let's organize this duel. Grapefruit at twenty paces."

As usual, under the influence of Mort's good humour, Dan feels himself loosening up, and in a few seconds his anger is all gone, and he's laughing at himself. Especially since he knows that he's going to get what he wants, anyway. After all, Mort and Nat and Eli have *their* favourite causes too, and some day they'll be coming to *him* for a contribution.

And so the meal goes on, more or less as it always goes every week-day of Dan's life. There are jokes, and political opinions, speculations on sports and business conditions, an occasional little spat, quickly made up again. Over coffee, Nat turns to Dan and says, "How's Drexell doing these days? My broker was advising me this morning to pick up a few more shares. But I thought I'd like to get the inside dope first."

"From the horse's mouth, you might say," says Mort.

Dan leans back, and lights up a cigar, and smiles importantly. It always makes him feel good when the subject of his leading client, the great Martin Drexell Enterprises, comes up. And he feels especially good when his advice is being asked. "This horse agrees with your broker," he says. "You can't go wrong with public utilities, you know. No matter what condition the country is in, the public still has to go on having its utilities, doesn't it?"

"Well, at least I won't lose any *more* with you and Drexell," Nat says, "than I'd lose with anybody else."

"Of course, one thing you have to understand," Dan adds quickly, knowing that underneath his sour un-enthusiastic manner Nat has the temperament and the instincts of a wild plunger. "It's never a good policy to put all your eggs in one basket, no matter how sound the proposition looks. You know my own system—seventy-five per cent in Government bonds, twenty-five per cent for speculation——"

"Well, here's a sound speculation—that nobody can turn down," says Mort. "Let's have some more coffee."

So they have some more coffee, and Mort tells the latest joke that he just heard—the one about the lady trombone-player and her boy friend who was a midget—and then it's time for them all to go back to their offices. They all move out to the street together, and Nat hails a cab and Eli asks for a lift uptown, and Dan and Mort start walking downtown together.

The conversation has been so pleasant that it's distracted Dan from the feelings that were occupying him before lunch. Now those feelings return to him, even a little more strongly than before. He begins to think that he wants to tell somebody about them, that he can get them off his mind by saying them out loud.

He starts off very casually, as if it's a matter of no importance to him. "You know, a funny thing happened to me this morning. You'd never guess what it was."

Right away that's an invitation for Mort to start guessing. "Your secretary threw herself into your arms and told you she loves you madly? You decided to quit work, and go to the South Sea Islands and become a beachcomber? You got a call from the President of the United States, he wants you to be the Secretary of the Treasury? Your bootlegger presented you with a case of genuine imported Scotch, absolutely free, because he's taken a personal liking to you? You got a letter from Greta Garbo——"

"For God's sake, shut up," Dan says, waving his arm. "This is no joke."

"No joke?" Mort stops dead in his tracks, claps his hand to his forehead, and stares at Dan in amazement. "My God, Dan boy, you don't mean it—you aren't saying it—you couldn't be serious. To think that Sarah is going to have another baby after all these years! Dan old pal, I'll tell you frankly, if I didn't hear it from your own mouth, I wouldn't have believed that you still had it in you."

"What happened to me was," Dan says, pushing on firmly, "I went to a birthday party. Old Abe Kugel, across the hall from me, was seventy-five years old to-day."

"And he celebrated the occasion by chasing his secretary around the room in her silk panties." Mort's humour, Dan has often noticed, has a way of bouncing back inevitably to one particular subject.

"He didn't do anything like that," Dan says. "He's a fine, dignified, respectable old man. And his grandson Mark was there. A wonderful boy—believe me, Mort, a really wonderful boy. And all the employees got together and gave him a cigarette lighter."

"The grandfather has a birthday, so they give the *grandson* a cigarette lighter?"

"No, not the grandson. The old man. My God, with you it's impossible to get in a serious word edge-wise."

"It's a beautiful day, Dan boy," Mort says, gesturing at the street around him. "The sun is out, and the people are happy, and business is wonderful. Do we have to spoil everything with serious words?"

Dan looks up at him, at the wide plump face, at the big cheerful grin, at the frizzly red hair that all the combs and brushes in the world couldn't keep down. In a moment Dan is grinning too. "Of course we don't," he says. "Serious words, who wants them?"

And so they go on with their walk, and Mort tells another one of his jokes—this time the one about the hunter who imitates the call of a female moose. And in front of Dan's building they stop and shake hands and say goodbye.

"Until to-night," Mort says. "You know you're giving Milly and me a dinner to-night."

"That's fine," Dan says. "We're having some people from the opera too."

" Good, good. I can try out my beautiful baritone on them." Mort tries out his beautiful baritone right then and there, paying no attention to the stares of the passers-by. Then he breaks off with a laugh, gives a wave of his hand, and disappears into the crowd.

VIII

MORT MELTZER is a true friend and a wonderful fellow, but he isn't anyone to talk out your deep, personal feelings with. And so, when Dan gets back to the office, the itch to unburden his mind is still on him.

He wonders if anything is to be gained by talking to Schultz.

"Did you hear the fuss across the hall?" he says, when he's sitting at his desk again. "They were giving old man Kugel a party for his seventy-fifth birthday."

"Is that a fact?" says Schultz. "Would you believe it, that a man his age could be so well preserved?"

"You should've seen the reception they gave him," Dan says. "Everybody turned out for the celebration— his grandson, and the salesmen, and the foreman from his factory, and the office staff. It's a remarkable thing, that a man should run an office for so many years, and still get such a reception from his office staff."

Schultz hesitates a moment, then puts on a stiff sort of smile and brings out a little awkwardly, "Well, you know how we all feel about you here, Mr. Waxman."

Dan stares at her a moment, puzzled. The next moment he lowers his head and blushes and feels awful. "No, it's not that," he stammers out, "I certainly didn't mean——" He gives a quick shake of his head, then gets very brisk and businesslike. "Those Drexell reports, will you get them for me from the files, please?

As soon as Schultz is out of the room, Dan mutters to himself and relieves his feelings by tearing up a pile of advertising circulars.

Later in the afternoon, he leaves the office and sets out for the climax, the highlight, the big moment of his business day—his regular conference with Martin Drexell. This means taking the car out to Drexell's home in the suburbs in almost, but not quite, the most fashionable suburb. Of course, Drexell also has an office in the city. He has several offices, a different one for each of his different enterprises, from Drexell Mid-West Light and

Electricity, the oldest and most respectable, to Trans-Drexell Airways Development, the youngest and fastest-growing. But Drexell usually makes the rounds of these offices no more than once a week, and the rest of the time he works at home. For this purpose his study is specially equipped with typewriters, files, a dictograph, and four or five phones with direct private lines to all his various offices.

It's a beautiful big mansion-type house, with tall white columns like the ancient Greeks, and a wide paved drive-way, and a long sweep of lawn down to the lake front. Dan can't deny it, he always gets a big thrill, stepping up to the high arched doorway, and he always rings the bell with confidence, because the butler knows him and calls him "Mr. Waxman". How many other men in his crowd could get through this door so easily? The closest most of them ever come to the great Martin Drexell is reading his regular pronouncements on "the future of the American investor" in the newspapers—and putting their money in his companies, of course.

The butler tells Dan that Mr. Drexell is on the phone to Paris, France, at the moment and doesn't want to be disturbed. So he puts Dan in the drawing-room to wait. For a while, Dan looks around at the antique furniture and the genuine gold-and-silver fixtures, and amuses himself trying to guess how much each item is worth, and how much more Mrs. Drexell paid for it. Then, when he gets tired of that game, he strolls over to the window and gazes out at the garden in back. This is one of his favourite views in Chicago—a genuine English garden, which Drexell is supposed to have brought over, bulb by bulb, rock by rock, seed by seed, from some famous Duke's ancestral estate in England.

And then Dan hears a noise behind him, the soft rustling of a woman's dress. He turns and sees Mrs.

Drexell in the doorway. She's the tall, willowy, perfectly-groomed type, and Dan has to admit that for a woman in her forties she's quite an impressive sight. Who could guess that twenty years ago she was working as a secretary in the office of a meat-packing company?

"Oh, Mr. Waxman, it's you," she says, giving him her cool look. "I didn't know you were here."

"I'll bet you didn't," Dan thinks. "Why, your day wouldn't be complete if you didn't pop in to take a few digs at me." His duel with Mrs. Drexell has been going on for years now, ever since her husband first hired him. It's an especially active duel because it's completely under cover—on the surface, the two of them are just as polite and friendly as can be. "Just waiting to see Mr. Drexell," Dan says out loud. "I'm not in your way, I hope." He makes it as clear as he can that he hopes he is.

"Certainly not, Mr. Waxman," she says, coming forward with her hand out. "You know it's always a pleasure to welcome you into my home." She puts just the slightest emphasis on the word "my".

"It's such a nice home," Dan says. "It's a pleasure when Mr. Drexell asks me up." *He* puts the emphasis on "Mr. Drexell".

Mrs. Drexell gestures gracefully at a chair. "Wouldn't you like to sit down, Mr. Waxman? You're looking tired." She gives a little laugh. "That husband of mine has so much energy himself, he thinks it entitles him to be a slave-driver to his employees."

"Now I wouldn't say that," Dan answers, not sitting down. "I'm on good terms with several of your husband's employees, and they tell me that he's a very fair boss."

There is a pause, while they study each other.

Then, with a gracious nod, Mrs. Drexell turns to leave.

"Well, I must be going out to the kitchen, Mr. Waxman. I'm giving a party to-night, and I have to make arrangements with the cook." At the door, she suddenly smiles. "How is your charming wife, Mr. Waxman? Please give her my regards. I'm looking forward to seeing her again some day."

The meaning of this is very clear; "Your charming wife, like all the other women in your seedy, unfashionable set, would give her mink coat to be invited to one of my parties—so I want you to know just what a fat chance she's got." And she nods even more graciously, to make sure that Dan gets the point.

Dan is very careful not to show the least bit of annoyance. "My wife will be flattered," he says. "She often thinks about you. Why, only this morning she was reading the society page, and she looked for your name among the guests at the Peyton-Terhune wedding reception."

The pleasant smile tightens a little. There are parties in this world that Mrs. Drexell would give *her* mink coat to be invited to.

"I'll say goodbye now, Mr. Waxman," she says. "In case I don't see you after Martin is finished with you." But this is really a pretty weak shot. She knows it herself, and she can't quite hide her irritation as she walks out of the room.

Dan laughs and lights up a cigar. Matching wits with Mrs. Drexell is one of his favourite amusements. Especially when he comes out of it as brilliantly as he has to-day.

But now the butler returns and tells him that Mr. Drexell will see him in the study. So Dan quickly crushes out his cigar and hurries after the butler.

Drexell, as usual, is in the middle of a flurry of activity. He stands behind his desk, barking into the phone, which he holds with one hand while the long bony fingers of his other hand are tapping impatiently against the blotter. Simultaneously, he manages somehow to nod at Dan, dismiss the butler, and take several puffs from that cigarette which droops permanently out of the corner of his mouth. Drexell is the only man Dan knows who can do a dozen things at once without making a single mistake at any of them. Why, the very first moment Dan ever set eyes on him, he was reeling off a mass of statistics at his secretary, snapping orders to his broker, and practising his golf swing, all at the same time—and what's more, he remembered the statistics perfectly, his stocks went up, and his golf game is in the middle eighties.

Will Dan ever forget the scene that took place then? He was terribly nervous for his first meeting with the Ohio farm-boy who had become a financial power overnight. And Drexell didn't put him at ease either, with that quick sharp way of his; "So you're Waxman," he said. "I hear you're an honest man. Also you're not a stuffed shirt. I'm not in business for the stuffed shirts. I'm in business for the man in the street. I'm building up a system, Waxman. The biggest system of public utilities in the world to-day. The man in the street is going to put his money into it, and the man in the street is going to pocket the money that comes out of it. All right, I'm a busy man, yes or no?"

Dan was still a little bowled over. "Yes or no what, Mr. Drexell?"

"Yes or no, are you working for me?"

Dan started to stammer out that it was an honour, that he certainly never expected——

"All right, all right," Drexell cut him off with a wave of his arm, "it's all settled, why go on talking about it?" And then suddenly, surprisingly, he threw off that brisk busy manner, strode forward, grabbed Dan's hand, and gave him the full force of the famous Drexell smile. "Happy to have you in the organization, Waxman," he said. "Only from now on the names are Dan and Martin. We're about to make history together, so we might as well be on friendly terms."

Dan laughed a little uneasily, and made the effort of calling the great Drexell "Martin"—and then suddenly, they were back to business again. "Now let's get started. I'll give you a quick rundown on the situation." The "quick rundown" took three solid hours, with Drexell talking, pacing, puffing cigarettes, waving his arms practically every minute. At the end of the time, Dan was exhausted, but Drexell just seemed to have more energy than ever.

As he showed Dan out the door, he suddenly grew genial and unbusinesslike again. "You know, Dan, I like Jews," he said. While Dan blinked at this one, Drexell went on, "Jews are realistic. They know what kind of a world this is. They aren't always being shocked, or standing up on their dignity, or showing off their refinement, or spouting a lot of high moral principles, while you know damn well they're ready to knife you in the back the first chance they get. I don't get the creeps when I'm with them, Dan. Jews are straight. Jews are down to earth. I like Jews." Then he gave a nod, and Dan knew that he was dismissed for the day.

He went away from that scene a convert. Like everybody who had ever worked for the man, like the thousands of investors who entrusted their money to him every year, Dan was under the Drexell spell. And to-day, after eight years, he's under it just as strongly as ever.

"Sit down, Dan, sit down," Drexell says, as soon as he's off the phone. "I'll sit down, too. It's been a hard day. The wolves are howling at me right and left. By

God, I need to relax for a minute or two. Don't talk business for a while, Dan. Do you know any good stories?"

"Good stories, Martin? Well, as a matter of fact, I heard a funny one at lunch to-day." And he tells Mort Meltzer's story about the lady trombonist.

Drexell laughs at it heartily. He throws his head back and booms out his laughter. He even takes the cigarette out of the corner of his mouth for the purpose. And yet, as soon as he decides that he's laughed enough, he has no trouble cutting it off and snapping right back to serious matters.

"I'm a little tired this afternoon, Dan," he says. "So we'll put aside the big stuff till to-morrow. We'll just polish off a few minor details."

For two and a half hours they work steadily on the minor details. And they might go on working another two and a half hours if Mrs. Drexell didn't stick her head in the door. "It's time for you to come up and dress, Martin," she says. "I'm sure Mr. Waxman won't be offended.

"*I'll* be offended," Drexell says, "if Mr. Waxman leaves this house without joining me in a good stiff shot of something."

"Martin dear, you have no idea how late it is——"

Dan starts to his feet. "As a matter of fact, Martin, I've got guests coming for dinner myself."

"Sit still, Dan." Dan sinks back into his chair, while Drexell turns to his wife. "Your stuffed-shirt friends can wait till I'm good and ready for them, Margaret. Stick a cocktail in their hands, and they'll be happy. As long as they're not paying for it."

Mrs. Drexell sighs. A dismayed but very genteel sigh. Dan can hardly keep himself from smirking a little, as she leaves the room.

From his desk Drexell takes a bottle and two glasses. "It just came over on the boat," he says. "Anyway, that's what they tell me." He pours out the whisky, then raises his glass. "What'll we drink to, Dan?"

For some reason, Dan is suddenly reminded of old Abe Kugel's birthday party this morning. A vague little shadow crosses his face. "What about friendship, Martin?"

"That's a good idea. To friendship—the only gilt-edged commodity on the market to-day." He tosses off his drink in one gulp. Then he gives a wink and adds, "Except for Drexell Enterprises, of course."

Riding home in the car that evening, Dan is tired and worn-out, but somehow in a wonderful mood. His heart pounds a little faster. He holds his head up high. He feels as if he's had a lot more than one quick shot of whisky.

That's how it always is after a session with Drexell.

IX

It's almost dark out when he gets back to Twelve Hundred Lake Shore Drive. In many ways it's the very nicest time of the day. The dim light makes everything look sort of unreal and magical. The lake is purple, the sky is silver, the wide boulevard seems to sweep away into a grey mist. Best of all is Twelve Hundred Lake Shore Drive itself, still the tallest, most beautiful building in sight. The twilight rounds off its sharp edges now, tones down the harsh gleam of whitestone and glass, smooths over the streaks of dirt and rust that have gathered through the years. In the early evening blur, with soft yellow light flickering out from behind a hundred window shades, Twelve Hundred Lake Shore Drive might almost be a Sultan's palace out of the storybooks that Dan used to love as a kid.

Since it's been a good day, with no more than the usual amount of exasperation and aggravation, he treats his family to one of his warmest greetings. He gives Sarah a big kiss at the door, and tells her that she's looking very attractive to-night, "just like a movie queen".

"Now what's this?" Sarah says, half pleased and half alarmed. "Have you got some bad news to break?"

"Bad news? What a worrier—she's always got bad news on her mind." He flops down on the sofa, and a second later he's stretched out comfortably on his back. "Why can't you be the calm, easy-going, level-headed type, like me?"

Bobby comes into the room like a whirlwind and throws herself on his neck.

"Whoa, whoa, hold the horses," Dan cries, as he returns her hugging and kissing—a little clumsily, because he's flat on his back. "Sarah, what are we bringing up in this household, a little girl or a wild Indian?"

"A wild Indian!" Bobby answers with a shout, and she starts to prance up and down, making war-whoops. Every once in a while Bobby bursts into one of these moods of crazy energy, and God knows what her arms and legs are going to do or what nonsense is going to come out of her mouth.

Dan loves these moods—just as he loves everything else about her, her shyness, her brightness, her fits of the giggles, and her fits of the sulks. He pretends, though, that he's in terrible pain. He puts his hands over his ears, contorts his face and cries out, "A madhouse. A regular madhouse. What a tragedy for a hard-working, clean-living man, to bring up a flock of lunatics under his own roof."

Bobby's war-whoops dissolve into giggles, and finally she subsides full-length on the floor, props up her chin with her fist, and absorbs herself in the comic section.

"Where does she get it from, all that energy?" Sarah says, smiling down at Bobby. "And the way she wears out her clothes. You know, Dan, I'm going to have to take her down to Marshall Field's again this week-end."

"Terrible, terrible," says Dan, shaking his head and putting on a look of great concern. "It's going to bank-rupt me. Pretty soon we'll all be out on the street, selling shoelaces."

"And you know what else she needs?" Sarah says. "Believe it or not, she needs a long evening dress. They're having some sort of a party or dance or some-thing at the school over Easter, and she says that all the girls will be wearing evening dresses."

Bobby looks up from the comic section with an expression of tremendous weariness. "I don't just *say* it, Mommy. It's *so*. You can ask any of the girls. You can ask Shirley Freed, or Marilyn Meltzer, or *any* of them."

"Evening dresses," Sarah says, with a sigh. "It seems like the younger generation is growing up quicker than it used to. When I was her age I can just imagine Papa letting me wear an evening dress."

Dan gives a laugh. "Your father is a grand old man, but a fashion plate I don't think anyone could ever have called him."

"Now I don't know about that, Dan. Papa knew how to dress in his younger days, you have to admit that. He had twenty different vests in his wardrobe."

"Sure, sure, but as far as women's clothes went, he's always been behind the times. In his opinion women's styles have stayed exactly the same since the year your mother died."

"Daddy," Bobby cries, her eyes widening, "you *are* going to let me have an evening dress, aren't you? Because if I don't show up with an evening dress, I'll look like a terrible dope——"

"Of course you're going to have it, dear," Sarah says, in her soothing voice. "We were just discussing."

Bobby nods her head, satisfied, and goes back to the comic section.

Dan looks down at her a while, and then he says, "You know, she'll look good in an evening dress at that. She's certainly going to make their eyes pop some day."

"She doesn't need artificial help," Sarah says, settling back in her chair and folding her hands in her lap. "Our daughter looks nice in whatever she wears."

Then, for a while, they all quiet down, busy with various sections of the newspaper. Then the doorbell rings, and the silence is over for the night, because Mort Meltzer and his wife Milly have arrived.

First of all, Mort makes a big fuss over Bobby. He grabs her in his arms, and lifts her up off her feet, and swings her around. "So how's my favourite girl friend to-day?" he says. "Have we still got a date on your sixteenth birthday?"

"Yes, I guess so, Uncle Mort," Bobby says, blushing a little. Bobby always gets shy with Mort.

"Better not stand me up," Mort says. "I'm a tiger when aroused." He puts Bobby down on her feet again, and begins to pant a little from the strain.

"Sit down and catch your breath, Tiger," says Milly.

About six-thirty, Bobby goes into the kitchen for her dinner. Ordinarily, of course, she sits at the table with the family, but to-night, with guests from the opera coming, they won't be eating till late. With Bobby gone, the men go off to one corner with their drinks, and the women settle down together on the couch. Milly is a lot like Mort—loud, and good-humoured, and talkative—so Dan can hear her voice rattling away at a fast pace, as a sort of background music to his conversation.

"I was with Drexell this afternoon," Dan says. "He predicts a big upswing in the Airways over the summer. So if you're interested in picking up a little extra change——"

"Now that, Dan boy, is an interest that it never takes much to stimulate in me. In fact, I'd have to be unconscious——"

"All right, all right," Dan breaks in, with a laugh, "I get the point.

"You know, you ought to be ashamed of yourself," Mort says, a sip or two later. "All this money you're making for me—what am I going to do with it all? I've used up all the normal, legal, ethical ways. Pretty soon I'll have to go in for exotic vices and depraved luxuries. And then you'll have me on your conscience for the rest of your life."

"Believe me, I'm not worried," Dan says. "Just exactly what exotic vices have you ever even heard about?"

"Oh, I've been around," Mort says. "In my free and easy days, before I got married——"

"What's this about before you got married?" Milly's voice carries clear across the room. "Before you got married, Mort Meltzer, you were an innocent little baby who trembled all over if a woman so much as looked at you."

"It flatters her vanity to believe that," Mort says, with a wink, "so why should I disillusion her?"

"It flatters *his* vanity to make up stories about his big, bad, adventurous past."

At seven-thirty Signor Mantini and his friends arrive. Actually they were invited for seven o'clock, but nobody

94

complains. Half an hour late, for Signor Mantini and his friends, is practically ahead of time. When he first got to know these opera people, Dan used to get annoyed at what he called their "irresponsible habits". Annoyed? He used to stamp up and down the living-room, waving his arms over his head and swearing loudly that he was "finished, absolutely and positively finished" with "those greasy Italians". Sometimes he would even shake his fist at the door and cry out, "I only want to see them once more—only once more—just so I can tell them to their face what I think of them!" Time, even from his earliest days, was a big problem with Dan. He couldn't stand waiting around for anything. It worked on his nerves, it frayed his temper, it grated against him physically, the way some people are affected by a ticking clock or a squeaking piece of chalk.

He never actually did "tell them to their face", of course. When they finally showed up for the appointment—no matter how late—he was always so glad to see them that he forgot all about his anger. And then pretty soon, as the years went by, he grew more and more used to it, until finally he got into the habit of making allowances for it. To-day he just naturally expects them to be late. In his mind he automatically translates seven o'clock into eight o'clock, and leaves it at that.

The truth of the matter is, Dan has never quite got over his awe in the presence of these opera people. He has never got over thinking of himself as an outsider, as not quite one of them—and maybe even as a little bit inferior to them. He remembers how he came to meet them all in the first place. It was through Drexell, of course. Drexell was one of the men who kept the opera going— Drexell was at least half responsible for the new opera house and for hiring all the expensive foreign singers— Drexell had a big reputation as a "patron of the arts", even though it was common knowledge that a certain little soprano from Oklahoma City was the big reason behind his patronship. So, anyway, when Dan mentioned to Drexell one day that he was fond of the opera, Drexell peered at him and said, "How would you like to be on the Board?" Dan thought he was joking and laughed a little, but Drexell just waved his hand and said, "All right, you're on the Board, I'll tell them about it to-morrow morning." And sure enough, ever since then Dan has been a leading member of the Opera Board and a personal acquaintance of all the *artistes*.

"Can't see why you make such a fuss over them," Drexell is always saying to him. "They're just like other people—only maybe a little dirtier." But Dan goes right on making the fuss. He can never forget that soprano who died so beautifully in *Trovatore*, way back before the War. How many times has he seen *Trovatore* since then? He couldn't even begin to count them. But it always makes him feel funny, and a little weak in the stomach, when that soprano starts to die.

"Signor Mantini, it's a pleasure," Dan cries, shaking hands with the white-haired long-nosed old man dressed in a crumpled blue suit. "How have you been? You're looking good."

"I don't feel good," Signor Mantini says. "My elbow is full of pain, like always. My stomach—no good. Last night I don't sleep one minute hardly." All the time he's saying this, Signor Mantini is shaking Dan's hand up and down, and bobbing his head, and smiling happily.

Signor Mantini then turns his attention to the women. He kisses their hands solemnly. Then he shakes hands with Mort.

"How's the boy, Signor?" Mort says, clapping the old man on the back. The presence of these opera people always seems to make Mort heartier, more boisterous, more Mort-ish somehow, than usual even. "I caught your show the other night," Mort says. "You did a pretty good job of waving your stick, Signor. But I have to tell you, I noticed a couple of places where you let those fellows sneak in a sour note."

"Sneak in? Excuse?" says Signor Mantini, wrinkling up his brow.

"It's a joke," Dan says, moving up quickly. "Mort's just kidding you a little."

"Joke? Oh, yes—joke." Signor Mantini begins to laugh, a quick high little cackle. "Mr. Meltzer—always joking. How is it I don't know you yet, Mr. Meltzer?"

With relief Dan joins in on the laughter at Mort's joke. And then Signor Mantini turns to introduce the two people he has brought with him. "Signora Da Croce you know already, no? And also it is my pleasure to introduce Herr Vogelschotz. Herr Vogelschotz is our new tenor—direct from Sweden he comes—he sings the Wagnerian."

Signora Da Croce, a large woman with thick ankles and a tremendous bosom, surges forward and embraces Dan enthusiastically. "Mr. Waxman," she cries, "I love you whenever I am with you." Then she repeats the embrace with Sarah—"Mrs. Waxman, your lovely expensive apartment, I would like to move into it forever." And finally somewhat smaller embraces for Milly and Mort.

Mort is the only one who gets a chance to answer the Signora's greeting. "So you're a soprano, Signora," he says. "You know, my father always warned me against sopranos."

Signora Da Croce's huge eyebrows lifted. "Why is this? What's the matter with the soprano?"

Mort leans forward and gives her a confidential little nudge. "Well, I don't know from personal experience, of course, but my father always said they were man-killers. He said a soprano would steal your heart away and break it in two, just for her own amusement."

Signora Da Croce roars with laughter at this. "Your Papa," she cries, "he's a very smart man!" And she gives Mort's arm a poke that practically knocks the wind out of him.

And now it's the turn of Herr Vogelschotz, the third member of the party. But Herr Vogelschotz, in contrast to his two companions, isn't the least bit emotional or demonstrative. He's a short, square, pudgy man with blond curly hair and a wide face. All his features are terribly little—button eyes, a pug nose, a rosebud mouth —and they're all set close together in the middle of his face with plenty of space around them. His cheeks are red, like a baby's. He acknowledges everybody's greeting by giving a stiff little bow and grunting, "So charmed." But he doesn't *look* very charmed. He doesn't look anything, in fact. He has absolutely no expression on his face whatsoever.

As they all move into the living-room, Signor Mantini apologizes for Herr Vogelschotz's abrupt manners. "He is in this country only a little time. He don't speak so good the language."

Dan makes cocktails for the guests. Signor Mantini bobs his head up and down, and thanks Dan for his cocktail at such great length that you'd think his life was being saved. Signora Da Croce takes one sip of hers and practically goes into a soprano aria over it. Herr Vogelschotz accepts his glass with a nod and gazes down at it blankly.

"Talking about opera singers," Mort says, "I heard a good story the other day. I wonder if you've ever heard the one about this opera singer who rode on to the stage on an elephant, and in the middle of his big number the elephant catches sight of this lady elephant on the other side of the stage——"

"Oh, come on, Mort," Milly breaks in, "you don't want to tell that one. That's a little too raw for this company."

"Now what's wrong with this company?" Mort says. "Signor Mantini here knows what the score is. He looks like a man who's been around. He hasn't spent his whole life waving a stick in front of a bunch of fiddle-players. Am I right, Signor?"

Signor Mantini is pleased and flustered. "Now, Mr. Meltzer, you make once more a joke—always a joke."

"And you too, Signora," Mort says, leaning forward and leering at Signora Da Croce. "I'll bet you could tell us a thing or two, couldn't you? A beautiful opera star like you, I'll bet you know what life is like."

Signora Da Croce laughs louder than ever and slaps herself on the knee. "I don't say yes," she says, "and I don't say no."

Dan smiles faintly. He's always a little nervous and embarrassed when Mort starts in on these opera people. And he's always surprised when they turn out to get a big kick out of Mort.

"Excuse me." A rumble from Herr Vogelschotz, who is sitting up stiffly in the corner. Dan turns and sees that Herr Vogelschotz has finished his drink and is holding out the empty glass.

"Coming right up," Dan says, hopping to his feet, and hurrying to refill Herr Vogelschotz's glass.

"You know there's one thing I've always wanted to speak to you about, Signor," says Mort, putting on a serious look which doesn't quite hide the grin underneath it. "How come these operas of yours are always in a foreign language? How do you expect people to listen to that stuff if they can't understand what's going on?"

Signor Mantini gives a small smile—a little bit like the smile you use when you're explaining something to a child. "This is a question—very complicated," he says. "How do I say it? Opera is written in a certain language, because—for the reason that this is the language that—it is written in."

"It's a self-evident question, Mort," Dan puts in, always glad of a chance to show what he knows about opera. "You take an opera that's in Italian, for instance. It just wouldn't sound right if you heard it in English."

"No, that is not true," says Signor Mantini, turning his small smile on Dan. "Mr. Meltzer makes a most interesting point. It is very complicated."

"Oh, well, naturally," Dan mutters, feeling squelched.

"Just you keep that in mind, Dan boy," Mort shouts out, in great delight. "I made a most interesting point. So I guess you're not the only opera expert around here."

Dan glares at Mort in silence. You know, sometimes Mort Meltzer can be a big pain in the neck.

"Here's the *hors-d'œuvre*," Sarah says, standing up and putting herself quickly between Dan and Mort. "Signora Da Croce, I'm sure you'd like some of these nice *hors-d'œuvre*. There's caviar, and stuffed eggs—or maybe a little bit of anchovy?"

A cry of pleasure goes up from Signora Da Croce and Signor Mantini as the maid passes the tray, and the question of opera is immediately forgotten.

"But so lovely. So appetizing," says Signor Mantini, taking four of them, and then after a moment's hesitation taking a fifth.

"This is why I love your home," cries Signora Da Croce. "Such delicious food to eat." And she too scoops in as many *hors-d'œuvre* as she can hold.

But when the tray comes to him, Herr Vogelschotz shakes his head. "Not for me. But please—this?" And once more he holds out his empty glass.

Now that the maid is out of the room, Dan tries to start in on opera again. "Signor Mantini, what's the story on Galli-Curci? Is it a fact that she's going back to Italy next month, and refuses to sing in America any more?"

"Galli-Curci—a great artist," says Signor Mantini. "Divine. Exquisite. A voice from the angels." He brings his fingers to his lips, and for a moment there is an ecstatic gleam in his eyes. Then the gleam changes—he leans forward and says, "Another one of these delicious little caviar *canapés*—if you don't mind please?"

"Galli-Curci," says Signora Da Croce, with a sniff. "She cares too much for the applause, that one. There is a certain vanity. There is a shallowness. The voice is pretty, but where is the feeling? Thank you so much." And she takes a couple of caviar *canapés* for herself.

Dinner is announced, and they all move into the dining-room, with Signor Mantini and Signora Da Croce in the lead. Herr Vogelschotz hangs back a moment, then follows them into the dining-room holding a full glass. Dan can't help giving him a quick worried little look—he's beginning to understand the reason for those red cheeks which make Herr Vogelschotz look so much like an overgrown little baby.

Conversation during dinner is carried on mostly by Mort and Milly. Mort tells a few stories—and as an introduction to each one of them, he and Milly carry on a friendly dispute about whether he ought to tell it or not. Dan makes a couple of attempts to draw his friends from the opera into the conversation. He asks Signor Mantini what he thinks of the Metropolitan Opera in New York— a question which can ordinarily start the old man talking and gesturing for hours. He asks Signora Da Croce whose operas she prefers, Verdi's or Puccini's. He even asks Herr Vogelschotz a question—whether he finds America much different from his native Sweden. But Dan gets only brief, polite, absent-minded reactions to these questions. His guests are busy. Signora Da Croce is gulping down her soup with much noise and flourish. Signor Mantini is using up rolls and butter at a terrific rate. Herr Vogelschotz hardly eats at all. He looks fidgety and unhappy.

Dan has an idea what will cheer him up. He leans forward and says, "You know, we've got a wonderful wine coming with the main course. Mrs. Waxman and I aren't big wine drinkers, but we know how much Signor Mantini likes it."

Right away Herr Vogelschotz looks much happier.

The main course is Signor Mantini's favourite, chicken Tetrazzini. When the maid brings it in on the platter, Signor Mantini's eyes light up, and once again he kisses his fingers. "Aha! Your sublime Tetrazzini. I think of it often. It is better than a restaurant."

"Cheaper than a restaurant, too," Mort calls out. "Am I right, Signor?"

Signor Mantini cackles and bobs his head. "You are right, you are right. Yes, yes, so right." When the maid gets to him, he helps himself eagerly to chicken Tetrazzini. He isn't bashful about taking a large portion.

At the end of the meal, they all go back to the living-room for coffee—a little idea that Dan picked up from the Drexells. And Mort, of course, can't resist making a comment on it. "Coffee in the living-room," he says "Aren't we hoity-toity?"

"What's so hoity-toity?" Dan says, a little loudly. "It's a pleasant custom. We do it all the time."

"Don't let him get your goat, Dan," Milly says. "He's

been living like a pig so long he thinks that's the way the whole world should live."

"It's not a bad life," Mort says, not the least bit offended. "We have a lot of fun down here, us pigs."

Coffee is finished, and Dan passes out brandy and cigars. Herr Vogelschotz refuses the cigar. But Signor Mantini makes up for this by taking two.

And so, for the next half-hour, they smoke and sip brandy and talk. And Signora Da Croce tells a long complicated story about how her favourite costumes for *Aïda* went down in a shipwreck. And then Signor Mantini glances at his watch, sighs, and looks very sad.

"Mr. Waxman—Mrs. Waxman—what misfortune. It is nine o'clock. We hate late rehearsing. We must go now."

He rises to his feet, and Signora Da Croce and Herr Vogelschotz rise along with him, as if at a signal.

"Well, now, this is disappointing," Dan says. "You're sure you couldn't stay just a while longer?

But Signor Mantini makes a spreading gesture with his hands—a very expressive gesture which tells how sorry he is to tear himself away, but also how cheerfully and philosophically he will resign himself to his sorrow.

Herr Vogelschotz pours down the last of his brandy.

Then they all move to the door and go through the ceremony of saying goodbye. Signor Mantini bobs his head, shakes the men's hands, and kisses the ladies' fingers. He even makes a pretty speech. "It is always so nice to accept your invitations, Mr. and Mrs. Waxman. So many business people—they have no understanding, no sympathy with the artistic and the cultural side of life. And the jokes of Mr. Meltzer!" Signor Mantini cackles softly.

Signora Da Croce doesn't have nearly as many words to say. She simply moves around to each one of them, embracing them and grinning broadly. When she gets to

Dan, she booms out in her loudest voice, "Very good dinner. I come again."

Herr Vogelschotz nods his head and says, "So charmed."

After they're gone, everybody goes back to the living-room. Dan feels that he can't let the silence go on too long. "They're fascinating people," he says. "You know, that old fellow is considered to be one of the great *maestros* in the world to-day. He's been compared to Toscanini."

"He's a good-looking man," Milly says.

"And that Signora Da Croce," Dan says, "did you ever hear her sing *Aïda*? She's got a voice that fills the whole opera house. Absolutely fills the house."

"Yes, she looks as if she's got quite a voice," Milly says. Then she adds quickly, "I mean—you can tell she's got a real artistic temperament."

For a while nobody says anything.

Dan lights up a cigar. "They're interesting people, though. It's always stimulating to be with them. A little eccentric maybe"—he gives a faint grin—"but you know what I mean, stimulating."

"No doubt about it," says Mort, coming forward and putting his hand down on Dan's shoulder. "Now if the lowbrow minority at this meeting can make a suggestion, let's have ourselves a stimulating game of bridge."

They play bridge till after midnight—Mort and Sarah against Dan and Milly, because Dan can never hold his temper when Sarah is his partner. It's a good game. Dan gets good cards, and he only makes a few mistakes—and whenever he makes one, Milly pulls him out of the hole. And what's more, Milly isn't the type who keeps reminding you every two minutes that she *did* pull you out of a hole.

In between rubbers, Mort tells jokes. Some of his best jokes, too—the one about the psychiatrist and the rabbits, the one about the plumber in the ladies' room—Dan has hardly heard any of them before. And so, what with chuckling all evening and piling up points, his spirits return to normal. By eleven-thirty Mort can even get away with telling a joke about a big fat opera soprano—and it doesn't upset Dan in the least.

But as soon as Mort and Milly have gone for the night, Dan falls silent again. A thoughtful look comes over his face. It's the same look that's been on his face more than once to-day. He sits forward on the sofa and watches Sarah tidying up the living-room. She moves back and forth, emptying ashtrays, gathering up cards, throwing away cigar wrappers. Then she goes to the light-switch, just over his head.

"Do you want to go to bed yet, Dan?"

He mutters something and shakes his head.

She stands looking down at him uncertainly. Then she tries a smile. "Did you have a nice day to-day, dear?"

"Nice day? Why shouldn't I have a nice day?"

"I mean—did anything special happen?"

For another moment they're silent. Then Dan gives a little sigh. "Sit down, Sarah," he says.

She sits down next to him on the sofa.

"They're a couple of good friends, aren't they?" he says. "Mort and Milly, that is."

Sarah nods. "We couldn't ask for better friends."

"And they're not the only ones, are they? We've got plenty of friends, haven't we? The Freeds, and the Nussbaums, and the Garfunkels, and all the others. Our life is full of good friends."

Sarah doesn't say anything.

Dan gives a little laugh. "They'll always stand by us, Won't they? All through the years, I mean. If we get to our seventy-fifth birthday, I mean—when they give us a party——"

Sarah just looks at him. He can feel her looking at him. But still she doesn't say anything.

"I'm not really talking about myself," Dan says quickly. "I'm talking in the abstract. I'm talking about any man. And what else should he hope for in this world, except for friendship, and the respect and admiration of his associates?"

Sarah looks at him a moment longer. And then, in a low serious voice, she speaks. "But that's what you've got," she says. "Right here in Chicago."

He doesn't have to see her expression. Her words are enough. He's calm and contented now. The tightness inside him is all gone, and he's more at peace with himself than he's been all day.

He smiles up at her a second later, and for the first time his contentment is written on his face. "I *am* a little tired," he says. "It's been a heavy day."

"To-morrow is Saturday," Sarah says. "You can sleep as late as you want." She switches off the light, and they go upstairs together.

At the door of their bedroom Dan stops suddenly and begins to laugh. "That Da Croce woman," he says. "Did you see the way she wolfed down her chicken?"

Sarah laughs, and says that she certainly did see.

And so the day comes to an end—an average day in my Uncle Dan's life, in the year 1928.

X

THE winter of 1929 and the spring of 1930 was a bad time for a lot of Chicago people. Contrary to popular superstition, the war veterans with apple-stands, the breadlines, and the groups of idle men on street-corners didn't spring up all of a sudden the morning after the Stock Market crashed. The only people affected at first were people who actually had money in the Market, and these people tended to keep their losses very much to themselves. They went on playing golf at their clubs and exchanging jokes with their friends. They postponed their vacations to Europe "because so much business has been piling up". They cut down their annual anniversary shindig from a hundred guests to an intimate family gathering—not for financial reasons, God forbid, but strictly because "we're getting a little too old for that sort of thing". Whatever economies or discomforts or fits of despair they may have indulged in private, they went on more or less the same as ever in public.

Among Dan's friends—the hundred or so people that he knew from his clubs, his business, his social life—there was a certain nervousness in the first days of November. Most of them had money—in some cases, a large slice of their money—in Drexell Enterprises. And most of them had been encouraged to put it there by Dan himself. Well, they might have put it there anyway, of course—plenty of people that Dan had never heard of had their money in Drexell—but still, you couldn't deny the effect of Dan's encouragement. And so, in those first days of November, with the newspapers full of scare headlines, and "reassuring" bulletins coming regularly out of the White House, with a dozen new rumours making the rounds every day, people *did* come up to Dan from time to time and ask him casual questions about what Drexell Enterprises was going to do, and whether they should hold on or sell out.

Dan was worried about the situation himself. Who wouldn't be? But his confidence in Drexell was a lot stronger than his worry. He soon worked out a careful, sensible little speech of advice which he delivered to anybody who approached him on the subject.

"Sell out? Look, Drexell is still going, isn't it? It's dropped a little, sure—everything's dropped. But take a close look, it's dropped a lot less than plenty of others. And it's dropping slower every day. You want my advice? I'll tell you frankly and truthfully exactly what *I'm* doing. No different from what I've always done— seventy-five per cent in good solid Government bonds. Not much profit, but nice and safe. The other twenty-five per cent for speculation. And when it comes to speculation, past experience and present facts prove that you absolutely can't beat Drexell."

"But look what's happening to *other* stocks," people said.

"Other stocks." Dan laughed and waved them away. "Don't you understand, that's exactly what Drexell thrives on. The more the others go down, the more Drexell goes up. Less competition."

And sure enough, events seemed to bear Dan out. Drexell Enterprises *was* falling slower and slower all the time. Then one day, around Christmas-time, it stopped falling completely. And then, with the New Year, to the amazement of all the professional prediction-makers, and contrary to all the rumours, it started to go up again. God knows how Drexell managed it. God knows what sort of a shot-in-the-arm he gave to his companies, but sure enough, by the beginning of the spring, Drexell Enterprises was right up on top again, almost up to where it had been before the crash.

Naturally, the people who had followed Dan's advice and held on to their Drexell stock, were full of feelings of self-congratulation. It was an early and a lovely spring. It was in the air by the first of April, a beautiful balmy sweet-smelling spring, which the Drexell stockholders enjoyed with a special zest because they knew that hardly anybody else was in the mood to appreciate it. It was a pleasant sight indeed to see two Drexell stockholders meeting on the street and hailing each other with broad smiles and waves, superbly conscious of belonging to a superior class of men. It was an even pleasanter sight to watch a Drexell stockholder shake his head sympathetically and cluck his tongue at a non-Drexell stockholder— or better still, at a former Drexell stockholder who had grown panicky in 1929 and unloaded.

The Drexell stockholders, to do them justice, were generous in their gratitude and appreciation for Dan. They listened more solemnly than ever when he opened up on business conditions. They went out of their way to tell him that they were planning to buy up even *more* Drexell stock than they had owned before the crash. One day in May—the day after Drexell Enterprises took an especially sharp rise—Dan walked into the dining-room of the club, and every man in the room rose to his feet, turned towards him, and applauded him. For the rest of the week Dan could hardly get over this. It was such a pride and satisfaction to know that you were being helpful and beneficial to your friends.

A short time later, towards the beginning of July, Dan began to hear the rumours.

He heard them first from Eli Glatz. Eli had just come back from a trip to New York, and over lunch at the club he was full of eagerness to tell Dan about it. "I had a talk with some friends of mine from Wall Street," Eli said, "and I feel that it's my duty to let you know about it. They had some very upsetting things to say about Drexell Enterprises. Very upsetting. Of course I don't put any stock in it myself. Heaven knows, I'm not the type who believes in idle rumours. Nevertheless, it *was* very upsetting, and so I felt that I owed it to our long friendship——"

"All right, all right, what'd they tell you, your friends?"

"Frankly, Dan," and Eli leaned forward and looked grave and sympathetic, "they told me that the bottom is going to drop out of Drexell Enterprises any day now. According to the rumours—strictly rumours, of course—Drexell has been up to some highly dubious activities the last few years. All these new companies he's started, and interlocking corporations, and so on—well, it seems that he's been building up an empire, so to speak, just for the sake of having more and more power, without any real assets or solid capital. Every time he has to pay the dividends on an old company—I'm just telling you the rumours, Dan, I'm not saying this is *my* opinion—every time he has to pay the dividends on an old company, he starts a new company, and sells shares in it, and collects a large amount of money which he uses to pay for the old company. And then, when the dividends fall due on the *new* company, he starts an even *newer* company—and so on and so on—and that's how he managed to get through the crash so well——"

"Wait a second, wait a second," Dan said. He had been itching to interrupt for a long time, and now he couldn't hold himself in any longer. "Do you know what you're describing? You're describing something which is not only very shaky business practice, but also unethical and illegal."

"Am I, Dan?" Eli looked more full of sympathy than ever. "I didn't know what I was describing. I don't really understand these questions of high finance. Buttons and laces is my line, and I've always stuck to it, and I've never put a penny into the Stock Market in my life. I'm only repeating what my friends told me. They said that

Drexell was bound to get into trouble eventually, and he finally has. All his dividends are coming due in a few weeks, and his mortgages, and the interest on his bank loans here in Chicago, and he doesn't have a single solid asset any more to pay his debts with. And according to the rumours, he's been taking trips to New York, in desperation, trying to raise the money *there*. He especially went to New York so that people in Chicago wouldn't find out what was up."

"Eli, you don't know what you're saying," Dan broke in. And his voice was so loud that people at the other tables turned around to look. "You're absolutely talking through your hat."

"Not so loud, Dan," Eli said. "We don't want this news to spread."

"Who cares if it spreads?" Dan said—automatically lowering his voice. "It's not news. It's a crazy lie. The same stories were spreading last year, isn't that so? And look how wrong they were. My God, is Martin Drexell a baby who was born yesterday and still has his ears wet— or is he the greatest financial genius in the country to-day? Would a man of his high calibre go in for a cheap swindle like your friends told you about?"

"Well, if you put it that way, Dan. Of course," and Eli looked mildly inquisitive, "it *is* true, isn't it, that he's been taking a lot of trips to New York lately?"

"What of it, what of it?" Dan said, a little louder. "He's been going to New York for relaxation. He likes to see shows, and what shows can you see during the summer in Chicago? Listen, Eli—listen to me." Dan shoved his chin forward, and his voice got more firm and positive. "I'm Drexell's chief accountant here in Chicago, isn't that so? If he was pulling anything fishy, I'd know about it, wouldn't I?"

"Would you, Dan?"

There was something so innocent in the way Eli asked this question that it made Dan frown for a second. But it was too late now, he was all wound up and he had to finish what he was saying. "Damned right I would. And I *don't* know anything about it. Because there's nothing to know, that's why."

"Would you personally vouch for that, Dan?" Eli said. "In case anybody repeats those rumours to me again, I mean."

"Would I personally vouch for it?" Dan shook off another vague little feeling of uneasiness, and began to nod his head hard. "I certainly would. I'm happy to vouch for Drexell. I give you my solemn word that his companies are just as sound and honest as the U.S. mint." And then Dan lowered his head and began to put away his rice pudding fast.

This talk with Eli Glatz stuck in his mind for the next few hours. And then, finally, he was able to forget about it. Eli Glatz is an old woman, he told himself. He gets pleasure out of repeating the nastiest gossip—always because it's his "duty", of course. Whatever Eli Glatz tells you, you know automatically that the truth is just the opposite.

And yet, in the next week or so, Dan heard Eli's rumour from a number of different sources. Never as clear and outright as Eli had put it himself. Only a little hint here, an indirect reference there, a disturbing word or two from some other direction. For instance, he would meet a friend on the street, and the friend would shake his hand and speak out very heartily, "Nice to see you, Dan. I was thinking about you to-day. Looking over my Drexell holdings. Saying to myself, 'Well, that's one investment I don't have to worry about. Not with Dan Waxman vouching for it.'" And somehow, though his friend's manner always seemed to be just as cheerful and good-humoured as possible, Dan would detect a certain small flicker of anxiety underneath it.

One time, leaving his office for the evening, Dan went down in the elevator with young Mark Kugel. All the way down Mark was polite and serious as always—he commented on the hot weather, he asked about Dan's health, he answered that he own health was fine. And Dan had the funniest feeling that there was something else on his mind.

Sure enough, when they got to the ground floor and walked out of the building together, the boy suddenly stopped and put his hand on Dan's arm. "Mr. Waxman— if you've got a minute or two—it's something I'd like to ask you about."

"Absolutely, Mark. Any number of minutes you'd like. If you've got some sort of trouble——"

"It isn't trouble, Mr. Waxman. It isn't anything important really." He gave a smile, to show how unimportant it was really—and the smile aroused Dan's fears right away. "It's about——" the boy went on. "Well, you know, Mr. Waxman, my grandfather is retired from the business now. He's living in a hotel now—I wanted him to come live with me, but he said an active young bachelor doesn't want an old man around—you know how Grandpa is, Mr. Waxman. So he's living in this hotel. It's a very nice hotel, and there's a lot of men his own age, and he gets a lot of time for playing pinochle and collecting his stamps and reading the newspapers and all. He's happy there, Mr. Waxman. Resting and relaxing for the first time in his life. He deserves it, God knows, after all these years."

"Yes, I see that," Dan said, wondering what the boy was getting at, but knowing it was better to let him take his own time.

"Well, the thing is, Mr. Waxman—Grandpa's business —it isn't really such a big business—it's a good little business, it means a lot to me—but it's never been so big really. And the last ten years or so, whatever free money there was—it was mainly for me he did it, Mr. Waxman, because he was thinking of my future—whatever free money there was, Grandpa put it in Drexell Mid-West Light and Electricity. And then, when Drexell Mid-West Light and Electricity started going up, and Grandpa's investment was really getting pretty valuable—well, he felt that for my sake, as a way of building up the business, you know, and making it worth more for me—he started borrowing on the strength of his Drexell shares, and re-investing, you know—and it worked out very nice on paper—and that's what the business is going on now, Mr. Waxman, what with the slump and everything. And that's what Grandpa is living on—— Well, I don't want to bore you with a lot of personal information——"

"Who says you're boring me?" Dan said, very quietly. "I think I know what's on your mind, Mark. Maybe I can save you the trouble of saying it. Your money is all tied up in Drexell Enterprises. You want to know whether the investment is going to be safe."

The boy nodded his head, and turned his eyes away, terribly pale and embarrassed. "I don't mean that I've got any doubts, Mr. Waxman," he said. "I wouldn't want to suggest such a thing for a minute. The respect that Grandpa and I have always had for you—— It's just that there are these rumours going around, and you can't help hearing what people are saying. And if anything happened to our Drexell shares, Mr. Waxman— well, it wouldn't be so bad for me, but Grandpa isn't a young man any more, how could he change his way of life at his age?"

Dan reached out and took the boy by the arm. And he

smiled his most reassuring smile, and spoke in his most confident voice. "He won't have to change his way of life. Nobody'll have to change anything. Those rumours you heard aren't true—there isn't any truth in them. Of course, speculation is speculation. Personally I don't advise putting more than twenty-five per cent of your spare money in it, on general principles. But aside from that, Drexell Enterprises is the safest stock on the Market to-day."

The boy looked up, the colour coming slowly back into his face. "Do you mean that, Mr. Waxman?"

"Do I mean it? Of course I mean it." Dan laughed and gave Mark's arm a nudge. "So put on a smile, and stop your worrying."

A moment later young Mark Kugel put on a smile.

But Dan wasn't smiling in the car riding home. And it was only when he finally got back to Twelve Hundred Lake Shore Drive that he was able to shake his head, and give a laugh, and say to himself, "That Eli Glatz. My God, he's been a busy little fellow this last week."

And then, a few days later, it happened again. It was Sunday, the maid's night out, and Bobby was away at summer camp, so Dan and Sarah went downtown for dinner at a steak place. And there in the same restaurant was Nat Garfunkel with his twin sons—tall dark-haired boys of fifteen, with already a touch of their father's worried, owlish expression on their faces.

Nat was just leaving the restaurant as Dan and Sarah got seated, so he stopped at their table to introduce the twins. "This is Ronny, and this is Donny," he said. "At least, that's what they tell me. Fifteen years, and I still have trouble knowing them apart."

Dan shook hands with them, and made a joke about what wonderful assets they would be to Nat in the real estate business some day. "One of them could make the promises to the client, and a few months later, when the client comes to complain, the other one could swear that he was away in Milwaukee at the time and never promised a thing."

Sarah shook hands with them too, and made a small fuss over them, saying how handsome they'd grown and how she hadn't seen them since they were so high.

"Wife's out of town visiting her mother," Nat said, "so the boys and I are making a night of it. We're on our way to see Charlie Chaplin."

Sarah made a remark about how nice it was when a father gave up so much of his time to his sons.

"Nice nothing," Nat said. "I can't get rid of them. They stick to me like glue. I think their mother gave them orders."

One of the twins was looking over at his father anxiously now, while tne other one cleared his throat and glanced down at his wrist-watch. But Nat wasn't quite ready to go along yet.

"Incidentally, Dan," he said, "when is the big blow-up expected? When am I going to be able to convert my Drexell shares into a cheap brand of toilet-paper?"

"I'm surprised at you, Nat," Dan said. "You aren't falling for those rumours are you? You aren't listening to that crazy Eli Glatz?"

"I don't know anything about Eli Glatz," Nat said. "And why should I need rumours? You know me, Dan, even without rumours, I always expect the worst to happen. I was only wondering, because I'm building this country place out in Glen Cove, and I've got a lot of money tied up in it——"

"Go ahead with your country place," Dan said. "Drexell is sound as a rock, I give you my word for that. Of course you shouldn't go *overboard*. That's only common sense——"

But Nat cut him off with a little grunt. "That's good enough for me," he said. "Except, of course, that I never take any man's word for anything."

Then he took his sons by the arm, nodded shortly at Sarah, and walked out of the restaurant.

"Honest to God," Dan said, making himself laugh, "Nat Garfunkel is going to worry himself into an early grave. What an imagination."

"Is it all his imagination, dear?" Sarah said, in a hesitant sort of voice. "You know, some of the girls were over for the Thursday bridge game, and that Mrs. Steinthal was talking—she does a lot of investing, you know, since her husband died and left her all those oil wells——"

"For God's sake, Sarah, not you too," Dan said, the colour beginning to rise to his neck. "Everywhere I go these days, that's all I hear—Drexell, Drexell, and Drexell. My God, I'm sick of hearing about Drexell."

Sarah lowered her eyes. "Yes, dear," she said, in a small voice. "Let's order our dinner."

And then the first week in August, just a month after his talk with Eli Glatz, the most disturbing thing of all happened to Dan. He got a telegram from his brother Herman in New York, saying that he was coming out to Chicago over the week-end.

Well, it wasn't the first time Herman had visited Chicago suddenly—Herman would travel across the Sahara Desert on a camel, Dan thought, if there was a potential buyer for a diamond necklace waiting for him on the other side. But there was something about the tone of this particular telegram that started Dan wondering. Something sort of sharp and urgent, which wasn't like Herman at all. Even in the early days, Herman had been the rigid, conservative type, and through the years he had been getting more and more so. To-day, at the age of forty-five, he was as ponderously cautious in his speech and stuffy in his opinions as any New England banker in his sixties. Under ordinary circumstances, you could pump him for hours, and not get anything more positive and emotional out of Herman than a disapproving cough.

"So why," Dan said to Sarah, turning Herman's telegram over and over between his fingers, "does he end up with a line like this? 'Vital business—must see you as soon as possible.' He could've said just plain 'must see you soon', and saved himself five words. What's so vital that Herman, of all people, loses interest in saving five words?" And it kept on worrying him until Herman finally showed up.

He arrived unexpectedly at nine o'clock that same night. Dan and Sarah were in the living-room, enjoying a quiet game of two-handed solitaire, when all of a sudden the doorbell rang, and there was Herman.

At first, in spite of this dramatic entrance, Dan could hardly believe that anything was wrong. Herman was so completely normal and absolutely the way Dan expected him to be. The same stiff straight way of holding himself, the same dark business suit, the same neat, prematurely grey hair, and the same solemn, dignified manner that was fine for selling jewellery, but deadly on a New Year's Eve party. And another thing was typical of Herman. Even though he had been riding on a train all day, with the sweat pouring down his face, he wouldn't sit down and take a drink until he had gone through all the formalities. He had to kiss Sarah, shake Dan's hand, inquire after Bobby, compliment the appearance of the apartment, and deliver an opinion on the weather.

Curious as he was about this visit, Dan couldn't keep away that little twinge of annoyance that invariably came over him when he was with his brother. Was there ever a time, Dan wondered, when Herman had felt a spontaneous unrehearsed emotion, when he had actually come out and said something just for the hell of it, just because he *wanted* to, and without thinking it out, debating it back and forth, and drawing up a blueprint on it beforehand? For awhile, after Herman got married, people thought he might change his ways. His wife, Doris, was such a cheerful, light-hearted little girl—she loved to dance, and go to night clubs, and laugh at jokes—and everyone was sure that Herman would loosen up under her influence. But it turned out just the opposite. Herman ended up by wearing Doris down. As the years passed, she laughed less and less, and forgot how to dance, and became sort of faded and mousy. Seven years ago, she faded away completely, and Herman, living alone again, grew more like himself than ever.

When the formalities were over, Herman took a seat, without sitting back and making himself comfortable in it, and accepted the drink that he drank on all occasions—a jigger of whisky and half a glass of soda—"one jigger please, no more, and *exactly* half a glass". Then, after three experimental sips, he decided that it was safe to come to the point. "I assume you're wondering why I'm here. Frankly speaking, it wasn't only on your account that I came. I'm meeting with some people tomorrow—a very wealthy meat-packing family, they're looking for a wedding-ring for their daughter's fiancé. However," and here Herman raised his finger to emphasize the solemn importance of this "however", "my appointment with them isn't until to-morrow afternoon. I've come almost a day early for the express purpose of taking up a very urgent matter with *you*."

"With such a build-up," Dan said, "it can only be a matter of life and death."

"I hope that isn't a joke," Herman said, drawing himself up a little. "Believe me, this isn't a joking matter."

And there was something in Herman's manner that impressed Dan in spite of himself. Impressed him, and worried him a little too. "Well, what is it?" he said, with an uneasy laugh.

"Some information has come into my hands," Herman said. "The origin of this information is confidential, I'm afraid. But you know I'm not the type of man who's given to exaggeration or hasty conclusions—so when I tell you that my informant is *absolutely* authoritative, I'm sure you won't have any trouble believing me."

"We believe you, we believe you," Dan said. "What's the information?"

Sarah started to her feet. "Maybe I'd better go to my room or something. This sounds like business."

"I'd rather you stayed here, Sarah," Herman said. "This concerns you too. It's a family matter." And the way he said the words "family matter", it practically sent a shiver up Dan's spine.

The next moment Herman leaned forward, and his voice became even more intent. "Listen to me, Dan." (He had long ago given up calling his brother by the undignified name of "Danny".) "Listen to me, Dan. Drexell Enterprises is going to collapse within a week or ten days. You have to get out while you still have the chance."

Dan gave a gasp at this. "What are you talking about?" he said. "You don't make sense——" He stammered on a little longer in the same way, but really he was shaken, terribly shaken. As long as it was only Eli Glatz, with his malicious tongue, or Nat Garfunkel, with his worrying nature—— But to hear it like this from his brother Herman—from his solid, sensible, responsible brother who hated to say "Good morning"

to you unless he verified it first with the Weather Bureau
—to hear such a thing from such a weighty source——
"But where did you get such an idea?" Dan said. "You
have to tell me who this mysterious informant is."

Herman raised an eyebrow, very frosty. "I don't have
to tell you any such thing. I respect confidences. How
long do you think I'd last in my business if I didn't?
I *will* tell you this much, however. My source is a leading
figure in the New York financial world, who holds
mortgages for a large sum of money on some of Martin
Drexell's most extensive holdings. And less than three
days ago, Drexell himself visited this man in an attempt to
persuade him to extend his notes. The attempt was met
with an out-and-out refusal, since the interest alone has
already become too large for Drexell to pay."

Dan was thinking furiously. Three days ago? What
was Drexell doing three days ago? Yes, he *was* in New
York. Just for one day he was there—"Visiting a little
friend of mine from the Follies." That's what he told
Dan before he left, and he gave one of those confidential
little winks that always made Dan feel as if he was an
important part of an exciting conspiracy.

Dan laughs again. "And this large sum of money that
you're being so cagey about," he said. "How much is it?
Just for the fun of it, I'd like to know."

Herman didn't bat an eyelash as he answered this. "Ten
million dollars," he said.

"Ten million——?" Dan repeated the words weakly.

Herman nodded. "Exactly. And my informant tells
me there are at least half a dozen other men around the
city with equally large claims. What's more, this money
didn't come out of Drexell's pocket. It came out of
Drexell Enterprises. By clever manipulation it's Drexell
Enterprises that will have to pay the bill when the whole
thing is brought up before the bankruptcy courts."

"Bankruptcy?"

And Sarah wailed out the word too. "Bankruptcy!" It was a word that had a frightening sound even to people who didn't know a thing about high finance.

"Bankruptcy," Herman repeated. "And a long drawn-out complicated business it's going to be. In the end, I suppose, the lawyers will get most of it. At any rate, that's not our problem. Our problem is, what are *you* going to do?"

"Me?"

"How are you going to get out of this with the least possible loss? To your bank account—and to your prestige."

"My prestige? I don't follow——"

"First things first," Herman said. "What about your bank account? How much have you got in Drexell Enterprises anyway? Every penny of your capital, I'll bet."

"No, no—I've always invested half and half. Half in Drexell, and half in Government bonds. Just on principle. Don't keep all your eggs——"

"Good, good. First thing to-morrow morning then, sell your Drexell shares. Sell every last share. You won't do badly on the deal, not if you hurry up about it. Second of all, for your prestige."

"Herman, what do you mean?" Sarah put in. "Where does Dan's prestige come into it?"

"Where indeed." Herman looked from Dan to Sarah and back again, as if he could hardly believe in their ignorance. "When this Drexell business breaks, what do you suppose people are going to say? I myself know differently, of course. I know my own brother. I know what his faults are—and what they aren't. But that won't stop people from talking. They'll remember that you were Drexell's chief accountant. They'll remember that you've been keeping his books all these years. And they won't hesitate to assume——"

"Just a minute," Dan said, shaking his head. "Not so fast, not so fast——"

"There's only one solution," Herman said. "The family reputation demands it as well as anything else. To-morrow morning, after you've disposed of your own shares, you'll start calling up your friends and acquaintances. You'll call up every one of them who owns any stock in Drexell Enterprises. Every one of them who really matters, that is. You'll tell them what you've found out, and you'll advise them to sell immediately. After that, it's up to them. Even if they ignore your advice, they can never blame you for what happens. It's the only way, Dan. Now promise me that you'll do it."

"The only way——" Dan blinked a little, still sort of dazed. But the first shock was beginning to wear off, his mind was beginning to clear up again, his common sense was coming back to him slowly. "The only way——" And all of a sudden, he gave his head a sharp shake. "You don't know what you're saying. You're babbling away like a little baby. All the way from New York, just to talk baby-talk."

Herman put on the pained, regretful look that he always put on when Dan raised his voice to him.

"Sell my Drexell shares?" Dan went on, using his hands. "Call up my friends? Give up my work? Baby-talk—pure baby-talk. And I sat here and listened to him say it. That's the part that really gets me. For a couple of minutes I was actually believing him."

Sarah now shifted her gaze uncertainly to Dan's face. Don't you think it's the truth, dear?"

"The truth? Of course it isn't the truth. Use your logic for a minute, will you? I'm Drexell's chief accountant, I've been keeping his books for years—didn't my alarmist brother just point this out himself? So if all this fancy manipulation and spending and borrowing was going on, wouldn't I know about it?" He jumped to his feet and faced Herman squarely. "All right, answer me, wouldn't I know about it?"

Herman met his glare without flinching. "Maybe," he said, "And maybe not."

It was this sort of pussyfooting half-and-half answer that always sent Dan into a fury. "What do you mean, maybe not? How maybe not? How maybe not?"

"I wonder if it ever occurred to you," Herman said, just as calm and even as before, "that the books you work on might not be the only books. The side of his business affairs which Drexell lets you see might not be the only side. He probably has a great many offices and a great many accountants all over the country, all of them working on different sections of his interests, and none of them knowing what the other ones are doing."

"But why? Why? What's the point? A man like Drexell, why should he go in for such foolishness, like a spy story or something?"

"A man like Drexell," Herman repeated Dan's words, putting into them the greatest amount of scorn that he could manage in his stiff, unemotional way. "Drexell is an adventurer. He's a modern type of pirate. A man like that automatically *thinks* in terms of tricks and plots and deceptions. He *prefers* to do things in an underhand way. And I assure you, it won't bother him for a minute to see you and others like you getting the blame for what he did. If you'll remember, I warned you about him ten years ago, when you first got involved with him——"

"That's it! Now I see it!" Dan shouted out suddenly, laughing sarcastically, pretending to be jubilant. "You warned me about him. It annoyed you, didn't it, when you heard I was being taken up by him. A man with imagination, and energy, and genius—who's willing to take a chance, and play a hunch, and thinks there's more to being a business-man than crawling into a hole and covering himself up with moss. You hated the idea that maybe, on account of my connection with him, people would look up to your little brother, and point their finger at him, and say, 'There goes a successful fellow.' You can't stand admitting that you've been wrong about me, and maybe I'm not such a dope and a no-good after all. So that's why you're coming to me now with this crazy story. It's your way of breaking things up between Drexell and me. It's your own clever little manipulation. I see it. Oh yes." Another explosion of sarcastic laughter from Dan, who was waving his arms and pacing the floor by now. "Oh yes indeed—I definitely see it!"

"Do you believe that?" Herman said. "Is that what you seriously believe about me?"

"Believe it?" Dan stopped pacing, and turned his full fury straight on his brother. "Damned right I believe it. It's the way you've always been. Bossy and possessive. You hear me? Eaten up by bossiness!"

"In that case," Herman said, rising to his feet with great dignity, "I think I'd better go."

"Go! Go!" Dan was practically hopping up and down in front of him. "Is that supposed to be a threat? Am I supposed to start shaking in my shoes? Go! Get out of here! Good riddance!"

"Dan, don't say such things," Sarah put in. "Herman, don't go. You two shouldn't fight like this——"

"Keep your nose out of this!" Dan shouted at her, over his shoulder.

"It's no use, Sarah," Herman said. "*I'm* not the one who's fighting. I'm *never* the one who fights. It's been exactly the same ever since we were small boys. Obstinate and mulish. Forty-odd years, and he still hasn't learned a thing."

"Obstinate!" Dan cried. "Who's obstinate? *I'm* obstinate?" But Herman was already out of the room. And a second later they heard the front door shut behind him.

Herman was gone, but Dan was still full of steam. So he went right on with the fight for the next half-hour. While Sarah watched anxiously from the sofa, he stamped up and down the living-room, muttered to himself, came out with sudden sentences in a loud voice, waved his arms at the air. It didn't seem to bother him at all that he didn't have anybody to fight with.

Then around ten-thirty he began to calm down. He let himself continue the fight from a sitting position. He picked up a handful of grapes from the bowl of fruit that Sarah had placed in front of him. He put one into his mouth. It tasted good. He picked up another handful. He hadn't realized how hungry he was. He told Sarah to bring him a liverwurst sandwich from the kitchen. While she was gone, he caught sight of the newspaper, and when she returned with the liverwurst sandwich he was deeply absorbed in the crossword puzzle.

Still, the talk with Herman didn't go right out of his mind. If the truth were known, it kept him awake that night long after the lights were turned out. And it filled up his whole ride down to the office next morning.

After pottering around at his desk for an hour or so, accomplishing nothing—except to make Schultz look at him darkly and say, "You're off your stride, Mr. Waxman, can I get you a bicarbonate?"—Dan finally gave a sigh and called up Drexell's home.

First, he got Mrs. Drexell. As a matter of principle, she tried to keep him from talking to her husband. "Must you disturb him, Mr. Waxman?" she said. "He had a very late night. We were entertaining some people from London. Lord and Lady——"

"Yes, I *must* disturb him," Dan broke in, not bothering to hide his annoyance. "This is business."

Through the receiver he could hear Mrs. Drexell's genteel sigh. "Very well then. If you're going to make a fuss."

It was her round, and Dan knew it, but he didn't even try to do anything about it. This was one time when he was in no mood for playing games with Mrs. Drexell.

A few minutes later Drexell's voice exploded into Dan's ear. "Hello, Dan. How are you? What's up?"

A funny little feeling shot through Dan at the sound of Drexell's voice. That rich, positive, down-to-earth voice —a hundred times more real and dependable, it seemed, than all the stuffy cold-blooded Hermans on earth. And yet, Dan's fears weren't gone by a long shot, and he just had to get them off his mind. "Martin," he began, already a little guiltily, "the reason why I called—I'm a little bit upset this morning. To tell the truth—I heard something last night. About Drexell Enterprises, that is."

Drexell's laugh was loud and hearty. "What's so upsetting about that, Dan? Can a man walk two blocks in the city of Chicago without hearing something about Drexell Enterprises?"

"No, of course not. But what I heard—well, it wasn't good, Martin. It was——"

"Wait a second, Dan." Drexell's voice wasn't sharp or annoyed or worried or anything like that. It was just sort of politely inquisitive. "Stop me if I'm wrong, mind you—but I think I can tell you what you heard."

A little weakly, Dan said, "You can tell me——?"

"You heard that Drexell Enterprises was on the verge of bankruptcy, didn't you?"

"Yes, Martin, I——"

"You heard that I went to New York to try and borrow money, didn't you?"

"Yes, Martin. But how did you——"

"You heard that I was keeping more than one set of books, and taking dividends from one group of stockholders to pay off another group of stockholders, and building up dummy organizations without any solid assets to back them up. That's what you heard, isn't it?"

"Yes, I did, Martin." Dan was completely confused by now. "But I just don't understand——"

"Dan my friend," and Drexell's voice had never been firmer, steadier, more full of strength and assurance, "you heard exactly what I *wanted* you to hear."

"You wanted me——?"

"Exactly. You and the rest of the world. It's a complicated situation, Dan. A question of strategy. Throwing dust in the eyes of my enemies, making the competition feel over-optimistic, lulling their suspicions—all a smokescreen for this big deal I'm coming up with now."

"A big deal, Martin?"

"The biggest yet. So big that it'll not only revolutionize Drexell Enterprises, but frankly, you can expect the whole country itself to be on its feet by—— But not another word. Not even to you, Dan. You won't be offended, will you?"

"Offended? Offended at you?" And quickly all of Dan's faith and trust was rushing back to him. "Martin— I don't know what to say. I'm ashamed of myself. A coward—jumping at shadows. Just because some big stuffed-shirt starts talking to me about 'authoritative information'——"

"Apologies accepted, Dan. As a matter of fact, you had just the reaction I anticipated. I'm proud of myself. Now they're ringing me on another phone——"

"Yes, yes, of course, Martin. I won't bother you any more. I'll see you this afternoon. I'm sorry."

Dan hung up the phone, shook his head, breathed a terrific sigh of relief. Thank God he had come to his senses again. How close he had been to spoiling his friendship with Drexell, his business relationship, the things that made his whole life worth living—thank God he was now completely recovered.

That same evening he had a chance to prove himself how completely he was recovered. Sarah and he went down to the railroad station to see Mort and Milly Meltzer off. They were taking the "Twentieth Century" to New York, and to-morrow morning they would sail off to Bermuda for a month's vacation. It was Mort's first vacation in years, and for weeks now he hadn't been talking about anything else. "Palm trees, and bicycles, and beaches," he said, putting on an ecstatic faraway look. "And hot tamales, and beautiful native girls. Ah, that's the life for a man."

"Let me catch you with those native girls," Milly said, "and it won't be a very long life."

So now they were all at the station, going through the usual exhibition of gaiety and tears that every trip ought to start out with. Sarah gave them a big box of candy, and Dan presented Mort with some gift-wrapped cigars. And Milly had a moment of alarm when she thought she couldn't find their boat tickets. And Sarah said, "Well, you won't really be away for so long. You'll be back in time for our Labour Day party." And then, Sarah and Milly fell sobbing into each other's arms.

So Mort took Dan by the arm and edged him over to the side. "Women," he said. "Babies, every one of them. It's a wonder us men haven't invented something to replace them."

"Listen, Mort," Dan said. "I'm glad the women are

busy just now. Because there's something I'd like to talk to you about. Before you leave, that is."

"Fire away, Dan boy."

"Well—I don't know how much this trip is costing you. But I was with Drexell for a couple of hours this afternoon, and he gave me an inside tip—Drexell Gas is due for a big rise in the next week or so. If you wanted to pick up a few extra shares right now—chances are, by the time you got back to Chicago, they'll have paid for your vacation. Of course," Dan added hastily, "if you don't feel like it, that's all right too. I know you've got a lot of money in Drexell already."

"Feel like it?" Mort said. "Since when don't I feel like getting a free ride to Bermuda? I'll give you my cheque right now, and you can handle the whole deal for me."

Dan smiled, but still not quite easily. "You mean, you're willing to take the risk? You haven't been listening to—the rumours that are going around?"

"How could I keep from listening to them?" Mort laughed. "My God, if I paid attention to all the rumours I listened to, I would've been in the nuthouse years ago."

Dan's smile grew bigger, his voice more assured. "Yes, I see your point. That's just how I feel about it myself."

"Besides which, Dan boy," Mort went on, slapping his hand down on Dan's shoulder, "believe it or not, I've got a lot of faith in you. If there was anything wrong with Drexell Enterprises, I'm sure you'd let your old pal in on it."

"Mort dear," Milly's voice broke in, "I think we'd better get to our compartment."

"Oh yes, we're in a big hurry," Mort said, with a wink at Dan. "Why, it's only half an hour till train time."

Less than one week later it happened. It happened so

quickly that even the gloomiest sceptics were taken by surprise. It began early in the morning, with Trans-Drexell Airways wobbling a little. An hour later Mid-West Electricity joined in. Then the wobbling changed to a definite falling, and one by one all the other Drexell Enterprises became a part of it. At lunchtime the pace increased. By the middle of the afternoon they were dropping so fast that no power on earth could stop them. Before the Stock Exchange closed that evening, Drexell Enterprises were down to nothing.

XI

EVEN before lunch, the phone calls started coming in to Dan's office. They were mostly from clients of his—or friends from the club—or fellows he played golf with. They were all Drexell stockholders who had been going around a week ago priding themselves on their business judgment. All they wanted now, at first, was to ask off-hand questions. "Doesn't mean anything, does it, Dan?" "No reason to get worried, is there, Dan?" Then the questions grew a little less offhand, a little more anxious. And the phone calls began to come faster.

It got so bad after lunch that Dan just couldn't keep up with them all. He had to instruct the switchboard girl to tell people that he was out of the office. Two lines he kept open, though. On one line he was in regular communication with his broker. A lot of good it did him, this regular communication. His broker was no help at all. "I'm completely in the dark, Dan," his broker said. "It's as much of a surprise to me as it is to anybody. All

I can say is, I'm confident the situation will stabilize itself. The situation always stabilizes itself."

On the other line Dan had Schultz making regular attempts to get in touch with Drexell. Every fifteen minutes she tried Drexell's number—and then every ten minutes—and always it was the same story; "The line is busy—the line is busy." Drexell must be going through the same business, Dan thought. He must be swamped by calls. And he told Schultz to try him every *five* minutes.

And then, at four-thirty, when it was absolutely clear what was happening—when Drexell Enterprises didn't have a chance in the world, and even Dan couldn't get around it—he just wasn't able to sit around the office doing nothing any more. "I'm going out there," he announced to Schultz, getting suddenly to his feet. "I'll speak to Drexell personally. I'm sure he's doing something about all this. I'm sure he's still got a few tricks up his sleeve." Then he told Schultz to call his home, tell Sarah he might be late, take down the names of anybody who called.

He was held back by just one more phone call. It was his broker again. "Nothing new on my end, Dan," said his broker, reeling off his message in a tired mechanical voice. "But all the indications are that the situation will stabilize itself. I'm confident that the situation——" Dan hung up on him, and hurried out the door.

Outside the heat was intense. It came blasting into Dan's face the moment he stepped out to the sidewalk. It was thick and sticky, it slowed him up, he had to move against it on his way to the car. And the sky was a dark dirty grey, gathering itself up for an explosion. And all around Dan, people were hurrying along with their heads down and anxious looks on their faces, hurrying to get home before the storm broke.

Dan got into the car and sat back in his seat and put a cigar in his mouth. But he didn't light it up. He just left it there, and forgot all about it.

Traffic downtown was thick. The car got caught in a jam at one corner, and Dan caught sight of a headline on a newsstand. "Wait a second, wait a second," he said to the chauffeur, as he was about to start the car again. Then, leaning his head out the window, "Paper, paper. Over here, will you." The paper was shoved at him from the street corner, and Dan opened it up with shaking fingers.

It was an extra edition. The tall black headlines almost seemed to be screaming at him, as the car jolted into motion again.

DREXELL FAILS:

WALL STREET PANIC

And in smaller headlines underneath:

GOVERNMENT CHARGES FRAUD:

INDICTMENT EXPECTED

Hastily, a little wildly, from the motion of the car and the confusion of his own feelings, Dan read the article through. It was a jumble of high-flown dramatic phrases, staggering sums of money, the rumours that he'd been hearing for the last month, rumours he hadn't ever heard before, dark references to "the Treasury Department" and "Money-Hungry Tycoons" and "the life savings of widows and orphans".

Dan crumpled the paper up and hurled it out of the window. Then he leaned forward and yelled at the chauffeur, "Hurry up, hurry up, what's the matter with you?"

The sky was black when his car pulled up to the Drexell mansion. And the house looked funny, some-how—queer and upsetting, somehow. The shades were down—Dan could see it at a glance—the shades were down on all the windows. And parked in the driveway was a long black car that Dan hadn't ever seen there before.

He practically ran up the front steps, and pushed the bell hard—and the door flew open so quick that it gave him a start. It was just as if the butler had been ready for him, had been waiting in the foyer with his hand on the doorknob.

But the butler hardly even bothered to look at him. "Mr. Waxman," he said. "I was just passing by—I heard your ring." And he turned right around and disappeared into the back of the house.

Dan just stood there a moment, wondering what was going on. Then, when nobody showed up to give him an explanation, he took a step towards the living-room. The high double doors of the living-room were shut tight—it was another queer thing, he hadn't ever known them to be shut like that before. He reached up a little uncertainly and gave a soft knock.

A moment later one of the doors opened. It opened just a little way, and a man came sliding out, and shut the door behind him quickly. He was a little man with a soft round face and an important look. He spoke in an accentuated whisper, the way people do in hospitals. "I'm Dr. Miller," he said. "Was there something you wanted?"

For some reason it irritated Dan, to dash all the way out here like this and come up against this whispering little busybody. "Was there something I wanted?" Dan answered him. "I wanted to see Mr. Drexell, that's what I wanted."

"Well perhaps, if you could tell me your business with him——"

"Tell you my business with him? I want to see him, that's my business. I'm Mr. Waxman, his accountant, and my business is with Mr. Drexell personally."

The little doctor began to shake his head. He shook it back and forth, slowly and sadly. "Oh, I'm afraid that's impossible. I'm afraid that's quite impossible."

"Impossible? What do you mean, impossible? Now listen to me——"

"It's all right, Doctor. I'll talk to Mr. Waxman."

The living-room doors were open wide now, and Mrs. Drexell was standing in the doorway.

"Really, Mrs. Drexell, you mustn't," said the doctor, shaking his head at her. "You really must lie down and rest. You really owe it to yourself."

"Do you want to see Martin, Mr. Waxman?" she said. "I'll take you up to see him right now."

Dr. Miller almost forgot his whisper at this. "But really, Mrs. Drexell——"

She turned to him with a quick gesture of impatience; "Oh, what does it matter, Doctor? And then she turned back to Dan. "Come this way, Mr. Waxman. Martin is in his bedroom."

She started up the stairs. And Dan followed just a little way behind her. And Dr. Miller bustled along behind *him*.

She didn't say another word to him. She didn't look back at him once. But Dan could see her face, half turned away from him. He could see the way she held her chin up, always so stiff and aristocratic, just like the society ladies on the stage. And he could see the cool superior look in her eyes, and the thin stern line of her mouth. And underneath it all, he could see something else—that is, he couldn't see it, but he could feel it, something sort of throbbing underneath, something she was holding in, and holding it in for dear life. "What is it?" he wanted to shout right out. "What's happened here, anyway?" But he couldn't say a word.

And then, on the second floor landing, they stopped in

front of a closed door. And Mrs. Drexell reached out and turned the knob softly and quietly pushed the door open. "Come in, Mr. Waxman," she said, in that same calm matter-of-fact voice.

The shades were drawn. The room was dark. Dan took a few steps inside, squinted around him, and suddenly stopped walking. His eyes had grown used to the darkness now, and he could see what was lying on the bed.

A little hiss of breath escaped him in spite of himself.

The uniformed nurse by the bed half rose in her seat.

"It's all right, Mrs. Neilsen," said Mrs. Drexell. "We'll only stay a moment."

Dan took another half-step forward. "Martin," he said, in a low voice. But even as he said it, he knew there wouldn't be any answer.

The next moment Dan turned away quickly. "I'd like to go," he mumbled. "I'm sorry." And he moved past Mrs. Drexell, and out of the room.

Mrs. Drexell followed him, shutting the door behind her.

They didn't go down the stairs again. Dan stood on the landing for a second or two, trying to get hold of himself. Finally he was able to look up at her and bring out his question. "What is it? What happened to him?"

"The doctors call it a stroke," she said. "His whole right side is paralysed. He can only see out of his left eye."

"But when—how——?"

"He was busy all day," she said. "He wasn't off the phone for a minute. He wouldn't even stop for his lunch." She paused. Not from emotion, but evidently just to collect her thoughts. Then she went on. "At three o'clock the news came. About the indictment. He began to talk strangely. He talked about all the money he made for people. And this was how they repaid him. He said he'd show them all. He said he'd issue a statement to the newspapers. Then he went into the study and slammed the door behind him. We could hear him switch on the dictating machine. We could hear him walking up and down and talking in a loud voice. Then we couldn't hear him talking any more. When we went into the study, he was sitting behind the desk. Just sitting there. You saw him for yourself."

"And—the way he looks——?" Dan said. Then broke off embarrassed.

"His mouth, you mean?" said Mrs. Drexell, very matter-of-fact, "I suppose he still thinks he's dictating. I don't see how we'll ever know." Her face was steady and unmoved a moment longer. And then, the next moment, her mouth puckered up, her eyes were red, and she was sobbing convulsively. And since Dan was standing closer to her than the doctor, she reached out at him instinctively, and sobbed into his shoulder.

Dan couldn't say how long he held her like that. It seemed like an endlessly long time, and every minute of it he was fidgeting and sweating, feeling awful for her and wanting to pat her on the shoulder and comfort her, and wondering if he really ought to do so.

It was a big relief when little Dr. Miller finally took her by the arm and gently separated her from Dan. Her eyes were red now, and her face was wrinkled and ugly. It was an old woman who looked up at Dan, blinking hard, confused and upset. And then Dr. Miller led her away.

Dan scrambled down the stairs and out of the house just as fast as his legs could carry him.

The storm broke on the way home. There were flashes of lightning, and crashes of thunder, and the rain slashed madly against the windows of the car. At the door of the apartment Sarah began to fuss over him. Was he all right? Did he get wet? Did he hear the news? Oh, it was terrible—it was just heartbreaking. Shouldn't he take a hot shower before dinner? He finally had to lash out at her angrily and tell her to leave him alone.

So it wasn't till much later on, till just before bedtime, that she dared to bring up the subject again. "Dan dear," she said, in a low voice, breaking into a long silence, "what does it come to, this Drexell business? I mean— how is it going to change things for us?"

He was feeling a little guilty, the way he talked to her earlier. So he smiled up at her as warmly and encouragingly as he could. "Don't worry about it, Sarah," he said. "We've got a lot of money in Drexell, of course. For a little while we may have to give up a few things. But we're not wiped out by any means. I've still got my work. And thank God for my principles—seventy-five per cent in Government bonds, only twenty-five per cent in speculation."

But the worried look didn't disappear from Sarah's face. "That wasn't what I meant exactly," she said.

Dan looked at her, a little puzzled. "I don't follow," he said. "What *else* could you mean?"

Sarah didn't answer him. Then, a moment later, her worried look changed to a smile. "Nothing," she said. "I'm just making noises like a woman."

XII

THE next week, it was one shock after another for Dan. The day after the Drexell failure, the Government men called on Dan. He had to show them all his files on Drexell, all his books, all his correspondence. He had to spend whole days in Government offices, in conferences, in endless round-and-round discussions with suspicious men from the tax department.

He found out things during this hectic week that he never would've believed a few days before. He met three men—three separate individual men, besides himself—who had been working on completely different sets of books for Drexell Enterprises. And each one of these three men was under the impression, just as Dan himself had been, that he was Drexell's chief accountant in the Mid-West. What's more, Dan saw records of Drexell Enterprises that hadn't ever appeared on any stock quotation. And he inspected huge bank accounts under names that he'd never even heard of. And he read letters in Drexell's handwriting that were so contrary to the things Drexell had been telling him for years that he almost couldn't believe the evidence of his own eyes. He even read one letter in which Drexell referred to him personally —and used an expression about him which made Dan wince for days and days afterwards.

How he drove himself that week! He came down to the office at eight every morning. He had his lunches brought in to him. He didn't get home till seven or eight at night. And then, after dinner, the chances are he'd go right downtown again. No theatres, no parties, no card games at the club—nothing but figures, ledgers, red and black ink, writing, writing, and more writing, until his head was pounding and his fingers were too cramped to lift a pen. He knew that it was the only cure for what was troubling him, for the shock and the confusion, for the terrible feeling of disillusionment.

As a result of all this work, he didn't get a chance to see any of his friends. He was much too busy to visit his clubs. There was no time to listen to what people were saying.

A few little things did manage to force themselves on his attention. One afternoon he passed a fellow from the club on the street. He started to say "hello"—but this fellow just went hurrying by without looking at him. Lost in a daydream, Dan thought, and he dismissed it from his mind.

Another day, he ran into another friend, riding up the elevator in his building. This friend greeted him warmly. He shook hands with him, he smiled at him. They talked about the weather. And then, just before he got out of the elevator, this friend made a remark. Only a casual remark—nothing important at all. "Haven't seen you out at the club for a long time, Dan"—that's all there was to it. Only there was something about the way he said it. Something about the little gleam in his eye. Once again Dan gave a shrug, and forgot all about it.

A day or so later he got a phone call at the office. It was Eli Glatz. The reason he gave for the call was that he wanted to check up on the exact time of the big Labour Day party that Dan was giving, and whether it was going to be formal or not. Only somehow, Dan got the peculiar feeling that this wasn't Eli's reason for calling at all. He got the feeling that the real reason didn't come out till the very end, just before Eli hung up. And even then, it was just a remark—just a casual, innocent-sounding, unimportant remark.

"I hope you're bearing up under it, Dan. I hope you're not letting it upset you too much."

"Drexell's failure? Of course it's upsetting me. It's upsetting everybody, isn't it?"

"Yes, yes, of course," Eli answered a little too quickly. "It's upsetting everybody, that's perfectly right."

Dan thought it over a few minutes, when Eli was off

the wire. Then he gave it up with a shake of his head, and went right back to his work.

But what happened the following evening, a shake of his head couldn't get rid of it so easy. When he got home from the office, he found Sarah sitting up very straight on the living-room couch. Her eyes were red, her lips were trembling a little. He could see that she'd been crying. He asked her what it was, but she wouldn't answer him. She just pressed her lips together, and gave her head a quick shake. And when he kept on asking her, the most she did was to blurt out suddenly, "That Steinthal woman, Dan. She's a nasty malicious person. Just because she lost a few hands at bridge——" And for the rest of the evening, Sarah wouldn't say another word about it.

And then, two days later, Dan got a letter from his brother Herman. He read it at breakfast, and it made him so mad that he slammed his fist down on the table and spilled half his coffee. "What's the matter with that man?" he cried out. "He's out of his head. That brother of mine is out of his head." He waved the letter in front of him furiously. "Look at this. Just look at it. Look at what he says." But he still held on to the letter and kept on waving it. " 'By now you have found out how right I was in everything I told you.' Patting himself on the back. Some people just can't resist the opportunity to tell themselves what smart fellows they are. And the way he goes on—'*everything* I told you.' Look how he underlines 'everything'—just look." Sarah didn't get much of a chance to look, because Dan still didn't let go of the letter. "What does he mean by that, underlining 'everything'? And what he writes after that—'Doubtless you will be making a change of location just as soon as possible.' What's so doubtless about it? Why should I be making any changes of location? Where does he get such a crazy idea, can you answer me that?"

141

"I don't know, Dan," Sarah said, looking down at her eggs.

"I don't know either. He's crazy, it's the only explanation. And at the end of the letter, look what he writes. Look what he's got the nerve to write to me. 'If you decide to come to New York, I can assure you there will be an excellent place for you in my own firm. Do not think of this as a mere gesture of family loyalty. A first-rate accountant is always a valuable asset to any business.'" Dan couldn't stand it any longer. He flung the letter across the table at Sarah, shouting out as he did so, "Read it. Read it. Read it for yourself. 'An excellent place for you.' 'Don't think of this as family loyalty.' *He'll* find a place for me. *He* thinks I'll be a valuable asset. Wait till I answer that letter—wait till I tell him about the excellent place that I'm recommending for *him*——"

"Dan," Sarah said, frowning over the letter. "he only meant to be helpful, you know—he wasn't trying to insult you——"

"No, no. He wasn't trying. He didn't *have* to try. It comes to him natural." Dan jumped up to his feet. "I'm leaving. I'm going down to the office. I'm sending him my answer by the morning mail." He stood for a moment, his neck burning, his hands clenching and unclenching. And then, in a final burst of fury, he gave a terrific kick at the table, rattling the dishes and the glasses. "This breakfast was *lousy*!" he cried. And he turned and stamped out of the room.

By the time he got down to the office, his anger had cooled off a little, and he started to feel ashamed of himself. Herman sends him an annoying letter, he told himself, so he takes it out on Sarah. What a louse he was sometimes—what an A-Number-One louse. And he told Schultz to call up the florist and order a dozen roses.

XIII

By the end of the week, Dan succeeded in finishing up his work on Drexell's affairs. The Government was satisfied. Dan was cleared of any implication in the shady side of Drexell Enterprises. He was only an innocent bystander now. The mess was in the hands of the lawyers, and the Government representatives, and the army of doctors and nurses who sent up a barrage of daily bulletins between Drexell and the rest of the world.

Dan felt a tremendous surge of relief, now that it was all over. And something else was over too—the dead, oppressive feeling which had been weighing on him ever since he went out to Drexell's house that day. The shock and the disillusionment were gone now. Well, not completely gone. It was still a terrible thing to think about, how completely fooled he'd been. It was still a little irritating to his pride, to realize that he could've been so mistaken in a man.

And that he could have misled his friends the way he did, that was the worst part of all. They asked his advice, they put their trust in him—and he let them down. In all innocence, of course—hurting himself as much as he hurt them, of course—but still you couldn't get around it. He let them down, and now he had to make up for it. By going to them frankly and openly and telling them how sorry he was. By working harder than ever for his clients. By being a hundred times more careful in the future, when he got involved with any big deals. And if there was anybody who needed a little more help than that—if there was anybody who had been put into a really big hole because of the Drexell failure—well, Dan could see his responsibility there too, and he swore that he'd do all he could.

In connection with this, his very first thought was of young Mark Kugel and his grandfather. He remembered what the boy had told him a few weeks ago—how his grandfather had tied up so much of his money in Drexell Enterprises. Dan wondered just how much this was. Not too much, he hoped. After all, he was the one who had encouraged the boy—though at the same time, he *had* warned him that too much speculation——

In a state of some confusion, Dan arrived at his office door on Friday morning—but instead of going in, he went across the hall to the door of Kugel's Klothes for Kiddies. He was about to knock, when suddenly the door pushed open. Dan stepped aside in surprise. Because it's a regular procession coming out of that door. It's a man carrying a chair, and another man carrying a lamp, and two more men grunting and sweating with a great big desk. And then, to bring up the rear of the procession, there was young Mark Kugel himself.

"What's the story?" Dan called out to him. "Are you redecorating the place?"

The boy stopped in front of him, and Dan couldn't help noticing how nervous and embarrassed he was over something. "No, no, it's nothing like that, Mr. Waxman. The fact is, we're—well, we're moving out."

"Moving out? You mean, you've found better office space?"

"Well, not exactly. The fact is—well, we're selling the business."

"Selling the business?" Dan's eyebrows really went up on this. "You're selling Kugel's Klothes for Kiddies? After all these years it's been going—and your grandpa built it up from a shoestring?"

"It's not such a new idea, Mr. Waxman," Mark put in very quickly. "Actually, we've been thinking about it for a long time. For years and years now. It's a pretty small business and we've had some nice offers—and Grandpa thought it would be better for me, less worries and headaches, you know, if I got a good job with some bigger firm. We discussed it back and forth, and Grandpa insisted on it, so I'm starting in next month with Silver and Sons. I'm going to be in the accounting department, Mr. Waxman—so we're really in the same line now, you might say——" And he trailed off with a little grin.

Standing in the hallway, looking up into the boy's face, Dan soon understood the whole thing. A terrible rush of sympathy came over him. He had to wait a moment before he could speak. "Well—it sounds like a very nice job. I'm sure you'll do very well at it. About the money, though. You mentioned once, what your Grandpa was living on——"

"Oh, it's all right, the money." The boy's embarrassment was greater than ever now. He couldn't meet Dan's eyes at all. "As a matter of fact, we won't even be needing as much money as we used to need. Because we're making another change—just a coincidence, that it should happen at just this time—well, Grandpa's moving out of his hotel. He's been getting a little lonely there. Nobody to talk to but a lot of old men. He's going to live with me from now on. We're taking a little apartment downtown. Near my new office that is. It's kind of convenient that way, and Grandpa will only be a few blocks from his stamp club——"

"Yes, I see that," Dan said. And his own embarrassment was just as great as the boy's now. "Well, it sounds pretty nice all around."

"Oh yes," said Mark, with a smile. "We're both very pleased about it. Grandpa and me. We expect we'll be very happy."

"Yes. Yes, I'm sure you will. And you know"—for

just a moment Dan let his voice grow more serious—
"if there's anything I can do. If you need help or anything."

"No, sir: no, sir," Mark said, shaking his head.
"That's kind of you, but why should you? I mean, we
certainly don't feel—I mean, we're all right, sir, you don't
have to worry."

"Yes, I know what you mean."

They stood for a while in silence, fidgeting, neither of
them knowing how to break away. Finally Dan held out
his hand. "Well, good luck to you, Mark. I'll be seeing
you before you're gone for good, won't I? So I can say
goodbye to you in detail."

"Yes. I'll drop in on you, Mr. Waxman."

The boy moved on down the hall behind the procession of furniture men.

Dan went to his office, and he was thoughtful all morning. It was sad, what the boy had told him. It was sad,
that a man of old Abe Kugel's age had to make such a
sudden change in his life. And yet—upset as he was,
Dan couldn't help seeing one good side of the situation.
The boy didn't hold him to blame. The boy realized that
Dan was a victim too, that Dan would've done anything
in the world to prevent this sadness from happening.
How could he keep from drawing encouragement out of
this little scene? If young Mark Kugel, who had lost so
much, didn't feel bitter towards him—well, why should
he expect anything less from the rest of his friends?

Life was coming back to Dan. His natural desire for
activity was asserting itself again. He could hardly wait
to get out to his club, speak his little piece of sympathy
and apology to as many people as possible, drink down
a quick one to the future, and plunge right in to a good
game of golf.

XIV

He was down for breakfast early on Saturday morning. It was a bright sunny day, so he wore his light suit and his golf shoes. He polished off three stacks of pancakes, told Sarah what he was going to do, and laughed at her nervous expression. Then he set right off for Pleasant Fairways.

It was crowded, the way it always was on a Saturday in the summer. In the entrance lobby six or seven men, some of them all dressed for their golf, were chatting in little groups, or leaning over at the desk to find out about their handicaps, or waiting impatiently for their wives to get dressed. Dan gave a quick glance around before anybody noticed him in the doorway. They were all people that he knew, but nobody he was particularly friendly with. So he started across to the inside writing-room, nodding and smiling as he went. He was answered with nods and smiles in return—and then, just as he reached the door, he realized sort of uncomfortably that the people in the room hadn't looked away from him and gone back to what they were doing. Their heads were still up, he could feel that, and their eyes were pointed at his back. Automatically—not because he was trying to catch anybody in anything, or anything like that—he gave a quick look over his shoulder. Right away all the heads went down, all the voices started chatting again. Dan gave a vague smile, then a shrug, then went on to the writing-room.

It was empty, except for Otto the steward, a lean sharp-faced attentive little man in his forties. He was straightening out one of the potted plants, but he raised his eyes at Dan's entrance—and for just a split second Dan caught a look of surprise in those eyes. It was funny, because Otto certainly knew Dan pretty well after all these years—and besides which, nothing ever surprised Otto.

A second later the look was gone. Otto's face was impassive again, he was saying his usual polite "How are *you* this morning, Mr. Waxman?" So maybe it was all in Dan's imagination.

"Pretty good, Otto, pretty good," Dan said. "Any of my cronies around? I'm looking for a good game of golf."

"There are a number of gentlemen still in the locker-room, sir. And I think I saw Mr. Garfunkel come in."

"Mr. Garfunkel? That's good enough for me. Thank you, Otto. So how are things with you? Haven't seen you for quite a while."

"Very well, thank you, sir. We haven't seen *you* for a while either, sir." Nothing significant or unusual about the way he said this. And yet, as Dan turned out of the room, he had that same funny feeling that Otto, like the men in the lobby, was staring after him.

Only this time Dan didn't look around to check up.

He went straight to the back of the building and down the stairs to the locker-room. Half-way down he could hear the usual noises—the laughing, the shouting, the clanging of metal doors. He got to the bottom of the stairs, and started down the aisle to his locker. As he passed by each row, he nodded to the men he saw there, fumbling into their clothes, absorbed in a story about their golf game, or just sitting back on the wooden bench and relaxing with a smoke.

"Hello, Charlie," Dan said. "How are you, Sam? Harry boy, you're looking good."

They answered him back, of course—Charlie with a wave that was wider than any wave Dan had ever seen him give: Sam with a short nod: Harry with a quick stiff smile, almost as if he'd been caught out in some guilty act. And the queerest thing of all—from the moment after Dan opened his mouth, it almost seemed as if the locker-room noises, the arguing and the horseplay, had somehow grown more subdued, not so hearty, had gone down to a low uneasy buzz.

"What's the matter with me to-day?" Dan asked himself. "I'm imagining things."

He got to his own row now, and saw that four or five of the men with neighbouring lockers were dressing there. Nat Garfunkel wasn't among them, though. Nat must be out on the course already.

"Gentlemen," Dan said, stopping at the end of the bench and smiling around at all of them, "it's a pleasure to see you. How's everybody to-day?"

It was a simple enough question, you'd think. Then why the funny awkward little moment of silence before anybody answered it? And why the long blank stares on their faces, as if there was something queer and unbelievable about him talking to them like this?

Finally Fred Dickstein spoke up. "How are you, Dan? Long time no see." Fred Dickstein was a large, fat man with an elegant little black moustache, and he was one of the most fashionable and expensive dentists in Chicago—so fashionable and expensive, in fact, that he didn't even call himself a dentist, he called himself a "dental surgeon".

"I've been pretty busy, I'm afraid," Dan said, moving down to the middle of the bench and taking a seat in front of his own locker. "Lots of work to clear up." His voice grew a little more serious. "This terrible Drexell mess."

Again there was that funny little pause—very quick, it didn't last more than two seconds. And then, as if they were in a terrible hurry, two men in the group got to their feet, smiled around at everybody—a little too much

149

smiling, it flashed into Dan's mind—called out "Got to get going. can't waste the whole day gabbing with you lazy bums"—and were especially careful to tell Dan how nice it was to see him again, before they went scooting out of the locker-room.

Dan looked after them, uncertain. Then he made himself turn back to the others, keeping up his serious look, determined to push through what he intended to say. "I don't know how you fellows were affected by this business," he began. "You had a little money in Drexell, didn't you, Fred? Believe me, when I think of how many friends of mine had money in Drexell—and in a way, I suppose, I'm the one who's responsible for it. Partly responsible, anyway——"

"Yes, yes," Fred Dickstein put in quickly. "Well, the fact is, Dan, I didn't have much money in Drexell at all, I got out of it in time actually, somebody gave me a tip——" He reached into his locker—practically dived into it, Dan thought—and fished around busily for his golf clubs.

The man next to them on the bench—it was little Cornelius Rosen, who owned a successful string of Turkish baths—was having a lot of trouble tying his shoelaces. This made it necessary for him to keep his head down between his knees.

Dan felt a little itch of discomfort. All right, all right, he told himself, he didn't want to embarrass them. As long as they preferred to forget about the whole thing, why not change the subject? "So how's the golf?" he said, forcing a smile. "What sort of a game are you playing these days, Fred?"

"Pretty good, Dan, pretty good," Fred said, smiling back. "Matter of fact, I had a little bad luck yesterday afternoon. Lou Bender and I went around for nine holes together, but I was off in my putting, I had a hard morning in the office." Fred was the only dentist Dan had ever heard of who could afford to take off in the afternoon and play golf.

"Well, that's how it goes, Fred," Dan said. "Maybe you'll be in better form to-day. You had the whole night to rest up in. You know, I'm feeling pretty hot myself."

My God, if there wasn't another one of those peculiar little pauses—and absolutely no reason for it, no reason that Dan could see.

And then Cornelius Rosen had his head up again, and he was mumbling at Fred, without looking at him or Dan. "Better be hurrying, Fred. You know Art is out there waiting.

"Yes, yes, sure," Fred nodded at him quickly, a little impatiently.

"Well, well," Cornelius got to his feet, "nice to see you, Dan—see you around." And he turned and hurried down the row and out of sight.

Fred started to his feet too.

"Wait up a minute," Dan said. "Maybe I can show you how to play the game of golf for a while."

Fred fidgeted a little. "Well, the fact is, Dan—Corny and I were meeting Art Cohen outside for a three-some."

"Well, that's fine," Dan said. "Why not make it a foursome? More competition that way."

Fred fidgeted even harder. A look of pain came over his face. Even his little black moustache seemed to be in pain. "Well, the fact is, Dan—don't know how to say it exactly——"

"What's the fact, Fred?" said Dan, still smiling and keeping his voice conversational.

"Well, it's Art Cohen, Dan—you know, he had quite a bit in Drexell—Light and Electricity, I think—and the last week or so, he's been talking a lot around the club about what he'd do if—well——"

Dan could feel that flush of red coming over his cheeks. He lowered his head, instinctively trying to hide it. "Yes, yes—well, maybe some other time, Fred——"

"Sure enough, Dan. We'll talk about it, we'll talk about it." Fred gave an agonized shake of his head and escaped as fast as he could.

Dan sat still for a moment, conscious of the looks and the whispers of a couple of men at the other end of the bench. At least, he *thought* they were looking at him, though their eyes were carefully turned away—and he *thought* it was him they were whispering about. He got to his feet abruptly. "Little hot for golf to-day," he brought out to nobody in particular. "What I need is a long cold drink."

He shut the door of his locker, and started down the aisle to the door. He moved his little legs fast. He kept his head down and didn't look at anybody.

The lobby was empty now. He was relieved at this. He actually caught himself feeling relieved at it.

He turned to the left and hurried into the cocktail lounge—a low-ceilinged dimly-lighted room, with hard-wood walls and anchors and stuffed fish and things, to give it a shipboard effect. It was practically empty too—only the bartender polishing glasses, and one man sitting at the bar. Dan gave a sigh, because he hated to drink alone—and then, the next moment, his face brightened up. He lifted his head and started across the room quite confidently, all his old cheerfulness right back with him. Because he saw now that the man at the bar was Nat Garfunkel.

Nat was sitting with his back to the door. And he was hunched over in a way that was absolutely typical—every part of Nat, even the slope of his back, expressed his natural pessimism and incurable gloominess. Silently Dan slipped into the chair next to Nat, waited a moment, then nudged him in the side.

"Drink up, drink up. You've got a date to get beaten at golf."

Nat turned his head slowly.

Dan's smile faded away. The sight of Nat's face was a shock. It was never the most cheerful, lively-looking face in the world, but *this* wasn't even its usual state of dilapidation. The cheeks were so hollow. The mouth was so white. The rings under his eyes were so much darker than they had ever been before, and there were so many more wrinkles in his forehead. It was just as if he'd grown ten years older since the last time Dan had seen him.

"Nat, what's the matter?" Dan began. "You've been sick or something——?" Then he stopped himself. It came to him now, what it was. It was worry, a terrible deep worry staring out of those bleary eyes. Dan could have kicked himself for not realizing it immediately. Hadn't he always suspected that Nat had been plunging much too heavily in Drexell shares? And a man like that, who's got a temperamental attraction for worry, who's half-way along the road to despair even under normal conditions—a man like that, it would naturally hit him harder than most people.

The words came out of Dan in a rush. "Nat, I should've known. What's the matter with me, anyway? All wrapped up in my own affairs. It hit you pretty hard, I guess. Coming so sudden, and everything—I'm sorry, I'm honestly sorry."

He paused a moment, looking anxiously at Nat for an answer. But Nat just looked back at him, and his face didn't show him a thing.

"And the thing is," Dan hurried on, "I can't get over

the idea that it's partly my fault. Because you came to me, you know. You asked my advice. And even though I meant it in good faith—— No, no, don't contradict me, you can't talk me out of it."

He paused again, then went on with a smile. "Just the same, Nat, it's not as bad as you're acting. I mean, why let it deprive you of your powers of speech?" He laughed a little. "It's only money, after all. Nothing to get an ulcer over. You'll get through it all right. We'll all be around to help you—me and Mort and all your friends." He hesitated a moment, then reached out and put his hand on Nat's arm.

There was a pause, and then, in one quick twist, Nat pulled away from Dan's hand. His face got tighter, his mouth worked a little, then his words came out very sharp and clear. "You son of a bitch," he said, "get your hands off me."

Dan drew back, as if he'd been slapped. "Nat——" he said.

"You made your killing," Nat said, a little louder. "Isn't it enough for you? Do you have to gloat over us too?"

Dan's head was spinning. He shook it back and forth, trying to clear his brain, trying to make sense out of what was happening to him. "But Nat," he said. "But listen to me, Nat. I lost out, too. Twenty-five per cent I had—I always said it to you, didn't I? Keep your speculations down to twenty-five per cent——"

"You couldn't tell me, could you?" Nat said. "You couldn't warn a friend ahead of time."

"Nat, I didn't know. I was just as much surprised as anybody——"

Steadying himself against the edge of the bar, Nat struggled shakily to his feet. He stopped in front of Dan, swaying a little, looking straight into Dan's face and it made Dan shudder, that look. Nobody had ever looked at him like that before. "You crook," Nat said. "You dirty son-of-a-bitching crook." He swayed a little more, then lifted his chin and moved with shaky dignity out of the cocktail lounge.

Dan was stunned for a few seconds longer. Then he could feel the bartender looking at him. Not staring or gaping or anything. Just looking up at him curiously. Bartenders never show any emotion over anything. So Dan didn't even order a drink. He mumbled something and walked quickly out of the room.

He kept going till he was out in front of the club building. There was an attendant there who called your car for you. But Dan didn't feel like talking to the attendant, he didn't want to answer the inevitable question. "Leaving so soon, Mr. Waxman?" So he avoided the attendant's eye. He sauntered along to the parking space in an attempt to look casual. The chauffeur was reading a newspaper in the front seat. He put it away quickly as Dan approached, and scrambled out to hold the door.

"Leaving so soon, Mr. Waxman?" he said.

"Never mind about that," Dan said, and he pushed past him into the car. "Take me home," he said. "Hurry up about it."

All through the ride he was hunched up in the seat, not even looking out of the window. Over and over again, in his mind, he went through the scene at the bar, and over and over again the pain shot through him. Once during the ride he looked down and saw his shoes, those big heavy shoes that he always wore for playing golf. He felt like a fool. Just like a silly damned fool.

Sarah was out. He was glad of it. He didn't want to talk to anybody for a while. He spent the afternoon in an easy chair. He listened to the radio without taking in a word. He held the newspaper on his lap without reading it. When Sarah got home around five o'clock, he didn't tell her what had happened. She asked him how his golf game went, and he grunted and turned a page in the newspaper. She mistook this for his usual reaction when his game was off, and he was happy to let her go on thinking so.

From that morning on, it was impossible for Dan to pretend that nothing was wrong. It just wouldn't go away, his pain at the things Nat had said to him. It cut into his work. It kept him from sleeping at night. He could never tell when it was all going to flash into his mind again, just as clear and vivid as if it had happened a few minutes before.

If only he could decide what he ought to think and feel about it. But his thoughts were all mixed up, his feelings wouldn't stay put. One minute he was angry at Nat. Of all the unreasonable people! My God, as if Dan personally had lost his money for him. And less than three months ago, he was one of the men who stood up and applauded Dan when he came into the club. But the next minute Dan was shaking his head and feeling miserable. Nat was right, he was telling himself. A crook was what he was, and no getting around it. Maybe not intentionally—but what difference does that make to a man with twin sons to support?

And of course, underneath all of this, was the biggest question of all, the question that now began to gnaw away at Dan every minute of the day. What about the rest of his friends? Were they going to feel the same way as Nat? A few malicious strangers—people who didn't know him very well, and enjoyed having a grudge to hold—well, he supposed he'd have to expect it from them. And an unstable individual like Nat—it was terrible, Dan would've given anything if it hadn't happened, but you have to face it, some people just don't have their emotions under control. But what about the others? What about the people who had known him all his life, the people whose homes he went to, the people he invited up for dinner—what about the Freeds and the Jacobsons, the Davises and the Nussbaums, and all the good friends that Sarah and he were so proud of? Surely those people wouldn't be so unfair. Surely they'd trust him and stand by him after all these years.

He discovered that he had a terrible fear of finding out the answer to this question. It was a sad thing to discover for a man who hadn't ever been afraid of anything before in his whole life. There it was, though, and he couldn't fight against it. In the next ten days, before Labour Day, he stayed away from both his clubs, he avoided the restaurants where he knew his friends liked to eat, he begged out of social engagements by telling Sarah that he was very busy. Not that he *really* had any doubts. But it was still too close to him, his scene with Nat. He couldn't stand it, for such a thing to happen again.

What Dan looked forward to most eagerly, almost a little desperately, was Mort Meltzer's return from Bermuda. Mort and Milly would get back to Chicago early Labour Day, just in time for the big party that Dan was giving. Dan would have lunch with Mort the day he got back, he would put the question to him squarely. "Do people blame me for it, Mort? Do they hold this Drexell business against me?" Mort was his closest friend in the world. He could count on Mort to tell him the truth.

Meanwhile he stuck close to his office during the day. He hardly budged from his easy chair at night. When he had to go out on the street, he kept his head down and walked along very fast.

In spite of all this, one or two little reminders somehow managed to get through to him.

One day, for instance, when he got back to the office from lunch, Schultz had a telephone message for him. It was a message from old Jake Perelman, the Perelman Panties Company, one of his clients for years. "It's kind of annoying, Mr. Waxman," she said. "He says you should clear up his account, he's taking his business somewhere else."

"Perelman? Perelman's taking his business somewhere else? I've been keeping his books since the days he couldn't add two and two."

"Well, that's what he says, Mr. Waxman."

"It's unbelievable. Does he give a reason?"

"No reason. He just says that he—he needs a change, that's all."

"That's the reason? He says that he needs a change?"

"That's all he said, Mr. Waxman." Schultz's voice was a little strained. Dan looked up at her sharply and saw that her eyes were turned away. The question rose to his lips—and then, all of a sudden, he couldn't ask it. All of a sudden he was afraid to hear the answer.

"All right, all right," he said, dismissing Schultz with his busy gesture, "I'll go into it later. He wasn't such a big client anyway. I only stuck with him because of old times."

The rest of the morning Dan couldn't get a bit of work done. He sat at his desk, with his chin in his hand. Or he stood by the window, staring out at the Lake and the city. Once, he picked up the phone, he dialled the number of Nat Garfunkel's office. But when he heard Nat's gruff "Hello" at the other end, he hung up without saying a word.

More than ever, he could hardly wait for Labour Day, and for Mort's return from Bermuda. He could hardly wait to see him, to pour out the story to him, to listen gratefully while Mort made a joke out of the whole thing.

XV

DAN began to think now about his big Labour Day party. It wasn't just a personal, private type of celebration, this party—like Thanksgiving or New Year's or birthdays. It was more in the nature of a fancy, official occasion, in honour of the new opera season, which was scheduled to begin at the end of September. For such a long time his friends had been kidding him about his personal connections with "those big opera stars" and asking him, in a joking way, "Why are you such a hog, Dan? Why do you always keep them to yourself?" And sometimes the tone of this question wasn't quite so joking. So Dan decided to do something about this situation. He decided to give a great big party, before the opening of the season, for the purpose of bringing together the two groups of people who meant most to him—his friends from his ordinary daily social life, and his friends from what he liked to think of as "the world of the opera". Just a gay, exciting evening, at which all these various people could get acquainted with one another. No attempts would be made to raise money for the opera.

For months now he'd been planning this affair. Invitations were sent out a long time ago, and practically everybody had written back that they could come. The opera people had been contacted directly over the phone by Dan himself. He even made a long-distance call to

San Francisco, just to make sure that Maestro Mantini would be available. The restaurant and ballroom of the Downtown Club had been rented for the whole evening. The chef would provide a big dinner, and a four-piece orchestra was hired to play dance-music.

But now, Dan began to worry about this party. He began to wonder if it was wise to go on with it. The reason for his worry, he told himself, was money. Wasn't it an extravagance now, what with the Drexell business? He and Sarah couldn't really afford too many parties like this for a while.

This wasn't the real reason, and he knew it perfectly well himself. It was that terrible morning at the club. It was Nat Garfunkel, and Perelman, and all the others. Only a small minority he kept insisting to himself. Three or four unreasonable people who would hold a grudge for a while and stay away from his party. Not enough, for God's sake, to spoil the fun. Or embarrass him, or anything like that. Or was it more than three or four people?

The argument would go back and forth in his head, until he had a headache. But he just couldn't make a decision, and so he didn't call the party off. And he began to think more and more about Mort.

The night before Labour Day he had a real fit of the fidgets. He couldn't sit still in his chair. He paced up and down the living-room—tripping over Bobby, who had come back from summer camp now, and taken up her usual position face down on the floor, with the comic section. He shouted at her to "Sit up in a chair like a human being." And three separate times, he had Sarah call up the Meltzer home and find out from the maid what train Mort and Milly would be coming in on to-morrow.

He was up at seven the next morning. Why up at

seven? Mort and Milly wouldn't be in till eleven o'clock. Still, he was up at seven, and he gobbled down his breakfast as if he was late for an appointment—and since the office was closed on Labour Day, he had nothing to do for the rest of the morning but fidget around the apartment, making a nuisance of himself. And then, at twelve o'clock sharp, he couldn't stand it any more. "I'm going out," he said to Sarah. "I'm going up to see Mort—he ought to be in by now."

"They'll be pretty busy, dear," Sarah said. "Unpacking and everything."

"Will they be too busy to pay attention to an old friend who wants to welcome them home?"

"But you could call up if you wanted to, Dan. Since we'll be seeing them at the party to-night."

"Who wants to see them at a party? That's the whole point, to see them by themselves."

Sarah rose from her chair. "Well, maybe I'll come along with you. Milly promised to bring me back some shawls from Bermuda——"

"Never mind, never mind," Dan said quickly. "Why should you come along? You'll be seeing them at the party to-night." And he hurried out of the apartment before Sarah could make a decision. His business with Mort had to be alone—he didn't want it held up by a lot of female chit-chat and gushing. When it was finally over, when it was off his mind once and for all, then the chit-chat and gushing would sound a lot better.

Mort and Milly lived with their three kids in a suite of rooms at the Belmont Biarritz, one of the big residential hotels on upper Michigan Avenue. You had to wait in the lobby, with the artificial palm trees, while the desk clerk called up and announced you. Dan was waiting there almost five minutes, and still no sign from the clerk that he should go up. "What's the matter?" he said, marching up to the desk. "They're home already, aren't they?"

"Oh, I'm sorry, sir," said the clerk, looking not the least bit sorry, with a bored expression on his face. "Mr. Meltzer says that he'll be down shortly."

"Down? Who's asking him to come down? I want to go *up*."

"I'm sorry, sir. That's what he said." And the clerk turned away with a scornful look, which plainly said, "If you can't understand simple English, that's certainly not *my* responsibility."

Dan began pacing up and down the lobby. It was annoying. There was no doubt about it, it was definitely annoying. That stupid clerk gets his message mixed up somehow, and now poor Mort has to make a whole extra trip in the elevator.

A few minutes later, he heard the elevator door opening. He swung around to look, and sure enough, right behind a lady with a little dog, there was Mort.

It was just wonderful to see him. The sight of his homely face and his loud summer suit started Dan trembling with affection. And the fears and worries which had tortured him the last few weeks, they just didn't seem to exist any more—one glimpse of that shock of untidy red hair, and you just couldn't imagine *anything* being wrong in the world.

Dan rushed forward to meet him, holding out his hand, nodding his head, calling out his name from halfway across the lobby. "Mort! Mort! How are you, for God's sake? A sight for sore eyes, like they say." He grabbed Mort's hand and pumped it up and down enthusiastically. "I missed you. Do you know that? It's something I hate to admit—but I actually missed you." He let go of Mort's hand, and stepped back a ways, so he could look him up and down. "Look at him will you.

He looks so healthy. And the tan on his face. A regular Tarzan he's turning into. So how was it down there? Did you have the most wonderful time of your life?"

But Mort didn't get a chance to answer, because the next moment Dan moved forward again, and he had his hand on Mort's arm. "Come on, come on, what're we doing down here anyway? Is this any place to carry on a conversation? That crazy desk clerk, he made a mistake, probably didn't even tell you my name right. Come on, while the elevator's still here, let's go on upstairs."

He gave Mort's arm a little tug—but Mort didn't move. "I came down on purpose, Dan," he said. "We'll have to talk down here."

Dan blinked at him. "Down here? But I don't follow you——" He stopped short, noticing for the first time what a funny look there was on Mort's face. So stiff and serious, not a twinkle in either eye, not the trace of a smile on his lips—well, it just wasn't like Mort's face at all. "What's the matter, Mort?" Dan said, trying to keep away the thought that was forcing itself into his mind.

"We'll have to talk here. Milly doesn't want you up in the apartment."

"Milly doesn't——?" With difficulty Dan controlled the shudder that passed over him. "Is it Drexell? Is it that terrible business? Has it affected Milly too?"

Mort didn't say anything. His mouth twitched a little, as if he wanted to—but in the end he kept his face stiff and serious.

"Listen, Mort," Dan said, "this attitude of Milly's—it's just what I came over to talk to you about. The last few weeks, it's been terrible. You've got no idea how it's been. Everybody I meet—the way they look at me. Most of them don't say anything, but most of them don't have to. I can see it in their looks. As if they thought I was—some sort of a swindler or something——" Dan broke off, realizing that his voice was getting louder, and bringing curious glances from the desk clerk.

"Listen, Mort," Dan said, lowering his voice, "suppose we go upstairs." He saw the expression on Mort's face, and he shook his head. "All right, all right, I don't want to upset Milly. But I haven't even told you the half of it. The other day at the country club, I ran into Nat Garfunkel. The things he said to me—he called me a crook. Me, a crook. I guess he lost pretty heavily in Drexell shares, I can understand what he's going through. But he didn't have to call me a crook. I lost a lot of money myself. It's lucky that I've got my Government bonds. And I always advised Nat to do the same thing. Don't put all your eggs in one basket, that's what I always said to him. You heard me yourself, Mort. You heard me say it to him many times——"

Dan broke off uncertainly. He searched Mort's face for some sign that he was going to speak. He didn't see one, though.

"Listen, Mort," Dan hurried on, "if we could only go upstairs. People are staring at us."

"Why go upstairs?" Mort answered quietly. "You don't have any more to say."

"I don't have any more——?" In an instant it rushed over Dan, the terrible fear that he had been trying to keep away. "Mort, you're not telling me——? My God," he almost laughed as he said it, "*you* don't believe those stories about me, do you?"

Mort wasn't laughing as he gave his answer. He wasn't even smiling a little. "I believe what I see," he said. "I believe in the facts."

"The facts?" Dan made a wild, awkward gesture with his arm—the sort of gesture a man might make when he's standing in the darkness and trying to ward off a blow, and he doesn't have any idea what direction it's going to come from. It was a desperate useless gesture, and so were the words that stammered out of him. "Mort—you're not saying this to me—of all the people in the world—after all the good times we've had——"

Mort kept up his stiff serious expression a second longer, and then he suddenly gave a sigh, a low tired sigh, the saddest sound that Dan had ever heard out of his friend. "All the good times we've had," he said. "I thought about them myself, Dan. When the news came to me in Bermuda, I did a lot of thinking about those times. I told myself that it couldn't be true. I know Dan Waxman, I told myself. He wouldn't pull a trick like that, I told myself. He wouldn't do such a low-down thing to his friends."

"I wouldn't, Mort, I didn't."

"Yes, you didn't." And for the first time there was just the touch of a smile on Mort's lips. It wasn't one of his cheerful, exuberant smiles. It was tight, and sort of bitter, and it didn't seem to belong on Mort's face at all. "Finally I couldn't think about it any more," he said. "It's that kind of a world, I told myself. You never know what a man's really like."

"You know what *I'm* like, Mort. I'm the same as I ever was. I've always been the same to you. My God, my God, I wouldn't do *anything* to hurt you. I wouldn't do *anything* to hurt you." He reached out and grabbed Mort's arm in his excitement.

Mort looked down at his arm. He looked down at it silently. And once again his face had become stiff and serious. Dan blushed and pulled his hand away. As soon as he did, Mort looked up again. "I'd better be going, Dan. Milly must be wondering what's kept me." And he turned away and started towards the elevator.

Dan hurried after him, grabbed hold of him, whirled him around. "Listen to me, Mort, listen to me now."

He took a breath, and brought out his words as firmly and clearly as he possibly could. "I *didn't* know what Drexell was up to. I thought that Drexell Enterprises was sound, and that's why I advised everybody to invest in it. I lost as much money in the failure as you did or almost anybody else. I swear that's the truth, Mort. I swear it on my word of honour."

Mort looked him up and down. His lips parted slightly, and for a second Dan felt a little spark of hope. But a second later, Mort closed his lips. He shook his head slowly. "I think you believe it," he said. "I think you've really talked yourself into it." He turned away again and pushed the button for the elevator.

Dan stood and looked at his back. There were tears in his eyes. *Tears* in his eyes—a grown-up man. His hands hung at his sides, and he clenched them and unclenched them, with a wild feeling that he had to *do* something, only what could he do? There was nothing he could do.

Then, from somewhere behind him, he heard a buzz— the soft, insinuating buzz of people whispering. He turned his head. Sure enough, there were a couple of old ladies behind him. They were watching him. They were whispering about him. And across the lobby, a bellboy was lounging near one of the palm trees—also watching him, smirking at him, getting a big kick out of the whole business.

In a moment, Dan felt the anger rising to his neck. What right did they have to watch him? Who told them that they could smirk at him? If he had actually *done* something—but he hadn't done a thing. He hadn't done a goddamned thing. It wasn't fair they should treat him like this. Like a leper or something—like a convicted murderer—like he wasn't even a member of the human race any more.

"All right, all right then," he shouted at Mort's back. "I don't *care* what you think. You understand me? I don't give a damn. What does it matter anyway, your opinion of me? I'm only glad to find out about it. I'm glad that you showed me what kind of a friend you are. A friend without any friendship—a friend without any feelings—who *wants* such a person for a friend?"

Mort turned around on this. And his face wasn't angry at all. Just sort of tired and regretful. "I'm not going to lose my temper at you, Dan. A week ago maybe—but now I've cooled down, and I only feel sorry for you."

"Sorry for me? Sorry for me?" Dan burst out with his harshest, most sarcastic laugh. "Save your sorrow please. Use it on somebody who needs it."

"*You're* the somebody who needs it. Don't you know what it's going to be like for you in Chicago now? Do you think you'll have a single friend left? Do you think there's anybody who wants to go on knowing you?"

"Friends: believe me, I've got plenty of friends. Thank God everybody isn't as unfair and ungrateful as you are. Thank God there are still some sensible open-minded people who remember what I've done for them in the past, and wouldn't hold one little mistake against a man. Believe me, don't worry about my friends. To-night I'm giving a party, and it's going to be full of my friends."

A worried look came over Mort's face. And there was almost a pleading note in his voice. "Call off your party, Dan. Nobody's going to show up at it. Nobody except your hungry opera singers. Everybody else is going to stay away."

"Stay away? Stay away?" Dan was so furious now that he could hardly speak. All he could do was gulp and gasp and turn redder and redder. "Stay away, he says! Stay away!"

"Please, Dan. Don't hurt yourself any more than you have to——" Then, with a shake of his head, Mort broke off. He turned and walked into the elevator, which had come down by now.

Dan gulped and gasped a moment longer, and then, just as the elevator door was sliding shut in front of Mort, he managed to find his voice again. "Jealous!" he shouted out. "Absolutely green with envy!"

But the elevator door was shut tight by then.

So Dan turned around and stamped across the lobby, still working his arms, still muttering to himself, "Stay-away—my friends are going to stay away—jealousy, pure jealousy——"

And as he passed the desk, he suddenly looked up at the smirking bellboy, and cried out, "Go to hell!"

And at least he had the satisfaction of seeing that smirk disappear from the bellboy's face.

XVI

STAY away from his party—not a friend left in Chicago— it kept running in his head for the rest of the day. He shouted out the whole story to Sarah, who turned dead white when she heard it—but still it kept stirring him up. He was muttering about it all the time he dressed for the party that evening. He took out his anger on his tie and his cuff-links and his gold shirt-studs, and still it was on his mind. It even spoiled his goodnight kiss to Bobby. And he talked about it all the way downtown in the car.

It was wrong what Mort told him, that nobody would

show up for the party. A number of people were there already, when Dan and Sarah arrived. Eli Glatz was there, and Eli's wife, and four or five of Eli's particular friends. They were there with sneaky little smiles and sympathetic looks. They were quick to tell him that Charlie Davis had called and said he couldn't make it, that Helen Freed had announced her intention of ignoring the whole thing, that Manny Mannheim and his wife didn't care one way or another themselves, but they were such close friends of the Garfunkels——

"And I talked to Fred Dickstein this afternoon," Eli said. "He had me in the dentist's chair, and when he told me that disgraceful story, about how you showed up at Pleasant Fairways to boast about your cleverness, I told him he ought to be ashamed of himself, to say such things about you——"

"Fred Dickstein," Dan said. "That fat little phoney. Who wants the company of Fred Dickstein anyway? And that gabby wife of his. There's plenty of other fish in the sea."

In the next hour two more couples drifted in. Dan greeted them genially—more genially than he usually greeted people. "Are we early?" they said. "No, no," he assured them, "lots of people coming yet, it's this Labour Day traffic, it's holding up everybody who lives in the suburbs."

At eight-thirty the crowd from the opera arrived. There was Signor Mantini, bobbing his head, and Signora Da Croce with her tremendous laugh, and scrawny little Signora Fillippo, Signora Da Croce's big rival soprano, trying to outlaugh her and failing. There was Herr Vogelschotz, silent and blank-faced as usual, and with him a whole troop of Swedes, equally silent and blank-faced, and of course they all headed straight for the drinks together. There were a number of others, Italians, and

Germans and Frenchmen, hallooing at each other, laughing, gulping liquor.

"It is a small gathering," said Signor Mantini. "I thought it was not to be such a small gathering. I do not even see that funny Mr. Meltzer with his jokes——"

"It's not so small," Dan said. "Some people are just a little late."

He turned away from Signor Mantini and circulated among the other guests. He felt Sarah tapping him on the shoulder. "Maybe we ought to start dinner, Dan."

"Start dinner? Nobody's here yet. That's a crazy idea, start dinner."

Sarah retreated in silence.

By nine o'clock it was clear that nobody else was coming. Eli Glatz felt that he had to point this out. "I hate to say it, Dan, but I really don't think that anybody else——"

"You hate to say it." Dan gave a laugh. "I'll bet you hate to say it."

Eli sighed and moved off. A few minutes later, Dan saw him moving among the opera people, talking away at a great rate.

And a few minutes after that Signor Mantini came up to him, bobbing his head. "You know, it is a delightful party," he said. "But there is to be a dinner, no?"

Signora Da Croce was right behind him. "So hungry," she bellowed. "I will eat a horse."

Dan looked around him, at the straggly little crowd, practically lost in the big reception-room. "All right, all right," he said. "We'll eat now, Sarah, where are you? Tell the dining-room we're ready now."

The crowd trickled into the dining-room. A dozen or so tables had been set up all around the room, and they were gleaming and glittering invitingly. "There are place cards," Dan called out. "Everybody find his place card."

Everybody went to their places. There were so many empty seats that not a single table had more than three people at it. And some tables didn't have any people. And one table had just one single person at it, Herr Vogelschotz. But Herr Vogelschotz didn't let it upset him. He just stood up and waved at the rest of the Swedes, and one of them shouted, "Look at Sigurd! Plenty room by Sigurd!" And they all deserted their own places, and clattered over to Herr Vogelschotz's table. "What do they think they're doing?" Dan said. "Fine manners."

"Why not forget about the place cards?" said Eli Glatz, leaning across from the table next to Dan's. "Is there any reason why the party shouldn't be nice and cosy?"

Dan was about to answer him, but Sarah leaned in front of him. "Here's the waiter, Dan. He's brought the shrimp cocktail."

The shrimp cocktail was placed in front of Dan, at the same time as waiters all over the room were placing it in front of everybody else. An especially large number of waiters had been hired to handle the crowd.

"And this place here, sir?" said Dan's waiter. "Is the gentleman expected?"

He was pointing to the seat next to Dan, to the place card that said "Mort Meltzer" on it.

"No, he's not coming. Throw it away, get rid of it." Dan attacked his shrimp cocktail.

The other people from the opera had now noticed what the Swedes had done. They thought it was a good idea, and they all began to regroup at two or three tables. The Italians went to Signor Mantini. The Frenchmen went to Monsieur Lucien Volet, the ballet master. Only the Germans stayed put. They were already too busy eating. And so, all through the opening course, the room was filled with shuffling chairs and people crossing the floor with shrimp cocktails in their hands.

Dan mumbled about it, but kept his head down.

"It's a delicious meal," said Sarah, later on. "They certainly know how to make a steak at the club."

"It's a rotten steak," Dan said. "It's too tough. And there's not enough gravy. And these onions are——"

He never got out his opinion of the onions. He was interrupted by a disturbance from the Swedish table. "Waiter, waiter," they were shouting, "where is the champagne?" The champagne had been flowing in a steady stream at the Swedish table, and the Swedes had lost a lot of their shyness.

"Human tanks," Dan muttered.

When the meal was over—even before everybody had time to finish the coffee—Dan got to his feet and tried to speak out over the noise. "Will you clear the dining-room, please, so they can get ready for the dancing? Will everybody clear the dining-room, please?" But nobody heard him. The Italians and the French were making too much noise. They were laughing gaily and listening to nobody but themselves. It was a wonderful evening for all these opera people. They got invited to a great many parties in Chicago, but mostly it wasn't much fun. Mostly they were forced to hold themselves in, and act polite, and display themselves to the rich men and their wives. It wasn't often that they got to a party like this, where they were in the majority, where they could enjoy the good food and the liquor together, where they could laugh at their own private jokes, where the host and his friends hardly even existed.

"Quiet, everybody. Quiet," Dan cried. "We have to clear the dining-room."

Gradually he began to make an impression. Gradually the guests got to their feet, many of them holding on to their wineglasses, and moved out to the other room. Here too they stayed in their little groups, they paid no attention to anybody else.

"It's a *lovely* party, Dan," said Mrs. Eli Glatz. "It's one of the most *interesting* parties of the year." She scurried away before Dan could answer.

"Now *there* was a marriage of soul-mates," Dan said. His neck was getting hotter and hotter. He looked around at the scene in front of him, at the tiny little group of Eli Glatz's friends huddled together in one corner, at the large group from the opera screaming and laughing and gesturing in another corner. It was all such a mess—it was all such a crazy mess.

"Mr. Waxman," said a little man with a moustache, "I'm the orchestra. The orchestra is ready."

"The orchestra is ready," Dan said to Sarah. "For God's sake, let's get them in for the dancing."

Dan could see that the sweat was coming down Sarah's face too. "Maybe it's not so wise, Dan. Maybe they don't care to dance, maybe they prefer to talk——"

"What do you mean, they don't care to dance? I hired the orchestra, it's costing me good money. What do you mean, they don't care?" He pushed forward towards the opera people. Behind him he heard Sarah's voice, "Dan, please don't——" He shut it out of his mind.

"Dancing in the other room," he called out from the edge of the group of opera people. Backs continued to be turned to him, laughing and shouting went on in spite of him. "Dancing in the other room," Dan repeated, in a louder voice. Nobody even noticed.

The line of backs, the laughing, the hand-waving—suddenly it seemed to Dan that this was all directed at him, all meant for him personally, all a way of insulting him, and rubbing it in, and deliberately getting another kick at him now that he was down.

"Dancing in the other room!" he roared out in his loudest voice.

The opera people stopped talking, and turned to look at him. They looked with amazement at this peculiar little man, standing in front of them, with his arms in the air, and his loud voice, and his red little face.

An instant later Dan didn't know what he was doing. The full force of his temper came bursting out of him, the full force of these last few weeks, of the snide remarks and the sideway glances, and the insults he'd swallowed, and the look of hatred in Nat Garfunkel's eyes, and young Mark Kugel's embarrassment, and the bellboy's smirk, and Mort Meltzer not even letting him up to the apartment. "Get out!" he was yelling. "Get out of here, all of you! Get out of here! Get out! Get out of here!"

He was conscious of the way they gaped at him. Their voices rang in his ears, a jumble of foreign voices. From the corner of his eye he saw the interested satisfied smiles on the faces of Eli Glatz's friends—one big smile gloating out at him from a dozen faces. And he was conscious of Eli himself by his side. "Now, Dan," Eli was saying, "this is unreasonable. A man may have troubles, but he should face them with a little dignity——"

"Dignity!" And Dan could feel his arm swinging around, swinging around with terrific force, and he would have hit Eli square across the face, only Eli dodged back in time, Eli was an agile little fellow.

And then the anger was too much for him. The first terrific force was all burned up, and a wave of sickness came over him. His head was pounding, and his stomach was queasy, it was just like he felt after playing too much golf in the sun.

Sarah was by his side, taking hold of his arm. "Are you sick, Dan? Can I get you some water?"

174

He shoved her away from him and stumbled out of the room.

The car wasn't waiting for him. He had told the chauffeur that he wouldn't be needed till midnight. So he hailed a cab, he yelled at it until it drove up in front of him. He pulled open the door and climbed in—and didn't notice till then that Sarah was right behind him, that she was getting into the cab too.

He shouted his address at the cab-driver, as if it was an insult. Then he went right on talking, not to Sarah, not to the driver, but just talking because he had to talk. "You know what it's all about, don't you? They think they're going to drive me out of town. Twenty-seven years I've been here. Twenty-seven years—a quarter of a century—and I worked hard all that time. I built myself up from a nobody. I made myself a respected member of the community. And I didn't do so bad for *them* either. I made a lot of money for *them* too. Now they want to get rid of me—they think they can ostracize me—they think they can make it so hard for me that I'll pack up and leave."

He paused, gasping for breath, continuing the speech only with his hands. Then his voice came again, "Well, they're not going to do it. I'll tell you that right now. I'll tell the whole bunch of them. Mort Meltzer, and Nat Garfunkel, and that snaky Eli Glatz. I'll stick it out in spite of all of them. Chicago is where I belong, and Chicago is where I'll stay. And what's more, I'll have them saying so themselves—I'll have them coming to me yet—I'll have them apologizing on bended knee."

And he kept it up all the way home. And back in the apartment he poured himself a drink, and went on with his speech between gulps. And Sarah sat on the couch and looked up at him with her eyes very wide.

And then, around midnight, the telephone rang.

175

"Now who the hell is that? Who's calling up at this time of night?" And he barked "Hello" into the phone at the top of his voice.

It was Eli Glatz. His voice was very strained, his manner was terribly formal. "I don't expect any apologies, Dan Waxman," Eli said. "That isn't the reason I'm calling. I may be one of the only true friends left to you in the world, I may be one of the few people who felt it was his duty to show up at your party to-night, in spite of the fact that such an action can only jeopardize my position among the rest of my acquaintances—I may have done all that for you, and I may have received fine thanks for my sacrifice—but I don't expect an apology, I'm not asking for an apology."

"All right, you won't get one. Is that why you called?"

"No, Dan." Very cool and high. "I called to tell you the news. I only heard about it myself when I got home just now."

"So get to the point. What news?"

"Don't talk to me like that, Dan. I'm upset enough already. And you'll be upset too when you hear it, and then you'll be sorry for how you talked to me." A pause, then Eli went on, "It's the news about Nat Garfunkel."

Right away Dan was on the defensive. "What about him?" he said, a little sharply.

"He killed himself, Dan. Early to-night he did it. He went out to that country home of his. It isn't even finished yet, loose boards and paint cans all around. But he wanted to get away from his family. He went out there with a gun, and he shot himself, and he died instantaneously."

"What is it, Dan?" Sarah said, running up to him. "What's come over you?"

176

"It's a terrible tragedy," Eli was going on. "He left a note, you know. To explain why he did it. Financial reverses, he said." Eli lingered a little on the last phrase.

Dan wet his lips. His voice was hoarse. His words came out painfully. "His family, Eli. Those twins of his. What's going to happen to them?"

"Nobody's very sure about that. He sacrificed his life insurance, of course. Doing it the way he did. I suppose his wife will be taking them back to St. Louis. I've heard that her brother is a big man in the produce business." Eli paused slightly, then finished up very quiet and satisfied. "Well, I just thought you'd like to know." And Dan heard the click of the receiver.

"What is it, Dan?" said Sarah. "Oh, my God, what is it?"

Slowly Dan replaced the phone and sank down on to the couch. "I'm sick," he said. "I'm just sick."

XVII

A WEEK later, the Waxman family left Chicago. That's how long it took Dan to clear up his affairs—to write Herman accepting his offer of work in New York: to sell the business: to sub-let the apartment for the rest of the lease: to resign from the Downtown Club and collect his golf bag from Pleasant Fairways: to break the news to Bobby, who couldn't understand why she had to leave all her friends: to find a job for Schultz, who broke into tears for the first time in Dan's memory and told him that she wasn't ever going to be able to stand a new boss.

Another thing that had to be done—flowers had to be

sent to Nat Garfunkel's wife. As for the funeral—it was a private one, and Dan and Sarah weren't invited.

So finally the week was up. They were ready to start off.

They left for the station early in the evening, just before dinner. It was the time of day that Dan had always loved best—that magical twilight time, when everything changed its colour and its shape. While the doorman went to the corner for a cab, they stood on the sidewalk among their suitcases. And none of them said anything, all three of them were busy with their own thoughts.

The breeze from Lake Michigan was soft and salty. It brushed against Dan's cheek. It seemed to be making fun of him.

The cab appeared. The suitcases were loaded into it, then Bobby got in, then Sarah got in. Dan put his foot up on the step. Then he turned for a moment and looked back at what he was leaving.

Twelve Hundred Lake Shore Drive rose up before him, shadowy and mysterious against the purple sky. The lights were on in the penthouse far above. Was the manager showing the new tenants around already? A smile came over Dan's face, as he thought of the day when he himself had moved in, and of all the breakfasts and dinners he had eaten up there, and the parties and the bridge games, and the jokes from Mort Meltzer. He frowned, shook his head, forced himself back to his angry mood. Chicago didn't want him now? All right then, that was Chicago's loss. He got into the cab, and they drove away to the station.

PART TWO

Everywhere Else

"By the rivers of Babylon, there we sat down, yea, we wept, when we remembered Zion."

PART TWO

Everywhere Else

I

In our family, photographs have always been a big thing. My mother's living-room, like the living-rooms of all her sisters and brothers, is crowded with them. All sizes all shapes, all possible types of relative, close or distant— everything from that old faded snapshot of Mother, Aunt Goldie, and an unidentified giggling young lady, dressed up in 1912 bathing-suits, with an Asbury Park back-ground, to that touched-up, elegantly-framed, formal portrait of myself, aged four, with a wide collar, short pants, and a deep brooding frown. My Uncle Irving (he's the intellectual in the family and also a bachelor) labelled this one; "Young John Keats, Mulling Over the Opening Lines of *Endymion*."

Among these photographs, which have followed my parents all over New York, from apartment to apart-ment, are two of my Uncle Dan. And even though it's been several years since I've lived at home, I can describe those two down to the smallest detail—for they are as much a part of my early memory as the wallpaper in my bedroom or my illustrated edition of *Baseball Joe in the Big Leagues*.

The first of them was taken in Chicago in 1926, the day of Uncle Dan's thirteenth wedding anniversary. It shows him all spruced up with a bow tie and a straw hat, and his hair combed back slickly. (There was still enough of it to comb back in those days.) On his face is a broad grin of the most tremendous confidence. Aunt Sarah is clinging to his arm. She is smiling too, but a little bit anxiously. Her mind is occupied with the effort to hunch down and slink into the background, so that she won't seem to be too much taller than Uncle Dan. She might as well have saved herself the effort. As much as she may tower over him actually, she doesn't give the *effect* of towering over him at all. With his superb self-assured air, he would steal the scene if he were surrounded by a family of giants.

The second picture shows Uncle Dan in 1931, just one year after he moved to New York. It is another wedding anniversary—my parents' wedding anniversary this time. We are given a panoramic view of all the guests, thirty-five or forty people at least, seated at the long sparkling table. If you look closely, you can see my Uncle Dan, off in a corner, among the smiling aunts, the smiling cousins, the smiling waiters. (One particular waiter is smiling so hard that he stands out from everybody else and completely overshadows the anniversary couple.) But Uncle Dan isn't smiling at all. The camera has caught him with a scowl—a sour, set kind of scowl that seems to be a permanent part of his face. His hair is almost all gone now, his dinner jacket doesn't fit him, his left arm is blurred, because he deliberately moved it when the photographer told everybody to be still. (He didn't like the photographer's "high-handed attitude.") Aunt Sarah sits next to him, smiling as in the earlier picture. And also as in the earlier picture, she looks a little bit anxious under the smile.

As a small boy, I used to wonder about the reason for Uncle Dan's scowl and Aunt Sarah's anxiety—such marked contrasts to the gaiety of the rest of the group. Just recently I found out what it was. Since his Chicago days, Uncle Dan had developed an intense dislike for shrimp cocktail. All the way over to the dinner that night, he had been telling Aunt Sarah, "If they give me shrimp cocktail, I walk out. You understand me? I walk right out." And then, just before the photographer got ready to take the picture, the waiters appeared with the shrimp cocktail.

For the first few months after he settled in New York, Uncle Dan went out of his way to say how much he liked it.

"Now this is a city," he'd say. "This is definitely what I'd call a city. Modern, up-to-date, progressive—none of your old-fashioned Mid-Western prejudices. Good-looking buildings, statues, parks, skyscrapers—not just a lot of glorified stockyards. This is where the business is—this is where you meet the important men, the financial geniuses, the big-shots that run the world—you don't find a bunch of narrow-minded clothing salesmen, with no vision beyond the end of their nose, here in New York. And as for culture—well, it goes without saying. Here are art galleries that *are* art galleries. And the theatre—plays, real plays, the finest plays, a lot classier than the tenth-rate road companies of *Charley's Aunt* that you get exclusively in certain other cities I could mention. And the opera—take it from me, as an expert of long standing, New York has got the finest opera company in the whole world. You heard me. The finest opera company in the whole world, with singers that are singers—not just beer guzzlers and spaghetti slurpers."

These were my Uncle Dan's sentiments about New York, and during the first few months he applied them vigorously to every move he made. First thing, for instance, he set about finding a place to live. "The finest street in town is where I want to be," he said to Herman. "I want to make it clear that this is definitely going to be *my* city. I'm not just slinking into it with my eyes on the ground and my collar pulled up—I'm marching in with my head up, and setting myself up with a big bang, and establishing myself on a solid, permanent scale. So tell me, what's the finest street in town?"

The finest street in town was Park Avenue, so Dan and Sarah spent a whole week marching up and down it, between the sixties and the eighties, looking for a suitable apartment. They ended up with a duplex penthouse on Eighty-Fifth Street. "A duplex penthouse is what we've always had," Dan said. "So that's what we're going to have now. Nobody's going to say that I lost interest in living a good life, just because I happened to want a change of scenery."

"But isn't it a little expensive?" Sarah said. "You said we might have to cut down on things."

"We'll cut down on things that people can't see," Dan said. "Cutting down is our own private business, and we're not broadcasting it to the whole world."

He applied this same principle to the rest of their activities, as they settled down in New York. He joined the oldest, most conservative, most luxurious card club in the city—his brother Herman got him in. He took a season's box at the Metropolitan Opera. He started an account with a small, exclusive tailor who was famous for the way he overcharged his customers. He went out and bought the most fashionable car on the market, a long sleek Pierce Arrow. And he enrolled Bobby, for her last two years of high school, in the smartest, most expensive private school he could find, a school in which nothing was used but the latest methods of progressive education, and nobody got the benefit of them but the richest Jewish children in New York.

To make up for this extravagance, Dan and Sarah shaved the edges in all sorts of little secret ways that nobody ever knew about except themselves. Who could guess, for instance, that the uniformed chauffeur who drove their new Pierce Arrow wasn't a regular employee at all, that he was hired from a local driving agency only on the nights they took friends out to the theatre? And if the friends happened to notice that *this* chauffeur wasn't the same man as the *last* chauffeur—well, it was a simple matter for Dan to refer, in an offhand way, to how hard it was "to find decent help nowadays. So many people out of work, you'd think *some* of them would be good for something."

In his business affairs, too, he started off in the same grand manner. The big story in the news just then was the building of the Empire State Building, so Dan immediately put in a reservation for a suite of offices in the Empire State Building. But since that wouldn't be for a year yet, he settled in the meantime for a suite in the Chrysler Building. "Until the Empire State is finished," he explained to Herman, "the Chrysler Building is the biggest one in New York. And I made up my mind that my offices are always going to be in the biggest building in New York."

Then he set about getting clients. Herman, of course, gave him a great deal of work right from the start. But he didn't want to be completely dependent on Herman. "People who tie themselves up too exclusively with one individual account, and do most of their business with that account, and get their name associated with that account, such people are riding strictly for a fall." That was Dan's philosophy of business just now. So he met the business-men that Herman introduced him to, he met some more on his own through the club, he met still more through old contacts of Drexell Enterprises, and pretty soon he was doing a nice comfortable day's work.

One thing he had been worried about from the first—

how would people in New York feel about his Drexell background? Would they look on him with mistrust, like various parties in other sections of the country? Well, it turned out that he didn't need to be worried at all. He found out quickly enough that the New York attitude towards business was a lot different from a certain other attitude. New Yorkers were more sophisticated, more practical and realistic, not so much dragging in personal feelings and letting their emotions run away with them. When people heard that he used to be Drexell's chief accountant, they didn't clear their throats uncertainly, or turn away their eyes, or stick up their noses. On the contrary, they looked at him with a new respect, even a kind of awe in their eyes. They smiled sort of pleased and confidential, and shook his hand up and down, and murmured with positive admiration, "Sad state of affairs, very sad state of affairs—still, people should have a little sense when it comes to investing their money—isn't that how you feel?"

It wasn't really how Dan felt. But he was so relieved just to find out they were friendly, how could he help but nod his head and agree with them that it was "all a question of business, in the last analysis?"

Finally, most important of all, this tremendous enthusiasm and good humour that Dan threw into his new business, his new apartment, his new style of living, carried over into his new social whirl.

"One thing about our life in New York," he announced to Sarah within a few days after their arrival, "we're going to have lots of friends. We're going to have a circle of friends in New York like we never dreamed of before. Because this is a city where you *can* have friends. Because the people you meet here are intelligent, they're up-to-date, they're well-informed on the important questions of the day. You go to a dinner party here in New

York, and you sit next to people that can carry on a conversation, they *know* something, a man of the world has something in common with them. Not just a bunch of small-town storekeepers that got rich by accident one night, and all they can talk about is how much money they've got. What I mean to say is, we're going to have friends here, Sarah. We're going to have more friends than we ever had before in our life. People are going to see that if certain groups don't take an interest in us, all right, there are other groups, there are *superior* groups——"

And he was true to his word, in those first few months. Never in the history of New York City was there such a mixer, such a joiner, such a hearty uninhibited back-slapper—at least, so it seemed to the members of the family who watched Dan from the side-lines. In his very first week, he and Sarah didn't spend a single night by themselves. Through Herman, through Sarah's family, through those few members of his own family who were still alive, Dan inveigled a different invitation for each different night. And every home he went to, he purposely struck up an acquaintance with everyone he could get his hands on.

Then, at the end of the week, he clinched his position by throwing a party—a huge, fancy, expensive house-warming party for his new Park Avenue penthouse—and inviting everybody he had met during the week, people he had talked to only a few minutes, people he had barely shaken hands with, not to mention their wives, their children, their in-laws. "It's really ridiculous," Herman said. "You haven't even bothered to be the least bit selective. Cousin Louis from the Stock Exchange and Armand Lefkowitz the poet, Mrs. Samuel Peyser with her big charity connections and your wife's sister Goldie, old Max Fox who just paid a twenty thousand-dollar fine for income-tax evasion and Judge Pearlman, the same judge who tried his case. You haven't even considered for a moment whether all these people will mix together."

But Dan just laughed at that. "I didn't invite them so they could mix together," he said. "I invited them because eventually they'll have to invite me back. How else do friendships get started in this world? If you weren't such an old hermit, shut up in your hotel room half your life, you'd understand the mechanics of these things. I invite them—then out of courtesy, they have to invite me back—so out of politeness, I have to invite them again—after which, out of good manners, they have to reciprocate and invite me—pretty soon it's like a perpetual motion machine, it *can't* be stopped, we *have* to be friends."

This was towards the middle of December. It was only a short while later—though Dan could never put his finger on the exact moment—that the whole thing began to go wrong.

He never knew the reason for it, because it just sort of crept up on him out of nowhere. One day he was walking along Fifth Avenue, and all of a sudden, darting his head to the left, he didn't see the Metropolitan Museum at all, he saw the grimy old front of the Chicago Art Institute. Another time, late at night, standing on the terrace of his penthouse in the chill December air, he looked out at the spires and the rooftops and the million lights—and suddenly the whole scene blurred before his eyes, and way off in the distance, there was Lake Michigan sparkling.

It began to happen more and more frequently. A chance remark over a game of cards would start it off. Or the sudden taste of something familiar, during a dinner party. Or a face passed for a moment on the street—or the first quick look of a building looming up before him unexpectedly as he turned a corner. Just like that, just like the click of a switch, and he'd be back in the middle of some old card game, dressing up for some old dinner party, walking up to some old familiar building, looking into a face that he'd never see again.

He found himself taking a funny interest in the newspapers. The headlines, and the sports section, and the Stock Market reports, they didn't attract his attention in the usual ways. He found himself leafing through the pages with a sharp eye out for a certain dateline, a certain place, a certain name that invariably sprang out of the page at him, even when it was buried in a mass of type.

His temper began to grow short again. He had been holding it in check pretty successfully these last few months. Since Labour Day, since that terrific outburst in the ballroom of the Downtown Club, he was careful to push back every impulse to raise his voice. But now he could feel it building up inside of him again.

One Sunday, at the club, he lost his temper over a pinochle hand. He was keeping score, and old Judge Pearlman suggested, in that rich quiet voice of his, that he had made a mistake in addition. "A mistake," Dan said, blinking down at the score sheet. "What do you mean, a mistake?" One of the other men laughed and winked and said, "So now it comes out, *there's* the reason for that fabulous Waxman luck." Dan looked up at him, just looked at him for a second or two, and then he exploded. "All right, do it yourself!" he cried, snatching up the score sheet and flinging it across the table. "You don't like the way I do it, so do it yourself!" And he pushed back his chair, and turned on his heel, and strode right out of the cardroom.

He was in the first-floor lobby two minutes later,

trembling a little, feeling ashamed of himself already, as the coloured attendant helped him on with his coat. But he didn't leave the club, because Judge Pearlman and the man who made that remark caught up with him. Judge Pearlman put on his most soothing, diplomatic voice. The other man apologized with such misery on his face that Dan agreed to go upstairs with them again.

The game continued for the rest of the evening, easy and natural, no more outbursts. But all the time Dan could tell that they were thinking about him, glancing at him sort of funny when they thought he wasn't looking. And he could imagine how the incident would be reported to their wives when they got home that evening.

He made up his mind that it wouldn't happen again. Crazy, he told himself. Absolutely crazy. All the wonderful new friends he'd made in New York—the wonderful new life he was starting up for himself—crazy, just crazy, to take a chance on throwing it all away. And for nothing, for no good reason in the world.

He stuck to his resolution for a long time. On plenty of occasions he stuck to it longer than he thought he possibly could. And then, one morning in March, a rainy dreary oppressive morning, it all came breaking out again.

It happened over Saturday morning breakfast, with Bobby and Sarah right there at the table with him. He was looking through his usual pile of mail, when he discovered that one of Sarah's letters had been put at his place by mistake. He started to hand it across to her, when he suddenly caught sight of that return address. It was just like leafing through the newspaper—there was one word that always sprang out at him, no matter how quick a look he might take.

"Chicago, Illinois?" Dan said. "You're getting a letter from Chicago, Illinois?"

Sarah squirmed a little and said, "It's nothing at all, dear, just some advertising circulars." And she reached across the table for the letter.

But by now Dan was examining the return address more closely. "Milly Meltzer?" he said. "What sort of an advertising circular is Milly Meltzer?"

"Is it from Milly?" Sarah said, squirming harder. "Now I wonder what she's writing to *me* for." But Sarah always was a lousy liar.

"If she's writing to you," Dan said, "it's probably because you wrote to her first. Why did you write to her?"

"Dan, I didn't——" But he just tightened his lips a little, and Sarah gave up the attempt with a sigh. "Well, I did write to Milly, dear. I wrote to her last week. Just a short note, that's all I wrote, really I did."

"And what was it about, this short note?"

"Just a friendly gesture, Dan—hardly anything at all. It just occurred to me—Milly and Mort were always so close to us—and it's been such a long time now, since we saw them last. It just seemed like a pity to me——"

"And that's what you wrote to her? You wrote her what a pity it was that we aren't friends any more?"

"Yes, that's what it was, Dan. Nothing more than that, I give you my word of honour——"

"Nothing more than that. She gives me her word of honour." He glared at her speechless with anger. Or at least, he pretended to be speechless with anger, because he knew how much it upset her. When he spoke up again, his voice was louder. "You don't have any pride. Do you know that? That's the trouble with you. You're like a worm—you hear me? You're just like a worm—crawling on your belly, crawling up to the people that just stepped on you—saying to them, 'Please, as a personal favour, would you kindly step on me again with the other foot?'"

"Dan——" Sarah said, in a low voice, biting her lip and glancing uneasily in the direction of Bobby.

Bobby's eyes were lowered and her face was red. She was pretending hard to go on with her breakfast, the way she always did when she found herself caught in the middle of one of these scenes.

Dan looked at them both, and the consciousness that he was giving them pain only goaded him on. He wanted to give them even more pain, he was suddenly filled with delight at the thought of it. He waved the letter before him, and put on his most sarcastic voice. "A friendly gesture. Wonderful, wonderful. All right, I only hope the miracle happened, I only hope you softened their hard hearts, I only hope they're in the mood to 'forgive the poor sinners'—I only hope it, so I can write them back, so I can tell them personally just what they can do with it, their friendly gesture." Then he jabbed the letter across the table at Sarah. "Here you are. Open it. Go ahead, open it."

Sarah took the letter, but she just held it between her fingers.

"What are you waiting for? Open it, open it."

With her fingers trembling a little, Sarah tore open the envelope, pulled out the letter inside, and unfolded it slowly. "Read it," Dan said. "Go ahead, read it."

Sarah lowered her eyes and began to read. For the first moment or two, her lips worked silently. And then, her lips stopped working, and Dan could see that her fingers were trembling harder than ever.

"What is it?" he said. "Read it out loud. Go ahead. So the rest of us can share your pleasure."

Still holding on to the letter, Sarah looked up at him again. And her eyes were scared, absolutely scared to death.

It infuriated Dan, that she should look so scared. Of

him she was scared—as if he was some sort of wild man, that you had to be scared of.

"Give it to me," he said, and grabbed the letter out of her hand. He stuck it up close to his eyes, and plunged right into reading it.

But he never got further than the first paragraph.

Dearest Sarah,
    You poor darling, of course I'm not insulted that you decided to write to me. It was wonderful to hear from you, it was just like old times again. Why shouldn't we write to each other? Am I a monster or something, Sarah dear? Can I hold you responsible for what *he* did? Is it your fault, the man you are married to? So why should you have to give up everything, why should you have to sacrifice, why should I make you suffer when everybody knows how blameless you are, and everybody says that's the worst of the whole dreadful business, that the punishment had to fall on you too.

Slowly Dan let the piece of paper drop to his plate. His face was white, it was just dead white.

"Of course I won't answer her, Dan dear," Sarah was saying. "You know I'm not going to answer her."

Dan stared at her just a moment, then he did the only thing he could do to relieve his feelings. He opened his mouth and he yelled, he yelled just as loud as he could, he yelled till his face was red, and his cheeks were tingling, and his throat was aching. "Answer her!" he yelled. "Go ahead, answer her! Don't do me any favours! *Answer her!*"

The offending letter caught his eye, and he struck out at it, sweeping a glass off the table in the same motion. And then he was out of the room.

He was so ashamed of himself later on that he didn't even dare to send the usual flowers. Anything he did would look cheap and mean and cowardly. All he wanted to do was forget the whole thing, drive it out of his mind, forget all about it.

He couldn't even bring himself to go home for dinner that night. He had his secretary call up Sarah and tell her he'd be eating dinner with some business people. It wasn't until ten-thirty that he finally got back to the apartment, slunk into the living-room, hunched up in his easy-chair like a criminal.

And yet, ashamed as he was, losing his temper came easier to him after that. He began to do it more and more often. In the club, in the office, even at strange people's dinner-tables, he found himself putting on a belligerent mood almost deliberately. He found himself picking fights over trifles, finding insults where he knew deep down that no insult was intended, pretending to suspect the most honest, and what's more the richest, men in his club of cheating at cards, yelling at waiters and servants and stenographers for the mildest, most inoffensive mistakes—and feeling, two minutes later, like the biggest heel in the world.

It had its effect on his new set of friends, of course—there was a little bit of talk, there was a small amount of annoyance, one or two people who had thought at first that Dan Waxman was "a wonderful guy" now recognized that he was a wonderful guy who could also be a pain in the neck at times. All right, so was there anybody on earth that you couldn't say that about? Another man might have a very even temper, but he told the most boring jokes anybody ever had to listen to. And another man told hilarious jokes, but God forbid you should ask him to lend you any money. This was all the effect it had on Dan's new friends—but even if this effect had been ten times worse, it couldn't have been as bad as Dan imagined it was.

For another thing was happening to Dan just now, something a lot more devastating to a man's peace of mind than all the outbursts of temper in the world. He was beginning to fall prey to a kind of steady, gnawing, underground suspicion of other people. What he suspected was that they were thinking terrible things about him. They all had a secret dislike for him, he suspected, and they talked about it behind his back. Sometimes he came upon them while they were in the middle of talking about it. And then, look how they immediately broke off their whispering—look at the guilty way they avoided each other's eyes—and what extra-special warmth and friendliness they put into their greeting. "Hello, Dan!" they cried, their faces lighting up with the biggest, phoniest smiles he'd ever seen. "How you been, Dan?" they said, pumping his hands up and down in an orgy of good humour. It was a dead giveaway, it was better than an out-and-out confession.

But the most insidious thing about this suspicion of Dan's was that he couldn't help feeling, half the time, that these people were right to say terrible things about him. Whatever they said, it was absolutely true, and he said a lot worse to himself twenty times a day. They couldn't *begin* to know the truth. They didn't see him at home. They didn't see the way he treated poor Sarah and Bobby, and the office boys, and the cook, a poor old lady who only wanted to please him. They were right to dislike him. He disliked himself.

That was only half the time. The other half of the time, he rebelled against the injustice of it all. He scowled, he growled, he went around in a state of constant irritability. He began to realize that New Yorkers weren't the gods on earth he had originally thought they were.

"They're human, like everybody else," he said.

And then, a little later on, "They're a race apart, these New Yorkers. Boast, boast, boast. Front, front, and more front. Big talk, that's their chief commodity here in New York. A lot of big talk, and what's behind it?"

And then, still later, "Nothing behind it. Absolutely nothing. You want to know why? Because they're hard-boiled. They don't have any feelings. With all this big social life of theirs, and always running here and there, and giving parties, and going to the theatre, most of them don't have a friend in the world. They wouldn't know what it means, having a friend. They slap you on the back, they have you up for dinner, and they don't care any more about you personally than they do about your chauffeur—and a lot less than they care about your Scotch."

One night early in June he got into a big argument at the club. It was a card-playing argument, and it wasn't really any worse than a lot of others he had been getting into recently. It was followed by the usual feeling of shame, the mumbled apologies, the short period of awkwardness slipping gradually back into easiness and geniality again. Only this time the slipping-back process didn't seem to take so successfully in Dan. He was all right on the surface. He laughed, he slapped backs, he called out friendly insults with the rest of them. But he didn't feel them underneath. Suddenly he was fed up. All this friendliness and geniality, it all seemed so point-less to him. Why bother with it? he thought. What was the good of it anyway?

A few days later the week-end began, and for the first time the weather was nice enough for golf out at the Pine Needle Country Club. It was just a few weeks earlier that he had received his official notice of election along with the engraved letter of congratulations, and the bill for the membership fee. So this was going to be a big moment in his life—his first day of golf at the club, his first entrance into the real social life of his new friends.

Sarah mentioned it to him at breakfast.

Without even looking up at her, he gave a wave of his

hand. "You go, you go," he said. "You'll enjoy it I prefer to stay home."

She blinked at him, and put on her concerned look, as if she thought he was sick.

"It's all right, it's all right," he said. "I'll be very happy not to go. A lot of big show-offs with flabby stomachs—pretending they're great athletes, bragging about the wonderful putts they've made—giving their golf ball a little kick in the right direction if you once turn your back on them. No, thank you, I'd rather not waste my time on that foolishness. I'm a busy man, I've got my work to do."

And a moment later, though Sarah hadn't said a word, he raised his head and spoke up a little sharply, "It's all right, I told you! So why don't you drop the subject?"

II

His short flirtation with social life was over now, and my Uncle Dan made a concerted effort to lose himself in business. This was the only real course of action for an active, enterprising man, anyway. To put his shoulder to the wheel, to build up his financial position, to provide for the future and security of his family—to accomplish something useful in this world, in other words, instead of throwing away his life at card tables and golf courses.

But he knew, even before he started in, that it wasn't going to turn out right. He went down to his office regularly every morning, he stuck close to his desk, he was just as conscientious about his clients' interests as he had ever been. But somehow it wasn't the same thing any more. The excitement had gone out of it—the fascination of figuring, juggling, untangling; the sharp quickening sensation of being on the inside of big doings, of standing behind the scenes while momentous deals and important events were being manipulated. Only a year ago, what a pleasure it was to stride into his office, wave at the telephone girls, plump himself down at his desk, rub his hands together and put on a businesslike look and cry out, "All right, let's go!"

The pleasure didn't come to him at all nowadays. Only a terrible weight of drudgery when the morning mail was put in front of him. And a feeling of being completely pooped out and squeezed dry by the end of the day.

Another funny thing was the trouble he had in keeping a secretary. Every one that he hired, there always seemed to be something the matter with her. She was loud and impertinent, she was lazy and incompetent, she had a squeaky voice that grated on his nerves, her face was perpetually covered with one of those sweet, sticky, old-lady smiles that drove him crazy every time he looked at it. Whatever it was, and even if there wasn't anything at all, he invariably managed to quarrel with her after a few weeks, and pretty soon he'd be looking for a new secretary.

Sometimes, in a dreary afternoon lull, he'd drift into a daydream, and start wondering about poor old Schultz. What ever became of her? he wondered. Was she all settled down in her new job? Was she happy with her new boss? Did they take a break in the middle of the morning, while she told him the latest stories about "that good-for-nothing bum"?

"Who cares?" he told himself, and he broke off his daydreaming sharply.

And then, there was something else about doing

business in New York, something he had never had to contend with back in—back where he used to be. There was his brother Herman.

It was so many years since he'd spent any amount of time with Herman—steady, unbroken time, that is. He'd actually forgotten what Herman could be like, in large doses. It all came back to him now, though. Three or four afternoons a week they had business conferences together. And after business hours, they were together socially; Herman was always inviting Dan and Sarah for dinner at his hotel, or being invited for dinner at their apartment. Oh, yes, Dan had plenty of opportunity to renew his acquaintance with all those little quirks and mannerisms which used to make his blood boil when they were boys.

It was so many years—and yet, after a few months of Herman's dry little coughs, his stern little lectures, his long disapproving face, it didn't seem to be any number of years at all. It seemed to be a direct continuation of the old days, as if Dan's whole life in between hadn't really happened at all.

What irritated him more than anything else was Herman's cautiousness. Cautiousness, did he say? Cautious was what Herman *used* to be—cautious was the way you'd describe him when he was ten or eleven years old maybe. Nowadays he wasn't just cautious, he was absolutely paralysed. He was afraid to scratch his nose unless he had the diagnosis of three specialists that it really itched. He was afraid to cross the street when the light turned green, because what guarantee did he have that the people who worked the light were honest and efficient? On the High Holy Days, when he went to temple, he was afraid to join in on the prayers, because they hadn't been checked first by his legal department. Dan spent a lot of time, especially after one of those exasperating afternoon conferences, making up new and wilder examples of Herman's cautiousness.

And he spent a lot of time getting into arguments with Herman, too. For instance, Dan wasn't really very political-minded. Democrats, Republicans—they were all a bunch of politicians, as far as he was concerned. The ones who weren't morons were crooks, and the ones who weren't crooks were windbags—and the majority of them were all three. But now that he was in such close contact with Herman, he found himself taking sides in politics, and doing it more violently and emotionally than he had ever thought he could do before.

The reason was that Herman was such a terrible cautious, old-fashioned, dyed-in-the-wool conservative Republican. It was almost a disease with him, being a Republican. Every time he opened his mouth, out would come a whole string of dull, dry catch-phrases that Dan had heard a thousand times before—"the American system of free enterprise," "dangerous radical tendencies," "a lot of college professors meddling in business affairs", "impractical theorists," "what we need in the White House is a good solid business-man." Over and over and over again Herman repeated these same sentiments, and always with the same long serious face, the same slowly wagging finger, the same solemn throat-clearing, as if what he had to say was so profound and original that the whole world had to stop and listen to him.

All right, so what kind of a reaction could a man like Dan possibly have to all this? He believed in the American system of free enterprise as much as anybody—but now, all of a sudden, he found himself tearing it down and arguing against it as strongly as any Socialist from Brooklyn. He didn't have any more faith in impractical theorists than any other sensible man, and he was certainly grown-up enough to realize the sort of mess college professors always made when they stuck their noses into business. But Herman was so infuriating. And he was so absolutely sure of himself, and looking down his nose all the time at anybody who might possibly dare to disagree with him—well, my God, you had to put up an argument if you wanted to hold on to your self-respect. How could you keep from raising your voice a little, and waving your arms a little, and coming out with one or two opinions that you maybe didn't exactly believe in completely? And then, as soon as you were on record with those opinions, weren't you sort of forced to stick by them for the future, and make a good case for them, and more or less act as if you really *did* believe them? And the worst of all this was, most of the time Herman had the advantage. Because Herman never raised his voice in their arguments together. Herman never lost his temper, Herman could be boiling with rage inside, but outside he was always the same, calm, cautious, dignified Herman. And, of course, the calmer Herman managed to stay, the more excited Dan got. And the more excited Dan got, the more Herman was able to shake his head and sigh and say, "Really, there's no point going on with the discussion if you're going to lose your temper."

Around the spring of 1932 it got especially bad. Because this was the time of the political conventions, elections were coming up, and the newspapers were full of nothing but Hoover and Roosevelt: "Throw the rascals out" and "Don't change horses in midstream."

Who can say what Dan would have been, or who he would have voted for, if he hadn't moved to New York? Being in New York, seeing so much of Herman, he obviously couldn't be anything except the most ardent Democrat. In fact, for the summer and fall of 1932, this became the very biggest thing in Dan's life. All his interest, all his enthusiasm, all his deepest, most secret wishes, were concentrated on the coming elections. It was the goal of his life, he hadn't been so excited over anything since he left Chicago—to kick the Republicans out, to elect Franklin D. Roosevelt, to show that pig-headed, reactionary Herman that his so-called ideas were a hundred years behind the times.

The way Dan threw himself into this job—the way he pleaded and reasoned and threatened with his friends; the way he read all the speeches and memorized the choice bits; the way he rang them out triumphantly, or sarcastically, or slyly, or offhandedly at his next meeting with Herman; the way he wore his Roosevelt button all over town, in his office, at the club, even at the dinner-table—well, it was a surprise to his family and his New York acquaintances. Until now they had been a little worried that Dan seemed sort of listless and out of sorts lately, irritable over a hundred minor things, with no real interest in any one thing. And it was the cause of anxiety to Sarah, who knew that it couldn't last.

Then came Election Night, and Dan and Sarah had a big gathering at their apartment—the first real party they had given in almost a year. Herman was there, and Sarah's family was there, and a few of Dan's card-playing friends and their wives were there, and Bobby was allowed to stay up late for the occasion. They all gathered around the living-room radio—one of those bit, dome-shaped cabinet radios that were the newest thing in those days—and drinks and sandwiches were served, and they listened to the returns. Every time a block of votes was announced for Roosevelt—even if it was only a couple of dozen votes from Chickasaw, Kansas—Dan gave a whoop, clapped his hands together, nodded around at everybody, shouting out, "You see, it's a trend—what did I tell you?" But every time a block of votes was announced for Hoover, he laughed sarcastically, shook his head, waved his hand with great confidence, "Doesn't mean a thing—just one of those obscure outlying sections—probably populated by his relatives." As the evening progressed, and it became clearer and clearer how the election was going, Dan grew more and more excited and high-spirited. He filled and refilled his glass, he couldn't sit still in his chair, he paced the floor, he waved his arms, he kept up a running stream of optimistic outcries, crowing noises, genially sarcastic remarks at Herman's expense.

Finally, late in the evening, President Hoover officially conceded the election. Dan went wild. Talk about jumping for joy—literally and physically that's what he did. He was all over the room, kissing the women, slapping the men on the back, making sweeping gestures, gaily announcing to Herman—an even more than usually stiff and withdrawn Herman—that he "wasn't the type who said 'I told you so.'" Then he caught up Bobby by the waist and swung her around, laughing and crying out, "We did it! Baby, we did it!" After which, he bustled out to the kitchen, hurried up the champagne, poured it all around with his own hands, then delivered a long, enthusiastic, ecstatically mixed-up toast to "the greatest man in the world to-day, Franklin D. Roosevelt." He couldn't have been more overjoyed if he had been elected President himself.

Well, it was just as Sarah predicted it would be. Dan's elation lasted him another few days, then sure enough the reaction set in. Roosevelt was elected now, and all the shouting was over. Nothing to wave and yell about any more, nothing to romp around for, no more enemies to squelch, no more fence-sitters to win over, nothing in sight but the same flat, dreary round from apartment to office and back again. Even the weather was conspiring to kill his enthusiasm. That sharp November chill was in the air now, and the sky was heavy and dark. He had to keep the lights on all day in his office.

One morning, cleaning out his desk, he found one of his old Roosevelt buttons. Looking at it for a moment, he felt a dull sour sensation in his stomach. He picked up the button and dropped it into the waste basket.

Two days later, the newspapers carried a story—way in the back pages they printed it—about the death of the former financial tycoon, Martin Drexell. The last three years of his life Drexell had spent in a sanatorium, unable to move his arms or legs, or to utter a coherent word. He passed away in his sleep without pain. "An ironic aspect of this story" caught the attention of the reporter who wrote the article. Drexell's death came only two days after the Government's indictment against him, on charges of fraud, was finally settled out of court.

That night, Herman came up for dinner, and Dan got into an especially violent argument with him.

It was over nothing at all, this argument. A minor matter that neither of them cared about for one minute. Herman was telling a story about the elevator man at his hotel. Edgar was the elevator man's name, and he was a short stocky fellow in his thirties. "Not the way he acts, however," Herman said. "The way he acts, you'd think he was a boy of ten. No common sense. No intelligence. Definitely the mind of a ten-year-old."

There was something so smug and superior about Herman's tone of voice that right away Dan spoke a little quickly and sharply. "What'd he do to you, this poor fellow, that you should accuse him of being a ten-year-old?"

"Me?" Herman raised an eyebrow slightly. "It's not what he did to *me*. I assure you he didn't do anything to me. It's what he's done to *himself*."

"All right, all right, you played the overture, let's get going with the first act."

Herman gave him a cool stare for just a moment, then went on quietly, "Judge for yourself, after you've heard my story. Two weeks ago, this elevator man is taking me down from my floor, and suddenly he stops the elevator and starts crying. I knew right away, of course, that he wanted to borrow money. I've had experience of that sort of thing. I'm not a hard man. I was willing to help him out in any reasonable cause. But I *was* in a big hurry that morning, I didn't have time for the usual long, rambling digression that people always seem to go through when they're building up to a thing like that. So I told him to stop his crying, and get to the point. So he sniffled a little more, and finally he came out with it. His wife was sick, she had just been taken to the hospital, an expensive operation was needed, and so on and so on— the usual business. The long and short of it was, he was ready to worship the ground I walked on for the rest of his life if I only came across with a hundred dollars."

Dan was beginning to get annoyed at the way Herman was warming to his story, at the way he leaned back in his seat and crossed his legs and even put on the vague suggestion of a smile, as he remembered the elevator man's predicament. "And you wouldn't give him the money," Dan broke in. "A man's wife is dying, he asks you for a few measly dollars—it's chicken-feed to you, but to him it's life and death——"

"I don't know what you're raving about," Herman said quietly. "Of course I gave him the money."

"Oh," said Dan, still half belligerently. "Oh, you did." And he settled back in his seat again, muttering.

"I gave him my cheque for a hundred dollars right there in the elevator. Then he took me down the rest of the way, and I put the whole matter out of my mind.

Now here's the point of the story. Two days later—in fact, it wasn't as much as two days later—I'm going *up* to my floor, and this same elevator man stops the elevator and starts crying all over again. 'Mr. Waxman,' he says to me, 'my wife is sick, they just took her to the hospital, I need a hundred dollars for an operation.' Well, naturally, my first thought was, 'This is some sort of racket.' The whole operation story was a lie from the start, he was trying it on everybody in the building, it had simply slipped his mind that he had already tried it on me. I was quite disturbed. I don't like it when people aren't absolutely straight and above-board with me in business matters. I started to tell him so. And now I come to the real point."

"I don't believe it," said Dan, to the floor.

"The real point," Herman said. "It turned out that this elevator man wasn't lying about his wife at all. She really did need an operation. And the day I gave him that hundred dollars, he actually started off for the hospital with it. Only on the way—listen to this now—on the way he passed a store, and in the window of the store was—a mandolin. A mandolin, mind you. And the price of the mandolin was exactly a hundred dollars. And this elevator man had always wanted a mandolin. That was his great ambition since boyhood, to own a mandolin. He didn't know how to *play* a mandolin, you understand. He hardly even knew what a mandolin *sounded* like. Nevertheless, to own a mandolin was, as far as I can see, the sole purpose of his life. And when he saw it in the window of that store, and when he realized he had a cheque for a hundred collars right there in his pocket—well, the long and short of it is, he went into that store and bought that mandolin with the money I'd given him. And he went on to the hospital and showed it to his wife. He showed it to his wife. And she got a big kick out of it. Believe it or not, she got a big kick out of it. And there he was, less than two days later, crying in the elevator and expecting me to cough up another hundred dollars."

Herman came to the end of his story. He nodded his head a few times. He made his face longer than ever. Then he raised his finger and in his most important voice, produced the moral. "It's no worse than what you'd expect, of course," he said. "If he had any brains in his head, would he still be an elevator operator?"

"Would he still be an elevator operator?" It was more than Dan could stand. He leaned forward in his seat, squeezed his hands together, spoke up in quick impatient tones: "How self-satisfied can you get? I ask you, how self-satisfied? A man is ignorant and uneducated, and beaten down by bad luck and people who think they're better than he is. And then his wife gets sick, he's half crazy with worry, he isn't thinking logically, he does an illogical thing—and you sniff down your nose at him and ask him why he's still an elevator operator."

"What happened?" Sarah said. "Did you give him the money?"

But Herman wasn't listening to her. His eyes were hard on Dan. "You talk about acting illogically. That's my whole point. A man with brains *doesn't* act illogically. A man who was meant to be better than an elevator operator knows how to act *logically*."

"A man with brains!" Dan barked out. "Listen to him, a man with brains. And *you've* never done an illogical thing in your life, I suppose? *You've* never lost your head? *You've* never made a mistake?"

"Frankly," Herman said, without changing his expression, "very seldom."

"Very seldom! Very seldom!" Dan's voice was rather loud now. "I believe it. You want to know, I really believe it. You don't *have* any feelings to lose your head over. You couldn't *be* so attached to anybody else that you'd act illogically for them. You're a dried-up old sour-puss—that was *your* childhood ambition, and you fulfilled it long ago."

Herman's lips just tightened a little. Even when you insulted him, he didn't lose control of himself. "You say that because the argument is going against you," he said. "You take refuge in nasty remarks."

"I wonder," said Sarah, softly. "Was he able to raise the money?"

"Nasty remarks?" said Dan. "I don't make nasty remarks. I'm telling you the truth—the plain un-varnished *truth*!"

"All right, you're telling me the truth. But you don't have to shout."

"Shout! Who's shouting!"

"You are. And I'm only a few feet away from you, I can hear you quite well in your normal voice."

"What's my voice got to do with it? What the hell do you mean, dragging my voice into it?"

"*You* dragged your voice into it. And very loudly too, that's what I'm trying to point out to you."

"Don't point it out to me. I'm not interested in what you point out to me. I'm sick and tired of your pointing out."

"Dan dear," said Sarah, with her hand on his arm. "Maybe if I made some coffee——"

"Never mind coffee, I don't want any coffee." He shook her hand off and whirled back on Herman. "I'm sick and tired, do you hear me? I'm sick and tired of your smug face, and your superior tone, and your high-and-mighty attitude. A prune. A dried-up prune, that's what I've got for a brother. Get out of my home. Go on, get out of my home." He waved his arm at the door, stamped up and down, and yelled out furiously, "Go on, what's holding you up? Get out!"

Herman rose to his feet, not forgetting to smooth out the crease in his pants as he did so. His face was pale, his lips were white—and that was his only sign of emotion. "If I go now, I'll never come back," he said. "You understand me? Never."

"Never, never" Dan cried. "I'm grateful! I hope that's a promise!"

Herman gave a short nod at Sarah, then turned and walked out of the apartment.

Dan went on pacing and yelling for another hour, until the last bit of anger was worked out of him. Sarah said nothing, except to murmur once or twice, "That poor woman. Oh, I hope she got her operation."

For a while it looked as if the rift between the brothers was really permanent. The wave of shame that came over Dan led him to call up Herman's office the next morning. But Herman was true to his word, he wouldn't even talk to Dan. And this made Dan mad all over again, he pounded his fist down on his desk and cried out, "All right, if that's how he wants it. All right, all right, what do *I* care?" And he sounded off at Sarah for another hour that night.

And as a matter of fact, it wasn't till a week later that Sarah arranged for the brothers to meet "just accidentally" at a family party. Then she manœuvred the rest of the family into another room in the most natural way in the world, placed herself between the two glaring, sulky men, smiled at them, took them each by the arm, murmured a few soothing words at them, and finally brought them together to shake hands.

"All right," said Dan, sort of half to Herman and half to a nearby lamp shade, "I apologize."

"Very well," said Herman, stiff and formal. "Apologies accepted."

The way he said it made Dan snap his head up, and he

almost burst right out with something that would have started it all up again. But he held himself back at the last moment, grunted, and turned away quickly.

That night, when he was alone with Sarah in their own bedroom, he sank into a chair, sighed, and passed his hand over what was left of his hair. "I'll stay out of his way from now on," he said. "I'll stay out of everybody's way. I'm no good for people any more."

III

IT was a dismal winter for Dan, the winter that began after his quarrel with Herman. It was a time of muttering and fidgeting, jumbled figures and flat dinners and bad weather, office hours that seemed to stretch on for ever, and long sleepless nights when he prayed under his breath for morning and the office.

It was getting worse and worse every day. It was having its effect on Dan's health, on the yellowness of his cheeks and the circles under his eyes. And the circles under Sarah's eyes too—they were right there, keeping pace with Dan's. The family was even starting to talk about it. "Where's it going to end?" my mother asked my father at dinner one night. But nobody liked to push the question any further.

God knows where it *would* have ended, if something hadn't happened in the spring that eased the tension and snapped my Uncle Dan back to the world again.

Bobby graduated from high school. She was seventeen years old now. She was pretty—not exactly Joan Crawford, but pretty enough for all normal purposes. She was bright—if she wasn't at the very head of her class, she wasn't at the other end of it either. Her disposition was just as shy and sweet and cheerful as it had ever been. Within a month after coming to New York, she had made as many friends as she ever had back in Chicago.

Now she was graduating from high school, and Dan and Sarah and a number of aunts and uncles gathered in the auditorium, with all the other relatives, to see the ceremonies. For the whole week leading up to this, Dan had been in one of his touchiest moods. The preparations got on his nerves—the excitement in the air, the gifts, the telegrams, the trying on of dresses, the constant consulting and chattering and general visiting back and forth of Sarah's sisters and aunts and nieces and cousins. "A bunch of kids get out of school," he said, "What's so special about that? Every single year it happens, millions of kids go through it. If you want my opinion," he said, "it's only an excuse, nothing but a complicated underhanded excuse for cluttering up my house with busybodies, relatives, and other female pests. Besides which," he said, "it's all a lot of hypocrisy and misleading propaganda. An innocent child moves one step closer to facing life and going out into the world, and you all smile at her and tell her 'Congratulations'. As if you didn't know damned good and well what's ahead of her."

On the actual day of graduation, Dan's irritability reached its height. He fretted and fumed all through breakfast. He was late getting to the car, then he yelled at everybody for the "delay". Down at the auditorium he complained in the loudest possible whisper about everything he could think of. Why was the room so hot and stuffy? Look at that high ceiling, you won't be able to hear a word those poor kids say. What a crowd of people—every one was more peculiar-looking than the next one—was this the sort of people his daughter had been associating with in high school? And why didn't they get things started, incidentally? What was holding them up? Ten o'clock, they said, and already it was five minutes after. What a nerve they had, just because they knew that you couldn't go to the box office and demand your money back——

Finally the lights grew dim, things were about to start. Dan continued to whisper. "What's wrong with this audience, why don't they shut up, can't they see it's time now?" "All right, all right, enough of this organ music, when do the kids get here?" "Opening hymn? Who wants an opening hymn?" "*And* a speech. Who is he, that big windbag? Who's listening to him? Let's have the kids."

The speech came to an end, there was a hush over the audience, then the organ music changed its character. The triumphal march from *Aïda* rang out slowly and solemnly, while necks craned to the back of the auditorium. Down the centre aisle, two by two in time to the music, came the girls of the graduating class of 1933. They were all in white. How tall they looked. And how grave and important, measuring their steps, holding their eyes straight ahead of them.

Already the irritation was melting out of Dan. The sight of all those young girls in white—it made him choke up somehow, though he didn't know most of them personally. Bobby was one of the last, because she was one of the tallest. From a distance, he spotted her coming through the door. The beat of the music brought her nearer. Her face was grave and her eyes were steady, just like all the others. She was almost up to his aisle now, and Dan felt his heart throbbing painfully. What was going through her mind at this moment? What was she thinking and feeling, this daughter of his, looking so serious and grown-up all of a sudden? She was his daughter, and she was a person too, and he didn't know the first thing about her, she was just like a stranger to him.

She was only a few feet away from him now. He could have reached out and touched the folds of her sleeve. And then she was past him, he was watching the back of her head and her swirling dress.

In that moment he loved his daughter more than he had ever loved her. And an idea came to him, a sharp urgent idea that filled him with excitement and impatience. Here was the big thing in his life, he told himself. Bobby was it. To bring himself close to her at long last, to watch her grow up, learn things, develop a mind of her own, turn into a wonderful happy woman— this was his life from now on, this was his ambition, he could hardly wait to get started.

He got started that very same morning. When the ceremonies were over, the audience of parents and relatives surged out to the sidewalk in front of the building. There was lots of handshaking back and forth. Traffic was held up all along the street. Then a side door opened, and the girls came bursting out, laughing, waving, rushing forward, a swarm of white birds starting suddenly into the air.

Bobby rushed up to Dan and Sarah and the family group. Her face was red, from shyness and excitement. She was breathing a little fast. She stretched out her arms while she was still several feet away, and Dan raised his own arms to meet her. A moment later she was on his neck, hugging him tight, kissing his cheek, laughing in his ear, like the old days when she had her outbursts of wild spirits and he played with her in the living-room. Just like the old days it was—back at Twelve Hundred Lake Shore Drive.

"Daddy, did it go all right? Did you notice me in all

that crowd? I hit a sour note in the class hymn, you don't think anybody heard me, do you? And when I walked up there for my diploma, I was *sure* I was going to trip and fall flat on my face. Oh, Daddy," laughing, talking, even crying a little, all at the same time, "I thought it would *never* be over!"

Dan didn't say a word. He just let her chatter on, while he patted her shoulder and smiled to himself. And one thought kept going through his head: This is it. This is certainly it. This is the answer to everything.

IV

"It's not normal," Dan said. "Frankly, I don't understand it. It just isn't something that a normal human being would do."

"She isn't a normal human being," Sarah said." She's a member of the younger generation, and we're simply her parents. It's not our business to understand what she does."

"That's supposed to be an answer? That's the silliest thing I ever heard. By that reasoning, when she was two years old and threw her cereal across the room, we should've kissed her and given her another bowl and told her to do it again."

"It's not the same thing, dear. Bobby is grown up now."

"Who says she's grown up? Twenty years old, since when is that grown up? And look at all the experience of life that she's got. Two and a half years at Vassar College—very grown up. Answer me just one thing. If she was so grown up, why would she do a crazy thing like this? Thanksgiving dinner—her own family that she hasn't seen for two months—and she's 'terribly sorry', she 'hates to eat and run', but she 'just happens to have this early date'. Early dates. All of a sudden our daughter has early dates on Thanksgiving."

"It's her life, Dan. She's capable of making her own decisions."

"Then why did she make *this* decision? There's the proof of what I'm saying. She isn't capable of blowing her nose."

"Maybe not. But we have to act as if she was."

"Why? Why? That's all I'm asking—why?"

"Because we're parents."

At which Dan threw up his hands and shouted out, "That's supposed to be an answer?"—and they started all over again from the beginning.

It was Thanksgiving, 1935. Dinner was over a long time ago, and the family, stuffed and puffing and red in the face, had straggled out to the air and their own homes. Behind them they left a trail of empty plates and full ashtrays. It was in the midst of this debris that Dan and Sarah had their talk.

And still later, with the debris cleared up and the living-room no more rumpled than usual, Dan continued to sit with an angry look on his face, and wait up for his daughter to come home. Sarah tried to persuade him not to do this. "We don't want her to think we don't trust her," Sarah said. But Dan just grunted and said, "Why not? It's the truth." Finally, around midnight, Sarah moved around the room, emptying out ashtrays, then stood for a moment in the archway. "Don't say anything you don't really mean, dear" were her last words before she went up to bed.

For the next hour and a half Dan sat and chewed a cigar—or paced up and down and chewed a cigar.

Finally, he heard Bobby's key in the front door. For a second he got a little flustered. It occurred to him suddenly, for the first time, that Bobby's new boy—this mysterious boy that nobody had ever seen or knew anything about, except that he could drag her away from her own family on Thanksgiving—might be with her now. Dan didn't know whether he should step out to the foyer and announce himself quick, or hunch down in his chair and keep very quiet. Before he could decide, the front door had opened and shut, and it was clear that Bobby was alone.

"Who's there?" came her voice. And then she was in the room with him, smiling, her face a little flushed. "Daddy, you didn't have to wait up."

"Who waited up? I was reading a detective story, and I lost track of the time."

"You and your detective stories." Bobby said it lightly and fondly, with maybe the smallest shade of superiority in her voice. Since she started going to Vassar, she had become just a little bit of an intellectual.

"Did you enjoy yourself to-night?" Dan said, trying to keep the gruffness out of his voice, and knowing he couldn't do it.

"Oh, I had a nice time," she said, in an offhand way. Three years ago she would have cried out "I had a *marvellous* time!" But that was another thing Vassar had taught her—the naïveté and immaturity of expressing enthusiasm.

"Where did you go? What did you do?"

"Oh, we went to lots of places. We made the usual tour of the Village." Bobby yawned delicately, and patted her mouth even more delicately. "Well, I'll see you in the morning, darling." She gave him a quick kiss on the forehead, then started to the door.

"Wait a second, what's the big hurry?" Dan said,

raising his voice a little. "Join me in a nightcap, why don't you? Then we can go upstairs together."

"I really *am* awfully tired."

But Dan couldn't just let her run off like this, he couldn't just go through the whole night with this thing on his mind. "It'll only be a quick one," he said, leaning forward a little and putting more urgency into his voice than he really wanted to.

Bobby hesitated a moment, then she smiled and nodded. "All right, just a quick one."

Dan was on his feet immediately, bustling up to the liquor cabinet, making the drinks with a great deal of excess motion, calling out very professionally, "Scotch is what you like, isn't it? I seem to remember your drink is Scotch." A few minutes later he was back in his easy-chair again, and they both had glasses in their hands, and they were facing each other across the room.

"You ran out of here pretty quick after dinner tonight," Dan said, finally. "This date of yours must've been pretty special."

"No, no, nothing special." Bobby sipped her liquor, rolled it around appreciatively in her mouth, gave a pleased little sigh as it warmed her stomach.

"What's his name, this fellow who's nothing special?"

"You've never heard of him, Daddy. He doesn't come from New York."

"People don't have names outside of New York?"

"Of course they do. What I mean is, his name won't have any particular significance to you."

"All right then, if it's so insignificant why not tell it to me? Why make such a big mystery out of it?"

"I'm not making a mystery, Daddy. His name is Harvey Harris."

Dan's eyes narrowed a little. "Jewish boy?"

"As a matter of fact, he is. Not that it really matters."

"If he isn't from New York, where is he from?"

"He's from Ohio. Beewick, Ohio—that's a small town right near Cincinnati."

"And what's he doing so far away from home? Does he go to college here in the city?"

"Oh, no. Harvey doesn't go to college. As a matter of fact, I don't think he's ever been to college. He's working now. He's in business with his elder brother, and he's in New York now to sell things."

"In business." Dan's belligerence eased up a little on this. The boy was in business—right away the two or three most horrible of Dan's fears went away. How mysterious could this Harvey Harris be, if he was in business? "What kind of business is he in?"

"Well"—Bobby laughed—"it isn't very romantic, I'm afraid. He makes soap. That is—his brother is in charge of making it, and Harvey spends most of his time trying to sell it. It's a small business still, but I guess they're doing very well."

"Soap." Dan thought it over a moment, then nodded his head, and even smiled a little. "What's wrong with the soap business? I was reading an article the other day, where it said that the United States of America uses one and a half times more soap daily per person than any other country in the world, except Switzerland." Dan could feel himself getting more genial every moment. He leaned back in his seat, and actually enjoyed his next mouthful of liquor. "How did you meet him, this young soap magnate? I thought you only got to meet a lot of crazy college kids with nothing on their minds but crew haircuts."

"Daddy, you've got such funny ideas about your own daughter. After all these years you should know that I don't care for that type any more than you do. Harvey was in Poughkeepsie on business, and he happened to go to one of the Vassar dances, and I realized right away that he was superior to the other boys."

And now, for the first time, there was a definite note of enthusiasm in her voice. And with it, the enthusiasm went right out of Dan's voice. He went on, full of suspicion, "How come he didn't pick you up at the apartment to-night, this fellow? Were you afraid to let us get a look at him?"

"Now you know that wasn't the reason. Harvey was busy with some buyers for cocktails, and he thought it would save time if I met him right at the restaurant."

"You went to the restaurant by yourself and waited for him there?"

"He was waiting for me, Daddy. Harvey is always on time, wherever he goes."

"And how come he didn't bring you home to-night?"

"He did bring me home. He let me off downstairs, in his car."

"Oh, he's got a car?"

"Yes. It's a used car—it's about three years old. He needs it for his work. Travelling all around the country and so on."

Dan grunted. He had a dissatisfied feeling. He felt that there were a lot of things he wanted to ask about this Harvey Harris, only he couldn't seem to think of them at the moment. And then, there was one big thing that he *could* think of at the moment—"How do you feel about this boy? Do you like him a lot? Do you like him particularly?" This was the question that popped into his head whenever Bobby went out on a date nowadays— and it was just the question that he could never bring himself to ask.

And then Bobby's voice was breaking into his thoughts. "I'm through with my quick one, Daddy. It's really awfully late."

Dan looked at her a moment longer. Then he nodded and got to his feet. "Yes. Sure. You're right."

They went up the stairs together. They kissed on the second-floor landing, and Dan turned towards the door of his bedroom. Then he stopped himself and turned back to Bobby. "I'd like to meet him, this boy. That is—if you're planning to see him again. If you're not, don't bother——"

"Of course you can meet him, darling. He'll be picking me up for dinner to-morrow night." Then she blew him a kiss and disappeared into her room.

Dan woke Sarah up and told her about it. Two nights in a row, he told her. And there were only three nights for her vacation. Didn't it look strange? Was it possible that something was up? What was Sarah's opinion? And when Sarah answered that she didn't have any opinion at all, Dan snorted and grunted and muttered irritably, "No opinion. She's your own daughter, isn't she? My God, you should have an opinion." And so, in five or ten minutes, he had muttered himself to sleep.

The way he fidgeted the next evening, before this Harvey Harris arrived, you'd think he was expecting somebody really important. You'd think a famous celebrity was coming, or an important client, instead of a nebbish little soap salesman from Nowhere, Ohio.

The first sight of Harvey Harris was a surprise. Whatever Dan may have been expecting, he certainly didn't expect a man in his thirties, a man at least twelve years older than Bobby was. He was tall and round-shouldered, with a long face and square rimless eye-glasses and a sort of fishy white complexion. When Bobby rushed up to him in the living-room archway, he patted her hand a little, and looked down at her with a thin smile, and said, "How are you this evening, Barbara? And right away, there was something about the way he said it. It was almost like a teacher giving a lesson to one of his pupils. It was almost as if—not in so many words, but strictly through the formal dignified tone of his voice—he was criticizing Bobby for showing how glad she was so see him.

And it made Dan wince a little, to see how Bobby herself seemed to get the point. She blushed, and then right away she made her face serious and dignified too. And as she introduced her guest around the room, Dan couldn't miss the nervous, uncertain looks that she kept stealing at him, to see if she was doing all right and if he approved of her manners.

But now this Harvey Harris was standing right in front of Dan, holding out his hand. "How are you, Mr. Waxman? I've been looking forward to meeting you. Barbara has told me so much about you."

Dan gave a grunt—the restrained, slightly sour grunt that he reserved for people who told him how much they'd been "looking forward" to meeting him. Then this Harvey Harris began to shake his hand—that is, he touched Dan's fingers, and applied a sort of flabby pressure, and pulled his hand away again leaving a wet clammy feeling behind.

As secretly as possible, Dan reached into his pocket and wiped his fingers on his handkerchief. Then he put on a smile, and tried to be hearty. "So how about a drink?" he said. "Scotch, rye, Canadian Club—a little sherry maybe? We've got a complete selection here at the Waxman Bar."

"No thank you, Mr. Waxman," Harvey Harris said, smiling his thin smile, and shaking his head. "The truth is, I never drink, except when business requires it of me. I believe in keeping my mind clear."

"Harvey says that he went through that stage when he was a boy in high school," Bobby put in, that same look of admiration in her eyes. "Now he's grown out of it."

Dan laughed a little uneasily. "Well, as one who hasn't grown out of it yet—you don't mind, I hope, if I——" He cut himself short and hurried over to the liquor cabinet.

"By all means, Mr. Waxman," said Harvey Harris. "I certainly don't mean to impose my own little ways of doing things on anybody else. I believe in tolerance and broadmindedness, if I believe in anything." Then he cleared his throat and added, "Besides, Barbara and I really must be going along."

"Are you sure you wouldn't like to stay for dinner?" Sarah said. "We've really got plenty."

"No, no, thank you so much, Mrs. Waxman," Harvey Harris said, once again shaking his head. "We have our plans all made."

"You wouldn't be interfering with anything," Sarah said. "Mr. Waxman and I were just going to spend a quiet evening at home. We could all have a game of bridge."

"Very kind of you, Mrs. Waxman. But unfortunately, you see, I don't play bridge."

"Okay, what about it?" Dan said, turning from the liquor cabinet and pushing into the conversation. "We could teach you how. A smart fellow like you should catch on in no time."

"Perhaps. No doubt." Harvey Harris pursed his lips together, and seemed to be smiling at some sort of private little joke. "But the truth is, I've never acquired the taste for playing cards. I was a poor boy, as Barbara may have told you, Mr. Waxman, and I've had to work very hard all my life, I never had time to play games, like people who were born with silver spoons in their mouths."

Bobby was looking at him all through this speech. And her eyes were sparkling. With pride and admiration they were sparkling. Dan could see it, and it made his stomach feel funny. "Harvey is a self-made man," Bobby said, still not taking her eyes from him. "He never had any of the advantages. He's worked himself up from the bottom."

"Well, I admire that," Dan said. "I'm a self-made man myself. Only it seems to me, a young fellow could enjoy himself too——"

Harvey Harris gave a laugh—another one of those satisfied school-teacher laughs. "When I get to be your age, Mr. Waxman," he said, "I'll be able to *afford* to enjoy myself." Then without waiting for Dan to answer him, he turned to Bobby; "It's really getting very late, Barbara. I'm not sure they'll hold our reservations. And I don't want to make a bad impression, because I take so many buyers to eat there."

"Yes, of course, Harvey," Bobby said, and she looked terribly concerned and worried for a moment.

Then Harvey Harris said goodnight, and how pleased he was to meet them, and how pleased he would be to see them again—and Dan got another handful of moisture. And then Bobby kissed him quickly on the cheek and said "Goodbye, Daddy." And obviously her mind was a thousand miles away. And so, the young couple was gone.

Dan did a lot of talking about them after they left. The fact is, he hardly talked about anything else for the rest of the night.

"What does she see in him?" he kept saying. "I don't get it, I just don't get it. A young, healthy, lively girl like Bobby—how can she go out with a fellow like that? He's old. He's a regular old man."

"He's only thirty-two, Dan," Sarah said. "Twelve years difference isn't so much nowadays. Look at my sister Nellie."

"*You* look at your sister Nellie. I'm not talking about years—years is bad enough, God knows, but I'm talking about the way he acts. The way he talks. The kind of fellow he is. Old! Like he hasn't been a young man for years and years."

"Well"—Sarah wavered a little, different feelings struggling with one another on her face—"at least he's mature and steady. That's a great deal in this world."

"Mature and steady. How many girls do I know, lively good-natured girls like Bobby, who got married to those mature steady old men, those mature steady *cold fish*—and look what happened to them, look what they got turned into in a few years. You remember my Cousin Wolfie, the kind of life he led my Cousin Martha? And Eli Glatz, with that nasty wife of his. And my own brother—my own brother Herman, God forgive me for saying it—look what poor little Doris was like before he married her, and look what she was like the day she died."

"You're exaggerating," Sarah said, with a little laugh. "There isn't going to be any marrying. She's only going out with the boy."

"There better not be!" Dan cried, with a sweep of his arm. "Marry that stuffed-shirt! I'd just like to see her try it—I'd come down on *that* so hard that they wouldn't know what hit them. Self-made man, is he? All my life I've had an admiration for self-made men—all my life I've been proud of the fact that I myself am a self-made man. And now, after two minutes of listening to that stuffed-shirt, I think I'd prefer it if she brought home a lazy good-for-nothing who wanted to live off my money."

And later in the evening, when it looked as if the subject had been dropped, he suddenly burst out with it again: "She's too good-natured. She's too kind-hearted. I always said it, didn't I? I always warned her, didn't I?

'Don't be such a good schnook all the time,' I said. 'It'll get you in trouble some day,' I said. And now it's happened, just like I said. This slimy little snake comes along, and gives her a story about what a poor boy he was and he never had the advantages and he's too hard-working to enjoy a decent healthy normal game of cards —and she falls for it hook, line, and sinker, she's all choked up and thinking what a wonderful fellow he is, and how superior he is to all the other poor dopes—and he's got her in the palm of his hand! My poor kind-hearted baby, she's an unhappy woman for life."

"Dan, it's not so serious," Sarah tries to tell him. "Don't worry so much, don't worry——" But her words just floated off in the air, and he went right on worrying.

He wanted to wait up again until Bobby came home, but Sarah convinced him he shouldn't. "It's nothing now," she told him. "There's nothing to it at all. But if you keep on waiting up, and pumping her with questions, and letting her know you're upset, then you never can tell, she might start thinking seriously, you might push her right into his arms."

Grudgingly Dan agreed, and he went up to the bed-room when Sarah did. But he couldn't fall asleep that night, he tossed and turned until he finally heard the sound of the front door downstairs. Then he sat up in bed and switched on the light and spoke up, "I'm going down. I want to talk to her." But Sarah sat up too, and reached out and put her hand on his arm. "Please, Dan," she said, "Please don't be foolish." He glared down at her hand for a moment, then without a word he switched off the light and lay back on his pillow. And he had to grit his teeth a little to keep himself still.

And then, the next morning, just before she dashed out for a luncheon date with one of her girl-friends,

Bobby announced that Harvey Harris was picking her up for dinner again to-night.

It was so upsetting to Dan that he didn't even go to the club for his Saturday afternoon pinochle game.

"The third time in a row," he said. "Every night of her vacation—every single night—and she spends them all with *him*. So it isn't serious, is it? So it'll all blow over, will it? Tell me that again. Tell me that it isn't serious."

He put on a scornful belligerent expression, as if he was challenging her to speak any such foolishness to him —and yet, underneath, he wanted the foolishness, he was waiting anxiously to hear it from her, he was depending on her for that soft easy tone of reassurance.

The reassurance didn't come. She lowered her eyes, and murmured quickly, "I don't know, Dan. I still don't think—I just don't know."

He grunted and buried himself behind the afternoon newspaper.

Harvey Harris came for Bobby on the dot. It was just like the night before—the same way of patting her hand, the same thin smile, the same wet handshake. And along with all this, there was a little laugh and an apology "for spiriting Barbara away from her home like this". But the reason, he explained, was "a most important one". "Mother is in town," he explained. "She's here for the annual convention of International Elocution Teachers. You know, that's how Mother got along and supported the family before my brother and I could work—before the age of fourteen, that is. She gave elocution lessons to wealthy children in Beewick. Now, of course, it isn't necessary for her to do so, but she still likes to keep active."

"Your mother sounds like a remarkable woman," said Sarah.

"She *is* remarkable," said Harvey Harris. "Naturally I'm very anxious for her to meet Barbara."

The words were on Dan's lips—"Why so anxious? Why so naturally?" But he didn't say them. There was a dryness in his throat, and he let the moment pass.

And then Bobby and Harvey Harris left for the evening, and he was alone with Sarah.

It was funny, how they stayed away from the subject. Without a word ahead of time, they both seemed to agree on this, and they talked of other things. Through dinner they talked about the food. After dinner they turned on the radio. They listened to Rudy Vallee, and they laughed at the jokes, and then they stopped laughing, they lowered their eyes, they gave themselves up to their own thoughts without any more pretending.

And then, when it was time for bed, Dan gave a sigh and a shake of his head. "I'll wait for her," he said. "She's taking such an early train to-morrow. It may be the last chance to talk to her."

And Sarah nodded just as easily and unprotestingly as if they had discussed this move in detail. "Yes, you'd better," she said. And after a moment, "She's always listened to you. She has a great respect for your opinion."

Then she got to her feet slowly, a little wearily. She made her usual round of the ashtrays, and ended up by kissing Dan goodnight. And for just a moment longer than usual she kept her hand in his. "I'll be waiting upstairs," she said. "I won't sleep."

When she was gone, Dan sank back into his easy-chair. The light was suddenly hard on his eyes. He switched it off, and sat back in the darkness, smoking his cigar, thinking about the past. "Sarah," says a voice—his own voice, sort of weak and faded, from a long, long distance —"what are we bringing up in this household, a little girl or a wild Indian?" "A wild Indian!" comes the answer in a shout—a shout as soft and delicate as the tinkle of a little bell. And there she is for a moment, dancing and prancing before his eyes. And there she is a moment later, stretched out on the floor, and her chin is in her hand and the Sunday comics are spread out in front of her——

"Daddy, you're not still up?"

The light blared out at him. He looked up and blinked, and for a moment it was a terrible shock, what he saw. It wasn't a little girl at all. It was a grown-up young woman, tall and good-looking, dressed in the newest fashion, with high heels on her shoes and lipstick on her face. And the only trace of that lively little girl was the spark of pleasure that was glowing out of her eyes.

"I didn't hear you come in," he said, still blinking and confused.

"You must've fallen asleep," she said. "Why did you do it, darling? Waiting up for me like that. You don't have to worry about me, as if I was a baby."

Why did he do it? It rushed back on him now, the great worry that was on his mind. He shook his head to get rid of the confusion. A heavy responsibility was ahead of him, and his senses had to be clear.

"Listen baby," he said. "Sit down, will you."

"Yes, Daddy." She laughed and perched herself on the edge of the sofa. Her cheeks were flushed. More so than usual—Dan couldn't help noticing it. It was happiness that caused it—he couldn't help noticing that too. Then he got hold of himself and pushed away stray thoughts.

"Let's have a little talk," he said. "It's a long time since we had one of our little talks."

"I know it, I know it," she said. "Poor Daddy, I've been neglecting you terribly, haven't I? Up at college, and going out all the time, and all. You make me feel so guilty."

"Guilty." He laughed, quick and a little nervous. "I don't want you to feel guilty. God knows, that's the last thing I want you to feel. It's your happiness that I want, baby. You know that, don't you?"

"You're the sweetest father in the world. You've spoiled me terribly."

"Spoiled you? Have I? I never thought about it. Maybe because I've been spoiling myself at the same time. But that's not the point," he went on hurriedly, "That's not what I want to talk about." He stuck out his jaw. Now is the moment, he told himself. Firm and courageous. Firm and courageous. After this, it'll be too late.

"It *is* the point, darling," she said, leaning forward suddenly and giving one of her brightest smiles. "You've always looked out for my happiness, and you've succeeded. I *have* been happy. I don't think a girl could ask to be happier. That is, I've been miserable too——"

"You've been miserable?" he put in quickly.

"Like all girls my age," she said, laughing. "A girl wouldn't be satisfied if she wasn't miserable every once in a while. And you know, I think that some men are like that too." She laughed again, then her face softened, and her smile grew gentler and more serious. "But now even *that* is all over. Now I won't ever be miserable any more. Because of what's ahead of me, Daddy. The biggest happiness of all. I can't really talk about it yet— it's not absolutely and completely settled—but it's coming any day now."

"It's coming?" Dan said. "Something is coming?"

Bobby got to her feet and moved up to him. "Let's not talk about it, Daddy. We'll talk about it later— pretty soon we won't be talking about anything else."

229

And she put her arms around him and kissed him, almost as affectionately and contentedly as she used to do when she was just a little girl.

The touch of her lips against his cheek made Dan weak. It set his knees to wobbling. Pull yourself together, he kept telling himself. But even as he told himself, he knew it was useless.

He returned her kiss softly, and a vague little smile came over his face. "All right, we won't talk," he said. "Whatever it is, baby—is it right for you? Then it's right for your mother and me."

They separated a few minutes later. And Dan went to his room and to Sarah. She was lying back on her pillow, and the light cast heavy shadows across her face. But her eyes were very wide, staring and anxious. Dan walked up to the bed without a word, looked at her, then turned away and started to undress for the night. It wasn't till he was in his own bed, and the lights were out, that he spoke up sharply, with sudden fierceness.

"All right, it's her life," he said. "She's old enough to make her own decisions."

And a silence came over the two of them, dark and heavy and oppressive. It was a long time before either of them could get to sleep.

V

Bobby got married to Harvey Harris in June.

Dan threw all his energy into the wedding and the reception that followed it. He was determined to make this the biggest, fanciest, most expensive party he had ever given. "How often does your only daughter get married?" he declared to everybody he came in contact with—and invited them to the wedding. In the end he had a guest list of over a hundred people, not including wives and visiting relations. To hold all these people he hired two big adjoining ballrooms in the Gloucester Arms on Central Park South. And he ordered crates and crates of the most expensive champagne from Paris, France. And he hired the swankiest caterers in town, a firm whose merest chopped liver *canapé* would cost a fortune. And he took his prospective son-in-law on shopping expeditions for suits and ties, he gave advice about the wedding-ring, he interviewed three leading rabbis personally until he found the one who could "put on the best show". He even had his fingers in various pies that are generally considered the exclusive business of the women—such as looking over Bobby's trousseau, and nodding his approval or screwing up his nose in disgust.

In short, he wasn't still for a minute. Rushing from one appointment to another, going over the bills as they poured in, throwing cocktail parties and interviewing help and yelling at various organizations over the phone, he kept himself busier than twenty men twice his size. He didn't give himself a moment for thinking.

And then, all of a sudden, it was on him, the day of Bobby's marriage. There was confusion at the temple, there was hysteria among the ushers, there was crying from the guests. Then he joined up with Bobby in the outer lobby, and was able to get just a quick sense of how she looked in her wedding-dress—and then they were marching down the aisle together. And for a while everything seemed to be suspended in air, his furious activity came to a sudden stop, like a long gasp for breath—and then it was all over, and the crowd surged out of the temple and downtown to the hotel, and Dan grew wilder and more active than ever.

To this day there are people who remember him at that wedding reception. They remember how fantastically happy he acted, how he drank and he laughed, how he ran from group to group slapping backs, telling jokes, putting his two cents into the conversation. He was everywhere, and he was nowhere—everybody saw him, everybody got a word from him, but nobody could pin him down.

And it all reached its climax with the toast, that wonderful elaborate toast that he delivered at the end of the party, full of compliments to the groom and hilarious memories about the bride, and ending up with his greatest feat of the evening, draining down a whole glass of champagne in one uninterrupted gulp with his mouth full of chopped liver.

A few minutes later Bobby sneaked off to a room in the hotel, and appeared again in her ordinary dress, and went from relative to relative to say goodbye. And Sarah hugged her and kissed her, and suddenly burst out into such dreadful sobs that she had to be led out of the room and everybody was embarrassed.

And then it was Dan's turn. He grabbed Bobby around the waist, he cried out "My married daughter!", he launched into a speech which he broke off after three words. "Little confused," he said. "Little too much to drink." Then he laughed in a friendly, stupid way just to prove the point.

Bobby gave him a funny, sharp look for just a moment, but Harvey was pulling at her sleeve. So she turned away from Dan, and a few minutes later the young couple had sneaked out a side door. They were on their way to Mexico City for their honeymoon—by way of Milwaukee, where Harvey had business.

The party was over now really. The guests were finishing up their drinks and hurrying out to their dinner appointments. But Dan just filled up his glass again, and then filled it up some more, and his laughter got so loud that Harvey's mother—a sharp-faced grey-haired little lady with a terribly refined voice—gave him some hard looks. But Dan laughed at that too, and he asked Mrs. Harris to join him in the polka—and he would have insisted, in spite of her hard looks, only he suddenly began to feel sick.

The next day he had bleary eyes and a pounding head, and a temper that made Sarah and the cook and everyone else around his household walk on tiptoe. He was through with breakfast at noon. He called up Herman, he called up his travel agent, he located his lawyer in the middle of a golf game. To each of them in turn, in a voice that didn't allow for contradiction or argument, he announced his decision. He had plenty of money saved up, and his Government bonds were bringing in nice dividends, and one of his old insurance policies was just begining to pay annuities now that he had turned fifty. So it was his intention to give up his accounting business, to sublet his office, to sell his furniture, to get rid of his car, and to set off for an indefinite length of time on a trip.

"It's crazy," Herman said. "Where do you think you're going to go?"

"Where? I don't know where. Away from New York. Away from this crazy business world, and running to the office every day like my life depended on it. I'm going to relax a little. I'm going to enjoy myself. Who knows, I might even improve my mind and get acquainted with the finer things of life. Some place like Europe. That's it exactly. I'm going to Europe, where people know how to live the right way and everybody isn't always thinking about money. I'm going to Europe, and I'm not so sure that I'll *ever* come back!"

Almost the last person that he told about this decision was Sarah. When he finally got around to barking it out at her, she didn't raise a word of objection. She lowered her head a little and murmured softly, "Yes, Dan. I'll start to pack our things."

Their passports came through at the end of June, and they reserved a first-class cabin on an English ship. On the fourth of July, late at night, Herman drove them down to the ship, and the three of them drank a token glass of champagne in the cabin. Then Herman went back to the privacy of his bachelor apartment, and Dan and Sarah slipped out of the country.

VI

When he said that he was going on a trip for an in-definite length of time, my Uncle Dan couldn't have guessed how terribly long that "indefinite length" would be. Europe was only the beginning. Europe was only the prelude to a life that was going to last Dan and Sarah for over nine years, a life of packing bags and running for trains, of restaurant food and hotel towels and railroad station waiting-rooms.

First there was London. Dan was energetically determined to like it. So he prepared himself all through the boat trip by praising everything about London, especially its faults, to the skies. "Now take the fog," he said. "Why do you think those Englishmen are so rough and ready? Because they're born and brought up in that fog, it toughens them up, it makes men out of them." Dan made this speech so many times that it was a little bit of shock, when he got to London, to find that there wasn't any fog at all. It was sunny and warm, with a nice light breeze just to make it comfortable. "Well, here's one piece of good luck," Sarah said. "We won't have to be so rough and ready after all." "That's not so funny," Dan snapped at her.

He was full of praises also for "the typical English character"—anyway, for his idea of it. "Unemotional and reserved," he explained to Sarah beforehand. "It takes a screwdriver to pry any conversation out of them. Especially with Americans. Don't expect a bunch of noisy blabbermouths, like you get in America." And here too he got a surprise.

It was just as if the English Government was out to contradict him deliberately, because from the first moment he set foot in Southampton he was besieged by talkative Englishmen. There was a tall, eager-looking man with black-rimmed glasses who insisted on directing him through the customs—and told him all about his impressions of American university life at the same time. There was a dumpy little woman on the boat-train who struck up a conversation without being asked—she described herself as "a cheerful spinster" and spent the whole trip showing Dan and Sarah pictures of her nieces and nephews. "My God," Dan whispered to Sarah once, "in her family they must multiply like rabbits." And it was the same thing once they got settled in their hotel—talkative desk clerks, talkative waiters, talkative bellboys, buck-teethed ladies who approached them with big smiles in the lobby and cried out, "Welcome to England! You'll find us plain and simple, but we've got our sense of humour!"

"It's because we're strangers," Dan muttered. "When they know us better, they won't talk to us so much."

Herman had given Dan a list of business people to look up—and when he looked them up, another one of his favourite illusions was shaken. This was his illusion about the leisurely, impractical business methods of the English. "Business, to these Englishmen, is practically a sideline," he said. "Most of the time they're out fox-hunting, and going to cricket games, and strolling through the park with their top hats and their monocles, and occasionally they pop into the office just to cash a cheque. That's why Americans are so much richer than Englishmen, and Englishmen are so much happier and more relaxed than Americans."

But the first luncheon Dan had, with a group of English jewellery men, everything turned out exactly upside down. First of all these men were about as un-leisurely and unrelaxed as anybody Dan had ever known. They gulped their food, kept looking at their watches all through the meal, talked in short nervous spurts, and took pills for their stomach trouble. Even before they were finished with their dessert, they pushed away from the table, shook hands quickly all around, and dashed back to their offices. And second of all, they were a lot richer than most of the business-men Dan knew. The way they tossed their money around, and spoke off-handedly about their town houses and their country houses, and sported big diamond rings and imported silk shirts and tailor-made gloves—well, it was a big surprise to Dan. But not really an unpleasant one. After a week in London, he actually began to sort of like it. The people talked his own language—well, approximately his own language. The hotel was clean, and the plumbing was up-to-date. The shows were good, and it was easy to get around. The only big drawback was the food but Dan hadn't been such a big eater in the last few years, anyway. Best of all, he found that Herman's business contacts, in spite of their rush and their money, were willing to be fairly friendly. He and Sarah even got a couple of week-end invitations for the month of

August. So he started talking about moving out of the hotel and renting a flat for the year.

"It wouldn't be a bad city to live in," Dan said. "We'd have a nice set of friends in no time. Nice people, not a bunch of flashy New York show-offs. And we wouldn't have to keep running around all the time, that's the big advantage. Here in London people lead a quiet life, you're not expected to wear yourself out at parties and theatres and so on, it's no disgrace to spend a quiet evening at home. And the women seem pretty nice too, don't they? Always smiling and polite—you've got some good friends already, haven't you, Sarah?"

"Yes," Sarah said, lowering her eyes.

"Nice Jewish people at that," Dan said. "Of course it's a nuisance that the only temples are strict orthodox—but who cares about that, with all the other assets? I tell you what, we'll think it over. We'll stay here for a month or so, till the end of the summer maybe. And if we like it enough, we'll look around for a permanent place."

Making this speech, warming up to his sales talk, Dan succeeded in convincing himself more strongly all the time. He went around for a week in a nice rosy glow, telling himself that London was definitely the answer to his problems, in London a man could really *live*.

Then, one night early in August, during the intermission at a play, a voice called out to them across the lobby. "Dan Waxman! And Sarah! Well, who would believe it?"

And a moment later this couple—this thin little man with a toothbrush moustache and sad eyes, and this sharp-faced, bright-eyed little woman—came rushing up to them and started pumping their hands up and down. That is, the woman pumped and the man just sort of smiled vaguely from the sidelines.

For a couple of seconds Dan couldn't place them—and then he remembered. Their name was Rosen—Arthur Rosen, and his wife Selma—and they used to live in Chicago, and this Rosen worked for the Chase National Bank. And then, sure enough, it all came back to Dan—around ten years ago, this Rosen was sent to London to take some job with the English branch of the bank, and a big farewell party was given for them. It was two or three years, Dan remembered, before he and Sarah left Chicago themselves. And right away, the usual question flashed through Dan's mind; Did these Rosens know about it, what had happened in Chicago, the Drexell business and all? And right away, with a little grunt, he gave himself the usual answer: How could they help but know about it? It was common gossip to the whole world.

"Dan and Sarah Waxman," this Rosen woman was saying. "Good Heavens, it's like seeing ghosts. Just like a couple of ghosts rising up out of the past. Isn't that a fact, Arthur?"

Mr. Rosen nodded and murmured something.

"Well, good Heavens, what brings *you* to dear old London?" Mrs. Rosen went on. "How long have you been here? Why didn't you look us up? We could show you all the sights, and introduce you to all the people— Arthur and I have been here so long now, we're practically Englishmen ourselves. That's jolly well so, isn't it, Arthur?"

Mr. Rosen mumbled.

Mrs. Rosen laughed. "You see what I mean? You couldn't tell Arthur's accent from the genuine English variety. Oh, there's the bell, and we haven't had a chance to talk at all—meet us afterwards, we'll have supper together—Arthur and I know the quaintest little place, all the real Englishmen go there—we'll have a wonderful gabfest, all about old times." And she was so insistent and talked so fast that the date was made before Sarah or Dan could catch their breath.

Back in their seats during the next act, Dan muttered about it to Sarah. "What'd you want to go out with *them* for?"

"There wasn't much I could do about it, dear. It won't be so bad. Selma was always a good-natured sort."

Dan clamped his lips shut, but his mind kept working. She better not say anything, he thought. She just better not make any cracks.

After the show they all met in the lobby again, and the Rosens whisked Dan and Sarah off to their "quaint little place". It turned out to be a Chinese restaurant in a dark, dismal street off the theatre section. One of the letters on the front marquee was broken, the waiters were short fat Chinese men who had to ask for the orders three times over and *still* got them mixed up, the food was very greasy and full of rice—in other words, it was exactly like any Chinese restaurant anywhere in New York or Chicago.

The restaurant was completely empty, except for the four of them and the waiters, so Mrs. Rosen's voice carried loudly as she repeated what a "wonderful little find" this was. Then she leaned forward, her eyes grew brighter, and she said, "Well now, let's get down to the business of the meeting. What *are* you doing here in London? What brings you such a long distance from the good old U.S.A.?"

Dan tightened up immediately. Right from the start he didn't like her tone. He was positive she was fishing for information. And Dan hated people who fished at him.

"We're just sort of travelling around," Sarah said. "It's our first trip."

"Your first trip! How wonderful for you. What a marvellous experience you have in store for you. Just like a couple of honeymooners. I always say, when you see Europe for the first time, it's just like going on another honeymoon. Do you remember *our* first time, Arthur?" And she sighed deeply.

Mr. Rosen gave his feeblest smile yet.

Then Mrs. Rosen was leaning forward again. "But isn't this a rather unusual decision for you to make? I mean, I never really thought of the two of you as the travelling kind. You were always such home bodies. That is, you always seemed to be so perfectly at home when you were—at home, so to speak."

Dan clenched his fists under the table, and peered at this Rosen woman hard. What she just said, was there some sort of a dirty dig hidden underneath it? Was she trying to be funny at his expense or something?"

"Well, we decided we'd waited long enough," Sarah said quickly—and Dan could see that the woman's remarks were getting her nervous too. "You know, people can change over the years."

"Yes, of course," said Mrs. Rosen, with another sigh. "You certainly hit the nail on the head. People do have a way of changing. And I suppose you two have changed a lot since the old days."

There was definitely a smirk on her face—Dan could definitely see it there. And he wasn't able to keep his mouth shut any longer. "Now just what do you mean by that?" he said.

"Dan, dear," Sarah murmured.

Mrs. Rosen was blinking at him. "Excuse me? What do I mean by what?"

"That last remark, about the way we've changed? What does it mean?"

"What does it mean? Why—I don't know what you're

—all I meant was, things must be very different for you since the last time we met."

"Different?" Dan's voice grew louder. "How do you mean, different? Why should anything be different?"

"Why? I don't know why. I just assumed——" Mrs. Rosen gave a puzzled look at Sarah, then turned back to Dan with a high nervous laugh. "Good Heavens, I was only inquiring about the old days in Chicago. You act as if you didn't *want* to talk about Chicago."

There it was. There was the straw that broke the camel. Dan got a quick glimpse of the agonized look spreading over Sarah's face, then he let go with his loudest snort. "You'd like that, wouldn't you? You'd like it for me to talk about Chicago. That's what you're poking and prying around for. That's why you finagled this little supper to-night."

"Finagled?" Mrs. Rosen's eyelids fluttered very fast. "What are you talking about? What's happened to him?"

"It's nothing," Sarah said, "it's a sort of spell——"

"A spell!" Dan lifted his arms in the air. "I'll show you what kind of a spell it is. I'll show you I won't stand for it, being poked at and pried at, and turned into a regular guinea-pig, so she can give a thrill to her dear old friends back home." He pushed back his chair and stamped to his feet. "Come on, Sarah, we're getting out of here. We don't sit here another minute. We don't let them insult us another minute."

"But who insulted you?" cried Mrs. Rosen. "What's it all about?"

"What's it all about? Very funny. She pretends she doesn't know what it's all about. She pretends she isn't absolutely full to the brim with what happened in Chicago. She pretends that wasn't her special reason for looking us up, and following us around the city, and bumping into us 'accidentally' in the theatre."

"*What* happened in Chicago?" Mrs. Rosen's eyes were bulging now—and it would have been hard to tell which emotion was strongest in her, horror at the way Dan was behaving or curiosity about what happened in Chicago.

"You have the nerve to ask?" Dan shouted. His arm shot out, and he pointed his finger accusingly at Mrs. Rosen. "Hypocrite! Liar! Putting on that phoney English act, and all the time pumping me for malicious gossip!"

"Phoney English act!" Mrs. Rosen stuck out her jaw, quivering with outraged dignity. "Arthur, what's the matter with you? Are you going to let him talk to me like that?"

Mr. Rosen half got to his feet, and put on a faint apologetic smile, and opened his mouth.

"Don't get belligerent, Rosen," Dan turned on him sharply, "otherwise I won't answer for myself." Then he grabbed Sarah by the arm. "Come on, we're getting out of here."

Sarah hung back a moment, stammering at the Rosens, "Selma, I'm sorry—Arthur, I'm sorry—wonderful to see you again——"

"Sarah! Come on!"

"It's a lovely little place——" That was all Sarah had time to say before Dan practically dragged her out of the restaurant.

They walked back to the hotel. It was a full mile, and the streets were crowded, but they walked just the same. Dan had to keep moving to get rid of the excess steam, to work the irritation out of his system. It was all gone when they finally got back to their room. Dan was tired out, and deep in another one of those moods when he hardly dared to look Sarah in the face. So he kept himself busy—he ordered sandwiches and whisky, he pulled off his tie and unbuttoned his collar, he paced the room restlessly, he overtipped the waiter and splashed out a highball for himself, and drained it off very quick. Now, at last, he was ready to make the effort. He forced himself to turn to Sarah and meet her gaze directly. And seeing that she was just sort of quietly waiting for his words, he grew more confident, he laughed, he went up to her and put his arm around her.

"I've been thinking," he said. "It's a pretty dull city, this London. Maybe, before we commit ourselves to it positively, we ought to travel around and look over some of the others. I mean, I could call up the desk right now and get reservations for Paris in the morning. Now frankly, how does that sound to you?"

"It sounds just fine, Dan."

"Sure it does." Dan let go of her, gave a laugh, and rubbed his hands together. "My God, we're not exactly nobodies, are we? We don't have to swallow down the first city they dish up to us. We can afford to take our pick."

So they went to Paris the next day. Paris was hot and sticky, and the gardens were beautiful. Dan suddenly became a tremendous sightseer. He was on the move every minute, visiting every famous building he'd ever heard of, marching conscientiously through hall after hall in the Louvre, eating in a different restaurant every meal, taking all the walks and buying all the souvenirs and attending all the performances that were recommended in the guide-book. He even picked up a few French phrases, and got a certain pleasure out of ringing them out with an offhand flourish *"L'addition, s'il vous plaît!" "Comment ça va, m'sieur?" "Donnez-moi à boire!" "Où est l'American Express?"* And then, after two weeks in Paris, it all began to get a little tiring. The march through the Louvre began to wear on his feet. He found that he had eaten just one snail too many. *"L'addition, s'il vous plaît"* suddenly sounded pretty damn silly coming out of his mouth.

A week later, getting back to the hotel late at night, Dan caught his cab-driver trying to short-change him. When he pointed this out in a quiet but firm voice, the cab-driver got very indignant, and began to wave his arms and shout. It was all Dan needed. His neck got red, and he waved his arms and shouted right back. He reeled off a stream of curses and insults and opinions on French culture that made the cab-driver gasp, in spite of the fact that he couldn't understand a word of English. Finally Dan grabbed the disputed fifty-franc note right out of the cab-driver's hand, brandished it under his nose for a while, then crumpled it up and threw it with all his might to the sidewalk. Then, while the cab-driver scrambled for the note, Dan swept up the steps and into the hotel and right up to the desk, and boomed out in a voice that everybody in the lobby could hear "I'm checking out of this dump. Get my bill ready for me by morning. We're getting away from this den of thieves just as fast as we can."

So the next day they took a train to Italy. The ride was boring for a while, and then, when the scenery stopped being French and started being Italian, Dan's spirits brightened up. "Look at it, look at it," he said, pointing out the window. "Look at those soft rolling hills. Look at that green grass. Look at those little houses. Look at those cows. Now this is a country that *is* a country. This is the place to be. Nice, pleasant, easy-going people. A little bit soft-hearted and impractical maybe. A little bit of a tendency to loaf around all day and play their accordions. But that's better than a lot of sharp confidence men, disguised as cab-drivers."

They went to Rome, where Dan was in raptures for the

244

whole month of September. He looked up some of Herman's business contacts, especially one sweet old Italian business-man with white hair and a little fat wife. They were friendly, and suave, and charming, and they gave Dan and Sarah more hospitality than they had ever received in their lives. Under the direction of Signor and Signora D'Antoni, Dan and Sarah took the prettiest walks through the cities, visited the churches when the tourists weren't there, sat at the most restful cafés sipping the most refreshing drinks. What's more, they discovered that Signor and Signora D'Antoni played wonderful bridge, and that there was an Italian card game which bore a strong resemblance to pinochle.

And then, one night in the last week of September, they went to the opera, which was presented outdoors against the background of one of the ancient Roman ruins. It was *Trovatore*, and Dan was having a wonderful blood-and-thunder time for the first three acts. And then, in the fourth act, when everything suddenly grew calmer and sadder, Dan began to feel this twinge inside of him, this funny pang close to his heart. It was something physical, that's what he thought at first. That piece of veal during dinner, maybe. And then he realized that it wasn't physical at all. The stage lights grew dim, and the music swelled up, and the soprano began to die. And slowly, a little unbelievingly, Dan realized that his eyes were wet, that in another moment tears were in danger of running down his cheeks. He felt Sarah's hand on his own—he brushed it away quickly. With a gulp he got hold of himself again.

The next morning, over breakfast, he cleared his throat and announced, very stiff and businesslike, "You know, I've been thinking, maybe we've had enough of Rome. Maybe we've had enough of this whole Italian atmosphere. It's pretty, all right. It's stimulating, definitely. Maybe it's *too* pretty and stimulating. It gets under a man's skin. It takes the energy and the ambition out of him, and fills him up with wild ideas. Like opium, if you know what I mean. Maybe we ought to go some place that's a little more up-to-date, and businesslike, and —and a colder climate, if you know what I mean. Anyway, I've made up my mind——"

So they said their goodbyes to Signor and Signora D'Antoni, and at the end of the week, which was also the end of the month of September, they set out for Switzerland. They didn't go to any of the big cities, though. Dan was sick of big cities. That's where all his troubles came from, he said. Big cities breed big problems, and big head-aches, and big doctors' bills. What he needed was to get out in the country, out close to nature, with only the sky and the flowers, and fresh air going through his lungs, and a fresh outlook on life. So he and Sarah went to a small resort in the mountains near Geneva —the place had been recommended to them by an old English couple they met in Rome—and they settled down to enjoy the blessings of quiet and solitude.

Dan wasn't there two hours before he knew he was going to be bored to death. But that's just what he wanted. He wanted to sit back and close his eyes and sink into boredom, a kind of thick soft boredom that would fold over him and nestle under him and float him through the days and the nights. "Why not spend the whole winter here?" he said to Sarah. "The climate's supposed to be pleasant all year round. They send tuberculosis patients here. Why not settle down here and clear some of the cobwebs out of our brains, and some of the butterflies out of our stomachs? Why not? I don't see why not." And he nodded and sighed, and shut his eyes and looked forward, a little tensely, to a whole future life with nothing to worry him, nothing to think about, nobody to get mad at and raise his voice to.

He actually got through a whole month like this. A whole month of waking up late in the morning, eating long heavy meals, snoozing on the sun-porch in between, playing cards at night with the same trio of slow plump German-Swiss business-men, retired—then, around midnight, lumbering off to bed and sinking into a dull, sodden sleep. And then, at the end of the month, a letter came from Bobby. It was long and chatty and full of Beewick, Ohio, like all her letters since she settled down there in July. Only, at the very end of it, she brought out her big news—she was going to have a baby, it was expected next April.

Dan and Sarah were so excited for the rest of the day that they hardly knew what they were doing. They jabbered their news to everybody else in the hotel. They wandered here and there with pleased, absent smiles on their faces. And then, when they were alone in their room that night, Sarah came out with the one thing that was on both their minds. "Let's go back to the States, Dan. Let's arrange to be with her when it happens. It's such an exciting time. And it only happens once in a girl's life—her first baby, I mean."

"Yes, we could do it," said Dan, nodding thoughtfully. "I could cable my man in New York, he'd arrange to have boat tickets waiting for us in Paris."

Sarah was flushed and happy, almost like the old days again. "A grandmother," she said. "I've always dreamed of it. Ever since I was a little girl."

"You dreamed of being a grandmother when you were a little girl?"

"Yes. I know it sounds silly. But I always thought I'd make such a *good* grandmother. Sweet, kindly old Grandma, you know what I mean?" She laughed, then suddenly reached out and took Dan's hand. "And you'll make a very distinguished Grandpa—did you know that, Dan dear?"

Dan smiled and murmured something modest. "Yes, absolutely, I'll send that cablegram in the morning."

But the mornings in Switzerland are brisk and clear. The light has a hardness and brightness that drives away wild notions and woolly daydreams.

"The cablegram, Dan?" Sarah said to him at breakfast.

Dan didn't look up from his coffee. "There isn't any point to it, Sarah," he said, sharp and abrupt. "Where are we going to do all this—this Grandpa and Grandma business? In Beewick, Ohio? With our darling son-in-law Harvey, maybe? With his charming old mother?"

Sarah didn't answer for a moment. Then, in a small voice, she said, "But, Dan——"

"No buts," he said. "We'll stay in Europe a little longer. We still aren't through with Europe."

So the cablegram they sent was a message of congratulations to Bobby and Harvey. They stayed in Switzerland a few days more, then they packed up and went down the mountain to Geneva, and took a train across France, and got on a boat and found themselves back in London.

"We didn't find what we wanted the first time," Dan said. "All right, we'll make the circle all over again. We'll do the whole tour a second time around. Who can tell, this time we might be in luck."

In the end, they made the tour three times around. The cold weather came, and they shivered in the London chill and complained about the bad Paris heating. Spring came, and they set off for the Italian Riviera—"Not so many American tourists as the French Riviera," Dan said.

And then, at the end of April, Dan suddenly threw up his hands and put a stop to the whole thing. What made him do it? He couldn't answer that himself. It was a warm sweaty afternoon, and he and Sarah were prowling around Notre Dame, wearily admiring the gargoyles, killing time before dinner. A little boy came running around the corner of the cathedral. He was just another little French boy, with very red cheeks and very pale eyes, a beret cocked on his head and a dark-blue cape flapping behind him. He was followed by an old nurse-maid, making little twitching motions and calling after him hopelessly.

With a loud excited whoop, the little boy ran headlong into Dan.

For a moment, Dan felt the wind knocked out of him. Then the blood rushed to his head, and his arm swung up violently. "You dirty little bast——" Then he stopped himself short.

Several things flashed before his eyes at once. The face of the little boy—wide frightened eyes, his mouth twisted in alarm. His own arm, poised over his head, his fist clenched, tightly clenched, ready for murder almost. Sarah by his side, the nursemaid at a distance, two old women staring at him in horror.

Dan turned away quickly, with a pang of shame. "My God, my God, he muttered all the way back to the hotel, what am I turning into? A madman, an animal, a beast in human form.

At dinner that night, he was calm and stiff, he seemed to be in control of himself. "It's this Europe that does it," he said. "Old and falling apart. Unhealthy. Dirty. It muddles up a man's brain. We have to get out of here. We have to go home again. Pretty soon it'll be too late."

Sarah reached across the table and touched his hand. "It'll be May when we get back," she said. "Everything is so lovely in May. We can go to some nice place for a vacation."

Dan looked at her. His face was still stiff and empty. His voice was soft. "What is there about me?" he said. "Isn't there any place at all for me in the whole damned world?"

Two days later they sailed for New York.

VII

On the ship going home, Dan slowly came to life again. The first night he shut himself up in the cabin, and wouldn't come out except for meals. But the next day, under the influence of the refreshing sea breeze and the restful luxurious atmosphere, the cabin didn't seem so attractive any more. He found that there were two enthusiastic bridge players at his dining-room table, and that accounted for the afternoon. And in the evening, he and Sarah went to the lounge and even put a few bets down on the horse races. The evening after that, he suggested to Sarah that it might be nice to go into the ballroom after dinner and maybe dance a little.

But it was really the following morning that the last trace of deadness passed from him. The first day out, looking over the passenger list, he and Sarah had noticed that they were sailing with none other than Mrs. Martin Drexell, Dan's great enemy from the old days. They tried their hardest to avoid her—they even made sure to put themselves in a different dinner sitting than she was in. Dan had never quite been able to forget his last conversation with her, in Drexell's mansion on the day of the big collapse. He remembered vividly the way she let herself go, and fell weeping into his arms, throwing away all her dignity and all her pride in front of a man she disliked. Now, with Drexell dead and all her former glory gone, Dan felt a little embarrassed about seeing her again—embarrassed not for himself but for her, because she could hardly help but be reminded of the circumstances of their last meeting.

And then, the morning of his fourth day aboard ship, he was taking a stroll along the deck while Sarah was at the hairdresser, and as he turned a corner he found himself face to face with Mrs. Drexell herself.

Right away Dan blushed, and tried to turn his eyes away, and gave that casual, confident little laugh which people always use for touchy situations. "Well—what a surprise," he said. "I had no idea——"

"Mr. Waxman, isn't it?" she said. "Are *you* on this boat?"

The coolness and steadiness of her tone made Dan look up at her in spite of himself. And he blinked at what he saw. No sign of dismay or nervousness in her, not the smallest spot of red in her cheeks, not even a vague shadow of the tearful, desperate woman who had thrown herself into his arms outside her husband's room. It was the old Mrs. Drexell who stood before him now—the tall, cool, beautifully-groomed woman, with a light fur wrap thrown over her shoulders and that high, polite, superior look in her eyes.

"Yes, I'm here," Dan said, still a little confused. "I was just in Europe—with my wife——"

"Oh, your wife." Mrs. Drexell's lip curled just slightly. "I remember her very well. Such a charming, simple little woman."

Dan shook the last of his confusion off. And something began to rise up in him, something of the old energy and competitive spirit. "You're looking good yourself, Mrs. Drexell," Dan said. "You gained weight since I saw you last."

"It won't be Mrs. Drexell any more in a few weeks, Mr. Waxman," she said, sailing smoothly over his last remark. "Lady Isaacson will be the name. I'm joining his Lordship in New York." Then, with an accommodating smile, she added, "That's English, you know. In England they have titles."

"Well, let me give you my sincerest congratulations," Dan said, "and I hope you'll be very happy. God knows, you deserve it—as I've been saying to myself ever since our last meeting."

Mrs. Drexell took this one without blinking. "Oh, yes, back in Chicago," she said. "I understand you don't live in Chicago any more, Mr. Waxman." And then, with a small but amiable nod, she excused herself and moved on down the deck.

Dan stood and looked after her until she had disappeared around another corner. A draw, he told himself. You definitely had to call it a draw! And then, to his own surprise, he shook his head and started chuckling. Waxman, you're not licked yet, he told himself. And with a brisker, more belligerent step, he continued his stroll.

By the time the ship reached New York he was so far recovered from his fit of lethargy that he was able to put up a bold, confident front for the family. When they asked him if he had come back because he was sick of Europe, he laughed and said, "Europe isn't the type of place you get sick of—but I'm an American, an American has to end up in America."

He expected Herman to be a little harder to deal with. The day after Dan's arrival in New York, Herman managed to invite him out for lunch, and look at him in his longest, solemnest way, and ask him, "What happens now? Europe seems to have been a failure. What are you going to do with yourself now?"

"Failure? Who said it was a failure? Europe was the most remarkable experience of my life. I got just what I wanted out of it. Did I ever say I was going to settle there permanently?"

"Well, we'll let that pass——" Herman said.

"No, we won't let that pass," Dan put in sharply. "And your second crack, we won't let that pass either. What am I going to do with myself now? Why am I suddenly somebody that has to 'do something' with himself? I'm a grown-up man, and I'll live like I please— in other words, without answering a lot of damn-fool questions."

Herman sighed softly. "I could never argue with you. I won't even try."

"Don't," Dan said. "We'll both be a lot happier."

So they faced each other across the table for a moment, the two brothers—Dan glaring, and Herman just watching, sort of sad and thoughtful. And something else on his face too, Dan noticed—a little pinch around his mouth, a tightness at the corner of his eyes. Like he was feeling a twinge of pain or something.

Dan worried about it for a second, then put it out of his mind in his unexpected pleasure that the victory over Herman had been so quick. He could even afford to be generous and admit a point. "Don't worry about me," he said. "Whatever I do, I'll be happy. Basically I'm a person who's easily satisfied."

He stayed in New York another week, seeing the family, saying "hello" to the boys at the club, catching up on the latest hit shows. And then, towards the end of May 1937, Dan and Sarah were on their way again.

VIII

DURING the next eight years, my Uncle Dan's restlessness was the talk of the family. That is, it was one of the hardy, indestructible staples of conversation, it was one of the things that his in-laws and his cousins and his nieces and nephews could always come back to when there was nothing else to talk about. It was in the same class as my Aunt Ida's heart condition which had kept her thin as a matchstick and on the brink of instant death for the last twenty-three years; as the social pretensions and snooty boasting of my cousin Arnold's second wife, who everyone knew was just a little salesgirl in Macy's before Arnold picked her up; as the stinginess of Uncle Walter, or the dreamy impracticalness of Uncle Irving, or my cousin Eric's airy indifference about living off his poor mother while he went on with his ballet lessons.

Where was Dan going to go next? That was the question that the family was constantly asking back and forth. Or more often it took the form: Where was he going to drag poor Sarah next? And when the next spot was finally decided on, and Dan and Sarah had settled down in it and rented a house and maybe joined a club or two, there was throughout the whole family, even among distant branches living hundreds of miles from New York, a kind of simultaneous crossing of fingers and holding of breaths and silent praying, "Maybe this is it—maybe this is finally it." Until Uncle Dan began to show signs of the old restlessness, the irritable look, the barking at employees, the quarrel-picking with his friends. At which the family would join once more in a general sigh and shaking of heads, and at a few dozen dinner-tables in a few dozen cities all over the country the age-old question would be revived: "Where is he going to drag poor Sarah next?"

I was a boy in school during those years, so even now I don't have a very clear idea of the details of Uncle Dan's wanderings. All I know is that he kept criss-crossing the country, from East to West, from North to South, more or less at six-months intervals. Wherever he went, there always turned out to be something wrong with it. Dallas, Texas, was too hot, and Detroit, Michigan, was too cold, but San Francisco wasn't enough of either— "No character," Dan said, "How can I live in a place that isn't even interesting and colourful enough to have a *temperature* of its own?" And then, sometimes the place was too big and noisy and full of people, like Washington, D.C.—"I feel like I'm lost in the crowd, a human being has to have breathing-space." So they would move somewhere different—out to a resort hotel in Arizona, for instance, and pretty soon Dan would be grumbling and muttering, "I feel like I'm lost in empty space, a human being has to have the company of his fellow man."

Only, in more than one place it was the company of his fellow man that finally drove Dan away. "What kind of a stuffy crowd have we got ourselves into?" he said to Sarah, after five and a half months in New Haven, Connecticut (to this day I don't know whatever prompted them to go to New Haven, Connecticut, in the first place). "No life to them. All they can do is sit around at night and glare at each other. It's this college here that's the cause of it—it gets in everybody's blood, it's so goddamned dignified and refined that a man might as well stretch right out in his grave and pull the dirt in after him." So they left New Haven and swung all the way across the country to Los Angeles, California—and within another five and a half months Dan was complaining about "this loud, flashy crowd that we've got ourselves into. Now God knows I'm not the type that makes a big fuss about people's vulgarity and so on—like my cold-fish brother—I enjoy a good time as much as the next man. But do they always have to have it at the absolute top of their lungs? And the way they brag about their money here—God forbid that your French poodle should show up on the street in last year's mink!"

It was during these eight years—around the year 1938, I think—that Dan and Sarah lived in Miami Beach, Florida. I have since found out that the day they picked me up at Dr. Porter's School, when I made so much trouble for everybody with my suitcase and my extended goodbyes and my polo coat, was also the day they were leaving Miami Beach for good. Dan had got himself involved in a wild and disastrous business deal, as silent partner in a firm that made coconut candies, and Miami Beach was poison to him just then. In fact, for years afterward he could hardly bear the sight of a palm tree. Knowing this now, I often wonder why he was satisfied on that memorable day simply to yell at me for my infuriating slowness—I often wonder why he didn't pick me up and shake me until my teeth rattled.

And then, of course, along with all the different places at which, with perennial optimism, Dan "settled down for good", there were also plenty of other places to which he made side trips along the way. He could never make up his mind, for instance, on any one place for his vacations. No resort hotel ever satisfied him more than once. There was something wrong with each one of them, bad service, or cramped rooms, or dirty silverware, or skimpy food, or impertinent waiters, or a lousy climate, or a dull clientele, or a rocky golf course—or if nothing else could be found, a manager whose face Dan just didn't happen to like.

Even greater complications were involved in his efforts to visit Bobby and his grandson, little Neil. (As a matter of course, Dan had objected to this name. "Neil? Who ever heard of such a fancy, inflated name? Especially for a little kid." But he didn't object too strongly—because he knew how much worse it might have been.) In spite of Bobby's frequent invitations, he wouldn't go to see her and the baby at Beewick. He gave her various excuses—sometimes it was "business", sometimes it was "health", sometimes it was "the wrong time, for a lot of reasons that I can't go into right now". The real reason was known only to him and Sarah, and it wasn't necessary for them to discuss it out loud—it made itself clear enough in the look that passed over Dan's face every time the name Harvey Harris was mentioned to him.

Anyway, the result was that all sorts of elaborate, annoying arrangements had to be made, so that Dan and his daughter and his grandson could meet on some middle ground, when his son-in-law would be some place else—and without letting Bobby guess what the idea was. Twice a year Harvey had to go to New York for the Soap Market, and Dan generally manœuvred it so that he and Sarah would take a "vacation" just then, and Bobby and Neil would take a vacation at the same place. These manœuvres never worked out exactly right. Somebody's schedule always went wrong, and in the end Dan usually found himself squeezing in two or three quick, uncomfortable days with Bobby and Neil, at some Atlantic City hotel maybe, with a convention in full swing around them. Most of these two or three days would be full of irritations and distractions—with a few moments in between, when a smile from Bobby, or the reflection of that smile on her baby's face, would make Dan feel that it was worth the trouble after all. Until the next irritation came along.

But Dan's restlessness during these eight years didn't show itself only in his constant wandering from place to place. His business life at this period was even more tangled and hectic.

Oh, yes, he was back in the business world again. Not an accountant, though. All of a sudden this seemed much too tame to him. "A bookkeeper, a glorified adding-machine who copies down figures—is that any sort of work for a man?" Overnight he began to plunge himself into wildcat schemes and risky manipulations that would have made him shudder in his older, more solid days. For instance, he bought into an oilwell—not in Texas, but in Providence, Rhode Island, where some old lady claimed to have discovered it in her backyard. He financed a man who had invented a permanent electric-light bulb, which would run for five years straight without flickering out. (The only trouble with it was, it had a way of blowing all the fuses in any building where it was installed.) He owned half-interest in a racehorse for a while. When the War came, he got involved somehow in the manufacture of diapers, and through his old Drexell connections he managed to land several big contracts from the Army.

And then, of course, he was continually taking a fling at the Market—buying this and selling that, according to the latest rumour that he had happened to pick up somewhere. Dan, at this time, was ready to believe practically any rumour at all, as long as it was whispered to him in a mysterious enough voice. Or better still, if he overheard it accidentally on a train or in a men's room. It was all part of his general feeling of excited suspicion. "Things are going on that we don't even dream of," he used to say. "Deals are being made in back rooms—undercover operations—a man has to keep his ears open——"

Naturally, everyone was sure that Dan was going to lose his shirt. The family was constantly shaking its head and saying, "It won't be long now." And Herman never lost an opportunity to warn Dan—either in long, involved letters, or during those rare, unexpected intervals when Dan and Sarah came swinging through New York, on their way to somewhere or from somewhere else. "You're riding for a fall," Herman used to tell him, with his most judicious nod and his gravest frown. "The ridiculous chances you're taking—by rights you should have been bankrupt ten times over already."

"What's life without chances?" Dan would snap back at him. "Some people can moulder away between a stuffy hotel room and a stuffy office—some people can go through their lives as if they were dead already. Not me. I'm not built that way. Action is what I need. Something to do, something on the fire, something to keep myself moving."

And the amazing part of it was, Dan *didn't* go bankrupt. Some of this was pure luck—for instance, one of the big power companies paid a huge amount of money for the complete rights to his permanent electric-light bulb, "for the purpose of controlling its release to the public until a more propitious time", and didn't find out till later about its fuse-blowing properties. But mostly Dan kept his head above water because he never stayed in one business long enough to lose too much money. After a few months, he got as impatient with his latest business venture as he did with his latest location. And so, the moment he saw the chance, he would sell out his interests, sometimes at a profit, sometimes at a loss, but never at as much of a loss as he would have suffered if he had stuck to it. And then he would be hopping around, interviewing prospects, making phone calls, on the look-out for something new, preferably something with as queer an angle to it as possible.

And so, during these eight years, more than any other time in his life, Dan was all energy, all fuss and flurry, all dashing here and rushing there and never a moment to catch his breath. And his emotions kept right up with his activity. It was impossible for him to feel any emotion just moderately, in a pleasant easy-going way. Everything, for him, was an extreme. Either he laughed so hard that his sides ached and his ears rang, or he got so angry that he couldn't see straight, and he screamed at the top of his voice, and he flailed his arms so wildly that it was a miracle he didn't disjoint them: or he sank into such a deep, overbearing depression that he charged around for days on end with his head down and a murderous frown on his face, and hardly bothered to answer when people talked to him.

Out of this period come most of the "Uncle Dan" stories which have delighted us members of the younger generation for years and years now. The story, for instance, of the big argument he got into during the Shriners' convention in Philadelphia—he was being kept awake by the parade that was going on outside his hotel room, and finally he stuck his head out of the window and yelled out some remarks about "grown men who get a kick from dressing up like kids at a party!" The big argument began after that. Or the story of his annoyance at the beef stew in the U.S. Senate Cafeteria in Washington, D.C., and the way he tried to get in to see the Vice-President himself about it. Or the story——

But I could go on with them endlessly. Uncle Dan's state of mind during these years is best illustrated perhaps by the way he reacted to the War, in 1941. Like everything else that he came in contact with, he took it personally. That is, he looked on the whole War as a kind of malicious plot to get at him and his loved ones. He saw the German and Japanese armies as marching forward with himself, wherever he might be, as their ultimate goal. This state of affairs made him as mad as he could get, and he was damned well going to fight back. He was too old for the Army, of course, but he poured all the extra money he had into War Bonds, Relief Committees, and Service Clubs. He followed the newspaper stories as keenly as if he was right there on the spot, dodging bullets. He listened to all the radio commentators, and believed everything they predicted, and went into a rage if anybody made a sound while they were broadcasting.

His great speciality was being kind to servicemen. Wherever he happened to be located, hardly a week-end went by that he didn't have one or two soldiers or sailors up for dinner. In a bar, in a hotel lobby, he would strike up conversations with them, and it was never long before he brought them home. Then he would bustle around for theatre tickets, or seats to the ball game—or simply to fix them up with dates. For this purpose he was ready to commandeer every unmarried girl between the ages of seventeen and thirty-seven that he had even the remotest connection with—not only his own nieces and second cousins, but the nieces and second cousins, not to mention the daughters, of his friends, his business associates, and vague acquaintances that he met along the way.

But his feelings about the War came out most violently in his attitude towards Hitler. Up until now, Dan had paid only the normal amount of attention to the headlines. In common with everybody else in his family and his set, he had frowned and worried and grown bitter or horrified over what was happening to the Jews in Germany. He had given his money, like everybody else, to the refugee organizations—and like everybody else, he had complained about the "snotty attitude" of the refugees. But now that the War was on, a much deeper, more intense feeling took over in Dan. Hitler was no longer just a name in the newspaper, he was a personal enemy, he was somebody that Dan lived with every day of his life, just as surely as he lived with Sarah or any of the other people around him. At the mention of Hitler's name, his eyes would glow, his jaw would tighten, his neck would start to get red. It took very little to get him started on his speech about "that murderer—that butcher—it's a fine world, where an inhuman being like that is allowed to run loose". And he usually went on to what he personally would do "if I ever get my hands on that Hitler". And the way his face contorted with hatred, nobody ever doubted for a moment that he would really do it.

Even when he was by himself, Hitler occupied his thoughts, and he carried on conversations with Hitler in a low, furious mutter "All right, you'll find out—you'll see what we do to your type here in the United States of America. You'll kill the Jews, will you? You'll try to conquer the world, will you? All right, we've got ways of handling you, and they're not such nice ways either. Oh, no you don't—none of your crying and pleading for mercy—you should've thought of that a long time ago."

"Dan, dear—who on earth are you talking to?" It was Sarah, who had come suddenly into the room.

"Nobody, nobody, who's talking?" Dan said, turning his eyes away, becoming absorbed in the newspaper. "What's the matter, you don't knock on the doors nowadays?"

It was during these War years, while he was living in

Washington, D.C., that Dan heard indirectly about young Mark Kugel from back in Chicago. Old Abe, his grandfather, had died three years before, passing away peacefully in his sleep at the age of eighty-six. Shortly afterwards Mark, who was in his late thirties, went into the Navy. He became an officer, and he was on a destroyer in the Pacific, and the destroyer was sunk with all hands lost. The news came to Dan over lunch one day, and for the rest of the afternoon he went through his routine mechanically, with his mind only half on what he was doing, and a kind of heaviness weighing him down. At dinner that night his appetite was bad and his temper was short. He was only hoping for Sarah to nag him about his eating, so that he could have a reason to yell at her. When she didn't nag him at all, this seemed like an even better reason. He yelled at her for "thinking things" and for "deliberately keeping them to yourself so you can feel superior to me". It was one of the most terrible rages that he had ever been in. It left him exhausted, and Sarah was white and trembling for the rest of the night.

She was so upset over that evening that she did something she had never done before in her life—she went to somebody to pour out her troubles and relieve her feelings. She went to her younger sister, my mother. Before she was half through with her story she was already beginning to regret that she had come. But she made an effort and pushed through to the end.

My mother is a woman with a tremendous capacity for being calm and clear-headed and reasonable in the face of trouble—other people's trouble, that is. "You poor darling," she said, when Sarah was finished and looking down at her lap uneasily. "I can't say this comes to me as much of a surprise. We've always known how badly he treated you. And anybody with half an eye can see that it's been getting worse and worse. You want my advice? Well, all I can say is, don't stand for it any more. Tell him he's got to stop this sort of thing, or else you just won't go on."

"Won't go on?" Sarah looked up at my mother slowly, with a kind of complete unbelieving amazement in her eyes. "But *he's* the one who can't go on. Don't you see, that's why I'm so upset. The way he's driving himself and pushing himself, don't you see, something has to happen, something terrible has to happen." And then, with a funny little laugh, "Good Heavens, who *else* would go on if *I* didn't?"

And my mother, seeing that Sarah was absolutely unshakable under her quiet manner, just shrugged and said, "Well, don't say I didn't warn you," and dismissed the whole matter from her mind.

IX

IN April 1945, Dan was between moves. He was winding up a business in San Francisco and thinking over another business in Boston, and waiting tensely, with everyone else, for the news of the end of the War. Into this state of suspended animation came a telegram from New York. His brother Herman was very sick, he'd better come at once.

Dan and Sarah rushed right from the airport to the hospital—the new, shiny, antiseptic-looking hospital on Upper Fifth Avenue. It was nearly midnight when they arrived, and went right up to the eighth floor. The nurse on duty told them to make themselves comfortable in the waiting-room while she got in touch with the doctor. Here in this waiting-room they found young Mr.

Draper, Herman's chief assistant in the jewellery business. Well, not quite so young maybe. Actually, he was a man in his late thirties. But he had one of those smooth baby-faces, with light blond hair and clear blue eyes, that often keep a man's friends calling him "Junior" until the end of his life.

Draper was one of the most correct and proper men Dan had ever met, and sure enough he was properly dressed for this occasion, in a neat grey suit—dark enough so that he didn't seem callous and indifferent, but not so dark as to suggest that he was too sure of the outcome. His voice and his face were restrained and troubled, also, in the proper spirit. "Mr. and Mrs. Waxman," he said, shaking hands with them politely but not over-politely, "thank Heavens you're here. He's in a bad way, I'm afraid. A very bad way."

Briefly and to the point, Draper sketched in the details of the situation. For a number of years now, the people who knew Herman best—that is, the people who worked with him in his business—had realized that something was wrong. Their boss just wasn't looking or acting like his usual self. His face, which had grown lined and grey fairly early in his life, seemed even greyer and more lined than it ought to be. Every once in a while, if you happened to be looking carefully enough, you could see a certain tight little something pass over it, something which was very much like a grimace of pain. (Dan nodded and remembered that he had seen the same thing on Herman's face almost eight years ago, when he got back from Europe. What a dope he was, not to pay any attention to it then!)

But the most significant and upsetting thing of all, Draper said, was that lately Herman hadn't been taking the same tremendous pains with his personal appearance as he used to take. His pants, always so impeccably creased, had begun to get a kind of rumpled, baggy look. He had fallen into the habit of repeating his neckties, sometimes three or four or even five days in a row—and everybody knew how careful he had once been to show up with a different necktie every day of the month. What's more, his hair just hadn't been right at all since the beginning of the year. That beautiful smooth iron-grey hair of his which he brushed regularly every morning—exactly fifty times: not forty-nine, not fifty-one, but exactly fifty—well, it had a way of coming apart now, of losing its gloss and its neatness, and looking rather disorderly and drab by the end of the day.

"Rumpled, baggy, disorderly," Dan kept murmuring all the way through this speech. "You're right, you're right—he's in a bad way."

"I can tell you frankly," Draper said, "this last year I've been worried about him. I spoke to him about it several times. I told him that he was working too hard, and that it was beginning to affect his health. He ought to take it easier, I told him, and perhaps put a little more of the responsibility into the hands of those of us who are just as devoted to the firm as himself. I told him that he mustn't by any means allow anything to happen to him, if not for his own sake, then for the sake of his loved ones and all of us who had worked with him for so many years. I told him that I myself was ready at any time to take some of the burden from his shoulders. This was the least I could do, I told him, in appreciation for these many years."

"That was wonderful of you, Mr. Draper," Sarah said, her mouth already trembling a little.

"It was nothing," Draper said. Then with a sad little shrug, "Less than nothing. Naturally he wouldn't listen to me. You know the sort of man your brother is, Mr. Waxman. Amazing self-reliance. A remarkably strong will, though he was sixty at his last birthday. He was convinced that things just couldn't go on without his full attention. And so—you see the results."

"But what are they, the results?" Dan said.

The doctor could best tell them that, Draper said. All he knew was that Herman hadn't shown up at the store the day before yesterday. And since he hadn't sent any message, Draper began to worry about him. He called him up at his hotel and received no answer. So immediately after lunch, he went up there to Central Park West, and persuaded the young man at the desk to go up to the room with him and open it with a passkey. They found Herman on the floor between the bed and the bathroom, breathing heavily but half-conscious, completely exhausted from some sort of attack. He was dressed in his bathrobe and his pyjamas, and his hand was still clutching hold of his big gold-handled hairbrush. Dr. Glazer was called immediately, of course, and announced after one look at Herman that it was his heart, he had warned Herman about this at his last medical check-up. And so an ambulance was called, Herman was rushed to the hospital where he had been lying ever since in a dazed state and a great deal of pain. And Draper had got in touch with his whole family—that is, his married sisters and his brother.

"But you're the only one who's come to New York. The others just sent telegrams wishing him a speedy convalescence."

Dan frowned and didn't say anything. He was thinking of all the money that Herman and he, between them, had been doling out regularly for the last twenty-five years to their sisters and their sisters' husbands.

And then the nurse looked into the waiting-room and told them that Dr. Glazer had just phoned from surgery, he was on his way up.

Draper went up to Dan and put his hand on his arm, and looked solemnly and sympathetically into his face. "Mr. Waxman", he said, "I don't think anything is going to happen. God knows I hope it won't. But Dr. Glazer will tell you how serious this is, and we have to face it, there *is* a chance—— Well, what I'm trying to say, Mr. Waxman, I have reason to believe that the business will go to you. There are no children, you know, and his wife is deceased, that makes you his closest relation. It's a fine business, Mr. Waxman. I myself have been associated with it for more than fifteen years now, and for the last five your brother has come to depend on me as his right hand, so to speak. What I'm saying, Mr. Waxman—I want you to know that you can always depend on me, my loyalty to the firm is well known, and in the event of an emergency I'm prepared to take over at a moment's——"

He was interrupted by the appearance of Dr. Glazer. Dan and Sarah were up to him in a moment. "How is he, Doctor? Is it bad?"

"Bad?" Dr. Glazer gave that ironic smile of his. "Bad is what it was a year ago. I wish somebody would explain something to me some day. What is it about you big business-men? You're so smart and efficient when it comes to squeezing an extra dollar out of one of your customers—how come you act like a bunch of helpless, dribbling little babies when it comes to taking care of your own health?"

"Can we see him?" Dan said.

"See him?" Dr. Glazer always answered people's questions by repeating what they said. "Why shouldn't you see him? He can see you all right, he isn't doing much sleeping these days." Then with a long sigh and a shake of his head, he said, "You better see him now, while you can."

Dan looked up sharply at this. "Doctor—listen—does that mean——?"

"Mean? You know what it means. We both know what it means." Then he waved his hand, wearily and a little impatiently. "Go on, the nurse will show you the way."

So Dan and Sarah started out of the waiting-room behind the nurse. Draper took a few steps after them, then stopped in the waiting-room door. "I won't go with you," he said. "You'll want to see him alone. Families, you know. Just tell him I'm here, will you, Mr. Waxman? Tell him I'm praying for him. You know my name, of course—Draper. Eugene Draper."

But he was out of earshot now. Dan and Sarah were hurrying down the hall, behind the nurse. They stopped in front of a door at the very end of the hall. And just before they went in, the nurse spoke in a low voice, "He's very weak. Don't let him talk too much."

Dan and Sarah both nodded. Then the nurse opened the door softly and motioned them inside the room.

The bed was hidden by a screen, and behind the screen they heard a kind of thick, muffled, wheezing noise. A moment later Dan realized that it was the noise of Herman breathing. Dan did his best to steady himself and put on a smile, and then, with Sarah hovering behind him, he stepped around the screen.

The first sight of Herman made him catch his breath in spite of himself. All Dan could see was a face, rising up from under the bedclothes. Only it was hardly even a face at all—just a long bone of a nose, a vague blue line for the mouth, a straggle of dirty white hair, and two dark blotches staring out from the middle. And so white, so terribly white, that the pillow looked grey next to it.

Dan found his smile again and drew a little closer.

"Herman," he said. "It's me. I've come to see you."

For a moment there was no reaction, and then there was a faint stirring around the corners of that sliver of a mouth. And then the thick, muffled wheeze slowly turned into words. "Dan? They told me. I expected you."

"So how are you?" Dan said. "You're looking better than I expected."

Herman made an effort to shake his head, and succeeded only in moving his eyes slightly from side to side. "Very serious," he said. "My heart. The indications are it's fatal."

"Fatal?" Dan gave a laugh. "What kind of foolishness are you talking now? You'll be out of here in a few weeks. I've got Dr. Glazer's word for it."

Again that effort to shake his head. "Untrue. We're grown men now. We can accept the inevitable."

Dan knew that it was up to him to say something now, some sort of hearty, comforting lie. But for the life of him he couldn't think of a thing to say. The terrible truth of Herman's words was too strong for him, all he could do was go on smiling as hard as possible.

And now, Herman's lips were stirring again. "Dan— important matter. You know—I'm leaving you the business."

"All right, all right," Dan said quickly, "is this any time for a business discussion?"

"Only time. Important matter." The words were barely understandable in that heavy, exhausted voice. "It's a good business. I did it all myself. Cousin Simon had small ideas. Unbusinesslike. It's doing big things now. Slow and steady. As you know, that's my philosophy of life."

"Yes, sure. You were always the business-man of the family, Herman."

Herman was silent, breathing hard for a moment, then he gathered himself up for more speaking. "Remember? Family conference—Uncle Meyer? He said you were restless. Restless and unsteady. No good for jewellery. Too much temptation."

"I remember, how could I forget?"

For a second Herman's mouth gave a small twitch that might almost have been a smile. "It merely goes to show. Now you're getting into jewellery anyway. Better late than never."

Dan smiled too, and reached out suddenly to touch the bed.

A moment later, Herman's hand was out of the covers, thin and dry like paper, holding on to Dan's wrist. And his voice, though it couldn't grow any louder, was amazingly urgent and intent. "Listen, Dan. Watch out— don't be like me. All alone—nobody in my life—office— hotel rooms—restaurants—— Dying all alone, Dan, it's terrible. Dan, it's terrible. Dan——"

His grip on Dan's wrist had become very tight, you wouldn't think he had the strength for such a tight grip. And then, a moment later, it relaxed, his hand dropped limply, the intentness went out of his voice. He was staring dully at the ceiling again, and his wheezing was slow and heavy. At first Dan thought he was in some sort of a coma, but then his mouth started working again. it trembled just a little, and it turned down slightly, and for a moment his face was stretched into that long, solemn expression which Dan had known so well and hated so deeply all his life.

His words came very quiet and clear, with his eyes off on the distance. "Be a good boy in Chicago," he said. "Uphold the family reputation. I'm counting on you, Danny."

Then he was silent, and a few seconds later the nurse

touched Dan on the arm and he and Sarah moved quietly around the screen and out of the room.

Dr. Glazer told them there was no point in waiting. He would get in touch with them if there were any developments. So they went downtown to their hotel, and wearily, silently, they went to bed. They were awakened at five o'clock in the morning with the news that Herman was dead.

In the week that followed, Dan was grateful for funerals. The complicated arrangements with undertakers, obituaries, condolence notes, and cemetery officials kept him hopping from morning to night. He didn't have time to think about his feelings, the slow ache that was throbbing inside of him. He didn't have time to look too deeply into the past, and wonder about his brother Herman and himself, what their lives had come to and what they had meant to each other.

On the day of the funeral, he was busier than ever—making sure that the rabbi remembered all the facts of Herman's life, taking care of the seating arrangements, checking up on the cars that would take everybody out to the cemetery, pretending to miss the point of young Mr. Draper's grief, calming down the sisters who were weeping hysterically, controlling himself in front of his sisters' husbands who kept looking at him sideways and remarking casually that "old Herman was a successful man, how much do you suppose he was worth, in round numbers?" He was so busy, in fact, that he hardly had a chance to say a word to Bobby, who flew in alone from Beewick and got to the temple just a few minutes before the service.

And then, at noon, the funeral was over, the cars drove back to the city, and Dan refused his sisters' invitations to lunch—that is, they wanted him to invite them to lunch—and headed straight for his hotel with Sarah and Bobby.

They ordered sandwiches up in the room, and Dan sat in the corner while the women talked in low voices about poor Herman, and how nice everything went off, and how moving it was when the rabbi got to that part about his "unselfish contributions to those less fortunate than himself".

Dan didn't listen to most of this. Now that all the fuss was over, his mind was free to start working again. And what it worked on most was that last sudden outburst that Herman had given from his deathbed. "Listen, Dan. Watch out. Don't be like me." And the energy that he managed to put into it—a dying man, every breath was painful to him, but still he had the energy to bring this out. "Hotel rooms—restaurants—all alone—it's terrible, Dan. It's terrible, Dan." It kept running through his head, weaving in and out of his thoughts, there was no way of getting rid of it. "Listen, Dan. Don't be like me."

Dan was jarred out of his brooding by Bobby shaking his arm. "Daddy, look. Don't you want to see them too?" She was showing off the latest pictures of Neil. He was eight years old already—just eight this month—and it was almost a year since Dan had seen him. How big he looked—and so much more serious and intelligent than the last time. And in another picture, what a smile he was wearing. A Casanova—he'll be a regular Casanova some day. It was hard to believe it, wasn't it? A big boy like this—and his own little girl was its mother. Only his own little girl was a grown woman now, a woman close to thirty already, calm and confident with a life of her own, and beginning to show just a sign, just the smallest slightest trace, that she might be getting a little stout. And he could remember when she was eight years old herself, and terribly shy with strangers——

"Daddy," Bobby said, "I've got something I'd like to talk to you about. She drew up a chair in front of him, and leaned forward, and smiled in a quiet sympathetic way, as if *he* was the child and *she* was the parent. "Mother and I have been talking——" she began.

And in a few minutes it all came out. Sarah and Bobby had been talking about what he was going to do next, where he and Sarah were going to go, and could they possibly keep it up, this wild running around from one part of the country to another? And Bobby herself had come up with the suggestion, why shouldn't they move out to Beewick, Ohio, and settle down there permanently? Dan could go into business if he wanted to, or he could take up accounting again, or he could just rest and live off the fat of the land (the money he realized from the sale of Herman's jewellery firm would make that possible). Whatever he decided to do, Beewick was the place to do it, wasn't it? His whole family was there, his only daughter and his only grandchild, and that's where he and Sarah ought to be too.

Dan just blinked a little when Bobby got through. "I don't know," he said. "It's such a sudden—— Parents shouldn't live with their married children."

"You wouldn't be living with us, darling. You and Mother could find a nice little house very near to us, and we'd see each other often. You'd simply be living in the same town as us, and lots of parents do that."

"But Harvey—he might not——"

"Harvey is delighted at the idea. I told him two days ago that I was going to ask you."

"Yes, but it's so complicated—a big move like that——"

"Why is it complicated? You're on the move right now, aren't you? You've got all your things packed up right here in this hotel room. I'm flying back to Beewick to-morrow, and there's no reason why you shouldn't come along with me."

"To-morrow?" Dan searched his mind for more obstacles, more objections. But all he could think of was, "It's so so sudden. Let me think it over——"

"All right, Daddy, think it over. I have a little shopping to do. We'll discuss it again at dinner."

As soon as Bobby was gone, Sarah began to move around the room, clearing up the lunch things, sweeping away stray cigarette butts and breadcrumbs. Dan sat where he was and watched her, and for a long time neither of them said a word.

And then Dan spoke. "It wouldn't work, would it? Living out in the sticks like that. Running around with that impossible Harris family every day of our lives."

"I don't know, Dan," Sarah said, not looking at him, still busy with her tidying up. "Maybe they're not so bad if you get to know them."

Dan grunted. Then a moment later, "If I thought Bobby really wanted us to. I mean, if it isn't just a gesture."

"A gesture?" Sarah stopped moving now and looked at him, anxious and timid. "It's no gesture, Dan. You should've seen her face when she mentioned the idea. She'll be so disappointed if you say no."

"Will she?" He narrowed his eyes suspiciously. "It's a fact she'll be disappointed?"

"Terribly disappointed." Sarah came right up to him and looked down at him. "It'll be a home for us, Dan. It'll be just like Ch—— like things used to be."

Dan shook his head and muttered, "Maybe, maybe——"

"You'll be fifty-nine years old in May, Dan. When a man reaches that age—when people reach *our* age—they ought to have a home."

It was just what Herman had said to him, and he trembled a little to remember it. And there was Sarah, looking down at him with her eyes terribly wide—Dan held out another few seconds, and then he gave a sigh. "All right, we'll go out there and look it over," he said. "What can I lose? I've tried everything else." And then, in a sharper voice, "But if this doesn't work—I'm warning you, Sarah——"

Sarah had her arms around him in a moment, she was laughing and kissing him and saying over and over, "It'll work, it'll work. You won't feel sorry, I promise you. Oh, Dan dear, how can I thank you——?"

X

It was five o'clock in the evening when their plane landed at Cincinnati. Since it was an hour's drive to Beewick, Harvey met them with his car.

Harvey had grown a lot plumper and more prosperous since his wedding-day nine years ago. The soap business had gone through a tremendous boom during the war— the Army and Navy used a great deal of soap, not to mention the Marines—and Harvey's elegantly-tailored sports jacket, his fancy hand-painted neckties, his substantial paunch, were some of the results of this boom.

His manner hadn't changed at all, though. How could it? How could a man possibly develop a more superior smirk, a more grating, self-righteous tone of voice, or a wetter handclasp? How could he approve of himself any more enthusiastically than he had done all his life?

His opening speech, the moment they stepped into the

airport waiting-room, was absolutely typical. "Dan and Sarah," he said, "this is really a big moment, isn't it? Let me welcome you officially to our little community. You'll find that we're simple, unpretentious people. But if you're willing to accommodate yourself to our little ways, then *we'll* be willing to take you to our hearts." And then, with this warning off his chest, he turned to Bobby and kissed her carefully on the cheek and said, "How are you, Barbara? We've missed you. We've discovered how hard it is to get along without our little matron."

"It's stuffy in here," Dan said. "Let's get going."

During the ride Harvey and Bobby talked almost steadily about local gossip, house repairs, and family affairs, things that Dan couldn't make head or tail out of half the time. "Oh, Harvey, it's been on my mind all the time I was gone—did you straighten out that television business with the Zoning Commission?" "I certainly did. I went down there the next day and explained my point of view in no uncertain terms. They agreed with me that old residents have certain privileges, especially since they knew *us* and they don't know *them*." "Well, thank Heaven for that, what would Neil do without his cowboys?" "Incidentally, Barbara, you'll be interested to know that everything is all arranged with the temple. Mother *will* take over the dramatics group next September." "She'll be so pleased. And Ethel Rugoff?" "She'll scream, as usual. But who's donating the new Torah?"

Dan shut his ears to the conversation, and stared out the window at the landscape. It was really kind of pretty. It wasn't flat and brown and nothing but corn-fields, the way the Mid-West is supposed to be, the way it was in whole sections beyond Chicago. There were plenty of trees and green grass, and criss-crossing hills that gave you sudden sweeping views for miles around. And everybody seemed to be growing flowers around their houses. I'm liking the looks of it, Dan told himself. Who knows, there might be other things he liked, he might turn out to be satisfied after all.

"You are now entering the city of Beewick," Harvey said. He gave his little laugh. "It's not New York or Paris, of course. We make no such claims. We wouldn't want to."

"You'll love it here, Daddy," Bobby said. "I know you will."

Sarah was turning her head back and forth, trying to look out of both sides of the car at once. "It's very nice. It's really very nice."

And Dan, looking out the window as they drove through the streets of Beewick, had to admit to himself that he was a little surprised. What he had expected, now that he considered it, was something pretty close to the typical ghost town in a Western movie—an unpaved street, a horse, a man on a cracker barrel in front of the general store, and plenty of dust. But Beewick was really a thriving little city. The buildings went as high as four or five storeys, and some of them were fairly modern-looking. They passed a bank, they passed a department store, they passed a couple of mortgage and loan offices, a movie house, a hotel, some mortgage and loan offices, a big garage with a ramp in front, drugstores, hat stores, a traffic policeman, several mortgage and loan offices——

"Not bad," Dan said, with a grunt. "Better than I thought it'd be."

"To your right is the temple," Harvey said. "I think I may say we're justifiably proud of that building. It's the biggest one in the State outside of Cleveland and Cincinnati. Our Jewish community here in Beewick may not be the largest in the world, but it has the wherewithal to support its own temple."

"Harvey was chairman of the fund-raising committee," Bobby said. She leaned over a little and gave a confidential laugh. "Whenever they want to get something done, they always call on Harvey."

Harvey cleared his throat and smiled in a modest way. "It's a question of community spirit," he said. "You'll find it's quite a different atmosphere from New York or Paris, Dan. In a town the size of Beewick, no man is an island. We take an interest in what goes on behind our neighbour's door."

"Harvey is on the Chamber of Commerce," Bobby said. "He's the only Jew."

They were silent for a while, and pretty soon the streets began to grow less city-like, fewer drugstores and more houses—big, dirty-white houses with green shutters and long porches and sign after sign saying, "Rooms to Rent".

"Not the best section of the city," Harvey said. "But every city has its eyesores, doesn't it? We'll soon be out in the nicer suburbs, and then you'll see some gorgeous homes."

"Mother and Daddy haven't seen *our* new house," Bobby said, suddenly quite excited. "Everyone says it's the loveliest new house in Beewick. It's at least three times as big as that little place we had when we were first married."

Sure enough, it wasn't long before the trees sprouted up around them again, the green grass reappeared, and the houses and lawns grew bigger and more luxurious. Sarah was terribly impressed. She kept gasping and pointing and saying, "Now who lives there? They must be *very* wealthy people." And Harvey kept answering in an offhand tone, "Oh, that's the Brewsters—Jack Brewster is the president of the bank, we have lunch together once a week——"

"Mrs. Brewster serves with me on the Better Beewick Committee," Barbara said. "She's a lovely person. Of course we're not very close to them socially."

"That's the women," Harvey said, his tone growing just a little uneasy. "They keep up these artificial distinctions. If it was in the hands of the men, you wouldn't be able to tell the difference between a Jew and a Gentile in Beewick."

"I don't know about that, Harvey," Bobby said. "You know what sort of a reputation that Mr. Pearson has, that big real estate man——"

"The exception that proves the rule," Harvey said. "Frankly, I consider Jack Brewster one of my closest personal friends."

For the rest of the ride they were silent. And then Bobby waved and cried, "There it is, there's our house." and a moment later they turned in at a wide driveway next to a big white house with the biggest garage and the best-kept lawn they had seen yet.

"Oh, Bobby," Sarah said, "it's magnificent."

"Do you need such a big place to live in?" Dan said.

"For ourselves, no," Harvey said. "My own tastes are simple. You know what I was accustomed to in my early days. That's exactly why my boy is going to grow up in a completely different atmosphere."

Dan squirmed a little and didn't say anything. From anybody else, this sentiment would have started him nodding with approval, but from Harvey Harris it somehow filled him with exasperation.

And then things started happening too fast for him to go on with this line of thought. First there was his meeting with his grandson—and his pleasure at the way the boy threw his arms around him and called him

Grandpa. "He remembers me," Dan said. "And it's over a year now." And he kept repeating it all through dinner. "You know, he's a smart boy, that little Neil. Over a year, and he remembered me."

And then after dinner, there were guests. "Just a few of our very closest friends," Bobby explained. "We asked them over especially to meet you." And Dan was surprised to find that they weren't much different from the people he'd been seeing all his life, even in big cities. Mostly it was a younger crowd, of course, couples in their thirties and early forties, to suit Bobby and Harvey. But their interests didn't seem to be very different from Dan's and Sarah's. They were all bridge-players, and they were all switching to gin rummy lately, and their easy-going chatter about their golf club, the temple, the price of clothes, the big heavyweight fight, the War, it was all a lot like the chatter which had been going on around Dan since he was a boy.

And sure enough, before the end of the evening, the men and women split up, and there were card games. And then, around eleven, they came together again for the final round of drinks, and everybody asked Dan and Sarah questions about New York and about their travels. These questions slipped gradually into questions about how they liked Beewick, wasn't it an up-and-coming little town, wasn't Dan proud of his big-shot son-in-law? Why, everybody said that Harvey Harris would own the town of Beewick in another ten years. And as for Barbara—the whole town was crazy about Barbara, they had fallen in love with her right from the beginning, she was now one of the most popular and sought-after girls in the young married set. And little Neil—everybody agreed that he was one of the brightest little boys they had ever seen. And good-looking! Definitely he had all his mother's looks.

How could Dan keep from swelling up a little as he listened to all this? And later on, when he and Sarah were alone in Bobby's guest room, wasn't it only natural for him to look thoughtful and nod his head and say, "It could work—there's a possibility—I'll know in a few more days——"

The next morning, Saturday, he and Sarah were separated. Bobby took Sarah off for a quick, preliminary look at houses, and also for lunch with some of the women who were closer to Sarah's age. Harvey took charge of Dan, showed him the downtown business section, introduced him at the bank, took him on a tour of his city club, where they ended up having lunch with Harvey's brother, Ira.

Ira was two years older than Harvey, but he looked about ten years older. He had a thin drawn face, and a high bald head, and a slow sarcastic tone of voice. In the beginning, Harvey and Ira had been partners in the soap business, but a few years ago Harvey bought Ira out, and Ira was now his general manager. This information was supplied within the first two minutes of the meal by Ira himself. And Dan got the feeling that he supplied the same information to everybody he met, and always within a few minutes after meeting them.

Later on in the meal, he said, "So what do you think of our fair city, Mr. Waxman? Quite a lively metropolis, isn't it? Wait till to-night, when the crowds come in for the triple-bill cowboy shows. Big Saturday night festivities—every farmer for miles, with his wife, his ten children, and his pet pig."

"Now I already warned Dan about that," Harvey said. "If he's looking for the Great White Way, he won't find it in Beewick. He'll have to go some place else for it."

"I never said I was looking for the Great White Way," said Dan, just a little annoyed.

"And what's your impression of my remarkable kid brother, Mr. Waxman?" Ira said. "Quite the civic leader, isn't he? How do you like that shiny new palace of his? The house that soap built."

Later in the afternoon Dan and Harvey went back to the house, where they met Bobby and Sarah. And Sarah's eyes were bright, she was quivering with excitement. She was so full of all the wonderful houses she had seen, any one of which would be an ideal dream-house for them, that she couldn't describe them one at a time, and Dan finally had to cut in and say, "Hold it, hold the horses. I'm not getting a word you're saying, better turn the floor over to Bobby."

And then, in a little while, Neil came in from his afternoon play, and Dan presented the boy with a cowboy pistol that shot soap bubbles, which he had bought for him in the Beewick five-and-ten after lunch.

That night they had dinner with Harvey's mother, who lived in a big terrace apartment in one of the modernistic new housing projects on the outskirts of Beewick. She gave them roast beef, but she didn't take any of it herself, because she was a vegetarian. "I have my principles, but I certainly don't expect anyone else to sympathize with them," she said, in her quiet refined way—and everybody fidgeted a little, while her plate was heaped with carrots, asparagus, and green peas. There were no cards after dinner, because Mrs. Harris didn't believe in cards, she felt that they "discouraged the precious art of conversation". So for a couple of hours after dinner they engaged in the precious art of conversation—that is, Mrs. Harris told stories about the last convention of the American Elocution Teachers, and about all the sweet things which the members said to her. And everybody went home early.

Dan wasn't in quite such a good mood when he and

Sarah went up to their room that night. And when she asked him the inevitable question—or rather, *looked* the inevitable question—he just gave a shake of his head and muttered, "I don't know yet. A few more days."

He lay awake a long time thinking about this. He thought about all the things he had gone through the last two days. The important thing, he told himself, was to be logical and reasonable. He couldn't let himself be influenced by crazy emotions. He couldn't afford to blind himself and turn away from the facts. Too many times in the past, too many times all his life, this is what he did, and every time he paid for it. He could feel it still sometimes, how he paid for it.

So this time it was going to be different. Logic—cold, inescapable logic—that's what he had to stick by, no matter what. And what did cold, inescapable logic show him, if not that this was a foolish idea, this whole idea of settling down in Beewick, Ohio? Right from the start, the moment he set eyes on Harvey Harris again, hadn't all his old feelings come rising up in him? And Bobby— it was good to be with her, that was true all right. He couldn't deny the pleasure of seeing her, watching her laugh and smile, listening to the admiration of her friends. But there was still cold inescapable logic to think of, to tell him that Bobby wasn't Bobby any more, she was Barbara, she was Mrs. Harvey Harris, she was pretty well accustomed after nine years to living without her old father. And cold inescapable logic reminded him, in a way that was all too close and real, of the trap that this sort of thinking about Bobby had led him into once, and the pain he had received for his trouble only nine years ago.

So much for cold inescapable logic. It didn't satisfy him. Somehow he continued to toss in his bed. Because there was something missing, there was something pulling at him, whispering to him in spite of his logic. What was it? What was holding him here in Beewick?

In the morning he woke up to a light tickling against his cheek. He blinked, and then, as his sleepiness faded away, his grandson's smile took shape before his eyes. The little boy was in his pyjamas, he was standing next to the bed shooting soap bubbles into Dan's face.

"I was trying out my new gun, Grandpa," he said. "Did I scare you?"

"Did you want to scare me?"

"Well, I was trying to."

"All right then, you scared me."

A moment later Dan reached out and pulled the boy towards him. And Neil with a laugh began to bounce up and down on Dan's chest. And it didn't even wear Dan out, the boy was as light as a feather.

At breakfast that morning, he spoke up a little abruptly, "Well, I've thought it over. I've decided why not. It's a growing community, and the real estate values are good. It's time we settled down anyway." Then he gave a brisk nod and went back to the morning newspaper, just to show that his decision was completely businesslike, no illogical emotions mixed up in it anywhere.

XI

As the weeks went by, it really looked as if Sarah's optimism hadn't been so foolish after all. Things *were* going to work out, Dan became surer of this every day.

For the first few weeks, he was caught up in the excitement and confusion of getting himself established. He went around with Sarah and Bobby to look at houses. He peered into bathrooms, slapped his hand against waterpipes, opened and closed windows. He sat down with real estate men and dickered back and forth about rents, repairs, guarantees. And nearly every night he was up late with Sarah, discussing the merits of this particular neighbourhood, the beauties of that particular landscape, the inconvenience of various zoning laws, the suspicious possibility that there was water in a certain cellar.

Under the influence of all this discussing and examining and dickering, a feeling began to grow in Dan, a feeling which he had thought was dead a long time ago. He had looked at plenty of houses and apartments in the last fifteen years, he had talked with plenty of real estate agents. But always there was a funny kind of unreality about it all, always he knew deep down that his heart wasn't in it. And now, slowly and uncertainly, he began to feel that maybe his heart *was* in it. With each new house, the idea of having a home of his own, a place that was actually his and not just a temporary step between railroad stations, seemed more and more attractive to him. Why not? he began to ask himself. To settle down at night in his own easy-chair, to eat at his own dining-room table without having to look over a menu or catch the eye of a waiter, to stretch out at night in a bed that was meant especially for him, between sheets that wouldn't be washed and ironed and doled out to some-body else the very next day—why shouldn't he have these pleasures after all? Where was it written down that it was too late?

And then, early in May, they found the house they wanted. It was small, white, two storeys high, with a lawn and a flower bed, and a porch where a man could relax on nice days with a highball, and good TV reception.

Best of all, it was only a ten-minute walk from Bobby, and from his grandson. So they signed the lease, with an option to buy in two years, and the next few weeks were spent in hunting for furniture, picking up a good new car, trying out three or four different maids and cooks. And Dan, realizing that he couldn't do nothing all day, began to look around for work. "Fifty-nine, going on sixty, isn't exactly being dead on your feet," he said. And as soon as the house was fairly settled, he discussed the problem with Harvey.

Harvey made one of his speeches. He talked about "the unlimited business opportunities" in Beewick. He hinted at his own "small influence". He suggested that, if Dan was interested in going back to his old accounting work, perhaps on a limited scale, there would be "very few individuals in Beewick" who would "ignore the claims of Harvey Harris's father-in-law". It made Dan a little uneasy, this proposition. He didn't much like the idea of being too grateful to Harvey Harris—there was still something about that man. And even more, Dan didn't like to feel that people were being bludgeoned into doing business with him. All his life he had managed to get along strictly on his own abilities and merits.

It bothered him, but he discovered that he was able to get around the bother. He told himself that this work would be strictly a sideline, just to keep him busy, so he wouldn't actually be dependent on Harvey at all. He also told himself that he was a damned good accountant, one of the best in the field, if he said so himself—so even if people didn't start off with him entirely of their own accord, they still wouldn't have any reason to be dissatisfied with him later on. He told himself this, and dismissed his doubts with no trouble at all, because to tell the truth, there was something inside him much stronger than these doubts. If Harvey had been twice as overbearing, if his new clients had been twice as unwilling, this something would have kept Dan in Beewick just the same.

Even during the hectic days of moving in and settling down, he realized what he was feeling for his grandson. It was a pleasure just to look at the boy, to watch him playing, to listen to him laugh. The laugh, especially, because every once in a while, in the right light, with the right toss of the head, that laugh was Bobby's laugh all over again, Bobby when she was a little girl.

It pulled Dan back to the old days, back to Twelve Hundred Lake Shore Drive. For the first time in years he didn't resist this pull. He let himself remember everything, all the details of that old apartment in the penthouse, the smudges on the carpets, the pictures on the walls, and stepping out of his car at the end of a hard day and looking up at the lights of his own living-room, blinking softly through the twilight. Especially he let himself remember Bobby in those days. Her shyness and sweetness, her outbursts of high spirits, the way she jumped on top of him and hugged him—or suddenly got very dignified and pushed him away with an exasperated "Daddy—please!"

His grandson Neil was very much like her, he told himself. Full of life and happiness, given to wild outbursts and pranks and dances for no reason except the sheer joy of letting himself go.

Dan was with him as much as he possibly could. When the boy came home from school in the afternoons—he was in the fourth grade already, terribly bright for his age—Dan was usually at Bobby's house waiting for him. Sometimes they would play together. There was one favourite game in which Neil grabbed for the heavy key-chain that hung from Dan's belt and tried to pull his keys and his cigar cutter out of his pocket, while Dan pretended to put up resistance. They could play this game for ten or fifteen minutes at a time, until Neil was all worn out from giggling.

Then he would grow quiet and serious, and ask Dan to tell him a story about what *he* was like when *he* was a little boy. And Dan would poke around among his memories, and dig up obscure escapades from his early Brooklyn days. There was one that Neil was specially fond of, the story of little Oscar Weissman who used to live next door, and one of his uncles sent him a monkey from South America, and all the boys in the neighbourhood had a wonderful time encouraging the monkey to steal things. Neil's delight in this monkey was never exhausted. New stories, old stories, he could listen to them all with complete fascination. It became one of his regular refrains, one of the phrases that stuck in Dan's mind for years afterwards, and always with a pang of tenderness—"Oscar Weissman's monkey, Grandpa! Come on, Grandpa, Oscar Weissman's monkey!"

And so it was spring, and the landscape turned quite gaudy and beautiful. And everything was so perfect for Dan that even one disturbing little note couldn't really spoil his happiness.

It was a beautiful morning towards the middle of June. School was over, so Neil was playing in front of his house with another boy. And Dan and Bobby were on the porch—Bobby knitting quietly (she had taken up knitting since she came to Beewick), Dan watching the two little boys. They were playing Americans and Japanese in the South Pacific. First Neil would be the American, and he would sneak up behind his friend and poke him in the back with his finger and say, "Hands up, you Jap, you're my prisoner!" Then they would switch parts, and the other boy would be the American and he would take Neil prisoner. Dan watched the game with great interest. And every so often, when Neil was the Japanese, he would call out, "Look out, it's a surprise attack!"

Just then the car pulled into the driveway, and Harvey got out—he often knocked off work before lunch on these warm days. He waved at them from the driveway and started up to the porch. Suddenly he caught sight of Neil and his friend and he stopped short. "Neil," he said, in a voice that was quiet and cool, but somehow managed to carry quite a distance. "You're getting all overheated. Tell Mickey goodbye and come into the house."

"But Dad, we just started——"

"Don't argue with me, Neil. What have I told you about family co-operation?"

There was a tone in Harvey's voice that would have impressed a man his own age or older. So what could an eight-year-old boy do? Neil lowered his head and muttered "G'bye, Mickey," and trudged up to the house, kicking a pebble all the way.

Harvey met him at the back door, and put his hand on his shoulder, and they went in together. Dan could hear their voices from the living-room—that is, Harvey's voice, a low unruffled buzz, would go on for quite a while, then a high quick interruption from Neil, then the low buzz again. And pretty soon it was only Harvey's voice, Neil wasn't talking at all.

"What's it all about?" Dan said, turning anxiously to Bobby. "What'd the boy do?"

"Do, Daddy?" She looked up from her knitting with a puzzled smile. "He didn't do anything, did he?"

A while later Sarah came down from the upstairs bedroom, where she had been looking over wallpaper samples, and they all had lunch on the porch. And now it came out, the reason for Harvey's funny behaviour.

"Barbara dear," he said, smiling at her in that sad, patient way of his, "I don't know what you could have been thinking of this morning. You were right there on the porch, you had the boy under your eye at all times."

Barbara reddened a little and said, "What's wrong, Harvey?"

"What's wrong?" Harvey gave just the smallest sigh. "Nothing, nothing at all. Only that I found Neil playing with that Katzenstein boy again."

"I don't know why you don't like Mickey," said Neil, into his soup. "He can whistle better than any other kid in school."

Harvey turned to Neil, and without raising his voice he spoke to him in a way that made Dan grow tense immediately. "You don't know," Harvey said. "How can you say you don't know, after all the things I told you less than an hour ago? How can you make a remark like that? Weren't you listening to a word I said?"

Neil didn't say anything. He pressed his lips together and kept his eyes steadily on his soup. And Dan knew why he wouldn't look up, because he was afraid he might start crying.

"I'm talking to you," Harvey said. "Isn't it the custom in this family to look at people while they're talking to you?"

"Listen, what's the trouble?" Dan put in quickly, with a little laugh, trying to stall Harvey off until Neil could get hold of himself. "What's so awful about this Katzenstein boy? I was watching them myself, they were playing very nice and friendly."

Harvey turned to Dan with a polite little smile. "You're not familiar with the situation, Dan," he said. "I've got nothing against the Katzenstein boy personally. He's a well-behaved child, if a little stupid. But Neil is growing up now, he isn't a baby any more. He has to

291

begin to accept a little responsibility and develop a more mature attitude. There are plenty of very nice boys right around here in this neighbourhood, boys from very nice families. From Neil's type of family. He has to learn while he's still young the importance of travelling with the right people and not getting involved with unfortunate associations."

"An eight-year-old kid? That's an unfortunate association?"

"He won't always be eight years old. And neither will Neil. The time will come when he'll have a certain position to uphold in his set. I've explained this to him again and again."

"You're trying to turn him into a snob," Dan said, surprised himself at the discovery. "A regular little snob."

"A snob?" Harvey laughed softly. "Certainly not. You know better than that, Dan. Nobody in the world is more democratic-minded than I am. I consider myself a liberal in politics, and a liberal in my daily living. You know my own background, and you know I've never been ashamed of it or tried to conceal it. This has nothing to do with snobbishness at all. It's a question of adjustment. All of us must learn to adjust to our society, and the earlier we begin the happier we'll be in the end."

"It's crazy," Dan said, shaking his head. "Absolutely crazy."

"Dan, dear——" Sarah began.

"Bobby." Dan turned to her sharply. "You're the mother, what do you think about this?"

Bobby fidgeted a moment, then she smiled and said, "I think we're all making a big mountain out of a little molehill. The Katzensteins are moving out of town in September anyway, so what's all the fuss about?"

Then Sarah spoke up again, with her opinion of the wallpaper samples she'd been looking at all morning, and Neil started to get interested in his soup, and the whole matter faded away.

Not from Dan's mind, though. In the next week, he began to notice things—little things, little remarks that Harvey dropped in front of his son, little pressures that he put on him. Worst of all, sometimes there were odd little echoes of Harvey's attitude in Neil's own speech. My God, wasn't there time enough yet to stuff his head with crazy ideas?

But before Dan could go any further than shaking his head, the first of July arrived and Neil was sent off to summer camp. It was his first year at camp, and Dan wondered if he wasn't a little too young for such an experience. But Harvey just smiled and said, "He can't depend on his father and mother for ever. He has to learn a little self-reliance, and how to stand on his two feet in a community situation. I was standing on *my* two feet when I was even younger than he is." And when Dan protested some more, Harvey raised his hand and said, "Excuse me, Dan, but I think I know best." And so the question of Neil's future, and what kind of a boy he was going to turn into, was postponed for the summer. Dan went about his business, enjoyed the weather and the scenery, and waited for September.

On Labour Day Neil came home from camp. They all went to the station to meet him. And when he stepped off the train, a pale skinny little figure with a big suitcase in one hand and a pair of Indian moccasins slung over his shoulders, Dan felt a surge of pleasure and affection. It was all he could do to hang back while the boy kissed his mother and shook hands with his father. On the ride home, Neil was full of stories about camp, and how he liked nature walks best, and he acted in a play, he was a Chinese mandarin, but he didn't like baseball, and whenever they put him and Eddy Davis in the outfield, the two of them used to sneak off behind the assembly hall and play mumbley-peg. Smiling at him and only half-listening to his chatter, Dan made a resolution about the boy. "I'll keep my mouth shut," he resolved. "I won't bring the subject up. But if Harvey does it again—if he starts in with the same crazy business—*then* I'll open my mouth."

Even as he made this resolution, Dan knew that Harvey *would* start in again. And sure enough, the very next night at the dinner-table, Harvey started pumping the boy about who he met at camp and what his friends' names were, and telling him in his cool superior way which ones he should go on writing to, which ones were "the sort of boys I like to see you cultivate".

Dan didn't say anything when he heard this. But he hardened up inside, and smiled to himself, and made up his mind what to do. After dinner, he asked Neil how he'd like to take a little walk with his old Grandpa and maybe hear a new story that he'd just remembered about Oscar Weissman's monkey. Neil clapped his hands together and said he'd love to, could he, please? And Harvey waved his hand genially and gave his permission. So the two of them strolled along in the dim evening glow. They went up the hill to look at the excavation for the new house that was being built. On the way Dan made up something or other about the monkey. And then, when they got to the excavation and were leaning against the wooden railing and looking down into the hole, Dan casually switched the conversation.

He asked Neil about camp, and got him talking about which boys he liked and which boys he didn't like. Neil said that he didn't like that Georgie Davidson so much, the one Dad told him he ought to write to, because he was a hitter. Whenever he stood behind you in line or something, he used to hit you in the back or on the shoulder, and when you turned around and told him to cut it out, he looked up in the air and pretended he didn't know what you were talking about. Dan nodded his head very solemn, and looked down into the boy's face and said, "If you don't like him, don't write to him. You want to know a secret? What counts is what people are, and whether you really get fun out of being with them. So if you really like somebody, don't you ever let *anybody* talk you out of it."

There was a hush in the air, and Neil looked solemn too. And Dan trembled a little with excitement, because he knew that he had started something now, something which he couldn't back out on, and didn't want to anyway. It was going to be a fight now, an undercover fight between himself and his son-in-law, and the stake in this fight was nothing less than the whole future happiness of this boy. Was he going to grow up and be a nice kid, a solid, upstanding young fellow, a man that anybody could be proud of? Or was he going to be a nasty little snotnose, a spoiled brat, a snob and a prig and—even worse? No, he wasn't, Dan told himself, clenching his fists a little. Because his Grandpa wouldn't stand for it. His Grandpa was here to protect him. As long as Dan Waxman was around, nobody was going to turn his grandson into another Harvey Harris.

"I'm tired, Grandpa," Neil said.

Dan took hold of his hand, and his voice was almost grim. "All right, I'll take you home."

In the days that followed, Dan launched his campaign, and kept is up as the weeks went by. It was a sniping campaign. It went on underground, in the enemy's own territory. The strategy was simple enough. It was just a question of keeping his eyes and his ears open, and staying close to his grandson, and not letting a single thing slip by. Whenever he caught the boy in a single offhand remark, a single little phrase that showed the Harvey Harris influence, Dan was down on him in an instant, not angrily or naggingly, but quiet and firm, with his hand on the boy's shoulder and a smile and a few words like, "You just listen to your old Grandpa, he knows a thing or two."

And when the pressure on the boy was strong, when there was some particular thing that his father wanted him to do, or he had to face a particularly big bawling-out, Dan made sure of being around as soon as possible afterwards. He encouraged the boy to talk to him, tell him his secrets, come out with his troubles. And he talked right back to the boy, comforting him, putting him at his ease, working hard to counteract the effect that Harvey had made, to sabotage the opinion that Harvey had forced on him, to undo the dirty work that Harvey had done.

All the time he was careful to keep it behind Harvey's back. In Harvey's presence he smiled and kept his opinions to himself. He forced himself to stay on friendly terms, because he knew that an open clash between them would make his job ten times as hard.

And it seemed to be working too. Harvey didn't notice a thing. He was so sure of himself, he sailed along so confidently. He didn't have a suspicion of this innocent-looking, grumpy old father-in-law of his. And Bobby was so cheerful and pleasant, and busy with her house and her ladies' organizations, that she didn't notice any-thing either. And Dan didn't see any point in bothering her. It was all for her own sake really, for the sake of her own child, that is. Some day, years and years from now, when Neil was a fine young man, Dan would tell her what he had done for her and give himself the pleasure of her gratitude.

The only one he couldn't hide it from was Sarah. It was around the middle of October when she began to suspect what was up—Dan could see it just from the way she looked at him, wide-eyed and worried, and then looked away again quickly the moment he met her gaze. She didn't say anything to him, though, until Thanksgiving Day. Harvey had given Neil a long lecture at the dinner-table about using certain words that were "vulgar" and "coarse"—and after the dinner, Dan had taken Neil off for one of their "strolls". And late that night, back at their own house, Sarah wet her lips and spoke up. "You shouldn't do it, Dan," she said. "You shouldn't interfere between a boy and his own parents."

"Interfere?" said Dan, not even looking up from his detective story. "I don't follow you." And then, a moment later, he added in the same offhand, apparently indifferent tone, "Besides, it isn't as if the boy is a complete stranger in *my* life either."

Sarah didn't say anything for a while. She just hovered over him anxiously. Finally she gave a little sigh, and said, "Everything's going along so beautifully. I couldn't stand it if something went wrong." Then she turned quickly and hurried out to the kitchen.

But Dan just grunted and turned a page.

He forgot all about Sarah's words in the days that followed. Because things got better and better, as autumn eased into winter. One day there was snow on the ground, and he bought Neil a big fancy sled. When the boy set eyes on it, he threw his arms around Dan's neck, and the two of them seemed to be closer than ever. Then the Christmas vacation began, and Neil was home from school, and Dan spent more time up at Bobby's house than he did at his own. And so it went until that terrible day, the day before Christmas.

XII

HE slept late that morning, because his office was shut for the long Christmas week-end. When he finally woke up, he still lay in bed for a while and gave himself up to a pleasant daydream, involving easy-chairs and monkeys and himself at the age of seventy-five blushing at the speeches during his big birthday dinner.

The phone rang. He picked it up and mumbled "hello", and then the cold, precise voice of his son-in-law drove away his drowsiness. "Dan, are you listening to me? I have a very important matter to discuss with you. Will you come over here as soon as possible, please."

"I'm not even awake yet," Dan said. "I was going to take it easy and lounge around the house this morning."

Harvey's voice grew a little sharper. "What I have to say is more important than lounging around the house."

Dan reacted just as sharply. "All right, if it's so important, you can come over here. I won't be going anywhere."

After a moment, Harvey said, "Very well. I'll be there in fifteen minutes." And he hung up at the other end of the line.

Dan gave a shrug. What was so important with young Mr. Big-Shot? Somebody probably just made him the chairman of something or appointed him to something, and he wanted to make sure that the whole world knew about it.

But now Sarah bustled into the room, and she was looking worried. "What did Harvey want? What's he coming over for?"

"You've taken up listening at phones these days?" Dan said, laughing, not the least bit mad.

"I answered the phone on the downstairs extension. I couldn't help overhearing," Sarah came up to the bed, shifted a little on her feet, and then said, "He sounded angry, Dan. Have you done something?"

"Sure I've done something," Dan said, swinging his legs out of bed and poking his feet into his slippers. "I just signed a contract with his biggest competitor. I'm giving them a testimonial. 'Harvey Harris's father-in-law wouldn't be caught dead using Harvey Harris's soap.' "

But Sarah just shook her head back and forth. "I don't think it's a joke. I think it's something serious."

"To you everything's serious," Dan said. "You're a serious-minded person. What a strain, that you have to be saddled with such a happy-go-lucky, irresponsible husband." On the way to the bathroom, he gave her a gentle pat on the backside just to show he was in a good mood.

He was downstairs, in the middle of his breakfast, when Harvey arrived. Harvey was all bundled up in a heavy fur-collared overcoat. His lips were blue, his ears and his nose were red, and there was a frosty mist on his glasses. "Sit down, sit down," said Dan, pointing at a chair. "Have a cup of hot coffee. You look like you need some thawing out."

"I won't sit down. What I have to say is better said standing."

Dan spread his hands. "It's your feet, and it's your frostbite. You don't mind if I go on eating, do you? One thing I can't stand in this world, and that's a cold fried egg."

Harvey nodded, then cleared his throat.

At this moment Sarah appeared in the dining-room doorway. "Oh, I'm sorry. I'll come back later——" But Dan could see that worried look still on her face, and he knew she had come in on purpose.

"You might as well stay," he said, "now that you're here."

"There's no reason why you shouldn't hear this, Sarah," Harvey said. "In fact, perhaps you'd better."

"You look terribly cold, Harvey dear," Sarah said. "Won't you have some hot coffee?"

"He prefers being cold," Dan said. "It's his blue blood." He said this with a laugh, but to tell the truth, Harvey's stern stiff manner was beginning to have its effect on him. He kept smiling and eating his food, evidently with the same satisfaction, but underneath he was beginning to get just a little bit nervous.

Harvey cleared his throat again, looked at Sarah politely to show that he knew she was in the room, then turned his back on her and spoke directly down at Dan. "I'm a man of few words. I'm not afraid to speak my mind frankly. I don't believe in beating around the bush. Dan—what have you been saying to my son about his Christmas party?"

"Have I been saying things to your son?" Dan said, without looking up from his eggs.

"I think you know the answer to that better than I. Now I want you to tell me what you said to him. Why is he screaming and crying his eyes out right this minute? What's the cause of his disobedience and lack of respect for his parents' wishes?"

"Oh, he's being disobedient?" Dan looked up at Harvey politely. "There's something you want him to do that he doesn't want to do?"

"I think you know the answer to that too. I think you

were in the room last week, when I told him that I'd be taking a personal look at the guest list for his party."

"And now he's objecting to some of the guests that you're asking him to invite?" Dan chuckled a little. "He's got a lot of spirit, that boy. It isn't hard to tell that he's half a Waxman."

Harvey was silent for a while, and Dan could see from his eyes that he was getting angry and trying to keep it from showing. So Dan pushed down his nervousness and kept smiling. Finally, very quietly, Harvey said, "I think you know my theories about bringing up the boy, Dan. I think I've explained to you in the past the effort I'm making to form his mind and his attitudes while he's still young, and to protect him from undesirable influences."

Dan gave a sharp laugh. "Oh, yes, you've definitely explained your theories. In fact, when aren't you explaining your theories?"

"Very well then. So I'll ask you once more, and I expect you to give me an honest answer. Have you been talking to my son behind my back? Did you encourage him to defy my wishes on this Christmas party matter?"

"You want an honest answer?" Dan said, meeting Harvey's eyes very steadily.

"I insist on it."

"All right, you've got it. The answer is yes."

Harvey didn't say anything. He just tightened his lips slightly.

A little less coolly, Dan went on, "Frankly, if you want my opinion, your wishes on the Christmas party matter don't make any sense. A boy looks forward all year to a big thing like that, you should certainly let him enjoy it with the friends that he likes."

"It's not a question of likes or dislikes. It's a question of grounding my son's personality and character on a firm basis. If you'll pardon me saying so, you're a very old-fashioned person, Dan, and you're out of touch with the latest developments in modern psychology."

"Modern psychology, what's that got to do with it? Am I some sort of a mental delinquent out of an institution, or something? I've been around in this world a long time, and I brought up a child of my own, and what's more we always got along together fine."

"Exactly. You always got along together fine. There you have it, the beginning and end of your conception of the responsibilities of parenthood. And doesn't it show in your own daughter? Didn't she come to me with all sorts of personality problems and difficult emotional attitudes which I had to cure her of?"

"You had to cure her? *You* had to cure my daughter? Listen, if you want to know, the only thing you ever cured Bobby of was being a nice, lively, happy girl without a care in the world——"

"Please, Dan," Sarah said.

"Don't stick your nose in, Sarah."

"Harvey, he didn't mean anything by it. It's only because he's so fond of little Neil. And these last few months, he's only been trying to *help* you and Bobby with the child."

"These last few months?" Harvey said. His eyes narrowed a little, then he gave a nod. "Yes, Now I understand. It's exactly what I've suspected. This accounts for the boy's peculiar behaviour."

"Peculiar?" Dan snorted. "Since I took him in hand, that boy never behaved better in his life. Now he's on his way to being a *real* boy, not just a namby-mamby little ——ventriloquist dummy."

Harvey's face turned somewhat whiter than usual. "With me as the ventriloquist, I presume," he said. And then, after a pause, "You had no right to interfere. Neil is my son."

"And he's my grandson."

"Yes. Unfortunately that can't be denied."

"Unfortunately? What do you mean, unfortunately?"

"I mean, a child has enough difficulties to face in this world without such an unfortunate example in his own family."

"Unfortunate example?" Dan could feel his neck growing hot. "What are you getting at? What's wrong with my example?"

"What's wrong with it?" Harvey gave his thin little laugh. "Everybody knows what you are. Everybody knows the kind of unstable, abnormal life you've made for yourself." He paused delicately for a moment, and then said, "And everybody knows about your, to say the least, unsavoury background."

"My background!" This was so stunning that Dan couldn't speak for a moment. He stared and his mouth worked furiously.

"Now there's no more to say on the subject," Harvey said, buttoning up his overcoat. "Except this. From now on, if you please, you'll keep away from my son. Your long walks with him will stop. You'll give him no more gifts, no matter how trivial—and if you attempt to do so, I'll make sure that he returns them to you. You'll be allowed to see him and talk to him, of course—as his blood relation you're entitled to that courtesy—but only in the presence of his mother or myself." And with a nod, Harvey turned towards the door.

"Wait a minute," Dan said, rising slowly to his feet. "What are you saying to me? You're telling me I can't see my own grandson? You're telling me I can't play with him? *You're* saying I can't give things to him? You're crazy—you're out of your head!"

Harvey shrugged. "Nevertheless, that's how it stands. I assure you, it's as painful to me as it is to you. But my principles demand it. Now if you'll excuse me——"

"No, I won't excuse you I'll repeat myself—you're crazy. Who told you that you could pull a thing like that? What makes you think you can get away with it?"

"Please," said Harvey, with a sigh. "There's no point to all this."

"Don't go on with it, Dan," Sarah said, moving up to him. "Maybe, after a few weeks, if you show Harvey that you see his point of view——"

"I'm on trial, am I?" Dan cried. "I'm on my good behaviour. Like a little boy in school—like a convict in prison. Thank you. Thank you so much." And suddenly he made a wide sweep of his arm. "Well, I won't stand for it. You hear me? I definitely don't have to take this. Big Cheese Harvey Harris, does he think he owns the world? Is he the only parent that poor kid's got? He's got a mother too, maybe you forgot about that. And she's my daughter, let me remind you of that. We'll ask *her* how she feels about this. We'll get *her* opinion. We'll find out if *she's* willing to treat her son's only grandfather like a convict!"

"I think you'll find that Barbara will agree with my point of view."

"Will she? Will she now? That's interesting, isn't it?" And Dan laughed very loudly. "Well, we'll see about that—we'll see about that right now—we'll go over there right now, and we'll ask her!"

"Dan," said Sarah, almost in a desperate voice, "please don't drag Bobby into this."

"Get my coat," Dan said. "Get my hat. Is it snow out? Get my rubbers. We'll go over there right now—we'll settle this once and for all!"

"I'm willing," Harvey said. "It's a waste of time, of course, but I'm perfectly willing.

Dan stamped out of the dining-room, rushed from

closet to closet collecting his things, threw his coat over his shoulders, slapped his muffler any which way around his neck. Then, crying out, "Come on, come on—what are you dawdling for? Don't you feel so sure of yourself any more?" he bustled Harvey and Sarah out of the house, and started down the road. He walked fast all the way, waved his arms, and muttered to himself—and Harvey and Sarah ran along a little ways behind him. As soon as the house was in sight, Dan began to call out, "Bobby! Bobby, are you there? It's Daddy! We got a question to ask you!"

Finally they were right up to the house, and Dan marched up the front walk, calling Bobby's name louder than ever. She came through the door and down the porch steps to meet him, her knitting still in her hands.

"Listen, baby," Dan said, "listen to me——"

But Sarah and Harvey had come up next to him now, and Harvey was saying, "Neil? Has he got over his crying fit yet?"

"He's up in his room, dear. I think he'll apologize to you if you tell him he can come down."

"Let him stay there a while longer. The lesson must be impressed on him."

"Bobby, listen——" Dan said.

"What is it, Daddy?" she said, smiling uncertainly at all of them. "Is something the matter?"

"Nothing," Dan said. "Nothing's the matter. Everything's fine. Just as soon as you answer this question."

"What question? What's fine?"

"Bobby, listen——" Dan reached out and caught hold of her arm. He squeezed tight, and smiled into her face, and put as much of his feeling as he could into his voice. "Do you know what that husband of yours just said to me? You don't know about it, do you? You wouldn't go along with a thing like that. Telling me to keep away from my own grandson, like I was a contagious disease or something."

Bobby's eyes widened—and Dan's heart gave a little skip, because he could see that he'd been right, she *hadn't* known what Harvey was going to ask him to do. "Keep away from Neil? But Daddy, why should you——?"

"Barbara dear," said Harvey, stepping forward. "It's this disgraceful business with Neil this morning. You knew I was going to talk to your father about it."

"Yes. Talk to him. But you didn't say——"

"It was necessary," Harvey said. "He refused to be reasonable. There was nothing I could do but forbid him to spend so much time with the boy—except under the supervision of one of us, of course."

"You see, you see?" Dan pushed in. "So what about it, baby? It's a lot of foolishness, isn't it? You wouldn't let a thing like that happen, would you?" And he squeezed her arm harder, as if he could squeeze the right words out of her.

"We'll leave it up to you, Barbara," Harvey said. "I'm quite sure," and he managed to get a funny note of emphasis into his voice, "you wouldn't do anything to jeopardize the welfare of your child."

Bobby stared at Harvey, and then back at Dan. Her mouth opened, but she didn't say anything, there was a look of confusion on her face. And even worse—a look of fright, Dan thought, the kind of look she used to have when she was a little girl and she was scared of the dark.

And then, the next moment, that look went away. She got hold of herself, she lifted her chin and smiled, and gently pulled her arm from Dan's grip. "You're getting excited for no reason, Daddy," she said. "Harvey isn't trying to hurt you or anything. He knows how fond you are of Neil."

306

"Yes, but baby, what he said to me——"

"Darling, I think you must have misunderstood what he said to you. Nobody's trying to keep you from seeing Neil. We want you to see a great deal of Neil. The only thing is, when you're alone with the boy, he gets all over-excited. He isn't really used to you yet, I suppose. So all Harvey means is, it's better for Neil, and for you too, Daddy, if somebody else is around——"

Dan's head began to move back and forth. "You're agreeing with him?" he said. "You're really agreeing with him?"

"But *you* agree with him too, darling. We all agree that Neil's welfare is the most important thing, don't we?"

"I don't believe it," Dan said. "My own daughter— my own baby—going against me like that——"

"Please, Daddy," Bobby said, fidgeting a little. "I'm not going against you. You mustn't say that."

"You are, you are." Dan's head began to nod. "You're sticking up for *him*"—he made a quick, fierce gesture in Harvey's direction. "You're deserting your own father for *him*!"

"Daddy, I'm not deserting you." Bobby put her hand softly on Dan's arm. "You don't seem to understand——" She turned suddenly to Harvey. "Darling— don't you think, maybe——" Then she stopped herself, and turned away from him, a look of misery on her face.

Dan looked into her eyes. He looked hard and deep, trying to find the answer, trying to spy out some sort of hope or meaning in all this. And finally, at the end of his long look, he saw what he should have seen from the very beginning, what he had told himself a hundred times since he moved to Beewick, but never really knew until now. In the last eight years his Bobby had changed. She wasn't the lively little baby any more, or the shy little schoolkid, or even the smart, good-looking college girl,

The shadow of his old Bobby was there—but only the shadow. And it was fading fast, its struggles grew more and more feeble deep down in those eyes, clearer and clearer the more he looked, was Beewick, Ohio, and her knitting and her furniture, her membership in the Ladies' Auxiliary of the temple, her pleasant position as the wife of the town's most up-and-coming young Jewish business-man. In her figure and her face maybe she wasn't the stout, comfortable, middle-aged matron yet— but Dan could see that middle-aged matron in her eyes, he could see her smiling calmly, with her knitting in her lap, waiting for the moment to make her appearance.

Wildly and hopelessly, he made one more attempt. "Let me talk to the boy," he cried. "I'll go up to him, I'll ask him what he thinks of his old Grandpa!"

"You heard my decision about that a short time ago," Harvey said quietly, not the least bit ruffled by the whole scene. "That decision goes into effect right now."

"Daddy darling," said Bobby, moving closer to him, "why not forget about the whole thing? After all, you know how we feel about you basically. We're your family, darling, and this is your home."

Dan stared at her just a moment longer, and then he gave a sharp shake of his head. "Home," he said in a quick, trembling voice. "This is no home. I don't *have* any home." He turned to Sarah, still shaking his head and blinking, half in a daze. "We're getting out of this town. We're going back to New York. And after that we're going—I don't know where we're going. I don't care where we're going. But we're getting out of Beewick to-day."

"Dan!" Sarah cried—a sharp, soft little cry of pain.

Dan pushed it out of his mind, and shook his head even harder. "To-day," he said. "Don't argue with me— to-day." And before anybody else could say a word to him he was down the front walk and striding along the road, with the house behind him, and his daughter and his grandson, and as far as he was concerned, everything else in the whole damned world.

Except Sarah, who caught up to him a moment later, and ran along by his side.

They got back to their own house—Dan called the airport in Cincinnati—he threw things into a suitcase. Sarah was wailing at his side. "But our clothes—the furniture—the house——" And he was shouting at her, "We'll worry about it later—we'll handle it all from New York——" Then they were driving out to the airport. He never drove so fast in his life. Three or four times he nearly smashed up the car. What did he care? He didn't even know it was happening. And then they were on the plane—the engines roaring, the hostess being sweet and annoying, the ground dropping away fast below them.

And now, strapped in his seat, nowhere to go, nothing more to do, the buzzing was out of his ears at last. He blinked and looked around him, as if he had no idea where he might be. Then he turned and his gaze stopped on Sarah.

Her head was pushed forward a little—that long wrinkled face, popeyed and flabby. And ugly—my God, what ever possessed him to get married to such an ugly woman? And her lower lip was stuck out now, and her chin was trembling, and her eyes were wide open—her typical look when she was upset over something. Poor little me, that look said. Don't you feel sorry for me? Don't you agree I'm a pitiful case? Isn't it terrible for a woman to go through her life with such an impossible, unreasonable husband? And suddenly it came over him —all through their life together, she had been putting on

309

this look, putting it on especially to get sympathy, and make people sigh over her, and show the world how wonderful *she* was and what a louse *he* was——

All through the trip he stared at her. He was fascinated, he couldn't take his eyes away. It was like seeing her for the first time in his life. And seeing her as she really was—and hating her for it. A tremendous, irresistible satisfaction came over him, as he gave himself up to hating her.

They got off the plane in New York. He practically dragged her along to the taxicab stand. "Please, Dan," she said, breathing hard. "I'm tired. You're hurting me."

He dragged her all the harder for it.

The cab took them to the city, to the hotel where they usually stayed. But it was full—it was Christmas Eve and every room was taken. "We'll go down the block," Dan said. "We'll go up and down Fifth Avenue. We'll find a room if it kills us."

"Dan," Sarah said, in a weak voice. "Maybe if we called up one of my family——"

"We don't stay with families. We're through with families."

He pulled her out of the hotel. They marched down Fifth Avenue. It was a blustering cold night—the chill went through your overcoat, through your clothes, it cut into your bones. One minute on the streets, and your ears were frozen already.

In front of the third hotel, Sarah was gasping hard. "Please, Dan. Please, dear——"

"Please, she says" Dan turned on her, right there on the sidewalk, with the people rushing by to their Christmas dinners, and the Salvation Army Santa Claus ringing his bell, and the store windows sparkling all around with red and green lights and silver bells. "Why should I please you? Tell me why, tell me why! Did you ever please me in your life! Did you ever do anything but

310

hurt me, and make a fool of me, and turn all my friends against me? Oh yes, I see it now! What a crazy idiot I was, that I never saw it before! All the trouble I've ever had—*you're* the cause of it! You're the one who's ruined my life!"

"Dan, don't say that——" And Dan could see a tear in her eye—one of those phoney tears that she was so good at.

"Stop your whining!" he shouted. "Get away from me, will you! I'd be a happy man to-day if I'd never set eyes on you!"

She was moaning now, and gasping at the same time. "Dan," she kept saying. "Dan—please don't——", in a pleading way, as if he was hitting her. And then her moans stopped short. The colour drained out of her face, and he saw her weave a little and clutch at her heart before she collapsed to the sidewalk.

XIII

Two seconds after Sarah's collapse she was surrounded by a ring of people. Two seconds after that the policeman rushed over from the corner and bent down next to her and held her head, while Dan stood above him helplessly. Then the policeman said he'd send for an ambulance, but already Dan was hating the crowd and the public spectacle, so he said no, he'd call a cab and take her up to a hospital where they knew him.

The policeman stopped a cab with his whistle, and the two of them helped Sarah to her feet. She was very wobbly, and her face was still that terrible white colour, and her eyes were turned up so that Dan almost couldn't see the pupils. They got her into the cab, where she slumped back in the corner, half lying down. Dan sat down next to her, thanked the policeman, and gave the driver the name of that hospital way up on Fifth Avenue where Herman had spent his last days. It was a short ride really, because it was almost six-thirty now and quite dark out, and most of the traffic was off the streets. But to Dan it seemed like that ride would never end. And every minute of it he kept a bewildered watch on Sarah's limp form, and he would have thought she was dead except for the low moaning sound that came from her mouth.

Dan was scared. He had never been so scared in his life.

The hospital was almost as hard to get into on Christmas Eve as the hotels had been. Even with a couple of orderlies helping Sarah into the waiting-room, the nurse on duty told Dan that there wasn't a single vacant room, he'd have to go elsewhere. He shook his head and said "No—she's sick, you got to take care of her"—over and over again, like a lesson. And it was only by forcing the nurse to call up Dr. Glazer at his home right then and there that Dan finally got Sarah assigned to a small room which had just been vacated on the children's floor.

And then Sarah fainted again, right there in the waiting-room. The orderlies hurried up with a stretcher, and Dan saw her rolled on to it like a bundle of clothes and hustled away into the patients' elevator. He took a step after the stretcher, but the nurse stopped him, she told him he'd have to wait until he was called for. So he sat in a chair for a while, he stood up and paced, he tried looking at a magazine. Every five minutes he was up at the desk, asking the nurse, "Where's Dr. Glazer? Didn't he get here yet? What's holding him up?" And then, finally, in between one of these five-minute intervals, the nurse called him over and told him that Dr. Glazer had just got in touch with her on the switchboard, he had come into the hospital by the doctors' entrance and he was up in Sarah's room right now.

Another long period of pacing and sitting and squeezing his hands together and bothering the nurse. Then the news came through that he could go upstairs now, Dr. Glazer would see him. He ran for the elevator, pushed the button, swore at the operator when the door didn't open in a split second, swore all the way up to Sarah's floor at "these old-fashioned broken-down machines that take ten years to get you anywhere".

Dr. Glazer was waiting for him by the nurse's desk on Sarah's floor. "Well, this is nice, isn't it?" Dr. Glazer said. "This is certainly a nice state of affairs. What've you been doing to that woman, anyway—making her carry water kegs on her head, like an Eskimo's wife?"

"What is it? What's wrong with her? Is it something serious?"

"Is it something serious? Only the most serious thing in the world. The one thing that happens to everybody, this side of mortality—so naturally it's the one thing that nobody ever takes care of or pays any attention to. I mean, Mr. Waxman, that every day in every way your wife is getting older and older, and weaker and weaker—along with the rest of us. I mean what just a small amount of ordinary common sense should tell you without my help—that a woman in her fifties can't rush around like a woman in her thirties. She can't do the things that she used to do. She can't stand the strains. The muscles are getting stiffer, and the nerves are wearing thinner, and the organs are slowing up."

"It's a heart condition?" Dan broke in quickly.

"Heart condition. So that's your diagnosis, is it,

Doctor! Of *course* it's a heart condition. It's the same heart condition that you've got and I've got and your Uncle Julius has got. It's the condition of having a human heart, which is a fragile and temporary piece of mechanism that can take just so much punishment, not an Army tank, a perpetual motion machine, or a non-breakable plastic punching-bag." Dr. Glazer paused to take a breath and pass his hands over his eyes. "And your wife's heart, Mr. Waxman, has been taking enough punishment for twenty hearts lately, if my stethoscope is still working right. It's got to stop, do you hear me? Two weeks' rest is the first thing she wants—two weeks flat on her back right here in this hospital, with no worries, no activities, no nothing. And after that—*for ever after*, if you follow plain English—whatever it is that's been doing this to her, it has to stop doing it. That's my advice, Mr. Waxman, and for not figuring it out by yourself you deserve the outrageously big bill that I'm going to send you."

Then Dr. Glazer snapped his medical bag shut and told Dan that he could see the patient for exactly two minutes and then he'd better go home and get some sleep himself —"if you don't want to be spending the next two weeks in the room right next to her"—and so, with a sharp nod, he marched off down the corridor.

Dan turned, hesitated a moment, then knocked softly on Sarah's door. It was opened for him by the nurse. And beyond the nurse he could see Sarah lying in the bed, looking very small and pale.

"I'm Mr. Waxman," Dan began to the nurse, in a low voice.

But Sarah's voice, thin and exhausted, cut him short. "Is that him?" she said. "Is that my husband, nurse?"

"Yes, it is, Mrs. Waxman."

"Can he see me? Did they say he could see me?"

"Only for a couple of minutes, Sarah," Dan called out.

But she didn't answer him. And a moment later, from his position in the doorway, he saw her head shaking back and forth on the pillow. "Don't let him in," she was saying. "Don't let him come any closer. For God's sake, make him go away."

The nurse cleared her throat and smiled faintly. "Mrs. Waxman is still very weak," she said. "She's a little bit delirious."

"I'm going," Dan said, almost as pale now as Sarah herself. And he turned quickly and left the room.

He had to keep himself busy. So he went downtown and once more made the rounds of the hotels. He was lucky this time. At one of the big hotels near Grand Central Station, somebody was called back suddenly to Arkansas or Wisconsin or somewhere, and Dan was right there when the room was vacated. He took it, and went up to it with his one suitcase, which he had been lugging around with him all day, all the way from Beewick, Ohio. But in spite of the fact that it was after ten o'clock, in spite of Dr. Glazer's advice, he couldn't possibly go to bed and fall asleep. Now that Sarah was safe in the hospital, it was beginning to grow on him, the memory of what he had done. He left his room and went downstairs again and plunged into the crowd of Christmas Eve drunks, and nightclub patrons, and party-goers who filled the streets.

God knows how long he walked. Or where. Every minute of it he was thinking hard, thinking desperately until it hurt. The things he had said to her! Not that he hadn't said a lot of terrible things to her in the past. He remembered the very first time, before they were even married—that rainy night in Chicago, when he couldn't get a cab and he took out his anger on her. He remembered a hundred more times after that. But none of them was as bad as to-night. Never before had he been so nasty, and cruel, and not even fit to call himself a human being. And now he was getting punished for it, wasn't he? She hated the sight of him. She wouldn't have anything more to do with him. And how could he blame her for it? He wasn't even a member of the human race any more. There was no place for him among the decent, self-respecting people of this world.

His mind rushed ahead to what life would be like without Sarah. And a terrible empty aching feeling shot through him. All these years of wandering and running away and raging like a madman whenever things went wrong, Sarah had stuck with him, hovering behind him at hotel registers, hurrying after him to airports and railroad stations, turning pale and tightening her fists as he worked himself up into another one of his stupid furies. And all of a sudden, looking back over the long stretch of years, it seemed to Dan as if that was the most important part of it all, that Sarah was always around. It seemed to him as if that was the only real thing that had happened to him since the day he rode out of Chicago. No more Sarah from now on——

"Something the matter, bud?" A tall hefty-looking young man, with a girl on his arm, was talking to him. And Dan realized that he had stopped short right in the middle of the sidewalk, and the tears were running down his cheeks in front of everybody.

"Nothing—thank you——" He lowered his head and hurried on.

A few minutes later, surprisingly, he found himself right back at his hotel. He must have been walking in a circle. It was only ten-thirty, and it suddenly occurred to him that he was hungry, he hadn't eaten a thing since breakfast. That breakfast back in Beewick, it seemed like a thousand years ago.

Hungry. As he started across the lobby to the hotel snack-shop, he smiled a little bitterly to himself. His life was over. The whole world was like a long flat empty desert to him—nowhere to go, no place to stop and rest his head and say to himself, "This is where I ought to be." And yet, he was thinking of food.

He went into the snack-shop. It was nearly empty, only a few customers at the counter. He went to one of the booths, and moved into it as far as he could, as if he was trying to hide from somebody. But he wasn't there more than a minute when a voice suddenly broke into his thoughts

"My God, it's Dan! My God, it's Dan Waxman!"

Dan looked up and saw this man coming over to him from the counter, smiling and holding out his hand. Just an ordinary-looking man in his fifties—tall, nicely dressed, thick features, a head of frizzly white hair. Very untidy hair, as if he'd been combing it for hours and still it wouldn't stay down——

And all of a sudden Dan grew weak. Because he recognized the man now. It was Mort Meltzer.

XIV

"DAN WAXMAN," Mort was saying over and over again, all the way across the room. "Dan, I can't believe it. Is it actually you? Is it definitely not a mirage?"

Dan rose to his feet, and a moment later the two men were facing each other. And in that moment, now that his first burst of enthusiasm was over, Mort suddenly turned very red and lowered his eyes—and Dan grew just as embarrassed himself.

After awhile, without looking up at Mort, Dan said, "Why don't we sit down. Have a cup of coffee together."

Quickly, with relief, they sat across from each other in the booth. And then, in a kind of hesitant experimental way, they tried looking up at each other.

"How've you been?" Mort said. "You're looking pretty good."

"You're looking good too," Dan said.

"How's Sarah?" Mort said.

"She's been sick," Dan said. "But she's better now." They were silent for a while, smiling a little stiffly, evidently taking in each other's good looks. Then Dan said, "So what're you doing in New York, Mort? You don't live in New York, do you?"

"Live in New York? Over my dead body. I'm only here for business. I've got a shipment coming in."

"Business is good?"

"Pretty good, pretty good. I'm not so active as I used to be. I've got a son-in-law back home now. Marilyn— you remember my Marilyn, who was in school with your Bobby—Marilyn's been married nine years now, and she's got three children, and I put her husband in the business with me. He's a very bright boy, he's doing wonderful—you'd think he was made for furs." Mort took a breath and a drink of water, then pushed on, "You should see the kids, Dan. They take right after Marilyn."

Dan smiled a little at this. He remembered Mort's little girl Marilyn—a noisy, uncontrollable girl with a voice like a trumpet. He could imagine the noise that three little Marilyns would make.

"And Milly?" Dan asked. "Is Milly with you?" He asked it cautiously, nervously. He remembered the lobby of Mort's hotel—and the way Milly wouldn't let him come upstairs.

For just a second Mort lowered his eyes again. "Milly passed away, Dan. Last year. She had a cancer."

"Mort, I'm sorry," Dan said, in a very low voice. He pushed that memory of the lobby out of his mind. He tried to bring back some earlier memories, happier ones—like the sound of Milly's voice, ringing out loudly and cheerfully over the dining-room table at Twelve Hundred Lake Shore Drive. "Mort, I'm terribly sorry."

"It wasn't as bad as it could've been," Mort said. "It was over very quick. It was the kind where there wasn't much pain."

They fell silent again, and stayed that way while the waitress served their coffee and their eggs. And then, when she was gone, Mort looked up again with a smile on his face. "So let's hear about yourself," he said. "What've you been doing with yourself all these years? How's the world been treating you, Dan boy?"

This "Dan boy" sent a little thrill through Dan. It was such a long time since anybody had called him that. He found himself answering Mort's question almost with a certain enthusiasm in his voice. "I've been kicking around, Mort. Here and there and everywhere. I've done a lot of travelling. I've been to Europe."

"Europe? Milly was always after me to take her to Europe, but I told her, what did I want with all those old statues and broken-down churches? One good office building in downtown Chicago was all the Europe I wanted. But you always *did* go in for that culture stuff, didn't you? Like the opera. Are you still such a big lover of the opera?"

"Well, to tell the truth, I haven't been to the opera for quite a while now. Not that I've lost my interest, of course. But I've been so busy lately."

"Busy in business, Dan?"

"Business for a while. I've been in and out of business. Now I'm retired."

"Retired—now that's the smart thing to do. That's the way for a man to arrange his life. Make your money early, then enjoy yourself on it for the rest of the time. Sometimes I think about it myself, Dan—but I don't dare leave the business to that son-in-law of mine. Between you and me, Dan, talking frankly now, he's a sub-moron, the man my daughter married. What he doesn't know about furs, even after nine years in the business! Listen, the *minks* know more about selling minks than he does."

"I don't know," Dan said. "It doesn't hurt a man to keep active either. A man should have something to do with his time."

"Sleep," Mort said. "I can't think of a better thing to do."

Another silence. But not such a strained one this time. They sipped their coffee and munched their food, and kept looking at each other with a funny shadow of the old fondness on their faces.

"And Bobby," Mort said finally. "Where is she now, that wonderful kid of yours?"

"Bobby's married now," Dan said, making himself smile. "Very successful young fellow out in Beewick— that's a small town in Ohio. He's in the soap business, and they've got a lovely little boy, and Bobby is terribly happy."

"In the soap business?" Mort said. "I pity the poor kid—he won't *ever* get away with not washing behind his ears." Then Mort gave a pleased little sigh. "No kidding, though, I'm glad to hear it, Dan. That she's happy, I mean. You know how crazy I was about her, your Bobby." And then, all of a sudden, Mort began to chuckle softly. "Say, Dan," he said, "do you remember way back, about twenty-four or twenty-five, I guess? When we took your Bobby and my Marilyn to the circus —you remember that? We were going to give the kids a treat, it was going to be a big sacrifice on our part. And we got such a kick out of it ourselves, even when the kids got bored and wanted to go home we wouldn't let them, we made them stay to the end."

"How well I remember it," Dan said, chuckling a little himself. "But do *you* remember the first year we sent them to summer camp? We were being so calm and cocky, with our noses in the air, when the women cried at the station and said how much they'd miss the kids. We were sneering at them, and telling them what a couple of silly females they were——"

"I remember it, I remember it," Mort broke in. "And three days after, we both sneaked out of the house and made long distance calls all the way up to Maine!"

"And when Bobby wrote me that she had poison ivy, I nearly threw up everything and took a train right out to her!"

"Don't I remember," Mort said, laughing and shaking his head. "Sarah called me up, and I practically had to chain you to your easy-chair. And Dan," he rushed on, "do you remember how I used to kid your Bobby, and make her blush? I used to tell her that I had a date with her on her sixteenth birthday, and I'd go mad with jealousy if she stood me up."

"I remember," said Dan. "The way she used to blush."

Mort's smile grew a little vague all of a sudden, and he spoke in a different voice. "We never did have that date, though," he said. "I've always been sorry about that." And then, after a moment, he leaned forward slightly and his voice was more intent. "I've been sorry about a lot of things, Dan.

The silence now was more than Dan could bear. He began to eat his eggs quickly and noisily. And then he stopped eating—he felt Mort's hand on his shoulder. He began to tremble under Mort's touch, and he just couldn't bring himself to look up.

"You've had a tough time, Dan boy," Mort was saying. "We've been getting reports back in Chicago. Eli Glatz is still around, you know—he makes it his business to find out when anything bad happens to people."

"Who said it was tough?" Dan mumbled. "I've had a fine time."

"Liar," said Mort softly. And the pressure of his hand was firmer. "Listen, Dan—why don't you come back home?"

Dan wet his lips, and it was a few seconds before he could trust himself to say the words. "Back to Chicago, you mean?"

"Why not? Why shouldn't you? The old thing—it's all forgotten now. Except by a few pig-headed sourpusses. I wouldn't pull the wool over your eyes, Dan. There are still a few pig-headed sourpusses. But is that going to stop you from doing what you want to do? Is a man going to let the sourpusses run his life?"

Dan began to shake his head. He spoke in a low strained voice. "How could I do it, Mort? How could I do it?"

Mort let go of Dan's shoulder, and his voice took on a strong, determined note. "By doing it, that's how. By saying to hell with them all, and just plain doing it."

Dan raised his eyes slowly. And for a moment something flickered on his face, something almost like hope. And then, it flickered right out again. He thought of Sarah in that hospital bed—her head shaking back and forth, those words coming out of her mouth, "For God's sake, make him go away."

"It's no good," Dan said softly. "It's too late."

For a long time neither of them said a word, and then

from a distance they heard the sound of bells, and voices shouting from out in the street.

Mort looked down at his watch and smiled a little sadly. "It's Christmas," he said. "Give me a Christmas present, won't you. Reconsider your decision."

"Give you a Christmas present?"

Mort nodded, and his face had never been so solemn and so serious. "You'd be doing me a favour, Dan. I'm alone in the world now. Chicago is a pretty big city when you're all alone."

Dan looked hard into Mort's face, and the heavy lines under Mort's eyes, and his dull white hair, which used to be such a fiery red. "I'll tell you what," he said. "There's something I have to do. I'll do it to-morrow morning. And if it turns out all right I'll—maybe we'll go back to Chicago together."

Mort looked serious just a split second more, just long enough to nod his head and say "Thanks". And then his smile flashed on again, and his arms started waving, and he was full of the life and high spirits that brought Dan back to the old days.

They ordered dessert, and Mort flirted a little with the waitress, and suddenly he cried out, "I heard a story the other day! Did you ever hear this story?" And he was off on one of his long elaborate dirty jokes, about a dignified society lady who walked into a Paris burlesque house thinking it was the Ritz Hotel. And he followed this up with another joke, about a man who climbed to the top of a mountain and found the most peculiar evidence of human civilization up there. And after that there was another one, and so it went on, and they didn't leave the snack-shop till it closed up at one in the morning.

Mort was staying at a different hotel, down the street, so the two men said "goodnight" on the sidewalk in between. They shook hands quickly, and Mort wished Dan luck in the morning, and Dan said he'd be sure and call Mort up as soon as everything was settled, and they both said how sleepy they were—and still they stood and looked at each other, as if they couldn't have enough of each other.

Finally Mort gave a laugh and broke away. "Goodnight, Dan," he said. "It's good to see you."

"It's good to see you, too," Dan said.

XV

JUST before he went to bed that night, Dan stood in front of the dresser in his hotel room and looked into the mirror. And it seemed to him that he was seeing himself for the first time in many years. What he saw was a man approaching sixty years of age, and showing every year of it. He was short and homely, with a pot belly and a double chin. His head was bald. All right, his head had been bald since the age of thirty-five. But it was balder than ever now, there was only an uneven ring of hair left around the bald spot, and a few tufts around the ears, and even what was left was thin and straggly and dirty-grey. And his face—it was full of lines and wrinkles. It wasn't a young man's face. The eyes that looked back at him from the mirror were tired, they were heavy and bloodshot with the worrying and fretting and muttering of nearly sixty years.

You're a tired old man, he told himself. Enough is enough.

The next morning he went up to the hospital. He

asked the nurse at the first-floor switchboard to call up and find out if Sarah would see him. And while he waited for the answer, he paced the floor and shook his head and told himself it was hopeless, she wouldn't even let him pass the door, what was the point of hanging around? He was all set to walk right out of the hospital when the nurse told him that Sarah wanted him to come right up. He blinked a little, and asked her if she was sure she had the message right, and then he went up to Sarah's floor.

He knocked softly on the door. A moment later he heard Sarah's voice from inside, still pretty weak, but nothing like last night. "Come in," Sarah said.

He opened the door and took a few steps into the room, and then stopped uncertainly.

Sarah was propped up in bed with a couple of pillows. Her hair was combed, and she even had a little lipstick on. She looked just as uncertain as he did. She gave a kind of smile. "Aren't you going to kiss me, Dan?"

Dan stood still for a moment. And then he came forward and sat on the edge of the bed and kissed her quickly on the cheek. "Listen, Sarah," he began, "how can I apologize——"

But she was talking almost at the same time. "How can I apologize——"

"You?" Dan cried. "After everything I've done to you. After all the things I said——" He broke off with a little shudder. And then he went on firmly, "For God's sake, Sarah, lose your temper with me. It's your right after all these years. Show me I'm not the only one in the world who's entitled to have a temper."

But Sarah just went on looking at him. Her smile grew gentler and more peaceful. She reached out and touched him softly on the cheek. "All right," she said. "I've lost my temper."

After a while he told her about his meeting with Mort

Meltzer. Her face brightened up just at the name. And it continued to get brighter as he went into the details— how Mort looked, and how Marilyn was married now, and how Mort's collection of jokes was as big as ever. And she sighed a little over Mort's hair—"That beautiful red hair!" she said. And a little tear came into her eye when she heard about Milly. But she brightened up again immediately, when Dan came to the most important part.

"Sarah," he said, reaching out and putting his hands on hers, "Mort made a suggestion. About Chicago."

"Chicago, Dan?" she said, hardly louder than a whisper.

"Would you like to go back there?" he said. "Would you like to see Chicago again?"

"For a visit, Dan?"

"For good," he said. "For the rest of our lives."

He didn't need her answer. He could see it all on her face, he could see it in the colour that came into her cheeks. "Could we really?" she said.

He was bursting with happiness—but he held it off a moment longer. "It may not be easy," he said. "There are still some people who don't want us. Want me, that is. It won't be any bed of roses."

"Who likes beds of roses?" Sarah said.

That was all he needed to hear. The next moment his arms were around her, he was hugging her tight, like a young married couple again.

"Poor Dan," she kept saying into his ear. "Poor darling, you deserve it. After all these years, you deserve it."

And so they stayed together for the rest of the morning, and talked and planned ahead and looked back, and did a lot of laughing. Only sometimes it was hard to tell it from crying.

My Uncle Dan's return to Chicago in January 1946 was as quiet and unspectacular as his very first arrival there forty-three years before, when he was a young boy with his whole life ahead of him.

Mort Meltzer stayed with Dan in New York until Sarah could leave the hospital, and then the three of them got on the train together. It was seven o'clock the next morning when they got off again. Chicago was cold and windy. A grey mist was over everything, hiding the tops of the buildings, covering up the dirt and the grime, giving the whole city a soft and muffled effect. Dan stood on the corner in front of the station for almost five minutes, just looking around him, just taking in the sweet, sooty air.

Mort wanted to bring them right back with him to his hotel, but Dan shook his head. "Whatever happened to Twelve Hundred Lake Shore Drive?" he said.

"It's an office building now," Mort said. "Mutual Life Insurance."

"Let's drive by and take a look at it," Dan said.

The news that Dan and Sarah were back in town spread quickly. People were calling up the hotel all day. And that night, in his apartment, Mort gave a kind of party for them. The room was crowded with people that Dan used to know: men that he had played golf with and done business with and argued over the card table with: their wives that he used to tease and pay compliments to and flirt with in a nice way. The men were grey now, and slower, and some of them a little deafer. The women didn't laugh as loud or move across the floor as gracefully as they used to do.

And the room was empty too. Every once in a while

he would catch himself looking around for a face, listening for a voice—and then he would remember what Mort had already told him. Helen Freed had died in an auto accident three years ago. Fred Dickstein, fatter and more pompous and less occupied with his patients than ever, had passed away in the fall. Somebody else was in a home for mental cases, and somebody else had left Chicago and was never heard of again, and somebody else had drifted away peacefully in his sleep.

Eli Glatz was the same as ever, only a little more bent over, a little more wrinkled up, a little more sharp in his eyes and squeaky in his voice. "Well, it's good to see you, Dan," he kept saying, every chance he got. "Well, it's certainly a big surprise. I mean, I never dreamed we'd be meeting again like this."

As soon as possible Dan and Sarah found an apartment —a smaller apartment than the old one, for after all there were only two of them now. And Dan renewed his membership in the Downtown Club and in Pleasant Fairways—which actually wasn't Pleasant Fairways any more it had merged with its biggest rival, Noble Oaks, to become Noble Fairways. And he opened a small office downtown and took on a limited amount of accounting work, "just to keep my hand in". And he even made a search for his old secretary Mrs. Schultz, but he couldn't find a trace of her anywhere.

My Uncle Dan was sixty-eight last May. He lives in Chicago still. He goes down to his office every morning, and plays cards once a week, and smokes his regular three cigars a day. His game of golf is amazing for a man of his age. And, of course, he goes to the opera. He has a regular box, and sits in it every Monday night, rain or shine, during the season. And he just shrugs or grunts when Mort Meltzer starts kidding him about it.

He has never been to Beewick, Ohio, again, and Bobby has brought Neil to Chicago only twice. But Sarah and Bobby write to each other regularly, so Dan gets all the news. And the truth of the matter is, that's about all he wants. Because Dan is leading his old life again, wrapped up in his old pleasures, surrounded by his old friends. And he gets along with these people wonderfully—just as wonderfully as he used to do in the days before the Drexell trouble. It's exactly like Mort Meltzer told him—that old business is completely forgotten.

Well, almost completely. Every once in a while, in the heat of a political argument, say, somebody makes a slip of the tongue—or somebody gives him a certain look—or maybe he just imagines it's a certain look. Generally, Dan tells himself that this is the explanation—and he quickly shrugs off the whole thing.

Most of the time he spends with Sarah. They're getting a little too old for night-clubbing or theatre-going, and they know each other's thoughts too well for a lot of conversation—but television has solved their problem. They have one of the new giant screens, and they watch it nearly every night. And nearly every night Dan shakes his head and says, "My God, the silly stuff they put on television!"

What about his temper? Well, I have to do him justice—the years have mellowed my Uncle Dan. He doesn't flare up like a Roman candle nearly as often or as quickly as he once did. Sarah has a good deal to do with this. Whenever that look comes into his eye, all she has to do is raise her hand to her heart, and Dan is likely to forget all about his anger and rush off for a glass of water. And I must say, to the family's surprise Sarah isn't above raising her hand to her heart even when it isn't exactly a pain that her heart is feeling.

And yet, at least one new "Uncle Dan" story has

reached us here in New York. The story is that he and Sarah were going into a restaurant, and the revolving door hit Uncle Dan in the leg. In an instant his neck turned red, and he whirled around, and he burst out at that door in his angriest voice, "What do you think you're doing, you goddamned idiot!"

This is still my favourite image of my Uncle Dan— waving his arms and yelling at the top of his voice.

THE END